THE ASHEN CITY

RITES OF RESURRECTION
BOOK TWO

MARSHALL J. MOORE

PART ONE
REST

CHAPTER ONE

Two soldiers stood awaiting my command. One of them was already dead.

The other stood behind his unliving counterpart with feet apart and knees bent, his shoulders tensed. Though he must have felt the eyes of his peers on his back, I could tell Titian was doing his best not to let their collective attention rattle him. His face was as composed as any Attendant's mask, other than a tightness about the jaw.

Seconds ticked by in still silence, save for the susurration of the river flowing behind them. Unease rippled through the students assembled beside me as they watched Titian hold the ready pose, wondering why I had not yet issued him a command.

I ignored them. My own attention was fixed upon Titian, whose arms trembled as he held his fists before his face like a boxer, a vein straining against his neck.

Too tense. I wanted to tell him to breathe, but that would spoil the point of the exercise. Instead, I gave the command my students had been waiting for.

"Begin."

Titian's nostrils flared as he lowered both fists to his sides, streams of spectral blue ghostfire running down his arms. Those same illusory flames gleamed to sudden life behind the mask of the unliving Attendant as its stiff limbs jerked to mirror Titian's, fists low and ready.

"The Rite of Communion." Titian's deep basso rang out over the rush of the River Providens. "First kata: The Body Walks."

"And in Ayu'li, Acolyte," I reminded him.

Titian cleared his throat. *"Hashti'nai lanek."*

I nodded my approval. Titian's pronunciation was rough, his accent nearly unintelligible. But at least he had gotten the words right.

It was a start.

Stepping into a wide lunge, Titian began the kata. His Attendant mirrored his movements, though its motions were stiff, jerky—a marionette on invisible strings.

Another step brought both soldiers back to standing, the living and the dead, each with a hand raised to block an over-hand strike from an imagined foe. Titian's shoulders began to relax somewhat as his body recalled the motions drilled into him through long hours of repetitive practice. He moved through the kata more swiftly, his motions sharp and explosive —though his Attendant was not the only one whose move-ments were stiff.

Titian's feet stomped against the grass, his arms jerking through each position. Step to left, cross arms. Step to right, uncross them. Step to right again, followed by a straight-hand jab. A kick, a pivot—

Titian overextended and fell with a crash to the muddy riverside. His Attendant toppled with him, its own collapse an exaggerated pratfall.

Beside me his fellow Acolytes gasped, though the tenor of

their surprise told me their next exhalation would be a gale of laughter. I quelled them with a look.

"Acolyte Titian," I said, stepping forward. "Rise."

He rose, eyes downcast as he wiped mud from his tunic.

"Look at me, Acolyte."

Titian did, chin jutted forward, no doubt hoping an expression of defiance might mask his shame and disappointment. "Yes, Bellator Calvus."

The emotions of the young were as easy to read as their motives. Titian was a stubborn sort, his pride easily wounded. But like any decent teacher, I had discovered ways around my students' barriers.

"Can you swim, Acolyte Titian?" I asked.

His defiance evaporated, leaving only confusion. "Sir?"

I nodded towards the Providens, its waters flowing white and swift behind him. We were high in the Albastine Valley, away from the city itself. Here the river was mostly rapids.

"I know it's a hot day out, Acolyte, but the time for taking a dip is after class, not during." I wiped at my brow, already glistening with a fine sheen of sweat. "Not that I can blame you. I might dive in myself, as soon as you're out of my hair."

A smattering of giggles from the Acolytes behind me was hastily stifled. Though I was no longer a Legate, I kept my scalp as shorn as that of these Acolytes who would one day ascend to that rank. Provided that I trained them well.

I schooled my face into a gentle smile and made sure to keep my tone conciliatory. "Can you tell me where you went wrong, Acolyte?"

Titian frowned, but did not bristle. I waited patiently as he considered, mentally reviewing his performance of The Body Walks.

Misdirection is the heart of all warfare, my own teacher had taught me. By making myself the subject of the class's amusement, I had diverted their attention, allowing Titian to reflect on his mistake without the added weight of his peers' judgment.

"I was too stiff," he said at last. "My motions didn't flow."

"Correct." I gave him an approving nod. "Can you tell me why?"

His frown deepened, and I saw a hint of stung pride threatening to reassert itself.

I tapped him lightly on the chest, right against the diaphragm. Titian gasped in surprise, a burst of air whooshing from his mouth.

"*That's* why," I said, before his anger could flare to life. "Breathe, Acolyte. Watch."

I turned away from him, ghostfire flickering up my arms as I commanded his Attendant to rise from the mud.

"The Body Dances with the Spear," I announced, my voice echoing off the steep cliffs of the high valley. "*Ken'nai lanek ka ro.*"

The motions of the more advanced kata came to me with easy familiarity. I stepped carefully through the intricate movements and motions, mimicking the graceful twirls of a spearman's careful thrust and sweeping flourish. Not the regimented, mechanical stand-and-stab of a legion phalanx, but the acrobatic leaps and slashes of a whirling dervish. Like the Rites itself, it was a relic of my heritage—a martial display of the Ayu'li of old.

Beside me the mud-splattered Attendant moved through the kata, mimicking my every gesture and pose. Its movements hewed far closer to mine than they had to Titian's. The fluidity of its limbs was very nearly human, hampered only by the inevitable stiffness of the joints that no amount of careful mummification could fully prevent.

Such mummification was the inevitable fate of all citizens

of Albastine. Upon death our bodies were turned over to the mortuary and treated with chemical compounds and balms to slow decay to a fraction of its natural rate. Once the mummification process was completed, a Legate would imbue the body with a fraction of his will, turning it into an automaton capable of performing simple tasks.

We called it the Rite of Rising, though like the first kata I had been teaching my Acolytes, it was only a pale facsimile of the ancient Ayu'li funerary rituals that were the hallmark of my religion. Ages ago, priests of the Old Faith had danced the funeral dances to summon the spirits of the dead so that they might celebrate weddings and births and harvests alongside their living kin. Such displays had ultimately seen my ancestors driven from their homes beside the River Ayu, forced into a long and wandering exile until they met and mingled with a fellow refugee people, the Extorani. Together the two peoples had settled the remote and unfriendly Albastine Valley, founding the Republic I had dedicated my life to serving.

By now I was sweating freely, the exertion of the kata exacting its toll upon my own body. I did not care. There was joy in each twirling step, in the graceful motion I had only just begun to recover after recuperating from my injuries. For the first time in a long time, I felt strong and confident in my body.

A final step brought me into a wide stance, hands outthrust as I pantomimed the spear striking home, burying itself in the chest of an invisible enemy. Perspiration trickled down my face and shoulders, but I held the position, chest rising and falling, my muscles aching pleasurably. My Attendant stood before me, its stance a perfect mirror of my own.

For a moment there was no sound save the murmuring river. Then, as if on cue, the Acolytes burst into applause.

"Save that," I said, but I could not help grinning as I straightened. My Attendant did the same.

I waved a basic command gesture, and the spectral light faded from behind the bronze mask. The Attendant's posture slackened, hands hanging lifelessly by its sides as it awaited a living soul's instructions.

"Breath," I repeated as my students quieted, "is the foundation of all martial skill. Whether in a fistfight or on a battlefield, performing the Rites or fighting with gladius and shield, your breathing determines whether you live or die. Master it, and you master yourself. Understand?"

They nodded in unison. I chose one at random: a light-skinned girl of mixed Ayu'li and Extorani heritage. "Acolyte Drusa. When I performed The Body Dances with the Spear, what was the pattern of my breathing?"

"I..." Drusa rubbed her scalp, a nervous habit she'd picked up after her long dark hair was shorn away. "Could you explain the question, sir?"

I gave her what I hoped was an encouraging smile. The answer might have seemed obvious to me, but I was new to teaching. If my students struggled to grasp a concept, that was my failing, not theirs.

"When did I exhale?" I rephrased. "When did I inhale?"

"Oh!" Drusa's eyes lit with new understanding. "Whenever you moved you breathed out."

"And breathed in?"

"Whenever you came to rest."

"Very good." I nodded my approval. "With every breath, you inhale strength."

I raised my hands to my diaphragm, palms down, lungs straining against my chest with a deep inhalation.

"Exhale power." I punctuated my point with a straight jab, adding flickering tendrils of ghostfire racing down my arm purely for dramatic effect. The light flared, and I was rewarded with a suitably impressed chorus of gasps from my students.

I fought to suppress a grin. Teaching, like any other art, involved an element of showmanship.

Only one Acolyte seemed unmoved by the performance and its underlying lesson. Titian stood a little apart, shoulders hunched and head lowered, silently glowering.

I had miscalculated, I realized. By hitting him, even gently, I had embarrassed him in front of his peers. His stung pride would keep him from learning the lesson I was trying to impart, and he would struggle all the more for it.

As in any art, those who taught failed from time to time.

I resolved to take Titian aside and explain what my intent had been. Later, though. The class was nearly at an end.

"Homework," I announced to general grumbling. "Practice The Body Walks for a full two hours tonight, with special attention paid to your breathing on each step. Whoever can perform it best next class gets a bag of my wife's candied dates."

Grumbles transmuted into excited murmurs. Candied dates were an Ayu'li delicacy, and Bahlanni had been perfecting her recipe since she and I were both younger than these Acolytes.

"Dismissed," I said, cupping my hands together and raising them to my brow as I bowed my head. "*Destri feh tyskal—*"

I trailed off, the traditional Ayu'li benediction dying on my lips at a raised hand. "Acolyte Titian?"

"Why do you have us do that?" he asked, lowering his hand to fold it across his chest. "Sign off in Asher."

Beside him, Drusa let out an outraged squeak.

"Ayu'li," I corrected, fighting to appear unruffled by the slur. "The language and people both are Ayu'li, Acolyte. As am I, and as are the arts I am instructing you in. If you wish to learn the Rites, you must do so with full appreciation of the history and culture behind them."

Titian remained unconvinced. "The old Bellator never made us."

"The old Bellator wanted to make you fighters," I said, fighting down the anger threatening to flare in me at the thought of Desmodius. "I am here to make you soldiers. I trust I need not explain the difference?"

Titian's face reddened, but he was smart enough not to dig himself a deeper hole by answering. He glared at me, something darker and uglier than a student's dislike for his teacher smoldering behind his eyes.

Small wonder. Titian's mother, the late Senator Lucilla Candorous, had been among those slaughtered in the failed coup the previous autumn. I had intervened, managing to save both Albastine's fragile democracy and a handful of Senators.

Titian's mother had not been among them. Now all that he had of his mother was the iron ring on his finger, the family crest denoting his station as head of house. Perhaps he had a right to hate me for that.

But he remained my student, and I his teacher. One day his life might depend upon the lessons I was trying to impart. Letting his disrespect go unpunished would do us both a disservice.

"Speaking of breath," I continued, trying to keep my tone light, "Acolyte Titian appears to still have plenty to spare. Which means the rest of you must as well."

A chorus of groans, and some dirty looks cast Titian's way. They knew what was coming.

"Jog to the White Gates and back." More groans as I waved towards the narrow mountain pass at the far end of the valley. "If you get started now, you might make it back to the barracks before midnight. Go!"

Grumbling and huffing, they took off, feet pounding down the rocky slopes towards the far end of the valley. Titian was the last, but I held out a hand to stop him.

"A word, Acolyte."

Titian folded his arms over his chest. I waited until the last of his fellow Acolytes had departed before I spoke. "I wanted to apologize."

He thrust his chin at me. "What for?"

"Hitting you." I tapped him lightly in the same spot, just between his bottom ribs. "It's not something I intend to make a habit of. I just wanted to demonstrate."

"The last Bellator hit me harder," Titian said, shrugging. "And more often."

I kept myself from wincing, but only just. My predecessor had been far more brutal in his method of instruction, as I could attest. But I was determined not to repeat his mistakes.

"Desmodius Meridius served his Republic well," I said carefully, lest invoking the name should trigger Titian's temper. "First as a Legate and then as a Bellator after honorable discharge."

Titian's gaze dropped to my left arm, which hung loosely by my side. These days I kept it covered in a segmented leather sleeve, not unlike the lorica armor I had worn on campaign in another life. I did not like looking at it uncovered.

"I'm aware of the parallels," I said drily. "But do you know what the difference between myself and Bellator Desmodius is?"

Titian shook his head.

"Desmodius carried his war with him," I said, thinking of the hollow, haunted eyes of the man who had been my own teacher. I had hated him, once, back when I was in Titian's place. But I understood him better now, and understanding is anathema to hatred. "It followed him home. He fought it again in his nightmares, found it waiting for him at the bottom of every bottle. He brought it to his students, took it out on them in hopes that it might spare them from the real thing. Spare *us* from the fate he suffered."

Titian's shoulders slackened, his brow creasing into a frown. Likely he had never thought of his previous teacher in such a light.

"Did it work?" he asked. "Did you bring your war home as well?"

Another memory rose to confront me: Quintus, dying in my arms, the last look upon his face a puzzled frown. I swallowed hard.

"Yes," I admitted. "Every soldier does. We don't get a choice in that. But the choice we *do* get is whether or not we keep fighting it. Understand?"

"I think so."

"Just don't do it again." I clapped him on the shoulder with my right hand—touching people with my left one made them uncomfortable, I'd discovered. "That'll be all, Acolyte Titian. If you hurry now you can catch up to your slower peers. So long as you mind your breath."

"Yes, sir." Titian pressed his fist to his heart in salute, then turned and hurried after his comrades.

As I watched him go, a shadow fell over me. I glanced up and realized with a start that the sun was already sinking below the valley's western peaks, casting the highlands where we stood into the shade of premature evening. My lesson must have run longer than I'd thought.

I'm going to be late.

I set off down the winding trail after my students, my feet pounding across the rocky ground as I raced the lowering sun.

I had an appointment to keep.

CHAPTER TWO

Situated in a narrow valley, Albastine and its white towers lay in shade throughout most of the day, save for when the sun shone directly overhead. This lent the streets a perpetually gloomy atmosphere, particularly when the mists rolling off the river rose to shroud the city in fog. Small wonder that neighboring peoples thought our lands haunted, when the mindless dead could come stumbling towards you from the fog at any moment.

Born and raised in Albastine as I was, neither mists nor Attendants held any fear for me. Yet anxiety still lent speed to my steps as I raced through the rapidly darkening streets.

My lungs and legs alike were burning by the time I crested a rise on the far side of the valley, climbing the steep mountainside trail until the Barrows stood before me, the familiar yellow bricks of its gated entrance flanked on either side by sandstone phoenixes.

I put my hands on my knees and bent over, fighting down the gorge threatening to rise in my throat. I had run fast and hard, soaking my tunic through with sweat.

It had not been enough. From behind the bars of the bronze gates came the faint sound of singing, echoing and distorted.

Once I had regained control of my breathing I turned my gaze skyward, saw the glitter of stars against a deep black sky. They glimmered as if in answer to the rhythmic chanting emanating from within the Barrows, words sung in the tongue of Ayu.

Disappointment twisted my heart. I had failed to keep my appointment.

I straightened, smoothing down my tunic as I approached the gate to the Old Faith's place of worship. Two guards flanked it, standing beneath either phoenix statue. They were dressed and armed in the traditional Ayu'li manner, bare above the waist save for bronze jewelry about their throats and forearms. Gray ash had been streaked across their brows in deference to the holy day that had begun with the sunset.

The traditional weapon of the Ayu'li people was the scimitar, but by law citizens were forbidden from carrying swords. In a concession to Albastine practicality, each guard held a bronze-tipped staff, which they crossed in front of the Barrows entrance as I approached.

"You're late," the taller of the two said, dark eyes fixed on me.

I glanced westward, where the last rays of sunlight streaked above the mountains. "Barely."

The guards remained unmoved. "You know the law, Akhenkatem. Once the sun has set, the Hours begin—"

"And none are permitted to interrupt them." I halted before the crossed staves and addressed the shorter guard directly. "Come on, Neftani. It's barely dark."

"The Hours start at sundown," he said. "You of all people should know that."

"Why do you think I hurried over so fast?"

"Because you were late," came a third voice, scarcely audible over the groan of the Barrows' doors opening. A slight young man stood behind them, dressed in the blue robes of the Old Faith priesthood. The kohl shading his eyes matched the ash upon his forehead. "Hello, Akhenkatem. May the blessings of the Hours of Remembrance fall upon you."

"And on you, Hupli," I answered with a stiff nod. That the junior priest had anticipated my late arrival was a bad sign. "I'm not *that* late."

"The high priestess thought you might have some difficulty in keeping your promise." Hupli's tone was placid, but the words stung. "She sent me to ensure that you were able to attend the service unhindered."

"Kind of her."

Hupli tilted his head in acknowledgment. "Her Reverence is munificent."

Even to the likes of you, he left unsaid. Though he had never spoken to me with anything but courtesy, Hupli had subtly made his dislike of me plain on multiple occasions.

Out of the corner of my eye I noticed the guards exchange an uncomfortable look.

"Mercy is among her many qualities," I said, electing to take the high road. "As is patience. But we shouldn't test hers any longer, should we?"

"No." Hupli turned to the guards. "Let him through."

That did the trick. Both guards stepped aside, leaving the Barrows open like a yawning mouth. I stepped inside, into the warmth and darkness and the echoing chants of my ancestral tongue.

Soft refrains of song resonated off the winding tunnel walls as Hupli and I made our way towards the central chamber, our path lit by gently flickering candles. The walls on either side were carved with the likenesses of Ayu'li past, their features seeming to move and dance in the candlelight. Old and young, male and female, long dead and recently passed: all stared down at me from the walls, memorialized forever in this sacred place in the heart of the mountains we had made our second home. If I ventured deeper into the Barrows' complex series of tunnels, I could find my own family's private chamber and lay eyes upon the likenesses of my parents and grandparents.

Later, I told myself, just as I told myself that it was the haze of incense clouding the air that was making my eyes water.

Ordinarily these altars were bare, save for small offerings laid at their feet. But now we had come to the Hours of Remembrance, the high holy day of the Old Faith's calendar. Beginning at sundown and lasting until midnight the following day, the time was divided into seven Hours, set aside to recall the history of our people and their exile from the banks of the Ayu, to grieve and celebrate our lost ancestors and our living kin. In token of this, nearly every statue was festooned with wreaths or small bits of jade jewelry, with soft green silks draped lovingly about their stone limbs. Green was the color of the first Hour, that of Rest.

"Do you have a favorite?" Hupli asked, apropos of nothing. After nearly a minute of walking in silence, his voice echoing off the tunnel walls made me jump.

"A favorite ancestor?" I frowned. "That's like asking a parent if they have a favorite child."

He looked at me, his face unreadable. "A favorite Hour, I mean."

"Ah." That made more sense, considering the decorated

memorials surrounding us. "I suppose I've always been partial to the Hour of Return."

"The last of the Hours," Hupli said. We rounded a corner, the chanting from the main chamber growing steadily louder. "The promise that one day things will be set right. Is that its appeal?"

"Not really," I admitted. "I just liked getting candy when I was a kid."

Another man would have snorted, but Hupli did not so much as frown. "Your glibness does you little credit, Akhenkatem."

My Ayu'li name sounded like a reprimand in his mouth. "Well. It was also the end of the Hours. When they were done I could see my grandfather again."

"I see." Was that thoughtfulness I detected in Hupli's flat monotone? Hard to say. "I remember your grandfather well."

"Really?" Hupli was barely into his twenties, and my grandfather had passed over a decade ago. "You would have been very young."

"I knew I would join the priesthood from an early age," he said, voice void of inflection. "I took a greater interest in the sermons than my peers. And your grandfather was quite gifted."

"That he was," I said, my voice coming out hoarse. Grief never entirely loses its sting.

Further down the tunnel the chanting grew in pitch and volume, the words coming more clearly as I drew nearer to the Barrows' central chamber. I recognized it as the Mother's Nocturne, a farewell to the day and welcome of the coming night.

Unlike many other peoples, we Ayu'li held no fear of the night in our hearts. Our genesis stories said that the first men and women were shaped from the mud of the River Ayu at night, and that to night and dust would each of us return, at the close of our days. Thus were our most sacred ceremonies held at night, the time when the world of the living and that of the lost most closely brushed against one another.

"Wait," Hupli said, coming to a sudden stop just beyond the entrance to the chamber.

"For what?" The Nocturne, the last chance for me to slip into the chamber unnoticed while the congregation was preoccupied with its song, was drawing to a close.

"You are not properly attired." Hupli reached into a pouch at his side. His hand came away coated in fine gray ash.

"Alright." I swallowed my mounting impatience and bowed my head.

"In remembrance of Ayu." Hupli's touch was cool, almost clammy. The ashes were a fine dusting against my brow. "And those we have lost. May the rhythm of our feet guide them home."

"And our song call them to us," I finished, straightening. "May I go in?"

Hupli nodded, expressionless. Without another word he turned and disappeared down a side tunnel, leaving me to enter the house of worship alone.

My streak of bad luck held. I emerged into the central chamber just as the Nocturne died away, my footfalls echoing in the sudden silence. For a moment I stood there in the tunnel entrance, blinking rapidly at the thousands of candles lining the walls, turning the cavern as bright as noon.

When my vision adjusted I found that nearly the entire congregation was staring at me, their expressions unreadable.

I stared past them to the woman standing on the central dais, elaborate ceremonial robes and jewelry dangling from her outstretched arms as she stood in a posture of benediction.

From across the length of the chamber I could feel her dark gaze boring into me.

My mouth felt sandpaper dry. I swallowed and gave a little wave, hoping my expression looked appropriately contrite.

My wife did not return the gesture.

Nor did she frown, or give any acknowledgment of my presence that the assembly might have noticed. Only a smile, so swift and fleeting that I almost thought I'd imagined it.

I returned the expression, my own smile a touch sheepish as I did my best to slink into the crowd. Bahlanni nodded, ever so slightly, then turned her attention back to her congregation, fixing them with her wide, white smile.

"Sisters and brothers," she said in Ayu'li, her ringing voice reverberating off the cavern walls. "Aunties and nieces, uncles and nephews. Grandparents and cousins all. I bid you welcome to the Hour of Rest, this night of feasting and remembrance. Before midnight we shall recall the names of those who came before us and those who have since passed beyond into the Quiet Fields. We shall drink to their memory and break bread in their names."

An approving murmur swept through the congregation. The long winter had been a time of strife and unrest as the Republic reeled from the coup that had very nearly toppled Albastine's democracy. Now, on the edge of spring, the chaos finally seemed to have subsided, leaving the people of Albastine eager for the coming season of growth and renewal. Tonight's sunset service coincided with the mood of the city exactly.

Bahlanni clasped her hands, bracelets jangling. The congregation silenced, staring up at her with worshipful expectation.

I breathed a sigh of relief. My gaffe had been forgotten —for now.

"But first," Bahlanni said, both her expression and tone sobering, "we must remember those we have lost."

Silence cast its heavy blanket over the chamber, bowing every head. All knew she was speaking of last autumn. The majority of the Senate had been killed, including all three heads of state, two of whom had been the conspirators responsible for the coup. Were it not for the intervention of dozens of brave Old Faith Ayu'li led by Bahlanni herself, the conspirators might have succeeded in installing themselves as dictators over a nation that would have been a Republic in name only.

Emergency elections had been held throughout Albastine and its provinces. Formerly the Senate's makeup had been predominantly composed of individuals elected to semi-hereditary seats, restricting membership to the oldest and wealthiest noble families of the Republic. Such restrictions were lifted in the wake of what was now being called the Lightfall Massacre. Our new crop of Senators was both more representative of the people they served and more aggressive in shaping policy so that they would not fall victim to the same complacency that had killed their predecessors.

Many of the new Senators were Ayu'li themselves, or of blended heritage. All of them, regardless of race, honored the sacrifice of those Ayu'li who had turned the tide against the coup's instigators, falling in defense of a Republic that had not always treated them as fully equal citizens. The families of the lost had mourned their fallen heroes privately, but tonight we would honor them together.

"Raphekten," Bahlanni began, closing her eyes as she lifted her face heavenwards. "Khafra his mother, Ahmoptis his father. Iahmti his wife, Meresankh their daughter. Fallen in battle in defense of his family and home. Now he resides in the Quiet Fields with his grandparents. We give thanks to him for his sacrifice."

"Raphekten," the congregation and I chorused. "Son of Khafra and Ahmoptis. We honor you and thank you."

I had not known Raphekten, but somewhere near at hand I heard the choked sound of a woman fighting down a sob. I wondered if it was Iahmti, wife to the fallen hero. Guilt settled around my shoulders like a leaden cloak, and this time I could not blame the stinging in my eyes on the incense.

This man's death lay at my feet. I had not struck the killing blow, but if I had found the root of the conspiracy sooner I could have stopped it before any lives were lost. Had I been faster, stronger, braver, Raphekten might have lived. Had I been any of the things I was not, Meresankh might still have both her parents.

Guilt dragged my head down, yet I could feel no solidarity with the others of the congregation standing in identical postures. Were it not for me, they would have no reason to mourn.

"Djehen," Bahlanni continued. "Anramet her mother, Khiap her father..."

A feeling of sudden clarity came over me as Bahlanni moved on to the name of the next fallen Ayu'li. This was the reason I had come late to the service, though I had not been willing to admit it even to myself. I had not wanted to hear the roll call of the dead, the list of people who might yet be alive had I not begged my estranged wife to intervene in the coup.

"Ramsi. Honsta her mother, Busat her father..."

I stood there and listened to my wife call out the names of those who had died for and because of me. Each of those names was a weight between my shoulders, bowing me down. The names of those relatives who survived them were knives in my gut, twisting with each loss I had inflicted upon them.

This is my penance, I thought. *My punishment for failing them. Failing all of them.*

Name upon name, one after the other. Each one the missing fragment of a shattered family. Each one a mark against my soul. My knees were shaking, my breath coming in unsteady gasps. I wanted to run away. To flee from the chamber, from the Barrows itself. But the press of bodies was too thick, so close that I might have fallen if their shoulders had not propped up my own. My tears watered the stone floor.

"Akhenkatem," Bahlanni called out.

My head jerked up at the sound of my own name, the one my grandfather had given me. But that could not be right. During the battle I had come close to the Quiet Fields, but not close enough. Why then was Bahlanni listing my name among the fallen?

Evidently, I was not the only one wondering. Others of the congregation moved away from me, leaving me in a sudden gap in the crowd. I could feel their eyes fixed on me, though I could not read what lay behind them.

"Akhenkatem," Bahlanni repeated, staring at me. I could not read what was in her gaze. "Ainkar his father, Nyeri his mother. Bahlanni his wife. Come forward."

Hands reached out, pulling me forward, the congregation receding before me like the tide. Dread seized me. I was being called to account for the deaths I had caused. To look the families of the lost in the eye and plead for their mercy. I wanted to run, to flee. But I could no more resist the gently insistent hands tugging me towards the dais than I could sprout wings and fly from the Barrows.

Whispers fluttered around me like moths as the congregants bore me towards the dais. I realized with a start that their words were soft, almost reverent. There was no venom in them.

Before I could register what this might mean I was being led onto the dais, to stand beside my wife. Bahlanni turned to me, embraced me, and murmured in my ear. "You were late, my love."

"Sorry," I croaked back. "I had...something to take care of. What are you doing?"

"The same thing I've been doing all through this sermon," she whispered as she broke from the embrace. "Honoring our heroes."

She turned to the congregation, bangles jingling. "Erkhanti, Mekhati her mother and Hastir her father. Come forward."

Again the congregation parted as it ushered a single worshipper forward. I blinked, realizing that I recognized this one, though she had been introduced to me by her Extorani name. A very young woman, all ropy dark muscle, her head shorn almost as close as mine.

"Elantine," I greeted her under my breath as she joined Bahlanni and me on the dais. "Fancy seeing you here."

"Don't tell me you didn't know she was planning this," the former Acolyte returned, nodding at Bahlanni, who had already begun to call the next name.

"Hadn't the slightest idea," I said, truthfully. Bahlanni had taken to rehearsing her sermons for me during my convalescence after Lightfall, but she had kept this one under wraps, deflecting every time I asked about it. Now I knew why.

Elantine frowned. "She's your wife."

I looked at my wife, whose arms were raised in welcome as the other survivors of the coup came forward, singly or in pairs. Their faces, like those of their fellow parishioners, were fixed on hers, alight with admiration. These were adherents so dedicated to the Old Faith that they had followed Bahlanni into battle, so certain was their faith in her own convictions. Prophets and queens were made of such charisma.

"You're right," I said to Elantine. "But she's our priestess, first."

Before long all the surviving Ayu'li veterans of the Lightfall Massacre stood on the dais.

"Praise them," Bahlanni said, turning to us and bowing her head. "They have done our ancestors proud, defended our homes. Heroes all, the living and the dead. Let us rejoice in their courage and take comfort in their strength, and in turn comfort them so that their scars may begin to heal."

She turned to me and embraced me more closely than before—a wife embracing her husband.

"You are safe, Akhenkatem," she whispered in my ear as around me the congregation pressed in, placing hands on the shoulders and backs and heads of my fellow survivors in silent benediction. "You are safe, and you are home."

I nodded, but found myself unable to speak. I laid my head on my wife's shoulder and felt the grief leak from me with every ugly, choking sob. Around me I heard the other veterans of the battle doing the same.

They held us there, silent companions and witnesses to our grief: the whole community of the Old Faith Ayu'li, united in their tenderness towards us. I do not know how long it lasted, only that when my tears had dried I felt remade, renewed, reborn.

CHAPTER THREE

"You hate this, don't you?" Bahlanni whispered to me half an hour later, beaming as the congregation mingled and swayed around us.

The formal opening of the Hours had concluded, giving way to the celebratory feasting that characterized the Hour of Rest. A goodly number of the congregation had already made their way to the long tables lining the walls, which were heavily laden with trays piled high with spiced meats and mountains of rice. My stomach grumbled at the aromas drifting over to where we stood upon the dais with the rest of the veterans of Lightfall, swamped by a small mob of well-wishers paying their respects.

"I don't love it," I murmured out of the corner of my mouth, my own smile fixed in place. My role in the events of six months ago had earned me no small acclaim amongst our people, and I'd had plenty of time to practice smiling at crowds instead of screaming. "If I'd wanted to be the center of attention I would have gone into theater."

"Not with your singing voice," Bahlanni said, her grin widening into something real.

An elderly couple approached, taking both Bahlanni's

hands and mine and kissing our knuckles. I stammered out an embarrassed thanks, but Bahlanni handled their attention with the poise and grace of one long accustomed to receiving such adulation. She thanked them with utter sincerity, then sent them on their way before turning back to me.

"I should have warned you," she said, her grin fading a little. "About honoring the fallen. I should have known it might be a burden to you."

"It's not..." I shook my head, remembering what I had told my students scant hours before. *Breathe.* "I just wish I could have...that there were more of them standing here with us, not..."

"My love." Bahlanni stepped closer, angling us away from another set of well-wishers. Out of the corner of my eye I saw Elantine step in to greet them. I felt a rush of affection for her.

"Akhenkatem." Bahlanni touched two fingers to my chin and turned me to face her. "What happened on Lightfall was not your fault."

My voice came out in a whisper. "It feels like it is."

"It was not." Bahlanni's tone brooked no argument. "I brought our people to the Senate. They followed me there, not you."

"Because I asked you for their help." I wanted to look away, but the deep pools of her dark eyes held me fast.

"And we gave it." Bahlanni leaned in and rested her brow against mine. I closed my eyes, feeling her breath on my lips. "Those who died, died well. Do not punish yourself for the choices they made, my love. Neither you nor they deserve that."

I nodded, eyes shut tight. A tear squeezed its way down my cheek, a hot droplet of guilt.

"You are a good man, my love," Bahlanni said, taking my hand in hers and pressing it to her lips. "I would not have married you were you not."

I laughed, shaking free more tears. Dimly I became aware that the other survivors on the dais had closed ranks around us, shielding my moment of weakness from the eyes of the congregation.

The press of bodies around us no longer felt like a weight, but an embrace. I took a shuddering breath, finding that my tears had vanished as swiftly as they had come.

"Thank you," I said, to her and those around me as well. "I... I need some air. Do you..."

"Of course." Bahlanni kissed my hand again and glanced in the direction of the laden tables. "I'll save you a plate?"

My stomach growled an affirmative, and I let out a shaky laugh. "You truly are the best of wives."

She grinned up at me. "And don't you forget it."

FRESH AIR WAS a sweet relief as I emerged from the Barrows and into the night. The guards standing vigil turned in surprise as I stepped out from the bronze gate.

"Akhenkatem?" Neftani's brows lifted. "I didn't think it would be over so soon."

"It's not," I assured him. "I just needed some quiet."

He nodded and leaned in conspiratorially. "Honestly, there's a reason I'm out here and not in there. Can't stand the hymns."

It felt good to laugh. I clapped Neftani on the shoulder, nodded my thanks to his companion, then set off down the trail, letting my feet carry me along.

I walked without purpose for a while, taking solace in the bracingly cold breeze blowing against my face, coolly refreshing after the warmth of the Barrows. The quiet too was a relief, leaving me space to be alone with my thoughts.

I had been blindsided by Bahlanni's public honoring of the

Lightfall survivors, but upon reflection, that was not truly her fault. Had I arrived on time, she might have told me about her intentions and given me the option to opt out—or at the very least, time to acclimate to the idea.

Rebuilding a marriage took time. After years of separation, our reconciliation was not and had not been smooth, nor easy. Communication was something we were both still working on, as were expectations. But we were improving with each day, with each conversation. One day, we hoped, things would be as they were for us in the beginning.

Until then, all we could do was be gracious with each other.

The wind changed, snatching at my cloak, and I found myself standing in a high place overlooking the valley. From here all Albastine lay spread out beneath me like a map, quiet and foggy.

The city's slender white spires rose from mist-shrouded streets, looking less like skeletal fingers and more like a forest of petrified trees.

Albastine. My home, my city. I had fought for her, bled for her, almost died for her.

Now, after the long chill of winter, I was finally discovering what it meant to live for her.

A metallic glint flashed in the corner of my eye, cutting through the mists that swirled at the foot of the mountain path.

Startled, I turned. My heartbeat hammered against my chest as I cast my eyes downslope, towards where I had seen the glimmer of light.

A shadow loomed in the fog. Mists swirled around it as it ascended the trail, obscuring its form. My breath caught in my throat, my hand falling by old habit to my side before I recalled that I no longer carried the gladius that was the Legate's badge of office.

The shape resolved itself into a human figure, cloaked and

unnaturally still. What little light pierced the fog glinted off its bronze mask.

I released the breath I hadn't realized I'd been holding. It came out as a laugh at my own foolishness. An Attendant. Of course. Who else would be out here in the dark and cold?

And yet...

What would an Attendant be doing up here on the heights? The unliving servants were forbidden in the Barrows, and there was no task it could possibly have been ordered to perform this late at night, on this lonely mountain path.

As I pondered this, the Attendant stood motionless. But it was not the inert dormancy of an automaton awaiting orders. The posture was wrong, somehow.

And it was looking right at me.

Unsettled, I took a step to my right. The bronze mask turned, the unseen eyes behind it tracking my movements.

Sweat beaded on my neck, colder than the mists. Attendants were passive automata, incapable of taking action of their own initiative, and they possessed only a rudimentary awareness of their surroundings. For this one to scrutinize me so closely meant that it was under the direct control of someone else trained in the Rites.

I was being watched.

The realization must have shown on my face, because whoever was puppeteering the Attendant made it take a step back. I reached out my hand, intending to wrest control of the Attendant, but before I could make even the most basic command gesture, it had faded back into the fog.

"Wait!" I plunged into the mists after the Attendant, my feet pounding down the uneven mountain slope. Ahead, my quarry was little more than a vague outline in the fog. Again I tried to seize control of it, but found that dividing my focus between giving chase and performing the gestures of command was counterproductive to both efforts. Though they had been stripped down from the elaborate Ayu'li dances to their most basic components, the Rites remained difficult to perform on the run.

Fine, then, I thought. *I'll catch it the old-fashioned way.*

I put my head down and put on speed, legs pumping rhythmically as I gave chase. The embalming process that fortified Attendant bodies against the ravages of decay also stiffened their ligaments, giving their motions a characteristic rigidity. Even the most well-preserved Attendant could never outrun the living.

Yet the distance between us closed only slowly, if at all. Partly it was the difficulty of running downhill on a winding footpath in the dark; a single misplaced step could result in an ankle badly twisted or even broken. But more than that, the Attendant was *fast.* It must have undergone the Rite of Rising only recently, because it moved with an adroitness that was nearly lifelike.

Several times it almost lost me in the fog, yet each time I managed to catch up. If I hadn't known better, I would have thought it was trying to make sure I was still following it. An unsettling thought.

The mist-shrouded world around us changed as I ran, the path beneath my feet leveling out to become the familiar cobblestone streets of Albastine, the high wall of the mountains being replaced by the towering shadows of the Pale City's spires.

The Attendant had slowed its pace, turning from a shadow in the fog to a more human shape. I was close enough to see that it was not dressed in the typical Attendant's tunic and cowl —a ragged black cloak trailed out behind it.

Stranger and stranger. Who took the time to *dress* their Attendants? It wasn't like they could feel the chill.

I chased it down a flight of stairs into a gloomy courtyard. Abruptly, the Attendant stopped.

I slowed to an unsteady halt, my heartbeat thudding loudly in my ears. I approached slowly, keeping a wary distance in case of some trick.

The Attendant turned to me, its bronze-masked face unreadable as it raised a hand.

Though it held no weapon, instinct took over. I made the most rudimentary command gesture, the grasping motion that would allow me to seize the Attendant's puppet strings myself.

Nothing happened.

I stared at the Attendant. Whoever was behind its smiling bronze mask stared back, unperturbed.

I tried again, pouring more of my will into the gesture. Again, nothing.

Sweat and mist mingled against my scalp. I had been prepared for the contest of wills that ensued whenever two Legates vied for control over the same Attendant. Instead, the Attendant had been wholly unaffected, my command sliding off it like water off a duck.

What was I dealing with here?

The Attendant's hand was still raised, but it made no move towards me. Bizarrely, it had one finger extended, pointing into the fog.

"You're trying to show me something." The revelation was so startling that I didn't realize I'd said it aloud. Not until the Attendant further unnerved me by giving a stiff, solemn nod.

As if on command, the mists parted, revealing something far more unsettling. Three bodies lay strewn about the courtyard, though no blood pooled beneath them. More Attendants, scattered in a macabre tableau beneath the wall of the nearest building. The pale marble had been vandalized with a message crudely scrawled in streaks of black soot: ALBASTINE IN ASHES.

I shivered, overcome by the sudden urge to wipe away the ashes adorning my brow.

Beneath the graffiti, one of the Attendants twitched feebly, and my stomach churned as I saw that all three had been badly mutilated. Each had had its legs cut off just above the knee, their bloodless stumps slowly twitching as the Attendants attempted to carry out whatever their last orders had been. Upon closer inspection, the same had been done to their arms.

For a moment the world swam with a weird sense of déjà vu. I had seen Attendants dismembered like this only once before, during my investigation into the events that led to the Lightfall Massacre.

My enemies had laid a trap for me, luring me to an estate where all the Attendants had been ordered to self-mutilate, depriving me of their use as weapons and forcing me into a straight fight with one of the conspirators.

The thought drew my attention back to the strange Attendant I had pursued—no, the Attendant that had *led* me to this place. It had come to me directly and made sure I followed it back to the site of this grisly crime.

Someone had wanted me to see this.

I found myself again reaching for a sword that was not there, goosebumps prickling along my arms as I scanned the mists for more assailants. I turned back to the Attendant, ready to lash out at whoever was controlling it, regardless of how futile such an attack would be.

But the Attendant was gone. It had faded back into the mists, phantasmal, as if it had never been there.

A dazed feeling swept over me, heightened by the unreality of the scene. I had taken the Attendant's strange behavior to mean that it was under someone's direct control.

Had there been an Attendant at all? Or was I going crazy? I had heard tales from other veterans about old campaigners who, upon retiring, started seeing enemies where there were none. I thought back to my conversation with Acolyte Titian and wondered if I had truly left my war behind me like I had claimed.

Worry about that later, the rational part of my mind told me. *These three Attendants are real, whether that one was or not.*

Just to be sure, I nudged one with my boot. It didn't react, which was as expected. Attendants ignored any and all stimuli that didn't impede their assigned tasks. But the reality of the damaged Attendant, grotesque as it was, provided some reassurance.

Who did this? I wondered, staring down at the Attendant's stump, which twitched rhythmically, trying to move the leg that was no longer there. *And why?*

All unskilled labor in Albastine was performed by the Attendants, from heavy lifting to threshing grain to street cleaning. Individually or in cohorts, Attendants could be loaned out to guilds or private citizens, but ultimately all were property of the state. To mutilate them like this was a crime against the Republic itself.

Who could possibly stand to gain from such senseless sabotage?

"By all the gods," came a voice sounding nearly as sickened as I felt. "What is this?"

I turned just in time to see a figure emerge from the fog on the far side of the courtyard: a petite woman, slightly built beneath the heavy robes that guarded her against the chill night. The silver of a magistrate's badge glinted on her chest.

Her gaze swept the courtyard, taking in the mangled Attendants and the ominous graffiti before settling on me. Her eyes widened, then narrowed as I saw her gaze track from the ashes on my brow to those on the marble wall, then back to me.

"Get on the ground," she said, drawing the baton that was every magistrate's sidearm.

I blinked. "What?"

"By the authority of Albastine and the Magisterium, I'm placing you under arrest." She took a step closer, keeping her weight on the balls of her feet. With her free hand she drew a pair of interconnected cords, each end weighted with a heavy stone. A bola, typically used by magistrates to apprehend fleeing suspects.

Oh.

"I..." Someone had glued my tongue to my mouth. I swallowed hard, tried again. "I didn't *do* this."

"Sure," the magistrate said, in a tone that implied no credulity whatsoever. She circled me with wary footsteps, a hum splitting the mists as she spun the bolas, turning the paired cords into a whirling blur with her hand at its center. "On the ground. Final warning."

"Listen," I said, desperation seizing hold of me as I took a step forward. "There was an Attendant—"

The magistrate let fly the bola.

It whipped end over end at me across the courtyard, faster than I would have believed. Before I could even raise a hand in defense, it slammed into my midsection, harder and faster than any punch I had ever received.

I gurgled as the blow knocked the air from me. The bola whirled around me, binding my arms tight against my sides. I tried to fight free of them, unbalanced and fell. A crack thundered in my ears as my head hit the cobblestones. The world wobbled.

A shadow approached from the mist, resolving itself into the figure of the magistrate standing over me, her expression grim as any Attendant's war mask.

Fool that I was, I still thought I could persuade the magistrate that this was a misunderstanding.

"The Attendant," I said, struggling to pull myself into a sitting position. "It was just here..."

My left arm had not been fully trapped by the bolas, but in my shock, I had forgotten to exercise control over the otherwise useless limb, letting it fall uselessly to my side. Instinctively I sent a burst of will running down it.

It was not the stupidest thing I had ever done. But it was close.

The magistrate gasped as ghostfire blazed to life from between the cracks in my leather sleeve. I looked up at her, still intent on explaining the strange circumstances that had led me to this courtyard, and saw her baton come falling towards me like a meteor.

Then I saw nothing at all.

CHAPTER FOUR

Albastine was not a society that put a great deal of stock into incarceration. The valley was too narrow and our farms too meager to allow those who lived within not to contribute to the betterment of all. Locking someone behind the bars of a prison cell was a drain on the collective resources of the entire city.

Yet even in a community as orderly and civic-minded as ours, crime still occurred. And wherever there was crime, there was need for a place to hold those apprehended until their misdeeds could be properly reviewed by the powers of order and justice. Since we lacked a dedicated jailhouse, other buildings were repurposed as the need arose.

Which is why I awoke in a meat locker, my teeth chattering as my breath misted before my eyes and a pounding headache threatened to split my skull from the inside. A lamp shining near the doorway alleviated the gloom enough for me to see the shapeless carcasses hanging on hooks from the ceiling.

Shivering, I pulled myself to my feet. The bolas were no longer wrapped about my middle, but in their place, someone had cuffed my wrists. The sturdy iron dug painfully into the skin of my right hand. My left was completely numb.

Of course it is, some cool and rational part of my brain reminded me. The investiture of will that animated my atrophied left arm only remained active while I was consciously focused on maintaining control over it. Sleep or distraction left it hanging uselessly at my side.

Most days I animated my arm the moment I awoke. But most days I didn't wake up in a strange place after being hit on the head.

I sighed and poured my will down my bad arm. Flickers of spectral blue light danced across the walls as muted sensation returned to my fingers.

"Neat party trick."

The magistrate who had arrested me stood beneath the lamp, a small shadow halfway obscured by the carcasses hanging from the ceiling.

"You didn't seem to think so the first time." I took a wary step forward, ready to throw myself to the side at the first telltale whirr of bolas. "You going to knock me down again?"

She shook her head. "There aren't any Attendants within a hundred yards of us. Make your little lights all you want."

"Smart of you," I said, moving between the rows of carcasses to a scarred and stained butcher's table. "May I sit?"

She jerked her head at the benches running alongside the table. "Go ahead."

I did, making sure to leave plenty of space for the magistrate. After a moment's consideration she padded over on soundless feet, taking a seat on the opposite bench, at the far end of the table.

The lamplight cast her in stark relief, giving me my first proper look at her. The short cut of her inky hair emphasized the sharpness of her features, turning what might have been porcelain delicacy on another woman into something severe.

I winced as my headache redoubled its attempts to escape my brain. "Can I ask why I've been arrested, Magistrate...?"

"Caprio." She put her baton on the table between us. "Lavinia Caprio. Magistrate of the Republic of Albastine. Sworn to uphold its laws."

"Thank you for your service." The words came automatically; respect for soldiers and lawkeepers alike had been ingrained in me from an early age. Only when Lavinia's eyes narrowed did I realize she'd thought I was being sarcastic.

"As for your arrest," she continued after a moment's frosty silence, "I have you on suspicion of sabotaging state property. Not to mention a possible charge of fomenting insurrection."

"Insurrection?" I frowned. Her eyes flickered up to the streak of ash across my brow, and I recalled the sinister graffiti smeared across the marble wall. "That wasn't..."

She said nothing, watching me. Waiting.

I trailed off, thinking. I *hadn't* dismembered those Attendants or scrawled those ashes on the wall. But anything I said might be misconstrued and used against me. If I was going to leave this meat locker without a criminal charge, I'd have to tread carefully.

"I think," I said, choosing each word with exaggerated deliberation, "that you're supposed to write my name and occupation first."

To her credit, she showed no outward sign of annoyance. Instead, she nodded crisply, as though I was a junior magistrate reminding his superior of a minor clerical detail she'd overlooked, and pulled a wax tablet and stylus from somewhere in her robes.

"Of course," she said. "State them both, for the record."

"Gaius Cassius Calvus. Bellator."

The stylus made no noise against the wax. "Any aliases?"

"My Ayu'li name is Akhenkatem."

Lavinia twitched, as though there were a fly buzzing around her ear. Curious.

"Something wrong?" I asked.

"No." She paused. "Your wife is Bahlanni Apenti? High priestess of the Old Faith Ayu'li?"

"That's right," I said, frowning. It was an odd line of questioning—our marriage wasn't exactly secret.

"And when was the last time you saw your wife, Bellator Calvus?"

"This evening," I said, fighting to ignore the pounding of my skull. "She led a sunset service for the Old Faith. There were about a thousand other people who saw her there."

"What about before that?"

"Why does it matter?"

"Answer the question, please."

"This morning, I guess. We had breakfast."

Lavinia raised a brow. "Is it normal for you to go an entire day without seeing each other?"

"Yes." Perhaps our recent reconciliation was making me defensive, but I felt the inexplicable need to justify my marriage to this magistrate. "Our duties both take up a great deal of our time."

"Your duties," Lavinia repeated. "As a Bellator, you're responsible for training Albastine's Acolytes in the Rites and battlefield tactics so that they can become capable Legates. But I confess I'm not as familiar with what the position of high priestess entails. I imagine it involves a great deal of time spent ministering to her flock?"

"You'd be correct."

"Is any of that time spent in communication with the Sons of Ash?"

I blinked. "The who?"

Lavinia studied me for a silent moment, apparently trying to determine whether my confusion was feigned.

"Let me phrase that another way," she said, tapping her finger against the tablet. "Have you noticed your wife meeting with any strange individuals lately?"

"Magistrate Caprio," I said, ignoring the question, "my wife's not under arrest, is she?"

Lavinia's mouth became a tight line. "No."

"Then I don't have to answer your questions about her." I leaned back, placing my manacled hands in my lap. I didn't know who the Sons of Ash were or why this magistrate thought that Bahlanni was somehow involved with them. But I wasn't going to tell her anything more until I'd had the chance to talk to my wife myself.

"Fine." The word sounded like it cost Lavinia something. "Let's return to tonight, then. What were you doing in the hour or so prior to your arrest?"

I told her, from the Hour of Rest to my departure from it, though I glossed over the reasons behind my hasty exit.

"Is it reasonable to assume you're also a practicing member of the Old Faith, considering your marriage?"

"Recently reconverted," I admitted. "I was raised in the church but drifted away as an adult."

"Why's that?"

"Crisis of faith." I looked down at my hands, the one healthy and whole, the other not. I thought of what being here today had cost me.

Lavinia's eyes, huge and dark like some nocturnal predator's, flickered to the ashes on my brow. "An ongoing one?"

"Like I said, I've recently returned." I covered my gloved hand with the other. "Dozens of people saw me leave the Hour of Rest, Magistrate. And the time between that and you hitting me in the head isn't long enough for me to have done whatever it is you think I've done."

"Certainly not." Lavinia set the stylus and tablet down with deliberate care. "Not if you were an ordinary citizen, anyway. But for a Legate..."

She let the implication hang in the air between us.

"Gods," I realized. "You think I commanded those Attendants to cut off their own limbs?"

Her mouth twitched at the corners. "You leapt to that conclusion rather quickly."

A grisly memory rose in my mind: the dark confines of Tycho Terrens's decaying estate. A line of Attendants, their limbs stacked beside them like firewood, the last in line hacking at its own legs with a rusting cleaver.

"Each of the Attendants had all four limbs removed," I said, my voice coming out calmer than I felt. "If that was the case, wouldn't one of them have still had the knife?"

Lavinia's face spasmed, so subtly I might have missed it if I hadn't been watching her closely. But for that brief moment I saw doubt in her dark eyes.

"You might have hidden it somewhere," she said. "Or passed it off to your associates."

"My associates," I repeated. "You're talking about these Sons of Ash?"

Lavinia shrugged. "Someone had to complete the mutilations. As you said, not all of these—that is, not all of the Attendants could have done it to themselves."

Her hesitation was brief, her correction smooth. Yet I had a sudden intuition that for the first time in our interview Lavinia had misspoken. Not *the* Attendants, but—

"*These* Attendants," I repeated, stressing the word slightly. Realization struck. My living fingers trembled against the table. "Gods. This isn't the first time this has happened. There are more dismembered Attendants, aren't there?"

Lavinia said nothing, though a muscle twitched in her jaw.

I leaned against the bench, the pieces falling together. The graffiti with its ominous proclamation: ALBASTINE IN ASHES. The mutilated Attendants. The Sons of Ash, and Lavinia's intimations of insurrection.

"You think there's another conspiracy out to destroy the Republic," I breathed. "And that Bahlanni and I are part of it."

Her silence was all the confirmation I needed.

CHAPTER FIVE

Maybe it was just my headache, or maybe it was the cloud of my own frigid breath down in the cold of the meat locker, but my vision went blurry for a moment. I put both hands on the table, steadying myself as a sense of unutterable exhaustion crashed down on me.

Hadn't I done enough already? I had uncovered one plot to overthrow Albastine only months ago, and had only narrowly averted that crisis. But the conspirators had all been rooted out and destroyed. How many groups of dissatisfied citizens could there be in this city?

"Who?" I asked. My voice sounded faint. "Who's behind it this time?"

Lavinia shrugged. "You tell me."

I laughed, the sound hollow and disbelieving. "My wife and I both risked our lives last fall to save the Republic. If we wanted it destroyed, we could have just stood by and let it happen."

"Wrong." Lavinia set her stylus down on the table. "If you'd done nothing, the wheels of government would have ground on as usual. The Senate would have passed the Act of Tyranny.

Venaria Hestis would have been elected tyrant until the threat of the Wodes and the Herracians was vanquished."

"At the cost of our democracy," I said. "Venaria manipulated that election. Do you remember how?"

For the first time, Lavinia's eyes shied away from mine.

"Senator Julius Catellus," I reminded her. "Murdered at Venaria's behest when he tried to double-cross her. His blood nearly bought her that seat. Would have, if not for me and Bahlanni."

"No." Lavinia's hand moved from stylus to baton, though she did not raise it. "Instead, two-thirds of the Senate died in a bloody massacre, coincidentally leaving their seats empty for a new generation of Senators. One that includes a ground-breaking proportion of Ayu'li representatives."

I felt the color drain from my face. "What are you saying?"

"I am saying," Lavinia said, her tone measured, "that there are no coincidences. I don't know when you first became aware of Venaria Hestis's plan to become tyrant, but you and your wife certainly positioned yourselves to take maximum advantage of the ensuing chaos—"

I leaned towards her, teeth bared against a snarl I fought to keep from escaping my throat. The words spilling from Lavinia's mouth hurt in a way that was almost physical. If I could just make her stop, just for a moment, so I could have time to *think*—

In half a heartbeat Lavinia was on her feet, pushing away from the table with her baton in hand. I reflexively raised my hands in supplication.

Only then did some semblance of rational thought return, and I realized how badly I had fucked up.

"Wait—" I started to say. But Lavinia was already in motion again, leaping onto the bench. Her first blow caught me on my bad arm, sending out a burst of pale ghostfire from beneath the segmented sleeve. I felt no pain, only a dull ache.

The baton fell again, but this time I was ready. I caught it in between my manacles, tangling it as I tried to pull it from Lavinia's grip.

I must have weighed half again what she did, but she did not let go of her weapon. She kept her grip as I inadvertently pulled her onto the table, lashing out with a round kick that glanced off my good shoulder. My breath misted the air as I grunted in pain.

"*Stop.*"

The word was not loud, but it hung in the stillness of the frigid room. More from surprise than compliance, Lavinia and I both obeyed, stilling our tabletop struggle.

A tall, slender figure stood framed in the door, his face half shadowed by the lamplight. But I knew the voice, cold and clear as a winter sky

"Gracchus," I said, fighting to disentangle myself from Lavinia. But my manacles were still wrapped tight around her baton, which she refused to relinquish. "I—"

"Imperator," Lavinia said over me, her words coming out in a rush. "You saw it! Bellator Calvus *attacked* me—"

Imperator Gracchus raised a hand, palm towards us. "Enough."

His silk-soft voice was unruffled by anger, yet strangely all the more commanding in its tranquility. In the ensuing silence, Lavinia and I managed to pull ourselves off the table and each other, though the baton lay between us on the tabletop.

Gracchus picked his way between the hanging carcasses, wrinkling his nose in distaste. His dark robes were interrupted only by the purple sash that was the Imperators' badge of office. Those things remained unchanged from the last time I had seen him, shortly after the Lightfall massacre.

Yet as he stepped into the light, I saw that Gracchus's appearance was startlingly transfigured from what it had been half a year prior. Once pure midnight, his black hair was now shot through with long streaks of gray. His face had become a roadmap of lines beneath sunken eyes, and stubble dusted his jaw.

He halted at the head of the table, hands clasped before him as he looked steadily at me and Lavinia. That flat, unreadable gaze was unchanged, at least.

"Have a seat," he told us.

We complied, sitting in the exact places we had before Gracchus's appearance. I felt absurd, like a schoolchild who'd been caught fighting and now braced for the inevitable scolding.

The feeling was only slightly abated by Gracchus turning his attention to Lavinia first. "Uncuff him."

"What?" Lavinia blanched. "Imperator, this man is in my custody—"

"You have the wrong man," Gracchus said, pulling a tightly rolled scroll from his cloak and handing it to Lavinia. "Here."

Lavinia's brows knitted together as she unfurled the scroll. "What is this?"

"Exoneration," Gracchus said, glancing at me. "A mortuary report on the sabotaged Attendants. The embalmers estimate that the mutilations must have occurred at least half an hour prior to your discovery of the crime."

"I was in the Barrows then," I said, before Lavinia could object.

She glared at me. "Allegedly."

"Here." Gracchus pressed another scroll into Lavinia's hands. "A witness statement from one Neftani Khannem, swearing that Gaius Cassius Calvus was in the Barrows at a Ayu'li religious ceremony until about two hours ago."

"That doesn't mean Citizen Calvus couldn't have used his

Rites to commit the crime," Lavinia argued, giving Neftani's statement a cursory glance before tossing both scrolls to the table. "He's Legate-trained—"

"Meaning he might have seized direct control of the Attendants remotely through the Rite of Communion?" Gracchus arched a brow. "The Rite requires various command gestures, which tend to be rather...involved. None of which Citizen Khannem mentions in his affidavit. Nor would any of the other dozens of citizens present at the service."

I silently resolved to light an extra candle at my family's altar in the Barrows in thanks. My renewed piety was already paying dividends. No doubt Bahlanni would be pleased to hear it.

Or not, considering the circumstances.

My relief faded in anticipation of the unpleasant conversation that surely awaited once I returned home. Bad enough that I had arrived late to the Hours of Remembrance, and worse that I had fled. Now those problems were compounded by my arrest and by Lavinia's evident suspicion that Bahlanni and I were involved with some kind of fringe group.

Best to lay those suspicions to rest posthaste.

"Imperator," I said, cutting through whatever argument in favor of my culpability Lavinia had been mustering. Both lawkeepers turned to me. "Who are the Sons of Ash?"

"Don't—" Lavinia started, but Gracchus silenced her with a wave of his hand.

"A problem," he said. "One I would appreciate your assistance in solving, Bellator Calvus."

Lavinia's calm façade crumbled at last. "This is my investigation, Imperator. You can't enlist this man's help over my objections—"

"I can do exactly that." Gracchus produced a third scroll and set it on the table for us both to read. The Triarchy's seal was a black mark against the pale vellum. "I have received permission from Triarch Ferra to oversee the investigation into the Sons of Ash. Now please, Magistrate Caprio. Uncuff Bellator Calvus."

The keys Lavinia pulled from her belt must have been extraordinarily heavy, judging by how long it took her to unlock my manacles. Freed, my good hand tingled numbly from cold and stiffness. From my left I felt nothing at all.

"Am I free to go?" I asked, ignoring Lavinia's glower.

"Technically," Gracchus said. "But I'd prefer you stay. We have some things to discuss."

Lavinia's head jerked towards him. "If Bellator Calvus is no longer a suspect—"

"Then he'll want to know why he and the..." Gracchus paused, perhaps reconsidering his choice of words. "Why he and his wife are under suspicion. And if there is one thing we have learned from the events of last autumn, it's that Bellator Calvus does not stop digging once he's uncovered something. That, and handcuffs pose little obstacle to him."

I gave Gracchus a wry smile, more to further aggravate Lavinia than out of any warm feeling towards the man. He was speaking from prior experience.

"It could compromise my investigation," Lavinia said. "Consider that, Imperator."

"Done," Gracchus said. "Now."

He moved around Lavinia, taking a seat on the bench opposite me. I was struck once more by the trials that the last half year had inflicted upon his face. There were bags under Gracchus's eyes, and the lines around his mouth had deepened. For a man who had once taken great pains to appear wholly unflappable in the face of strife and danger, it was a startling transformation.

"Bellator Calvus," he said, resting his hands on the table.

His long white fingers were startlingly pale against the scarred and pitted wood.

"Imperator," I said. "It's been quite some time."

"A long time," he agreed, lips curling into a sardonic smile. "And a difficult one."

I could imagine. It had taken months to quell the unrest in the provinces, to say nothing of the incursions on Albastine's borders by our more hostile neighbors. Only the winter snows and the hasty dispatch of all available legions had forestalled outright invasion from the more militant of the Herracian princes. As the enforcers of the Senate's will, the Imperators were powerful, but their ranks were few. The current crisis must have taxed their resources to the absolute brink.

"So," I said, "there have been other mutilations?"

"Several, in fact."

"*Imperator*," Lavinia hissed, not even attempting to hide her anger. "I have to protest—"

"Then do it outside," Gracchus snapped, his cool veneer falling away with such vehemence that Lavinia flinched. "I'll speak with you once I'm done briefing Bellator Calvus."

Lavinia's expression turned stony. Her fist brushed her heart in the most perfunctory of salutes before she gathered up her stylus, tablet, and baton. She stalked out of the cellar, not bothering to close the door behind her as she ascended the steps.

"I take it you know each other," I said into the ensuing silence.

Gracchus's breath frosted the air. "She was a candidate for the Imperators."

"I can believe that," I said, rubbing at the throbbing bruise on my head. "She didn't make the cut?"

"No." Gracchus drummed his fingers against the table. "The Imperators require a certain...flexibility in our approach to maintaining peace and order in the Republic. One Magistrate Caprio sadly lacks."

"What kind of flexibility?"

Gracchus smiled thinly. "The moral kind."

"I find that hard to believe," I said, wincing at the throbbing in my temples.

"She does have a tendency towards overzealousness in the pursuit of her duties," Gracchus admitted. "One tempered by her commitment to the laws of our Republic."

I raised an eyebrow. "And that was the reason she wasn't qualified to do your job?"

"As I said," Gracchus stated smoothly, "*my* duty is to maintain order and peace within the Republic. Laws are of secondary concern to that goal, which upon occasion may require they be interpreted creatively."

"I see." I drummed my fingers on the table, thinking. Gracchus had shown me no love in the past—had suspected me of plotting to overthrow the Republic, in fact, and acted against me to stop it. His rescue of me tonight, while not unwelcome, was surprising. "Is this a setup?"

Gracchus did not so much as blink. "How do you mean?"

"It's a little convenient, don't you think?" I asked, toying with the manacles lying open upon the table. "I come across a bunch of sabotaged Attendants and a message about overthrowing the Republic just in time for Magistrate Caprio to find me at the scene of the crime. Then you swoop in here with precisely the documents required to exonerate me."

"It's good to see that retirement has not dulled your wits," Gracchus said, shaking his head. "Nor your paranoia. But I'm afraid in this case the latter is unfounded."

"Not from where I'm sitting."

Gracchus rubbed his chin, wincing slightly at the unfamiliar growth of stubble he found there. "Ordinarily I'd be disinclined to explain myself to you, Citizen Calvus—"

"Bellator."

"*Bellator* Calvus," he corrected without breaking stride, "but considering your prior service to the Republic and the discomfort Magistrate Caprio has inflicted upon you—"

"Gracchus," I interrupted, leaning forward, "playing good magistrate to Caprio's bad magistrate doesn't really suit you."

"Fine." His voice tightened. "I have had ears to the ground, as it were, for any activity in the city related to the Sons of Ash, and devoted resources towards rapid response to said activities. That is how Magistrate Caprio came across tonight's rather macabre display. The question, Bellator Calvus, is how you came to be involved."

"The Attendant—" I stopped myself. Thus far Gracchus had said nothing about any Attendants behaving erratically. If the one that had led me to the sabotage of its fellows had been under the control of another Legate, he either didn't know about it or didn't want me to think he knew.

And besides, the mere threat of a rogue Legate had been the cause of his animosity towards me last year. Better to not mention it until I knew more.

"The Attendants," I said. "They were mutilated by these Sons of Ash?"

"Likely." Gracchus glanced at the ash smeared across my brow. "As a member of the Ayu'li religion, I assume you're familiar with them?"

"I don't think so," I said, sensing I should tread lightly. "They have something to do with the Old Faith?"

"Not precisely." Gracchus leaned his elbows on the table, steepling his fingers together. "They're a group of Ayu'li whose views on your people's integration into broader Albastine society is somewhat...extreme."

"Extreme how?" I asked. It was true that the Ayu'li were the less populous of the two peoples who had founded Albastine, and much of our native culture had been subsumed into the greater society of the Republic during the intervening centuries. But like our Extorani counterparts, most of us considered our Albastine citizenship the foundation of our identity, with our ethnic and religious affiliations complementary to it.

"They're secessionists," Gracchus said, staring at me with unblinking dark eyes. "They think that Albastine has disregarded the tenets of your Old Faith for too long. That the Republic's use of Attendants is incompatible with the ancestral worship of your heritage."

The first Ayu'li settlers had practiced the rituals of the Old Faith to their fullest, including the sacred dances that called the spirits of the deceased back to the prepared vessels of their mummified bodies. But the necessity of Attendants to work the fields during the early plague years had put a stop to that, as every pair of hands was needed to see our fledgling city through the winter.

Upon death, the body of every citizen became property of the state, to be made into an Attendant in service of the People. Such laws took precedence over the Old Faith's religious practices. To my knowledge, no one had performed the original rituals in hundreds of years.

"They're not wrong," I admitted. Gracchus's mouth twitched downwards.

"One would think that you'd be grateful to live in the society we do," he said. "It seems to me that surrendering some old superstitions in favor of a democratic society is more than a fair trade."

Anger flared in me at his casual disregard for my religion, but I pressed on before the conversation devolved further. "But secession is impossible. Where would they even go? Ayu is a continent away, and the people living there are the descendants of the ones who drove our ancestors into exile in the first place."

"Correct," Gracchus said. "But that's the thing about extremists, Bellator. The practical considerations of their plans carry far less weight for them than the purity of their principles. As it happens, these Sons are fixed on returning the faithful to Ayu, Republic and reality alike be damned."

"And they're not above disregarding Albastine law to do so," I finished. "You're sure that they dismembered those Attendants?"

"We don't have incontrovertible proof," Gracchus said slowly, as though he were thinking over each word. Weighing how much he could tell me. "Tonight was certainly a...spectacle. We hadn't found any bodies before now."

He sounded galled by the lack of a concrete link between tonight's mutilations and these Sons, whoever they were.

"What have you found, then?"

"I'm afraid that information isn't freely available," Gracchus said, his sardonic smile returning. I had the distinct feeling that he was enjoying this game, dangling the question before me so that I would be forced to answer.

For a moment I considered just getting up and walking out. I was no longer under arrest, and by now the Hour of Rest must be at an end. Bahlanni would be wondering where I had gotten to.

But if these Sons of Ash were linked to the Old Faith, as Gracchus indicated, then they might be a threat not just to Albastine in general, but to the Ayu'li specifically. And I could not leave this frigid room without ensuring the safety of my people and my wife.

I sighed and took the bait. "I'd like to know, Imperator. Maybe I can be of help."

The cold smile widened. "Oh, I'm certain you can."

"Stop dancing about it, then. What have you discovered?"

"That Attendants are going missing." Gracchus's gaze flickered towards the door, then back to me as he leaned in, lowering his voice. "Not many, and not all at once. Couriers sent with letters never arrive, or farmhands disappear on the way back from the fields."

"That is strange." Attendants were intently single-minded, dedicated to carrying out their instructions until they were physically incapable of doing so. They could not get lost, distracted, or wander off. "Have any been recovered?"

Gracchus showed his teeth. "Only parts of them."

"But why these Sons of Ash?" I asked. "Plenty of Ayu'li object to the Republic's laws against the rituals which allow us to commune with our departed dead. But it's one thing to feel that your faith is being stifled, and another to commit deliberate sabotage in objection to those laws."

An objection I privately held mixed feelings about. It was true that the Republic's laws surrounding the creation of Attendants superseded our religious ceremonies, but such prohibition was not born from a place of discrimination. To the Old Faith, the dead were sacred. To the Republic, they were tools. The friction between those two views was the defining tension of my life and had no easy answer.

Gracchus nodded. "Indeed. Yet you've just begun to celebrate your holy day, in a time when the Ayu'li and their culture are making a resurgence in Albastine—in large part due to the contributions of you and your wife."

"I gather that's not a change everyone is comfortable with."

"Indeed not," Gracchus said. "There are those who might say you were overstepping your place in society. Popularity aside, your people and their religion comprise only a fraction of the Republic's population."

"And you?" The words slipped from me before I could stop them. "You think we're forgetting our place?"

Gracchus showed no outward sign of anger, but his tone chilled. "I think your place is as citizens of this Republic, before and above anything else. Only when you forget that do I have any...misgivings about your people."

"The Republic is made up of *all* its people," I reminded him. "Ayu'li, Extorani, provincials, immigrants. The texture of the society changes as its people do."

"And change *is* inevitable." Gracchus nodded. "Yet whenever it occurs, there are those who want to push for more, faster and harder. These Sons of Ash fall firmly within that camp, and I fear that their actions will only grow more drastic as the Hours of Remembrance draw on."

"You seem to have a high estimation of their capabilities," I observed. "I've never even heard of them before."

"Unsurprising," Gracchus said, unfazed. "They've been disbanded for several years now, and the times of their greatest influence coincided with your own deployments abroad. Coupled with your absence from the Ayu'li religious community..."

I shifted in my seat, uncomfortable with Gracchus's assessment of my personal history. "Like ships in the night."

"An apt metaphor." Gracchus looked down at the scrolls he had brought into the cellar. "However, lately my intelligence suggests that they are planning a resurgence. The recent mutilations confirm it."

He ran a hand through his graying hair, seeming older than I'd ever seen him. "But as you might expect, the scope of our jurisdiction as it pertains to the Ayu'li is limited by your religious protections."

"Like how you can't just storm into the Barrows," I said, not missing the resentment in his tone. We'd come to the crux of it, the reason Gracchus had rolled into this frigid cellar like the god of guile himself. "So you want me to hunt them down for you."

"A dramatic turn of phrase," Gracchus sniffed. "I simply want us to work together again, Bellator Calvus. For the good of the Republic and your religion both."

"How?" I asked, though I suspected I already knew.

"The Sons of Ash are reclusive," Gracchus said. "Secretive. They won't talk with the magistrates. But you already have an in with them."

"Bahlanni?" My wife's name came out in a croak.

"That's right," Gracchus said without a trace of shame. "As her husband, your commitment to the Old Faith is unquestionable. If you sought an audience with the Sons, I can't imagine they would refuse you."

"And Bahlanni?" I said, my voice still tight. "Are you asking me to lie to her?"

"Your marriage is your own affair, Calvus." Gracchus waved a hand, as if said marriage were an irritating insect buzzing about his head. "But if you want to keep her name clean, determining whether or not the Sons of Ash are responsible for these mutilations may be the best way to do so. I suggest you broach the subject with your wife carefully."

"Classic Imperator," I said, "maneuvering me into a position where you know I can't say no. Well done."

Gracchus stared at me with flat, unreadable eyes. "Duty comes before all else, Bellator. Mine and yours. I won't apologize for that."

"I wouldn't expect you to," I said. I looked down at my hands, lying flat on the table. One living and dark against the pale wood of the scarred table, the other pale beneath its leather sheath. "But I think you and Magistrate Caprio have one thing in common."

"Oh?"

"You've both got the wrong man." I raised my sheathed hand, forestalling any objection. "I'm not who I was. Before Silva Incognita, or before Lightfall. My priorities have changed."

The words felt right as I said them. Once I might have leapt at the chance to uncover a hidden plot against the Republic—I'd done exactly that, in fact.

But coming close to dying in service of my city had cured me of the desire to complete the act. Then I had been alone, friendless. Now I had a community, a relationship with my spouse. A life. All things worth protecting, but not at the whims of a manipulator like Imperator Gracchus.

He looked at me for a long time, his flat gaze unreadable. I expected him to try to cajole me further, maybe even threaten me. Instead, he did the one thing I hadn't expected.

"Fine." I was taken aback by how much vitriol Gracchus packed into that lone syllable. "I suppose you feel you've done all you can for the Republic already. Paid your dues."

That stung like a slap. "Imperator—"

"Your wife will be wondering where you are." He rose, gathering the scrolls he had brought. As he stalked out of the cellar in a whirl of cold air, his parting words were like a physical blow. "Go home, Citizen Calvus. Enjoy your retirement, while you can."

I was left alone in the cold darkness, wondering if I had made the wrong choice.

CHAPTER SIX

Alone light flickered in the window of my familial estate when I returned home. It put me in mind of stories I'd heard of sailor's widows who would light a single candle in their homes each night, hoping to guide home the wandering spirits of their loved ones lost at sea. Once Bahlanni had thought of me as such a lost soul. I hoped she no longer did.

I took a deep breath, gathered my courage, and opened the door to my home.

"Akhenkatem?" Bahlanni's voice echoed from down the hall.

"I'm home."

"In here," my wife called from the bath. "Are you alright?"

"Fine." I walked down the hall, my steps inordinately heavy. Ever since my grandfather's passing the estate was too large and empty. Until my injury I had never dwelled there for more than a month at a time, constantly deployed as a Legate guarding Albastine's borders. Among my dead soldiers I was secure in my purpose, even comfortable. Home was a place of ghosts.

So it was again, now that my wife had joined me in cohabitation. The hall was lined with white marble busts of her ancestors and mine. Though each was carved in the Extorani style, Bahlanni had turned them into proper Ayu'li altars, festooning them with garlands and candles and small piles of votive offerings. Somehow these adornments made the estate's long corridors feel closer, less lonesome. Or maybe it was simply the knowledge that this was no longer solely my dwelling. That however small we might be, Bahlanni and I were a family once again.

In Ayu'li fashion, the busts were ordered in lineal descent, with the oldest individuals' likenesses placed nearest the entrance. Only as I drew near to the end of the hall did the features become familiar. I bowed my head in respect to my grandparents, their marble faces sterner than I had ever seen them in life. I wondered at the amount of coaxing it must have taken Grandmother to convince Grandfather to sit still long enough for the sculptor to get his likeness.

Light spilled from the bathroom at the end of the hall, as warm and inviting as Bahlanni's gentle humming. The melody was hymnal, familiar, but I could not place it. Perhaps I had known it once, but had forgotten in my apostasy.

My parents' busts stood sentinel at either hand just before the bath. I stopped before them as I always did, wondering at the proud lines of my mother's face, the sad almost-smile gracing my father's lips. I wondered whether I had ever seen these expressions on them in life. If I had, it was buried in a fog of memory deeper even than that of Bahlanni's hymn.

I bowed my head to my parents and entered the bath. Bahlanni stood waist-deep, steam swirling about her, wearing only a brightly patterned vermillion headwrap to protect her braids from the water. Her back was to me, but I must have made a sound, for she glanced over her shoulder as I entered.

"Akhenkatem." Her voice was soft, tone inscrutable. "Welcome home."

"Sorry it took me so long," I said, hoping I hadn't worried her. "I—"

"Had quite the eventful night, I hear." She turned to face me, water running down her shoulders in rivulets. "Neftani told me that Gracchus came asking after you."

"He did," I admitted. "There was a…misunderstanding with a magistrate."

"One significant enough for an Imperator's attention?"

"I can tell you more about it in the bath," I said, shrugging out of my cloak.

Bahlanni smiled. "Come in, then." She reached a cupped hand into the bath and let the hot water run between her slender fingers. "It's still warm."

I nodded and began to undress. In a few moments I was as naked as she was, save for the leather sleeve around my left arm.

Bahlanni turned, facing me full on, the gentle curves of her body half shrouded in steam. My pulse quickened at the graceful swell of her hips, the sharp outline of her collarbones above her breasts. Abruptly I felt seventeen again, all awkward longing and desire at the sight of my naked wife.

Something glimmered in Bahlanni's eyes, dark and mischievous. She reached out both hands and beckoned me forward, a coy smile playing on her lips.

There had been reasons for the gap in our marriage, but a lack of desire was not among them.

I stepped into the pool, feeling the warm water seep between my toes, up my ankles. Another step and it was to my knees.

"Wait."

I froze, suddenly filled with an almost adolescent self-consciousness.

"Take it off," Bahlanni said, gesturing at my left hand.

"I..." I looked down at the black sleeve that covered my arm from shoulder to fingertip. "I don't like looking at it."

"I know." Bahlanni's smile faded. She had seen what lay beneath the sleeve, and the nauseated expression on her face had been etched indelibly into my memory. "But you don't want to wet the leather."

"I'll be careful."

"I've a better idea." A few steps brought her closer to me, enough that I could tell the heat of her breath from that of the steam around us. I started to say something, but Bahlanni placed a finger against my lips.

"Flesh of my flesh," she said, slipping into Ayu'li as easily as breathing, "close your eyes."

I did. Bahlanni removed her finger and took my sheathed hand in both of hers. I started to protest, but she stopped my mouth with hers. Surprise and desire met, mingled, and rendered me utterly incapable of speech or thought.

With a lover's gentleness, Bahlanni removed the leather sleeve from my arm. I braced myself for the inevitable sound of her disgust, but none came. Instead, she took my withered hand in hers, though I could feel her fingers only distantly through my deadened nerves.

"Come, my love," she said softly, and led me into the pool. The water slipped up my legs and past my groin, warmly inviting. Only when we reached the center of the pool did Bahlanni let go, her hands traveling up my bare chest to my shoulders. She turned me around and pressed me down until I was submerged to the neck, warm water enveloping me.

"Open."

I did, seeing the candlelight flickering off the walls with

new eyes. Bahlanni sat in the bath opposite me, smiling slightly. "Better?"

I looked down and found I could neither see nor feel my offending arm beneath the reflected candlelight.

I swallowed the sudden lump in my throat, nodded. "Thank you."

"You are my husband," she said as though that were answer enough.

Silence, save for the lapping of water against the tiles. Bahlanni wetted a towel and began wiping at her face, clearing away the black kohl and ceremonial makeup she had worn for the Hours. Washing away the priestess until only the woman remained.

"You haven't asked me," I said.

She wiped at her neck. "About?"

"Tonight. Gracchus, and the magistrate."

"You will tell me in your own time." Bahlanni handed me her towel. "Wash my back?"

I took it in my good hand. She turned around, droplets running down her shoulders. I rubbed the towel in slow circles, feeling her muscles stiffening and then relaxing beneath my touch.

"It was a misunderstanding," I said. "There was...I found something. A crime, I guess."

"And you leapt in to intervene?" Bahlanni's voice was gently teasing. "My husband, ever the hero?"

"Nothing like that," I assured her. "It was...grisly, though."

She turned, the smile on her face fading. "Was someone hurt?"

"Not exactly." I filled her in on the mutilated Attendants and the graffiti declaring the Republic's downfall.

"Who would do such a thing?" she asked.

I debated telling her about the Sons of Ash, recalling Gracchus's warning to broach the subject carefully. But Bahlanni was a traditionalist, not a radical. I could not believe that she would involve herself with a separatist faction like the Sons.

And more than that, I trusted my wife.

"Have you ever heard of the Sons of Ash?"

Bahlanni stiffened, then nodded. "I know of them. Are they under suspicion?"

"Gracchus said as much. Even asked for my help investigating them."

Bahlanni folded her arms across her chest. "What did you tell him?"

"That it's not my job," I said. "But who are they?"

"A group of malcontents using our religion to justify their political aims," Bahlanni said with uncharacteristic rancor.

I blinked. It was seldom that Bahlanni allowed her personal feelings to penetrate her carefully cultivated air of mystical serenity. "How so?"

"They want to return us to Ayu." She shook her head. "As if such a thing were possible."

"They're a minority sect, then?"

"Nothing so organized." Bahlanni pursed her lips, thinking. "More a clique of like-minded individuals."

"How come I've never heard of them before tonight?"

"You were gone."

My reaction must have showed, because she gave me an apologetic smile and cupped my face again.

"They came about during your time with the legions," she said, sidestepping the reminder of our separation. "While you were on the Isbenian border, I think. Enjoyed a brief surge of popularity, then faded just as quickly after their ringleader departed."

"Who was that?"

"Khefnar Djaru," Bahlanni said. "He was the one who started the movement."

Albastine in Ashes. "What's he like?"

"Like you'd expect the leader of that sort of group to be," Bahlanni said, looking away. "Outspoken, eloquent. Fierce in his convictions and wholly convinced of their rightness."

"Sounds familiar."

Bahlanni gave an annoyed snort and splashed water at me.

"It was a compliment!" I protested, raising my good hand in mock surrender. Bahlanni snorted again.

"He was more like you than me, in truth," she said. "As much a fighter as a leader. A soldier, once. A scout, I think."

I lowered my hand, frowning. An army without scouts was blind, and I had worked closely with many over my years commanding the Republic's legions. "I've never met him."

"Khefnar retired just before you became an Acolyte," Bahlanni said. "Spent several years traveling, I believe. Returned to Albastine during one of your deployments abroad."

"He came to stay?"

"Only briefly," Bahlanni said, leaning against the side of the pool. "He'd remain in Albastine a few weeks, just long enough for the Imperators to grow uneasy with his continued presence. Then he'd disappear again, once he'd sufficiently stirred up his secessionist sentiments among the Old Faith. Months would go by, then he'd come back with just as little warning."

I couldn't help but notice the past tense. "What happened to him?"

"No one knows." Bahlanni frowned. "Last time Khefnar appeared was four to five years ago. He made a lot of noise about how the Attendants were an affront to our ancestors, about how there was no possibility of practicing our faith in earnest so long as we were part of the Republic. He urged all the faithful to join him in a pilgrimage back to Ayu."

I let out a low whistle. The lush watershed of the River Ayu was thousands of miles from Albastine, a journey of many months across mountains, deserts, and seas. Though our ancestral homeland still occupied a significant place in the minds of the Ayu'li faithful, such a voyage was both arduous and fraught with peril—our ancestors had wandered through many alien countries in their years of exile, and the tales of that era were often not peaceable ones.

These days only the most ardent disciples of the Old Faith dared make the pilgrimage to Ayu, and even those only seldom. The last one I'd known to successfully complete the journey was my grandfather, and that had been when I was only a small child.

"Did anyone join him?"

"A handful," Bahlanni said. "All self-proclaimed Sons of Ash. None of them have been heard from since."

"Until tonight," I said, thinking again of the ominous graffiti. "'Albastine in Ashes.'"

Bahlanni rubbed her temples. "Khefnar's ideas were most popular with some of the younger Ayu'li. No doubt that slogan was the work of one of those, still riding high on the excitement of our holy day."

"Maybe," I said, though doubt still gnawed at me. Misaimed youthful rebellion was one thing, the cold-blooded mutilation of Attendants another.

I ambled over to the side of the bath, grabbed a towel, and began scrubbing with my good hand. Only being able to reach half my body quickly became an exercise in frustration, but I couldn't bring myself to use my bad arm, not here in this rare moment of tranquility.

Water sluiced down Bahlanni's body as she came over and took the towel from me.

"Here," she said, and began firmly but gently washing the side I was having trouble reaching.

"Thank you," I said, relaxing into her touch.

"You're welcome." The towel made slow, easy circles against my shoulder. "Do you think that Gracchus and this magistrate are going to be trouble for us?"

"I don't know." I shook my head. "Gracchus was cagey about it, but he seemed pretty convinced that the Sons were behind it. The magistrate seemed to agree."

"And you?" Bahlanni asked quietly. "What do you make of all this, my husband?"

I had taken the time to mull things over on my walk home. "The way I see it, there are two options. Either these Sons really are still active and looking to stir up trouble—"

A disapproving sound from Bahlanni indicated her feelings on that possibility.

"—or," I said, "we're meant to think that they are."

The motion of the towel stopped. "What?"

"Maybe," I said, considering each word, "someone's trying to stir up resentment against the Ayu'li now that we have so many Senate seats. The Republic has seen a lot of change these last few months, and not everyone takes kindly to it."

"You think it's a setup?" Bahlanni asked, a hint of real fear in her voice.

"You say the Sons are defunct, but someone still had to sabotage those Attendants and put up that graffiti. The magistrates will want to make a swift arrest."

"So we are in danger." Bahlanni withdrew the towel, leaving me shivering as droplets ran down my upper body. "That's why you want to help Gracchus investigate."

"I don't *want* to," I said. "But if whoever's behind it is a threat to the Faith…"

"Then duty compels you to stop them," Bahlanni said, a sad, wry smile on her face.

"I told him no." I turned, took her hand in my good one, and raised her fingers to my lips. "There are more important things to me now."

She considered that, then slowly nodded. "And you're certain you're at peace with that?"

In answer, I pulled Bahlanni close with my good arm. She tensed, then relaxed into my embrace. A pleasant shiver trickled down my spine, one that had nothing to do with the cool air against my damp skin.

We stayed that way for a long time, my wife and I, resting in one another's arms. Until the heat of our bodies overpowered the warmth of the bath, and rest became the furthest thing from our minds.

PART TWO
REFUGE

CHAPTER SEVEN

The second Hour of Remembrance came with the sunrise.

I awoke well before the gray dawn, still weary. Bahlanni was already up, seated at the mirrored vanity she had moved into my bedroom.

Our bedroom, I reminded myself. I sat up, rubbing my eyes.

"Good morning," Bahlanni said, though it was still deep night. Already dressed in her priestly vestments, she was busily applying the final touches of her ceremonial makeup, the candles beneath the vanity mirror illuminating her reflection.

"Morning." I tried to say more, but only yawned.

Bahlanni smiled at me in the mirror. "Still tired, I see."

I returned her smile. Groggy as I was, I could not complain about the lack of sleep.

"There's tea in the kitchen," she said as she applied kohl beneath her eyes. "Have some before you leave for the Barrows."

"We're not going together?" I asked, struggling to disentangle myself from the bedsheets.

"Not unless you're planning on going like that," Bahlanni said, her bracelets jingling as she gestured at me.

I looked down at my naked body tangled in the sheets. "I think I'll save that for the Hour of Rising."

Laughing, Bahlanni swept over to lean in and plant a kiss on my cheek. "I'll see you there?"

The question in her tone tugged at my heart. I turned her head towards me with two fingers and leaned in, breathing in her sweet smell.

"Count on it," I said, and kissed her.

THE SKY WAS gray twilight as I climbed the slope towards the Barrows, one more parishioner in a line already stretching down the mountain path into the valley below. Ahead of me were families, their children rubbing sleepily at their eyes and babies wailing at the early hour. Yet despite that there was a festive air among the crowd, an excited buzz leaping like a spark from one group to the next. The Hours were a time of holiday, and Refuge the most joyous of them.

I found myself smiling as I approached the Barrows, its bronze gates open wide and inviting to the Old Faith's adherents. The sphinxes flanking them were festooned with pale white flowers, lending a touch of life to their ordinarily austere appearance. In Ayu, their decorations would have been lotuses, but such species struggled to survive in the alpine climate of Albastine, and so we made do with edelweiss instead.

As ever, a pair of guards stood sentinel beneath the sphinxes, but today their presence was perfunctory. Hupli stood between them, greeting each member of the Faith as they approached to receive his benediction before entering our place of worship.

"Akhenkatem," he said, raising his hand in greeting once I was next in line. "Son of Ainkar and Nyeri. Blessings of all the ancestors be upon you."

"And upon you," I said, bowing to Hupli as he dipped his hand into the ceremonial urn tucked beneath his arm.

"I am glad to see you here so early," he said, pulling out an ash-covered hand. "As I am sure the high priestess shall be."

"I certainly hope so," I said, impervious to his attempt to spoil my newfound cheer. Today was a new day, after all. "She was in a good mood when we parted this morning."

"That is well." He drew two fingers across my forehead, leaving a wavy line of ash to represent the River Ayu. "May you find refuge within these walls, Akhenkatem."

"And you," I said, glancing over my shoulder at the line of worshippers behind me. "Whenever you're able."

What might have been a frown flickered across Hupli's features. "It is my privilege to welcome all the sons and daughters of Ayu to the Hour of Refuge."

"Enjoy it," I said, looking downhill as another group of families joined the line. Ash anointing my brow, I moved past him and into our holy place, my steps feeling lighter than they had in a long time.

THE CENTRAL CHAMBER of the Barrows was dimmer than it had been the night before, lit by only enough candles to keep total darkness at bay. The air was hot with the press of bodies and thick with murmured exclamations of excitement. I found myself holding my breath, waiting for the panicked quickening of my heart amidst such a crowd.

To my surprise, it did not come. The unease was still there, lurking at the corners of my mind, but Bahlanni's assurances from the night before kept it at bay. And though the people around me were little more than shadows, the glimpses of kohl-blackened eyes and ash-marked brows reminded me that I was no different from them. That we were all the children of Ayu, come to this place far from the river's distant banks, gathered to remember and rejoice.

A low humming echoed through the chamber, at first from a single throat before another voice joined it, and then another, and another. The tune was a hymn without words, a strong and thrumming melody meant to resemble the steady, flowing strength of the river as it coursed through us, finding voice in each of the faithful. Its power trembled through me, a connection as ancient as the stone around us.

Such power could not be restrained, and as one we swayed in time to the song, our feet stamping out an instinctive, primal rhythm. The spirit of the dance coursed through us like the river we sang our praises to, a wordless tribute to the place of our origin, to the ancestors who had lived and loved and suffered before us.

The steps of the dance were intimately familiar to me, for they were the motions that had been pared down to their basest element as the Legate's Rites. Now they were resurrected like the spirits of the dead they honored, restored to the fullness of their purpose. I could almost sense my grandfather's presence, guiding me through the steps just as he had so many years ago.

The song rose to a crescendo, reverberating off the chamber walls as a single voice cut through it in a piercing alto at once joyous and mournful. Light grew in the chamber as more candles were lit, and the song resolved itself into a single word of Old Ayu'li: *Welcome.*

A lone figure rose above the crowd upon the central dais.

Bahlanni, her arms upraised as they had been the night before, the light of a thousand candles reflecting off her bronze and gold jewelry, head thrown back as she held the final note of the song. A storm of fierce pride swept through me as I watched her in her element, surrounded by the adoring faces of our fellow believers.

This is where she belongs. The thought struck me with an intense pang of longing. Whether for that same adulation or for the unity of place and purpose it entailed, I could not say.

The song ended, the final note echoing into the silence. Bahlanni's eyes swept the chamber, her smile wide and inviting. A shiver thrilled through me at the hush of anticipation, the rush of countless breaths all held at the same moment.

"First," she said, "there was a river."

An excited ripple of exhalations spread through the congregation as she recited the Old Ayu'li words: the beginning of the canticles that were both history and scripture to us.

"The river's name was Ayu, and from him all life sprang. The reeds and lotuses, the palms and dates. Fish and frogs, the hippo and the crocodile, even cows and sheep. Yet among all these things there were none that could speak, and so the god Ayu grew lonely."

I relaxed into the familiar rhythm of the story of our origin, the words unchanged from its first recitation countless years past. The same words once spoken in my grandfather's resounding baritone found new life and meaning in Bahlanni's voice, her chosen pauses and emphases subtly lending weight to different parts of the story until it was as though I were hearing it for the first time.

I closed my eyes, letting her voice wash over and through me as she told how Ayu created the first man and the first woman, of how their children married the river god's own children so that his waters became our blood, and of the towns and cities that grew along the banks. Ayu, our home and sanctuary, forever our first refuge. And, according to the prophecies sung at the Hour of Revelation, forever fated to be our last.

"Yet that refuge lies behind us," she said, and the silence that enveloped the chamber grew tense. "Years behind us, and miles away. For the children of Ayu were not the only ones to walk the wide world. Others came, with iron in their hands and hate in their hearts—"

"Cassius?"

The whispered sound of my name—my Extorani name— jolted me from the reverie of remembrance. I opened my eyes and found a slight young woman standing before me, her expression apprehensive. I recognized her, but in this setting, it took me a moment to place her.

"I'm sorry," she said, misreading my silence. "I mean, Bellator Calvus?"

"Drusa?" I blinked, looking around. None of those nearest us had noticed our whispered interruption of Bahlanni's holy recitation, which was now delving into the bloody conflict that had seen our ancestors driven from Ayu. "I didn't know you followed the Old Faith."

"I don't." Drusa touched the ash on her brow, which was already smudged. She must have absently wiped at it and was consciously resisting the urge to do so again.

"Then what are you doing here?" I asked. "Today's training doesn't start until noon."

Drusa rubbed her scalp, avoiding my eyes. "I came here looking for you."

I blinked. Any student-teacher relationship necessitated firm boundaries, and I had been careful to maintain those between myself and my Acolytes. Drusa's interruption of the

Hours was a flagrant breach of them, one I wouldn't have thought her capable of.

On the dais Bahlanni's recitation had moved on to our ancestor's flight from Ayu and their subsequent years in wandering exile.

"Acolyte Drusa." I leaned in so as not to further disrupt the ceremony, putting my sheathed hand on her shoulder. Drusa flinched. "What is this about?"

Drusa was a model student: quick to learn, studious, and respectful. Her presence here was extremely out of character—whatever had brought her must have been important.

"It's about Titian."

My frown deepened. "What about him?"

Drusa bit her lip, still nervous. Behind me, Bahlanni continued her sermon.

"...until their wandering steps led them high into the mountains," she was saying. "Until they came at last to the deep and narrow valley of white marble. The folk of the neighboring lowlands called it Albastine, but to the wanderers it became a place of refuge. A home where they might settle at last, free from persecution. A democracy where all might have a say in their fate. A beacon of harmony to the world—"

"Founded upon a lie," a deep basso voice cut in.

A murmur of discontent rippled through the congregation as dozens of heads turned to see who had interrupted. Out of the corner of my eye I caught Bahlanni's shocked expression, scarcely able to believe someone would dare interrupt the holy recitation.

"A threefold lie that the Exturani fed us," the speaker continued, stepping forward. His features remained hidden in deep shadow. "The lie that they saw us as equals, rather than allies of necessity. The lie that they held any respect for our faith, save as a tool they might use and shape to their own ends.

And the final lie—that they hold anything in reverence, save their own power."

Another step brought him fully into the candlelight, eliciting startled gasps from the congregation. In a moment, I saw why.

Among the Old Faith, raised ritual scars were the hallmark of the priesthood. Bahlanni wore seven: three beneath each eye and one upon her chin. Hupli, as a junior priest, had only three. By the time he passed, my grandfather had possessed over a dozen.

This man's scars were beyond counting. They ran under his eyes, down his cheeks, along his jaw. The only part of his face that remained unmarked was his brow—and that had been anointed with the same holy ash as the rest of the faithful.

A sharp hiss of breath from Bahlanni drew my eye. She was staring at him, her face pale, and though I had never seen the man before I knew his name in the moment before it fell from my wife's lips.

"Khefnar."

The scarred giant inclined his head to the priestess upon the dais, the gesture at once respectful and challenging. "Blessings of the Hours be upon you, Sister Bahlanni, daughter of Kihsret and Nayameh. May the ancestors smile upon your steps."

"As they may light yours," she responded stiffly. "Now, permit me to continue the canticle—"

"Why?"

Bahlanni's mouth worked soundlessly, surprise and outrage warring across her face. An Extorani observer might struggle to understand why this interruption had affected her so profoundly, but every Ayu'li in the room instinctively understood the tension that had engulfed the chamber.

For the Old Faith, recitation was holy. The words first set to rhythm and song by our ancestors three centuries past were committed to memory in the canticles, with no deviation or alteration permitted. Barring our more ancient but forbidden Rite of Awakening, it was the best way for us to honor the memory of our ancestors. Interruption was as indisputably blasphemous as absconding with a golden idol would be to the more material faiths.

"Why?" Khefnar repeated, pressing towards the dais. A quartet of robed Ayu'li followed close behind, flanking him like an honor guard, each holding an elaborately inlaid wooden box to their chest. The crowd parted before them, moved by the sheer weight of Khefnar's presence. Or perhaps in deference to his physical weight—the man stood closer to seven feet than six. "Why should we dwell always upon the past, when the present itself is a choking vine strangling everything we hold dear?"

A murmur swept through the congregation. I caught only snatches, but the voices ranged from bewildered to outraged, doubtful to fervent. Disconcertingly, I glimpsed more than a few people nodding their agreement. It seemed Bahlanni had understated the popularity of Khefnar's ideals among her congregation last night, and I was too out of touch with the Ayu'li zeitgeist to have realized it. The thought made me acutely aware of my long absence from the faith.

"You are speaking of the Republic's proscription against calling forth the souls of our ancestors," Bahlanni said, recovering.

"I am," Khefnar said as he reached the dais where Bahlanni stood. He ascended the first step, bringing him almost eye level with her. "And more besides. The perversion of our sacred dead into Attendants. The Rites used to control them, stripped of all the ritual and ceremony of our ancient dances. The deepest mysteries of our faith, whored out to the Extorani dogs—and for what?"

He was not quite yelling, but his deep voice echoed around the chamber, booming in the silence that had fallen over the Hour of Refuge.

No one dared answer. Khefnar's eyes swept the crowd, but none were willing to meet his gaze.

Until his eyes fell on me. For just a moment, a frown shadowed his scarred face, alongside a glimmer of what might have been recognition. I caught myself uneasily shifting my weight into a fighting stance, the fingers of my good hand curling into a fist.

"Don't," Drusa whispered, tugging at my sleeve.

I looked down and saw that a flicker of ghostfire danced along my fingertips. I let out a breath I hadn't known I'd been holding, and the spectral flames vanished.

When I looked back up, Khefnar had already returned his attention to Bahlanni.

"For survival?" he pressed, taking another step up the dais. "For our people to live bereft of the practices we hold most dear. To live sundered from the ancient wisdom of those who have crossed the Quiet Fields. What sort of life is that?"

"The one we were born into," Bahlanni answered, moving towards him. "None among us may choose the span of our lives. Ayu lies years and miles behind—"

"Away," Khefnar corrected, turning his scarred face to the congregation once more. "The journey to Ayu is long, but it is not beyond our reach, for I have braved it and returned."

Another murmur swept the congregation, this one thrilling with nervous anticipation. It had been nearly thirty years since my grandfather's pilgrimage to our ancestral homeland. If Khefnar had truly repeated the feat, it would make him a living saint in the eyes of the faithful.

And how could Bahlanni, respected as she was, compete with that?

"Brother Khefnar," Bahlanni said. I could hear the tension in her voice as she strove to keep her tone even. "You are welcome among us as we celebrate the Hours of Remembrance. But this is not the place or the time to debate—"

"And why is that?" Khefnar challenged, ascending to the final step before the dais so that he towered over Bahlanni. "What better time to discuss our people's future than while we remember our past?"

"It is against the customs laid down by our ancestors," Bahlanni said, no longer bothering to mask the heat behind her words. "Those same ancestors you disrespect even as you claim to venerate them."

Khefnar did not answer immediately. He let her words hang in the air, echoing off the chamber as the congregation watched in tense, fascinated silence. A queasy feeling settled in my gut as I realized how masterfully Khefnar was playing to the crowd. Compared to his passionate but reasoned arguments, her riposte seemed like the emotional outburst of a frustrated child —a comparison only enhanced by their physical contrast. Khefnar was so huge that Bahlanni appeared to be a child beside him.

"Tell me, High Priestess," he said before the whispers could start again, "did the ancestors appoint you to your station?"

Bahlanni flinched. In the ancient days the high priest or priestess of the Old Faith was chosen by the ancestors themselves, anointed in a sacred ritual that called forth the spirits of each of her predecessors stretching back to the very beginning of our faith. Such a ritual had not been held since we had departed Ayu.

"I was apprenticed to the high priest before me," Bahlanni said. She glanced briefly past Khefnar, at me, before she said my grandfather's name. "Khaimesu, who was himself apprenticed to Syoris, high priestess. And so on, in direct line all the way back to the waters of Ayu itself."

"And that is where you draw your authority from?" Khefnar pressed. "The choices of a single living man, rather than the wisdom of uncounted centuries? The legacy of our homeland, which you have never seen?"

I saw Bahlanni's mistake. By not immediately asserting her authority as priestess, she had tacitly lent legitimacy to Khefnar's interruption of the Hours. By stooping to debate him, she only strengthened his position.

A fearful premonition seized me as I realized what was about to come next.

"Don't," I whispered, trying to catch my wife's eye from my place in the crowd. But Bahlanni's gaze was fixed wholly on Khefnar, the anger in her eyes unmistakable.

"And you have?" she asked, practically snarling.

Khefnar smiled, showing even white teeth. "Yes."

The tide burst, a wave of voices rippling across the congregation at the news. Cries of joy and disbelief, shouted prayers and whispered skepticisms.

"I have crossed the trackless wastes and scaled the mountains that lie between Albastine and Ayu," Khefnar said, his thundering voice quelling the room once more. "I have braved the screaming deserts and howling seas, until I laid eyes upon the pyramids raised by our forefathers."

He ascended to the dais, brushing past Bahlanni to its center. "Beneath the full moon on the banks of the River Ayu, I danced the ancient rites handed down to us by our ancestors. I called forth their spirits from the living waters, and with those waters they baptized me Khefnar, son of Feri and Yadennu, priest and prophet."

He spread his arms wide, forcing Bahlanni to take a step backwards to avoid being swept off the dais.

"This I swear to you, upon all the souls of those who have come before us: I shall lead us away from this valley and the blasphemers who have debased us. Follow me, faithful sons and daughters of Ayu, and I shall lead us home to the land of our birth."

CHAPTER EIGHT

Silence greeted Khefnar's proclamation.

They don't believe him, I thought with a sudden swell of hope. *He has no way to prove his claims. He—*

Nearby, just ahead of me in the crowd, someone let out a high, keening wail. An old woman fell to her knees, the wordless cry still erupting from her lips.

I tried to move to help her, but the crowd was too close, and I could only glimpse her between the shoulders of my fellow faithful. Tears streamed down her wrinkled face, her body convulsing with huge, shuddering sobs.

"Praise be to all the ancestors!" she half screamed, her creaking voice echoing off the chamber walls. "Home, home, home to Ayu!"

"Home," someone else echoed, his tone wondering. "Home to Ayu, at last!"

"Home!" shouted another.

More voices took up the cry until it grew into a chant, a single thought sung from hundreds of mouths: *"Home! Home! Home to Ayu!"*

I pushed forward through the crowd, only vaguely aware of

Drusa's panicked squeal as the press of bodies cut her off from me. There was a frenzied energy in the air, one I feared might turn riotous if not given a safer outlet.

I reached the foot of the dais, but could get no closer through the press of people crowding it. I caught Bahlanni's eye and reached my good hand towards her.

She shook her head.

In that moment I wanted nothing more than to seize my wife and pull her from that dais. To flee back to our home, or somewhere else where we would be safe. But doing so would only further erode her already tottering authority.

I let my hand drop to my side.

Khefnar had raised his own hands for silence, but before he could speak Bahlanni seized her moment.

"Brother Khefnar," she said, practically shouting, "the waters of Ayu flow through the veins of every soul in this room. You are welcome here among us, but you are certainly *not* these people's high priest. If you *truly* have completed the pilgrimage to Ayu and returned—"

There was a collective intake of breath at the slight emphasis on "truly." But Khefnar merely smiled.

"—then we honor your return and shall add your remembrances to the canticles. Later. Now is the Hour of Refuge, and you have dishonored it enough already."

Eyes moved between the two figures on the dais, swinging back and forth like scales of judgment. Their high priestess stood petite but unbowed beneath Khefnar's towering presence. Bahlanni had been among them all her life, had dedicated the last decade to the succor and well-being of her people. She was a pillar amongst them, steady and steadfast.

Opposed to her, Khefnar was a river, fierce and raging as he railed against the injustices we had suffered. He offered something Bahlanni did not: a future where our wrongs were redressed, our ancestral home restored to us. A return, and a reckoning.

I held my breath, waiting to see whom my people chose.

"You're right," Khefnar said into the silence.

Bahlanni's mouth dropped open in astonishment, eliciting a low chuckle from Khefnar.

"Of course you're right," he said. "After all, you have the better claim to the high priesthood, don't you? For all you know I could be lying about my journeys. Perhaps I merely spent these last years lazing away in the pleasure houses of Zantyum. Such a thing must have crossed your mind, Sister Bahlanni."

Bahlanni did not deign to answer that directly. "There is no way to verify your claim, Brother Khefnar."

Khefnar smiled. "What if there was?"

At a wave of his hand, the four robed figures who had accompanied him into the chamber joined him on the dais. Each set the ornately decorated wooden box he or she carried at Khefnar's feet.

"What is this?" Bahlanni demanded, incredulous.

"Proof." Khefnar knelt and pried open the lid of the first box. "Behold the treasures of Ayu."

From the box he drew a goblet of gold and turquoise, its twin handles worked in the form of winged sphinxes.

"The Chalice of Thukan," Khefnar said, holding it high for all to see. Someone to the left of me gasped as it shone brightly in the candlelight. "Hidden away beneath the pyramid at Kheost, until the spirits within bestowed it upon me."

He passed it to Bahlanni, who accepted it after a moment's hesitation. Her ash-marked brow furrowed as she examined it.

"Well?" Khefnar asked her.

"It...appears genuine," Bahlanni admitted, her reluctance plain.

Khefnar opened the other chests, displaying more treasures to the crowd before handing them to Bahlanni for inspection. The second was a wickedly curved, ruby-encrusted dagger, while the third was a pair of enameled bronze bracers. Bahlanni examined them all in minute detail but could find no fault. As close as I was to the stage, I could not miss the way her fingers trembled as she handed the bracers back to Khefnar. Even she was beginning to believe his claim.

"Are you satisfied?" he asked both her and the crowd in a raised voice.

An approving murmur stirred through the congregation, but Bahlanni was not ready to concede yet.

"And that one?" she asked, gesturing at the fourth box. "What holy relic have you hidden away in there, Brother Khefnar? The dusty bones of the first children of Ayu? Or is it full of river water?"

Khefnar smiled. "What if it was?"

"I am afraid I cannot tell the mud of one river from another."

A woman behind me laughed nervously, but she was the only one.

"No," Khefnar said, shaking his huge head slowly. "It is the final proof of my words."

He knelt, reaching into the box—

"*Bellator!*" Drusa had reached my side, pulled at my sleeve. "Bellator Calvus, please—"

I shook her off, returning my attention to Khefnar. Whatever Drusa had been about to say died on her lips as she saw what he took from the box.

It was a skull.

Time had bleached it as white as the teeth that grinned from its naked jaw, but it bore no other signs of wear or damage. In Khefnar's massive hand it looked so absurdly small that for a stomach-churning moment I thought it might have belonged to a child.

"What is this?" Bahlanni demanded, her face contorting into an indignant mask.

"This," Khefnar said, cradling the skull in his hands as if it were eggshell-delicate, "is Ostakri, my oldest friend, who accompanied me to Ayu."

Bahlanni's scowl deepened. "We are not heathen barbarians who desecrate our dead to make idols of their skulls—"

"Ostakri saw what I saw," Khefnar said, speaking over her. "He witnessed the miracles I did, watched me commune with the most ancient of our ancestral spirits. You ask me to prove that I have done the things I say I have. That proof lies within this skull."

The silence that followed was so absolute that I could hear the blood pumping through my veins.

"You are speaking of the gravesight," Bahlanni said, her voice trembling only a little.

"I am." Khefnar lifted the skull so that all could see it. "I have mastered that ancient rite. Are there any among you who have done the same?"

Hope rose in me. The esoteric rite of gravesite was all but forbidden by Albastinian law, and practiced by scant few Ayu'li. Even a people as devoted to their dead as we were shied away from reliving the experiences of the deceased. As far as I knew, I was the only member of the congregation who had used it.

Which meant I could call out Khefnar's story as the lie I desperately hoped it was. A look in the skull might reveal this Ostakri's memories—or it might show me nothing at all. Gravesight usually only worked on the recently departed, not their dry bones.

"Anyone?" Khefnar repeated, his brow furrowed. "Is there

anyone who knows our ancient mysteries and possesses the courage to delve into another's memories?"

I began raising my hand, but suddenly Drusa was in front of me, pushing me back into the crowd with what little strength she possessed. She succeeded in sending me back a few paces, more out of surprise than anything else.

"Titian is missing!" she hissed before I could say anything. "I think...Bellator, I think he might be hurt!"

Powerless to defend my wife and having failed to protect my students, I felt as though all the things I valued in this life had turned to sand, slipping through my useless fingers.

I opened my mouth to question Drusa more closely, but someone else spoke before I could, his voice flat and uninflected.

"I will dare the gravesight."

The crowd before the dais parted, forming a narrow aisle down which a slight figure in blue robes came striding: Hupli, his head held high, eyes fixed upon the skull in Khefnar's hands. The big man watched him come, and only then did I realize that he would have had to pass Hupli to reach the Barrows' central chamber—to say nothing of the ash anointing Khefnar's brow.

Hupli had been a part of this from the beginning.

"Hupli?" Bahlanni said, her voice hoarse as her one-time apprentice ascended the steps of the dais. He did not spare her so much as a glance.

"I am Hupli, son of Narom and Skeyan," he said, coming to a halt on Khefnar's other side, opposite Bahlanni. "Priest of the Old Faith."

"Priest?" a man behind me murmured before his neighbor furiously shushed him. But the sentiment was echoed by many around us. That Hupli had omitted his junior status and announced himself as full priest was not lost on the congregation.

Nor was it lost on Bahlanni, who continued to stare stricken at him, blank incomprehension on her face. I wondered how long Hupli had been in contact with Khefnar and his disciples. Wondered how long it had taken before he had turned against Bahlanni, once Khefnar had dangled the offer of full priesthood before him.

"I have studied the mysteries of our forefathers," Hupli continued, ignoring the whispers fluttering mothlike about the chamber. "I have committed each canticle to memory, know each step to the holy dances. As for courage, I cannot say."

He took a deep breath. Bahlanni's mouth worked silently, the unsaid word plain upon her lips: *Please.*

Hupli held out his hands towards Khefnar, palms up, as though awaiting the scarred giant's benediction. "But I will look into the skull."

"Very well." With a delicacy that belied his size, Khefnar placed the skull into Hupli's waiting hands. "May the blessings of your forefathers and foremothers guide you through this trial, Hupli, son of Narom and Skeyan."

Hupli turned, raising the skull high so that all the congregation could see it. Then he brought it to his eye level and stared into its empty sockets.

Nothing happened.

Moments crawled by as Hupli continued to stare into the skull's empty eyes, his ash-marked brow furrowed with concentration. He looked like he was attempting to decipher another language's alphabet, not commune with a departed soul.

Doubtful murmurings creeped into the silence, and I had another wild rush of hope. Like any of the Rites, the gravesight was a skill that took years to develop and master. I had learned it late in my training, and then only because my grandfather had insisted that another carry on that archaic tradition after his passing. For Hupli to assume he could learn this most esoteric Rite through nothing more than study was laughable—

Two points of light appeared in the skull's empty eye sockets.

The congregation hissed as one, shock rippling through the field of bodies. Even Khefnar took a step back, his triumphant smile momentarily inflected with surprise. He hadn't known—or hadn't been sure—that Hupli really could perform the gravesight.

The points of light grew, becoming swirling vortexes of pale ghostfire reflected in Hupli's own eyes. He leaned in closer, the brow of the skull smearing the ashes on his forehead, the swirling lights all but devouring his vision.

Until they did exactly that.

I had never observed the gravesight being used by another. The last time I had done so had been in Horatia's company. She had looked shaken once I had risen from the deluge of a dead man's memories, but at the time I had attributed her reaction to the terrible revelation the gravesight had revealed to me.

Now, watching from the outside, I realized that perhaps it had been the ancient rite itself that had drained all color from my friend's face.

Ghostfire leapt from the skull, tendrils of flickering wan light stabbing into Hupli's eyes. I watched in paralyzed fascination as those tendrils grew, clinging leechlike to his face. Globes of illumination pulsed along them, traveling from Hupli's living skull to Ostakri's dead one and back.

Memories, I thought. Yet the exchange did not look like an even one to me. It looked more like the skull was consuming Hupli's memories, drawing them into itself. For every lucent globule he pulled from the skull, two of his own disappeared into that terrible light.

"Stop it!" someone cried out, voice high and hysterical. "It's killing him! *STOP!*"

Dark brown hands wrapped about the skull, wrenching it from Hupli's grasp. Someone in the congregation screamed as Bahlanni raised it above her head, the flickering ghostfire transforming her face into an outraged rictus. Hupli slumped bonelessly to the dais.

Khefnar reached for the skull with an inarticulate cry. Too late. Bahlanni jerked it out of his reach, then hurled the skull to the floor. A hundred shards of fragmented bone spilled across the steps of the dais.

"How *dare* you!" Khefnar snarled, towering over Bahlanni. Fear lanced through me at the thought that he might strike her. I reached out with my good hand, ghostfire lighting my fingers as I reached for anything that might help save my wife from Khefnar's grasp.

A groan from the dais forestalled whatever violence had been imminent as both Bahlanni and Khefnar turned to Hupli, still prostrate on the steps. Bahlanni knelt and pulled him into a sitting position.

"Are you alright?" she asked, concern for one of her flock overriding even Hupli's betrayal of her trust.

"Dark," Hupli said, his eyes still squeezed shut. "So dark and cold. All shrouded in a fog."

But the voice was not Hupli's usual expressionless monotone. It was pitched higher and broke on the word *cold.*

Hupli opened his eyes, and the murmurs transmuted into startled gasps. The pale ghostfire still gleamed in his pupils.

"Khefnar?" he asked, still in that high voice. Unease tinged my gut as I wondered how young Ostakri had been at his passing. "Khefnar, are you there?"

"I am." Khefnar's voice and face softened as he knelt on

Hupli's other side, opposite Bahlanni. "I'm here, Ostakri. With you."

Hupli's attempt to speak was interrupted by a shudder that swept over his whole body, and he convulsed like a man in the grips of fever. Bahlanni rubbed at his brow, smudging the anointment ashes.

"Khefnar," Hupli said again once the convulsions slowed. "Khefnar, are we in…"

"Albastine," Khefnar said softly. "Yes. We've returned, my friend. As I promised you we would."

Hupli let out a long, shuddering sigh. "And am I…?"

Khefnar's voice was gentle. "You are."

"Oh." Hupli sagged against Bahlanni. "I…yes. I am here, but I am not here. On the far side of the Quiet Fields again. But these hands are not mine. This body…"

Another spasm rocked him.

"Stop it!" Bahlanni hissed, reaching across to grab Khefnar by the wrist. "Can't you see this is killing him?"

Khefnar nodded and took Hupli's face between his hands, leaning down so that their foreheads touched. "It is over, my friend. Rest well. I will see you again in time."

Hupli gave a final, shuddering nod and closed his eyes. Khefnar murmured a word in Old Ayu'li, one that sent tendrils of ghostfire flickering from Hupli's temples and up the big man's arms. Hupli slumped again, and only Bahlanni's and Khefnar's combined efforts kept him from falling to the dais.

When Hupli's eyes opened again they were his own, dark and flat. He looked around blearily, as if the dim light of the chamber were too strong for his eyes.

"Hupli?" Bahlanni asked, a tremor in her voice.

"I was," he said, his own voice low and ragged. "I was Hupli, and I was Ostakri. I saw…no, I *lived* as he did…"

His confusion was familiar to me, though that familiarity

did nothing to lessen the unease it engendered. I recalled vividly the way I had relived the memories of Julius Catellus, from his earliest days to his abrupt murder. How easily I might have lost myself in those same memories, until I could no longer tell where he ended and I began.

"I saw," Hupli said again, his voice stronger. "The great river. Ayu, from which we all sprang. The ancient spirits called back to dance and tell their ancient secrets..."

He looked up at Khefnar, a light in his eyes that had nothing to do with ghostfire. "To dance with you. Khefnar, chosen priest of Ayu."

"Ancestors be praised!" someone shouted on the far side of the dais. Khefnar straightened, looking once more upon the congregation.

"You have heard it from the mouth of your own priest," he boomed, ignoring Bahlanni and her stricken expression. "I have been baptized in the waters of Ayu, anointed by the ancestors themselves to be your high priest and lead you out of this land where the dead find no rest. For you I have only one question."

He spread his arms wide, all but sweeping Bahlanni from the dais. "Will you follow me?"

I opened my mouth to shout *no,* but another voice spoke first from somewhere in the crowd. "Khefnar!"

"Ayu!" called another. Within moments more voices joined in, turning the two names into a chant:

"Khefnar!"

"Ayu!"

"Khefnar! Ayu!"

More and more, until the chamber resounded with the chant. Not every voice was raised, but enough that when I next turned to Bahlanni I could see teardrops glistening in her eyes.

I reached for her, with my heart and with my hand. But the crowd was pressing forward, streaming and shoving past me to the dais as the faithful surged towards Khefnar. Their fingers brushed his robe, his legs, all wanting to touch the living saint. Others stooped to collect the shards of Ostakri's skull, claiming bits of what would soon become a holy relic for themselves.

Bahlanni stood behind him, forgotten and forsaken by those who had turned their adoring faces to her mere minutes ago. I had never seen her look so lost, or so alone.

Khefnar reached out to the nearest of the crowd, placing a hand on her brow and murmuring a benediction. The sight sent a surge of anger through me. How dare he usurp Bahlanni's place amongst the faithful, after so many years of her tireless labor? How dare these people cast her aside so easily for the false hopes Khefnar promised them?

I dove back into the crowd, ready to fight my way through to my wife's side if I had to. But something snagged at my cloak, pulling me backwards.

I whirled around to see Acolyte Drusa standing there, clutching the hem of my cloak in her white-knuckled hands. Her expression was fearful but defiant.

"Bellator!" she shouted over the noise of the chanting crowd. "*Please!* I think...I think someone's kidnapped Titian!"

Her words cut through my anger at Khefnar and my fear for Bahlanni, replacing them with fear of a wholly different kind.

"Why?" I asked, my voice coming out harsh and raw. "What makes you think that, Acolyte?"

Drusa bit her lip, glancing around at the crowd streaming past us. We might as well have been invisible—every eye in the Barrows was fixed on Khefnar.

"Because of these." Drusa reached into a satchel I hadn't even noticed she'd been carrying and pulled out a cloth that might have been white before it had been stained red. "I found them on his pillow this morning."

Bile rose in my throat as I took the cloth from her, unfolding it clumsily with my one good hand. I uttered a silent prayer to the ancestors that it was not what I thought it was.

They must not have been listening.

I unfolded the bloodstained cloth and saw something pale and slender. A finger, cut off at the first knuckle, still wearing an iron ring. On its face, the crest of the Candorous family glimmered back at me.

CHAPTER NINE

"What are we doing here?" Drusa frowned up at the towering spire of the Magisterium rising into the morning sky on the peak above us. We'd arrived just as the first light peered over the eastern mountains, painting the white marble golden. The sky was streaked purple and orange, and there seemed to be no sound in the world but the wind sighing through the crags.

The beauty of the scene did little to improve my mood.

"We're finding out what happened to Acolyte Titian," I said over my shoulder, not slowing my stride even as Drusa struggled to keep pace with her shorter legs. Both Magisterium and Senate sat at the valley's highest point, and the road leading up to them was correspondingly steep.

"You think he could be here?" Drusa said, glancing doubtfully first at the needlelike spire of the Magisterium, then at the great dome of the Senate rotunda. "But if he was kidnapped... the finger..."

"I think," I said, panting only slightly as we crested the rise and found ourselves on level ground once more, "that Acolyte Titian's disappearance isn't something for me to handle."

"But you're his teacher—"

"Exactly," I said. "Not a magistrate. Not even a Legate, anymore."

I paused to let Drusa catch up and wiped my brow. The ache in my legs from our swift ascent felt good. Felt like I was doing *something,* even if it was only moving from one place to another.

"But you've dealt with that kind of thing before," Drusa protested, panting as she caught up to me. "Last autumn, I mean—"

"I more or less stumbled into that mess," I said. "My job is to teach you, not investigate crimes."

A shadow passed between me and the sun. I looked up and saw the familiar statue of Vigilance, her arms outstretched. She stood facing the Senate dome, marble eyes impassive, a sword in one hand and a lantern in the other.

"Fortunately," I continued as we ascended the Magisterium steps, "I know someone who does."

"AND THE LAST place you saw Citizen Candorous was near the White Gates?" Magistrate Lavinia Caprio asked, stylus hovering over her tablet.

As she had with every question previously, Drusa glanced sidelong at me before answering. I nodded.

"That's right," Drusa said, returning her attention to Lavinia. "About a mile up the valley from the Gates, I think."

Lavinia nodded and marked something on her tablet. We sat in her office, a cramped little room on one of the Magisterium's middle levels. Most of the floor space was taken up by the heavy oak desk. Lavinia sat on one side, Drusa and I on the other. Between us on the table lay the bloody finger of Titian Candorous.

"What time?" Lavinia asked, coming to the end of her wax tablet. She reached behind her and pulled a fresh one from the wall, setting the other aside.

In true Albastinian fashion, Lavinia had used as much of her scant space as possible for practical purposes. Her files were carefully organized and tucked into honeycomb-patterned niches lining the wall, while books of law and public records were kept on the higher shelves so as not to impede her daily work. The only concessions to sentiment seemed to be a hand-woven blanket draped over the back of her chair and the small mountain of coffee mugs precariously piled on the room's sole end table.

"A few hours before midnight." Another glance at me, but this time I resolutely ignored it. Lavinia was making no effort to hide her skepticism, and I did not need her thinking I had coached my student on her responses.

"Could you be more specific?"

"Nine o'clock?" Drusa said. "Maybe nine-thirty. I was on my way down to the Gates and he was coming back."

Lavinia's stylus scratched against wax. "Was he behaving strangely?"

"I don't think so." Drusa chewed her lip, considering. "But..."

Lavinia looked up from her tablet, gaze darting between Drusa's face and mine. She must have been satisfied with what she saw. "But?"

"It wasn't that he was *acting* strange," Drusa clarified, looking anywhere but at Lavinia. The petite magistrate's intent gaze did a far better job unnerving my student than it had me. "But...Titian is tall. Was tall, I guess, if anything's happened to him."

"Let's not use the past tense until he's been fitted for an Attendant's mask," Lavinia said. Her expression softened fractionally. "Was your friend tall before last night, or was his being tall the strange part?"

I didn't find any humor in it, not with the bloody finger pointing accusingly at me. But the comment forced a near-hysterical laugh from Drusa.

"He was always tall," she said with a nervous giggle. "I mean, it was strange that I ran into him there. He's one of the faster runners in our class. It's a long jog from one end of the Valley to the other, but he should have passed me on the way back well before that point."

"So having a lead of only two miles on you was uncharacteristic?"

"Very." Drusa nodded, encouraged. "I didn't think much of it at the time. Honestly, I sort of assumed maybe he'd wandered off for a bit after his fight with..."

She trailed off, realizing she'd said too much.

Don't look at me, I thought. She did, of course.

"I see," Lavinia said, giving me a pointed look.

"Acolyte Candorous was the reason they were on a night-time jog," I said, attempting to allay her suspicions. "He disrespected me directly before an audience of his peers."

"So you gave them a few miles to think it over," Lavinia said, drumming her stylus against her tablet. She returned her attention to Drusa. "You think he went somewhere along the way?"

"Maybe." Drusa shifted uncomfortably. "Or maybe on the way back. I never saw him come back to the Barracks."

"And this?" Lavinia waved her stylus over the finger, her nose wrinkling in distaste.

"It was on his pillow this morning," Drusa said, turning a little green. "My bunk's the next one down from his..."

"So you took it and brought it to your teacher," Lavinia finished. "How'd you know where to find Bellator Calvus?"

"I make no secret of my religion," I said, perhaps a shade more defensively than I had intended to. "My students knew I would be worshipping in the Barrows this morning."

"Right," Lavinia said. "The Hours. This morning's was Refuge, I believe?"

I nodded, surprised that she knew. Most Extorani were vaguely aware of the Hours, but not many could name them in order offhand. Especially not those who had displayed Lavinia's level of hostility towards the Old Faith.

"So you found Bellator Calvus at the ceremony," Lavinia finished, "and he brought you here. Anything else?"

"At the ceremony—" Drusa began, but I held up a hand to stop her.

"I'll tell Magistrate Caprio about the Hours," I said. "I think you've earned a break. Go get yourself some breakfast from the canteen."

Drusa looked from me to Lavinia, who acquiesced with a grudging nod. The young Acolyte practically bolted from her seat, the door slamming shut behind her as she fled Lavinia's imperious gaze.

"So," the magistrate said, returning her raptor's gaze to me, "what is it you don't want your Acolyte telling me about the Hours?"

"Nothing," I said, readjusting my seat. "I just wanted you to hear it from me first."

"I'm sure I'm going to love whatever it is," she said. "First, though, I want to know what game you're playing at, Bellator."

"No game." I shook my head. "One of my students is missing. Possibly hurt, maybe dead. If that's not a matter for the Magisterium to handle, what is?"

"I'm not disputing the gravity of the matter." Lavinia's gaze flickered briefly to the bloody finger on her desk. "Just wondering why you chose to come to me and not one of the dozen other magistrates currently in this building. Especially after our, ah, *encounter* last night."

I laid both hands flat on the desk, steeling myself. Once I said what I was about to say, there could be no going back.

"Because," I said, eyes fixed on Lavinia's, "Khefnar's back."

His name had not been mentioned during my interrogation the night before, but the color draining from Lavinia's face was proof enough of recognition.

As succinctly as I could, I recounted everything that had occurred at the Hour of Refuge, beginning with Bahlanni's recitation and Khefnar's subsequent interruption. Lavinia was silent throughout, save for the furious scratching of her stylus as she noted down everything I had said. Only when I finished did she speak, to ask about Hupli's use of the gravesight on Ostakri's skull.

"Isn't it illegal to perform this ritual on the dead?"

"Technically, no," I said. That same technicality had saved me from imprisonment half a year before. "It's illegal to use the gravesight on an Attendant. But seeing as Ostakri's only remains was a skull..."

"I see." Lavinia made a dissatisfied sound in her throat. "Is there any chance this junior priest—"

"Hupli."

"Hupli," she repeated, only slightly mispronouncing the Ayu'li name. "Is there any possibility that he might have faked this gravesight?"

"None." I shook my head, recalling once again how the ghostfire had streamed hungrily from the skull to Hupli, its frantic pulsing as he dove into the memories within. "Whatever he saw in there was real. Khefnar may have really been to Ayu. For all I know, he might actually have been chosen by the ancestors as the new high priest."

I shifted uneasily in my seat, dismayed by the thought. Until now I had not been willing to entertain the possibility that Khefnar had been telling the truth about his pilgrimage.

"Is there any way to verify his claim?" Lavinia asked, frowning down at her notes.

"Not anymore." I shook my head. "Gravesight requires a body, or a large enough piece of one. The skull was smashed." I did not say by who.

Lavinia scowled. "So there's no way to counter Khefnar's claim to your wife's title."

"Not..." I hesitated, realizing even as I spoke that there *was* a way Bahlanni might reclaim her place as high priestess of the Old Faith. It might be dangerous, perhaps even impossible. But it was a chance.

"Ah," Lavinia said, reading into my silence. "So there is a way."

"Maybe," I said. "But only as a last resort. It'd be easier to prove that there's a link between Titian's disappearance and Khefnar's return."

"Assuming there is one." Lavinia gave me a hard look. "And if there was, are you certain that would convince your people to turn against their newfound messiah?"

"We're not savages, Magistrate," I said, biting back the harsher word that had threatened to leap from my tongue. "There are a few extremists like Khefnar among the Old Faith, I'll grant you. But the rest are merely caught up in his zeal. We're still citizens of Albastine, still subject to her laws. If it turns out Khefnar is behind Titian's kidnapping and the mutilated Attendants, they won't intervene when the Republic's justice comes for him."

A moment of silence hung in the air between us. Lavinia studied me carefully. "You seem awfully certain of that."

I raised my chin. "Which part?"

"That Khefnar is behind your student's kidnapping."

I shrugged. "First the dismembered Attendants, then Khefnar, and now this kidnapping. I don't believe in coincidence, Magistrate."

"Me neither," Lavinia admitted, running a hand through her hair. "Alright, Calvus. I'll enlist a few magistrates. We'll round up a posse of deputies, head to the Barrows. With any luck Khefnar—"

"No," I said.

Lavinia's mouth worked soundlessly. I pressed on before she could recover her voice.

"You asked earlier why I came to you," I said. "This is why. So that you'd see that not all of us are of Khefnar's party. That we're citizens of the Republic *and* Ayu'li of the Old Faith, and that there's no reason we should have to choose between the two."

"Khefnar is here illegally," Lavinia objected. "His last departure from Albastine was under punishment of exile. By law he should have alerted the provincial governors of his return to the Republic and lobbied them for permission to enter the valley. As it stands, I have every right to dispatch a posse to arrest him this very moment."

"And what happens when you send them into the Barrows during our holy Hours, when Khefnar's stirred half the souls inside into a frenzy?" I demanded. "Do you think you can apprehend him without violence breaking out?"

"So long as your people don't intervene—"

"Magistrate," I said, leaning over the desk. Lavinia's hand twitched towards her baton, but to my relief she elected not to repeat last night's mishaps. "We agree that Khefnar is dangerous. Yes?"

Lavinia nodded warily.

"If you go to the Barrows now," I said, "then innocent

people *will* get hurt, regardless of how things play out. And Khefnar will be expecting you to apprehend him. You'll be playing into his hands."

Lavinia chewed her lip, considering. "You're just trying to protect your wife."

"I want to protect *everyone*," I insisted. "Let me help you."

Her owlish eyes bored holes into mine, searching for some hint of duplicity. I refused to look away or even blink.

"How?" Lavinia demanded at last.

"As it stands," I said, "Khefnar's only current crime is entering Albastine without license. What's the penalty for that?"

"A fine," Lavinia said, resuming her seat. "And a month-long expulsion from the city."

"A fine his supporters will no doubt foot the bill for," I pointed out. "And a brief exile he can easily return from."

"True," she admitted. "On the other hand, the penalties for sabotaging an Attendant are far more severe."

"As are those for kidnapping," I said. I leaned forward, knowing this was my one chance to convince her. "My wife is still officially the high priestess of the Old Faith, Magistrate, even if Khefnar's reappearance has her congregation besotted. That gives me influence among the Ayu'li. I can go places you can't, find the evidence you need to connect these crimes."

I wanted to say more, but was wary of pressing too hard, too fast. Instead, I sat, suddenly exhausted. The adrenaline of the last few hours finally gave way to the crushing weight of all that had transpired and the daunting task that lay before me.

Lavinia did not answer immediately. Her eyes roved over the notes she had taken on her tablet, though her expression did not change enough for me to believe she was really reading what she had written.

"Fine," she said, the word coming out tight and brittle. "I

don't like it, Bellator Calvus. But you're right. Dealing with Khefnar and the Sons of Ash will require finesse."

I let out a breath I hadn't realized I'd been holding. "Thank you."

She thrust a hand towards me, so sudden and stiff that I flinched away. Two dots of color appeared high on her cheeks, and only then did I realize it had been extended in offering, not as a blow.

We shook once, brief and perfunctory. Lavinia turned from me and took her belt from the wall.

"Where will you go?" she asked. "Back to the Barrows?"

I nodded, though I didn't tell her it wasn't Khefnar I intended to see there. Not at first, anyway. "What about you?"

"I've got to search for your missing student," she said, buckling the belt around her middle. "Though I must confess my doubts about the one you brought here this morning."

"Drusa's got promise," I said, struck by a sudden feeling of defensiveness. "It took courage for her to come to me in the Barrows this morning. She's not of the Old Faith."

"Not all Ayu'li are," Lavinia agreed, her voice strangely soft. "Maybe you're right about her, then. I'm about to find out in any case."

She held her office door open, gesturing for me to leave. I paused in the hall, turned back to her.

"Take care of her, Magistrate," I said, keeping my eyes on Lavinia's. "I don't want to lose another Acolyte today."

"You won't," Lavinia said, resting a hand on her baton. "Swear it by all the gods."

I paid no homage to the gods of the Extorani, but I recognized the solemnity of the promise.

"Good hunting, Magistrate Caprio," I said, pressing my fist against my heart in salute.

After a moment's hesitation she returned the gesture. "Good hunting, Bellator Calvus."

CHAPTER TEN

At first the Barrows appeared unchanged from only a few hours prior. Incense still hung heavy in the air, and candlelight flickered against the statues carved into the walls. Hymns still echoed through the winding tunnels, but now they had taken on a subtly different cadence: not the gentle, soothing rhythms characteristic of the Hour of Refuge, but the deeper, slower intonations associated with the mystic Hour of Revelation.

I ground my teeth. In a span of hours, Khefnar had upended the celebrations Bahlanni had labored for weeks to prepare. I shuddered to think what he might do with more time.

Yet I did not proceed to the main chamber to confront him. Instead, my steps led me to a side passage, down a winding series of turns as the tunnels branched and forked. Albastine's valley was sparsely wooded, and the first settlers had lacked the materials necessary to build enough homes before the onset of winter. They had instead taken refuge in the winding cave system we now called the Barrows, each family claiming for themselves one of the smaller chambers within. With the spring thaw those first citizens of Albastine, Ayu'li and Extorani alike, had departed the caves to construct more traditional dwellings, but those of the Old Faith continued to visit and maintain the shrines they had erected to their familial ancestors in what would one day become the Barrows.

I turned a corner and arrived outside the chamber that had belonged to Bahlanni's family since before the Autumn Fever. Making an obeisant gesture to the statue of the guardian ancestor who stood at the entrance, I softly called out. "Bahlanni? Can I come in?"

No answer. I stepped inside anyway.

Bahlanni knelt before her family's shrine, her back to me. Candlelit faces of her ancestors were carved into the walls, looking down at her with gazes that were variously gentle, stern, jovial or dour. Fleetingly, I wondered what expression my stone face would bear when my passing came. Not a smile, I'd guess.

I approached quietly, not wanting to disturb her. I stopped a pace behind her and to the left, the proper position of respect when visiting the shrine to another's ancestors. I knelt, my posture mirroring Bahlanni's. She glanced at me, then turned quickly away. Not so quickly that I did not see the streaks running down her face, where tears had marred the ceremonial makeup she had so carefully applied that morning.

"I'm sorry," I said into the silence.

"For what?" Bahlanni's voice was flat, hoarse. "You did not invite Khefnar into Albastine, or into the Barrows. You did not cast aside years of tradition and ceremony for promises of a lost homeland."

You did not cast me aside, she did not say. I bit my lip and leaned forward to put a hand on her shoulder. She tensed, then relaxed beneath my touch.

"But I did disappear." The words cut like a knife, yet I forced myself to say them anyway. "I'm sorry."

She turned, her face in profile to me. "Where did you go?"

"It was an emergency. Someone was in danger."

Still kneeling, Bahlanni turned around fully so that we were facing each other. "Who?"

"One of my Acolytes disappeared."

Her eyes widened. "Are they hurt?"

The worry in Bahlanni's voice ran deep, utterly sincere. I marveled that she could immediately shift her concerns from herself to another with such ease.

"Yeah," I said, my throat threatening to close up. "They... whoever took him. They left me his finger."

"Ancestors preserve us." Bahlanni's face looked ashen beneath her makeup. "Whose?"

I told her what I knew. Bahlanni frowned at Drusa's admission to the Barrows, no doubt due to the Acolyte's status as an agnostic to the Old Faith, but did not interrupt.

"And now the magistrates are investigating?" she asked at last.

I nodded. "One of them is with Drusa right now, looking in the last place she says she saw Titian. Hopefully they can work out what happened to him."

"I see." Bahlanni bit her lip, looking down at her hands folded in her lap. "That's why you left when you did."

"Time was of the essence." I touched two fingers to her chin and lifted her face to mine. "Drusa wanted me to investigate myself. Instead, I went to the Magisterium so that they could handle it. I came back here as soon as I was able. I..."

There was more I wanted to say, but my tongue felt heavy, the words formed in my mind disconnected from my mouth.

"Akhenkatem." She reached out and ran one hand along my cheek. "Blood of my blood. It's all right."

"No." I shook my head. "I should have been there for you. *Here* for you. When your world was falling apart and I..."

"My husband," she murmured, placing her other hand on my other cheek so that I could not look away from the deep pools of her eyes, "I know what kind of man I married."

"And what kind is that?" I asked, trying and failing to summon even a weak smile, for I found I dreaded the answer.

Bahlanni did not smile either, but one corner of her mouth curled upwards. "The dutiful kind."

"But my first duty should be to you."

"Every soul is bound by obligation," she said, her tone shifting to that she used in her sermons. "And as different fruit ripens at different seasons, so too do different duties come to the fore at different times—"

"Bahlanni," I said, slipping into the speech of Old Ayu. "Please. Just listen."

She fell silent and sat back on her heels, waiting.

"There are things I have to say," I said, the words coming back to me rusty with years of disuse. "Things I should have said a long time since. And the first of these is that I am sorry. I am so, so sorry."

Bahlanni bit her trembling lip, but refrained from saying more, nodding for me to continue.

"I am sorry I left you," I told her, not for the first time. As I spoke I placed both palms flat against the chamber floor, feeling the cool stone beneath my living hand. "Sorry for the rift that grew between us in my absence. And I am sorry that I have not become the man you had hoped I would be in that time."

Again the lights blurred around me. "But I am trying."

Silence, save for the distant reverberations of hymns echoing from the main chamber.

"My husband," Bahlanni said at last, in the common speech of Albastine. I could not see her face from this angle, but I knew well the sad smile that accompanied that tone. "My sad, sweet, noble husband. Don't you see?"

Her hand rested lightly on the top of my head, as though she were about to bless me. "I have never needed you to be other than what you were."

I dared look up at her, saw her tearstained smile. "But when we separated—"

"We were young," she said, though her smile grew somewhat brittle. "Both then, and when we wed. We both expected things the other could not give, and were both wrong to do so. Time has made us wiser, I hope."

I could only nod.

"Akhenkatem," Bahlanni said. "Listen to me. I have forgiven you. Have you forgiven me?"

In answer I pressed her hand to my mouth, kissed her lightly on the palm.

"Then you must make me a promise," she said, her voice growing grave. "You must stop punishing yourself for the past."

The ghost of old feeling thrilled down my bad arm. "I can't just forget it."

Bahlanni's laugh echoed off the carven faces of her ancestors. "We are Ayu'li. We cannot forget the past. Instead, we learn from it. We let it give us strength."

From somewhere deeper in the Barrows, I heard the gentle echo of hymns.

"You're right." I took her hand in both of mine, the bare and the sheathed. "We cannot return to what we were. All the Rites in the world cannot wind back time. Yet after everything, here we are again."

I kissed her hand. "Building something new. Together. If you'll have me."

Bahlanni did not so much embrace me as collapse into me. There were no tears, no wracking sobs—all of that she had done alone, in the span of this small absence that had so painfully reminded her of my greater one.

I held her, letting her cling to me as a rock in a storm. I had not been there for her for so long. But I was now.

It must have only been minutes that we stayed there, bent together beneath the watching eyes of her ancestors' effigies. But it felt like years. I listened as her heart pulsed steadily against mine, each beat fading into the next as time ceased to have any meaning.

When we finally broke apart Bahlanni's dark eyes were shining, but her cheeks were dry.

"You were not there for me when I looked for you," she said, gently enough that I knew the words were not a reproach. "But you are here for me now, and that is worth something."

"Worth more than that," I said, and heard the newfound confidence in my voice. "I'm here to help you, blood of my blood. We're going to take back everything Khefnar took from you."

Her laugh was short. "You cannot take hearts, Akhenkatem, no matter how much you might will them to love you."

"You can win them, though," I said. "The faithful *love* you, Bahlanni. You are their priestess. They followed you into battle. Fought and died for you. Khefnar showing up with some wild stories and a few treasures may distract them for a day, maybe two. But when the moment comes, it's you they'll turn to. I'd bet my last denar on it."

"That certain?" Bahlanni managed a strained laugh. "A pity, then, that the Hours last only a few days."

"Actually," I began, "I have an idea on how we could use that—"

My attempt to explain how the sacred ceremonies might rewin Bahlanni her rightful place was cut off by her hand against my mouth. My heart thudded against my chest as I fell silent, listening.

Footfalls echoed down the tunnel leading to Bahlanni's

family shrine, not far off. A moment later a shadow crawled up the wall, the candles making it dance and sway as it drew near us. Only when its bearer rounded the bend to stand in the entryway did I realize who it was.

"*You.*"

Anger propelled me to my feet as ghostfire flared between the cracks of my leather sleeve. I started towards the intruder, only to be pulled back by Bahlanni's hands on my living one.

"Akhenkatem," Hupli answered, unperturbed by my outburst. He looked past me at his former mentor. "Bahlanni."

"Hupli," my wife cut in before I could. Her voice had gone frostily polite. "Be welcome in the house of my grandsires."

He bowed in acknowledgment of the traditional invitation, then took a perfunctory step past the guardian ancestor statue. I had a sudden, vicious fantasy of toppling it over on top of him.

"Thank you," Hupli said, not moving from his place just inside the chamber. "I have come here with an invitation. Brother Khefnar wishes to meet with you."

I barked out a laugh before Bahlanni could answer. "After humiliating her publicly like that? He's got some nerve—"

"Flesh of my flesh," Bahlanni interrupted, twining her fingers with mine and pulling me towards her. "You are being rude to my apprentice."

"Your *apprentice*," I said, glaring at Hupli's impassive expression, "should be crawling here to beg your forgiveness for betraying you like he did."

"I betrayed no one," Hupli said, as blandly as though he were remarking upon the weather. "Brother Khefnar asked if anyone among the faithful was willing and able to verify his claims by use of gravesight. I was."

"How?" I demanded, unwilling to back down. "You never underwent Legate training."

"Of course not." The annoyance in Hupli's voice would have

been red-faced indignation on another man. "I would never dishonor our ways with the watered-down Rites you teach the Extorani, Bellator. But the canticles and the dirges remain open to those of the Old Faith who wish to study the ancient rituals in full."

My outrage found itself warring against begrudging admiration. "You learned how to perform the gravesight from a book?"

Hupli lifted his chin. "Seeing as there was no better teacher available."

That stung more than it should have. I opened my mouth to retort, but was stopped by Bahlanni's fingers tightening vicelike around my own.

"Akhenkatem," she hissed in my ear. "*Enough.*"

Duly chastised, I shut my mouth. Despite Hupli's role in Khefnar's spectacle this morning, venting my anger on him would do no one any good.

"I would be glad to accept Brother Khefnar's invitation," she told Hupli, still frostily polite. "I look forward to hearing the full tale of his travels to Ayu, along with a more complete explanation of his reasons for disrupting the Hours of Remembrance."

"Excellent," Hupli said tonelessly. "I am sure he will oblige you on both counts. If you would follow me?"

He bowed, turned, and slowly walked back up the tunnel. I watched him, alert for any false move.

"Akhenkatem?"

"Mm?"

"You're hurting my hand."

"Oh." I let go. "Sorry."

Bahlanni flexed her fingers, then marched up the tunnel. I followed.

"It might be a trap," I said, not caring overmuch whether

Hupli heard me or not. "Could be trying to lure you someplace vulnerable."

"My love," Bahlanni answered, her voice still low, "faith does not necessitate stupidity."

"What?"

"Every follower of the Old Faith just saw Khefnar usurp my leadership before a congregation of thousands. Do you think they would ask no questions if I inexplicably disappeared immediately afterwards?"

"Oh," I said, feeling foolish for not thinking of it. As we passed a stand of votive candles I thought I saw Bahlanni's mouth quirk upwards at the corner, though that may have just been a trick of the light.

"Hupli is leading us to a parley," she said quietly, "not an assassination. Whatever he's planning will be easier with my cooperation than without."

"Quite right." Hupli's voice echoed back down the tunnel, making me jump. The man's hearing was damnably sharp. He turned, looking over his shoulder at us both with that placid expression I was beginning to find exceedingly creepy. "And Khefnar is quite looking forward to meeting you both."

CHAPTER ELEVEN

I had expected Hupli to lead us to the traditional seat of the Old Faith priesthood: the sacred chamber whose walls were carved with murals retelling the history of the Ayu'li people as it was sung in the canticles, from the first children born of the River Ayu to their exile and settlement in this distant valley. By tradition, that was where the high priestess made herself available to the faithful for counsel.

Instead, Hupli led us up a different path, one that wound steadily upwards. The sloping tunnel floor became steep stairs, evoking sharp complaint from the muscles in my calves. Though I kept myself in reasonably good shape through constant drilling of katas and daily runs through the valley, I was panting by the time the floor leveled out.

"Here," Hupli said, turning down a side passage. I was somewhat gratified that even he was out of breath.

The walls of this tunnel were of rawer stone than those of the lower levels, the ancestral statues carved into them of rougher craftsmanship, with fewer candles or other offerings. We passed several familial chambers, yet most of those lay dark and empty.

I glanced at Bahlanni, but she was lost in her own thoughts, her gaze far away.

Ahead of us, Hupli halted before one of the only chambers candles flickered in. The ancestral statue at the entrance was as crudely carved as the rest of those in this hall, though there was a certain artistry in the rough lines of its face that made me wonder if its simplistic design was an intentional choice.

From within came a resounding vibration so deep that it took me a moment to believe it could come from a human throat. Yet the rhythm was unmistakably that of the hymns of Refuge.

"Brother Khefnar," Hupli called softly.

The vibration ceased, replaced with Khefnar's deep voice. "Brother Hupli. Sister Bahlanni, Brother Akhenkatem. Be welcome in the humble house of my grandsires."

Hupli and Bahlanni bowed reflexively in answer. So did I, albeit with greater reluctance, before entering Khefnar's family chamber.

Its cramped confines put me bizarrely in mind of Lavinia's office, though that was where any similarity between the two spaces ended. The ancestral statues carved into the walls mirrored those outside, only vaguely evocative of distinct faces. A faint layer of dust clung to them, testament to the years of neglect they had suffered during Khefnar's sojourn to Ayu.

A scattering of candles had been lit to the ancestors, but the chamber's primary illumination came from the small fire in its center. As we entered I wondered why it hadn't filled the chamber with smoke. The answer was a low moaning from overhead. I looked up to see a natural skylight in the roof of the chamber, exposing it to the elements but also providing ventilation.

"Welcome." Khefnar sat cross-legged on the opposite side of the fire, flanked on either side by the disciples who had brought the supposed treasures of Ayu into the Hour of Refuge. The Sons of Ash, although half of them were women.

"Please," Khefnar said, "have a seat."

Bahlanni sat, folding her legs beneath her. After a moment's hesitation I did likewise, though my unease was heightened by the fact that Hupli had elected to remain standing behind us, a shadow outside the ring of firelight.

"Brother Hupli," Khefnar said, waving a broad hand over the fire. "That is all. You may go."

Hupli departed without a word.

"First you interrupt the Hour of Refuge," Bahlanni said in the wake of Hupli's departing footsteps. "Now you're ordering my apprentice about as though he were your own. But if you expect me to relinquish leadership of our people as easily, prepare yourself for disappointment."

"Sister Bahlanni," Khefnar said, his grin wide and white, "let me assure you. If there is one thing I believe you will *not* do, it is disappoint."

Bahlanni's nostrils flared, but Khefnar continued before she could interrupt. "As for orders, I have given none to your apprentice. Nor to any other, for that matter. All those who follow me do so freely, of their own volition."

"It's true," one of the female Sons said. She was startlingly pretty, with ink-dark skin and cheekbones that could have cut glass. She bowed her head to Bahlanni. "My name is Shahkti. Before I left Albastine, I was engaged to marry a man I did not know. A stranger."

"The Republic does not permit forced marriage," Bahlanni objected, shifting uncomfortably. Yet that argument left her on uneven footing. Arranged marriage had been common practice amongst the Ayu'li both in our homeland and in the years of exile—unsurprising for a people who placed such a great emphasis on family lines. Albastine's laws were more flexible in regard to marriage arrangements, permitting both freedom of choice and the possibility of divorce, though the more traditional amongst the Old Faith frowned upon both practices.

"Indeed it does not," Shahkti agreed, her eyes flashing. "My husband-to-be reneged on the match. No man of Ayu'li bloodline would consent to marry a woman thus scorned, and I was left a pariah. When Brother Khefnar offered to take me with him on his pilgrimage to our ancient home, I agreed without hesitation."

Bahlanni and I exchanged an uncomfortable glance. Traditionalist as my wife was, even she balked at the idea of forcing a couple into an unwanted union. Yet the implication of Shahkti's story was plain: had we been in Ayu, she might never have suffered such needless disgrace.

"You see?" Khefnar asked, smiling. He had maneuvered Bahlanni into a position where any objection she voiced to Shahkti's plight would be tacit support of Albastine's laws over our own traditions. "Her loyalty is a gift freely given, one I take care to treat with the respect it is due. The same with these others."

He nodded to his right, where an older man sat with his legs folded beneath him. His carefully braided hair was cloudy white, his face and hands wrinkled, but his dark eyes were bright and alert as he smiled at me.

"Akhenkatem," he said, a faint wheezing in his voice. "Or perhaps I should call you by your outer name, Gaius Cassius Calvus. It is good to see you."

Out of the corner of my eye I saw a muscle twitch in Bahlanni's jaw, her displeasure at the use of my Extorani name evident—even in this remote corner of the Barrows, we were still inside a sacred place.

"Do I know you?" I frowned. There was indeed something

vaguely familiar about the old man, but if we had met before today it was buried in the fog of memory.

He nodded, holding his weathered hands to the fire. "You did once. I served with your grandfather when we were both far younger men. Back when he was a Legate, and I—"

"A cavalryman," I finished, startled. Time had carved its lines into his face, but the calloused hands were the same. Once, when I had been but a young boy, those hands had gifted me a carved wooden horse. "Uncle Laurent?"

Khefnar's smile faded, though the old man beside him merely chuckled, unperturbed. "Extorani names are easier in the army, and that's where Octavio—I'm sorry, Khaimesu—and I met. These days I go by my Ayu'li name, Imnatt. But you can still call me Uncle Laurent, outside these walls."

Yes, I remembered now. Uncle Laurent, his familiar face a staple at the holidays and festivals that were the punctuation marks to my earliest childhood. Yet how old had I been when I had last laid eyes upon him? Five, six?

"Where have you been all this time?" I asked, my throat constricting suddenly. "Grandfather said you'd disappeared."

"He was right." Laurent shrugged. "I found retirement... uncomfortable. Purposeless. So I took what fortune I had, and I wandered, until my feet led me to the banks of Ayu. A less direct pilgrimage than the one your grandfather underwent, perhaps, yet the ancestors brought us to the same place in the end. How is he, by the way?"

Grief wrapped its invisible fingers around my throat.

"Brother Khaimesu has been with the ancestors these last ten years," Bahlanni put in, laying a hand on my shoulder.

"Oh." Laurent's face fell. "May they guide his spirit safely across the gray veil."

"And lead him to the peace of the Quiet Fields," Khefnar

added, looking strangely at me. "You have my condolences, Akhenkatem."

"Thank you," I said reflexively, though I was loath to accept his sympathy. Eager to change topics, I shifted my attention back to Laurent. "So Khefnar found you in Ayu?"

"The other way around, actually." Laurent's smile returned, now tinged with mischief. "But that is a longer tale for a later time. Suffice to say that he impressed me enough to win me to his cause."

"His cause," Bahlanni repeated, leaning forward so that the leaping flames danced and glimmered in her eyes. "I think we have danced around that enough, *Brother* Khefnar. What is your purpose in returning to Albastine?"

"Did you not hear me at the Hour of Refuge?" Khefnar's frown seemed almost genuine. "I have come to lead our people home, Sister."

Bahlanni's eyes locked on his in a silent contest of wills. I glanced at the Sons seated beside their leader, but found only quiet adoration in their expressions—a mirror of the same feeling the faithful had displayed towards Bahlanni only hours earlier, before Khefnar stole their adulation from her.

A sinking feeling settled into my gut. Until now I had clung to the faint hope that Khefnar was lying, that his pilgrimage to Ayu had been a cover for whatever more ignoble actions he had undertaken in his exile from Albastine. But mere charlatanry could not inspire the devotion that shone upon the faces of Laurent, Shahkti, and the others.

Which meant that all of them were in on the deception, or Khefnar truly had made the journey he had claimed—perhaps even had communed with those long-departed spirits. If that were true, had they really chosen him as their instrument to lead their long-sundered people back to the lands of their birth?

And if so, did Bahlanni and I have any right to keep our people from their promised land?

"Brother Khefnar," Bahlanni said, speaking low enough that he too had to lean towards the fire to hear her, "if you have truly been to Ayu, as you claim, I honor your achievement and praise your courage in making so difficult a journey. The same for your companions. But I will not allow you to lead our people astray—"

"Astray?" the other female Son practically spat. She was the most physically intimidating of the group besides Khefnar, taller and broader than me, with raised knots of scar tissue upon her bare arms. "How can it be going astray, Sister, to lead our people to their destined home?"

"Because to lead them home is to lead them to their death!" Bahlanni snapped, her strained patience giving way at last. "The east bank of the Ayu belongs to the Emmaiyad Caliphate, the west to the dozen sultans and sheiks of the Ghrabesh tribes. Tell me, *Brother* Khefnar, have either of those peoples grown friendlier towards our own over the course of three centuries?"

"Somewhat," he said, unperturbed by her outburst. "We pilgrims are no longer turned away at the gates of Aghrabesh, at any rate."

"The Ghrabeshi might tolerate the presence of a few followers of the Old Faith wishing to visit the lands their ancestors came from," I said, hoping to temper Bahlanni's impassioned argument with reason. "But I expect they would take a far dimmer view of thousands of Ayu'li at their doorstep, demanding the return of the lands they drove us from."

"Your expectation is correct," said the last of the Sons. His speech was thickened with a heavy accent, one unfamiliar to me. "It would not be a warm welcome."

He had been sitting so quietly that I had scarcely noticed him, but now I realized with a start that he was not even Ayu'li.

His skin was more bronze than dark, his large nose almost perfectly straight, with a hard line to his jaw that would put even the most sharp-featured Extorani aristocrat to shame.

"You're Ghrabeshi," I said stupidly.

He smiled, making a little bow with a distinctly foreign flair to it. "Nakmond an-Swerati, at your service. Son of Nizar and Lenaka—"

"Take it off," Bahlanni hissed beside me. She stood and leveled an accusing finger at Nakmond an-Swerati—or more specifically, at the wavy line of holy ash upon his brow. "Wipe that sacrament from your disbelieving face, Ghrabeshi, or I will do it for you."

"Why?" he asked, sounding genuinely puzzled. "It is the custom to wear the ashmark during the Hours of Remembrance, is it not? Especially in a place of worship."

"You profane this temple with your very presence!" Bahlanni's shout echoed in the cramped confines of the cave. "Your people drove us from Ayu centuries ago! You butchered us, ransacked our temples, desecrated our dead!"

"Sister Bahlanni—" Khefnar rose, real concern etched upon his ritually scarred face for perhaps the first time. His bulk seemed to fill the little chamber, but Bahlanni whirled on him with a fury even greater than the vitriol she had shown Nakmond.

"And *you*," she snarled, "bringing a scion of the desecrators into the last holy place remaining to us—"

"*SISTER*," Khefnar boomed, his face as stony as those of his carven ancestors, "find yourself a more civil tongue towards your guest. Brother Nakmond is a follower of the Old Faith, as much as you or I."

Bahlanni's mouth worked soundlessly as she tried to make sense of what Khefnar had said.

"He's not even Ayu'li," she managed at last.

"Yet I revere my ancestors, just as you do," Nakmond an-Swerati said placidly. "Some of them, at any rate. Others I abhor for their actions. Those who drove your own predecessors away from Ayu, for example."

"You're an apologist," I said, finding my own voice again. "And a convert?"

Such things were not unheard of, but they were exceedingly rare—the Old Faith was not a proselytizing religion, and its core tenet of ancestral worship made conversion both unappealing and difficult to obtain. Those few outsiders who adopted our faith typically did so as part of their marriage to one of the Ayu'li race, bringing themselves into the lines of our ancestral heritage. And even then, those rare converts tended to continue praying to whatever gods they had worshiped previously—the lack of a distinct pantheon of deities meant that the Old Faith was a syncretic one.

"I am." Nakmond's gaze flickered over to the female Son who had last spoken—not Shahkti, but the other one, who must have been a full head taller than him. Seeing him looking, she flushed and turned away.

Well. That was one mystery solved, at any rate.

"Be welcome in the temple of our ancestors," Bahlanni said stiffly, without bowing. "Nakmond an-Swerati, son of..."

"Nizar and Lenaka," he supplied, unperturbed, before returning his attention to me. "Nizar an-Swerati, my father, is one of the twelve sultans of Aghrabesh. And you are right in assuming that he would be ill-disposed towards a sea of Ayu'li rising from the desert to storm his city."

"Yet you've thrown your lot in with a man who wants that storm to crash against your father's gates," I observed, wondering how much of an-Swerati's conversion was genuine faith, and how much was the attempt of a younger son to seize power from his father and brothers. The labyrinthine web of power plays and betrayals that characterized the Ghrabeshi sultanate's politics was well-known, even this far removed from those desert sands.

"Crash indeed," Bahlanni said, sounding more tired than I'd ever heard her. "It would be a massacre. Even if every man, woman, and child among the Ayu'li left Albastine and survived the journey, they would be slaughtered by your father's soldiers the moment he learned of their intent."

"True," Khefnar admitted, "if the people were to approach unguarded and unarmed. I intend for neither to happen."

"What *do* you intend, then?" Bahlanni asked, uncharacteristically blunt. "I am tired of playing games with you, Khefnar, son of Feri and Yadennu. You say you wish to lead our people back to Ayu, even knowing the dangers inherent in such a journey. Perhaps some will even follow you there, after the spectacle you put on. But you must know those who follow you will fall, either from the perils of the journey or beneath Ghrabeshi blades."

She took a step closer, until she had to crane her neck to stare Khefnar in the face. "And I swear to you, upon the graves of every ancestor I have, from now back to Ayu, I will not permit you to lead a single soul out of this valley and towards certain doom."

Her words echoed off the cave walls, into the uneasy silence that followed. The Sons of Ash exchanged apprehensive looks.

"Your commitment to your people is admirable," Khefnar said, scarcely audible over the crackling flames. "And I would welcome your spirit on such a journey, were your heart to change."

Bahlanni sneered. "Don't hold your breath."

"What if there were?" Shahkti blurted. "Khefnar, we should tell them—"

"No," Khefnar said, raising a hand to forestall her. "Not yet.

We invited Sister Bahlanni and Brother Akhenkatem here to see what they thought of our pilgrimage. She has voiced her doubts, and we must marshal our arguments to convince her otherwise."

Bahlanni's sneer deepened, but before she could say anything, Khefnar's gaze fell on me. "Yet her husband has remained quiet throughout. Tell me, Legate, would you lead your people back to Ayu, given the chance?""

"Me?" I blinked. "I'm not a priest."

"Yet your grandfather was," Laurent reminded me. "Leadership runs in your blood as surely as it does his."

"I..." I trailed off, startled to discover that I honestly had no answer to the question.

I had traveled beyond Albastine, often for years at a time. Yet the city had always been home to me. My family estate was here, alongside all of the people that I knew and loved. More than that, the Republic to which I had devoted my life was founded in this foggy valley, and though its reach now stretched to provinces beyond, the Pale City remained its beating heart. So too its people—*all* its people, for the oaths of service I had sworn were not to the Ayu'li alone.

My home, my family, my life's work. Could I abandon all of that to chase after a half-mythical homeland, one neither I nor anyone I loved who still lived had ever laid eyes upon?

I wanted to say no, but still found my tongue tied. Khefnar and Bahlanni agreed upon one thing: so long as the Republic's laws forbade the rituals which called the dead back to the land of the living, we would never be fully equal citizens. For a fleeting moment I allowed myself to wonder—perhaps even to hope—what a land without such restrictions might be like. A place where we could worship at the tombs of our forefathers and foremothers rather than building them effigies of stone. A place where we might call forth their spirits during the holy

Hours, to dance and sing and share the tales of their long-gone days with their living kin.

A place I might see my grandfather again.

Smoke stung my eyes. I rubbed at them, ignoring the watching faces awaiting my response. Even Bahlanni had turned away from her confrontation with Khefnar, her fierce passion crumbling to uncertainty as she looked at me.

"No," I said, my voice coming out hoarse. "No. Ayu is our past. Albastine is our future."

Doubt still gnawed at me, but the words felt right. My grandparents were dead, as were my parents. But Bahlanni was here, now, alive.

A scowl darkened Khefnar's scarred face. "I might have figured as much from a Legate. You cannot be both a member of the Old Faith and a lapdog of the Republic."

"Khefnar!" Laurent chided. "Don't judge the boy so harshly. It's a terrible thing to ask, to leave the only home one has ever known behind in search of an uncertain future."

Nakmond nodded his agreement, his light green eyes fixed on me. "A great sacrifice. One not every man possesses the will to make."

The challenge in his voice went unanswered, for Khefnar began to speak again.

"So," he said, his low rumble filling the cave, "neither the high priestess nor her husband is convinced of our cause. Not yet."

"Do not expect that to change," Bahlanni said. "And speaking of the high priesthood, was it not your intent in coming here to usurp me of that station?"

"My *intent*, Sister, is to lead our people home. I had hoped to secure your aid in doing so, as well as your husband's. But seeing as the ancestors have chosen me to be our prophet—"

"Not all." Bahlanni spoke softly, yet there was a quiet conviction in the words that drew every ear.

Khefnar's heavy brows furrowed. "All what?"

"All of the ancestors," Bahlanni said, and though her voice held steady I could see her clasping her hands together to keep them from shaking. "You claim to have communed with our forebears of old in Ayu itself, that they elected you their representative. I cannot dispute that."

She looked down at her hands, no doubt recalling how she had used them to smash Ostakri's skull before I could use the gravesight upon it. "Yet even if you had been anointed by every high priest of Ayu since the river god himself shaped us, your selection would not be unanimous. What of Chyset, who gathered the survivors of the Night of Broken Bricks about herself? Or Nalametth, who safeguarded the Ayu'li across the Biting Sands? Or brave Janarri, who gave himself to the Emperor of Zyantime to buy his people's safe passage?"

An uneasy murmur from the fire. I caught Laurent's gaze on me as Bahlanni recited the names of our heroes, the high priests and priestesses who had led the exiled Ayu'li through deadly danger, surrounded on all sides by bitter foes. I knew the old man and I were both thinking of my grandfather in that moment, for he had been high priest before Bahlanni, and heir to that same legacy.

"Or Ynfep, first priestess to dwell within these very walls," Bahlanni continued, placing a trembling hand against the smooth Barrows stone. "Sixteen high priests and priestesses have come between her and I, serving our people. Providing them with counsel and comfort, leading them in praise and supplication. I have followed their example to the best of my ability."

She turned back to Khefnar. Pride surged in me at the fierce light in her eyes, rekindled for the first time since the disastrous events of the Hour of Rest. "Have you consulted them, Khefnar, son of Feri and Yadennu? Were the ancestors who have guided us through the years of our hardship there to give you their blessing, or only those whose living days were spent beside the Ayu, who knew nothing of want and persecution?"

"The *true* ancestors—" Khefnar growled, but Bahlanni's harsh laugh silenced him.

"If you do not think those I named worthy of the title," she said, "then you may as well renounce your own claim to be an Ayu'li, for it was from those ancestors and their contemporaries that every one of us in this room sprang, save the Ghrabeshi. They did not give you leave to usurp my priesthood, Khefnar, nor do I."

Khefnar stepped closer, towering over Bahlanni, looking as though he might strike her. I rose to my feet, reaching by habit for the gladius I no longer carried. But Laurent and the female Son whose name I didn't know stood, blocking me.

"Easy, son," Laurent said, putting a gnarled hand on my arm. Over his shoulder Bahlanni and Khefnar stood square to one another, like boxers at a ludicrously mismatched weigh-in, neither willing to look away.

"You have something in mind," Khefnar said at last, more statement than question.

"I do." Bahlanni nodded up at him. "The Rite of Awakening."

My jaw fell to the floor. The Rite of Awakening, holiest of all our ancient ritual dances, was the Rite that would call forth the spirits of the departed back to their mortal shells, to walk and speak with their living kin once more. It was the Rite that Khefnar claimed to have performed upon the banks of Ayu.

The Rite forbidden above all others under Republic law.

"Bahlanni," I said, trying to catch her eye over Laurent's shoulder. "You can't—"

"Interesting," Khefnar said thoughtfully, as though I were not speaking. "You think your predecessors will side with you over me. That they will want to keep our people imprisoned in this thrice-bedamned valley."

Bahlanni's smile was as vicious as I'd ever seen it. "Why don't we ask them and see?"

"Very well," Khefnar said, nodding slowly. "We shall do it in sight of all the faithful. At the Hour of Revelation."

Bahlanni frowned, but only briefly. "I'd planned to hold Revelation outdoors. In the city's market square."

"Among outsiders?" Khefnar smirked, though there was little amusement in his voice.

"Among our fellow citizens," Bahlanni corrected. "Many of the Extorani remain wary of our faith. By holding the grandest of the Hours of Remembrance amongst them, I hoped to dispel that mistrust."

"An admirable sentiment," Khefnar said, "though a misguided one. Still, I do not object. At the Hour of Revelation, then."

"Bahlanni!" I hissed, no longer able to contain myself. "You'll be arrested!"

They both turned to look at me.

"It's illegal," I reminded them. "Using the Rite of Awakening in Albastine. You can't call forth a spirit when its body is an Attendant or gone—"

"Forgive me, Akhenkatem," Khefnar said, a self-satisfied smile creeping over his ritually scarred face, "but you can."

I blinked. "What?"

"Those secrets our forebears carried with them out of Ayu are the least of those their own ancestors held," Khefnar said. "I have learned others deeper still—including ways to call upon the ancestors without making use of their mortal remains."

Bahlanni's breath caught. "Truly? But how—"

"That would be telling," Khefnar said, the faintest smile playing upon his scarred face. "Suffice to say that I have done it and can do it again."

"Liar," Bahlanni said, immediately and without heat. But almost against my will, I turned towards Laurent. The old man raised his bushy brows.

"It's true," he said, his voice barely audible over the crackling fire. "I saw it with my own eyes, Cassius. Swear on your grandfather's memory."

I turned to Bahlanni, who was watching me with an unspoken question in her eyes: *can we trust him?*

I didn't know, not for certain. But I could read the sincerity in the old man's eyes enough to hazard a guess.

I nodded. Bahlanni bit her lip, then turned back to Khefnar.

"Very well," she said, moving to join me beside the fire. "At the Hour of Revelation, we will let the spirits of those who came before decide who their descendants will follow."

Khefnar's smile widened. "Pray they choose well, Sister."

And silently, I did.

PART THREE
RENDING

CHAPTER TWELVE

"You think this is a bad idea," Bahlanni said as we descended the long flight of steps from Khefnar's family chamber.

"Yes." I saw no point in tact. "The Rite's illegal, Bahlanni."

"It's also the cornerstone of our religion. One that's been denied us for far too long." She paused. "And if Khefnar's right and there is a way to conduct the Rite without the bodies... My love, do you realize what that would mean?"

I did, though the confrontation with the Sons of Ash had left me little time to grasp the implications. Now they came crashing down upon me.

"There would be no reason for the Rite to be outlawed." My heart began a slow crawl up my throat. "We could... Gods, Bahlanni, we could commune with our ancestors again. With your parents, and mine. With—"

"Your grandfather," she said softly.

My heart nestled itself in the place just behind my vocal cords, cutting off speech entirely. I forced it back down.

"Khefnar's not offering up what he knows for free, though,"

I said once my throat had cleared. "The fact that he's even willing to leave the choice up to the ancestors means he's confident they'll choose him. And if they do, what's to stop him from leading the faithful on his suicide mission back to Ayu?"

"Us," Bahlanni said. She bit her lip. "But...if he's right, and the ancestors *do* choose him as the leader of the faithful...do we even have a right to stand in the way?"

I stared. "Don't tell me you're agreeing with him."

"With his principles? Yes." Bahlanni ran a hand along the stone wall. "But not with his goals. Ayu is miles and years away. If it were closer..."

We paused on a landing decorated with the stone effigies of a mother holding two children: one a babe in swaddling clothes, the other perhaps three or four years old. My throat tightened at the sight. These were almost certainly victims of the Autumn Fever, the plague that had spread through the valley in the earliest years of our settlement, killing huge swathes of the Ayu'li and Extorani refugees who dwelled there. Had our numbers not been so badly depleted—and their unburied bodies less plentiful—then we might never have resorted to creating Attendants in the first place.

"But wishes are as useless as teats on a snake," Bahlanni said, braids swaying as she shook her head. "Khefnar will lead our people to their doom if he holds sway over them."

"Hey," I said, reaching out to rest a hand on her arm. "We won't let that happen, alright?"

Bahlanni looked up at me, then back to the memorial to mother and child. "How can you be certain?"

"Because no one—ancestor or living soul—would follow him over you," I said, squeezing her arm.

A faint smile came over my wife's face. It made what I had to say next all the harder.

"But," I continued, my tone growing serious, "you can't lead the faithful from exile."

Her smile faded.

"The Rite's still illegal," I pressed on. "Even if Khefnar has some way of calling back the ancestors without their bodies so that it wouldn't require using Attendants, it would still take the Senate time to draft and vote on legislation authorizing that version of the Rite."

"Time we don't have," Bahlanni said.

I nodded. "Exactly. Please, love. Don't go through with it. Let Khefnar perform the Rite alone. The magistrates can arrest him, and—"

"Akhenkatem." Bahlanni placed her hand on my chest, just above my beating heart. "Please."

That word, so small and tired and soft, silenced me. I placed my own hand over hers. My bad hand, though by the time I realized that I could not gracefully withdraw it.

"Listen," Bahlanni said gently, "you saw what happened at the Hour of Refuge. How they flocked to Khefnar when Hupli performed the gravesight. Do you think their adoration would lessen if he performed the Rite of Awakening alone? At least this way I will have some way of softening his influence."

"They'll arrest you both," I said, my own voice coming out in a whisper. "We...the faithful need you. *I* need you."

"As I need you," she said, still in that gently conciliatory tone. "But as I said, different obligations take precedence at different times. What is that maxim you're so fond of quoting?"

I knew the one she meant, but for the first time the words came unwillingly. "All Serve the People."

Bahlanni smiled sadly.

"You have sacrificed so much for your people," my wife murmured, her thumb circling my leather sheath. "Please. If... when my time comes to do the same, let me."

I nodded, not trusting myself to speak.

"If Khefnar has his way," Bahlanni continued, "then he will try to lead the faithful from the city. Not all of them will follow, but enough that we will never be what we are now again. They will perish in the wilderness or find themselves beset by enemies. I cannot allow that to happen."

"And if..." I did not want to say it, did not want to voice any doubt in her. But the possibility needed to be addressed, however much I hated it. "If the spirits side against you? If the high priests and priestesses who came before agree with Khefnar?"

Bahlanni looked over her shoulder, at the mother and her children carved into the stone. Perhaps she was thinking of what they had endured to come to this valley: the perils they had faced, the relief they must have felt upon reaching sanctuary here.

Or perhaps she simply did not want me to see her face.

"Then I will honor their wishes," she said. "No matter the cost."

To whom, she did not say. I squeezed her hand tight, willing her to feel my heartbeat beneath her fingers.

We did not speak again as we walked through the Barrows tunnels, each deep in our own thoughts about our people, our nation, our future. Each measuring hope against dread, fear against our ability to act. Each preparing for the further challenges this day was sure to bring.

Bahlanni and I parted ways at her family chamber. She needed to prepare for the remaining Hours of Remembrance, for regardless of what happened at Revelation there were still three ceremonies in between: Rending, Reckoning, and Ruin. I kissed her goodbye, saying that I would try to make it to all three, but that nothing was certain.

"Nothing except us," was her reply.

As I departed the Barrows' bronze gates, the sentries halted me.

"There's an Attendant," Neftani said, pointing with his staff down the slope to where a bronze-masked figure stood with unnatural stillness. "It's here for you, Brother Akhenkatem."

"For me?" My mind flashed back to last night, to the strange Attendant that had led me through the mists to the site of its mutilated kindred. Once more I found myself wondering who might have been puppeteering its strings.

"Yes," Neftani said, giving me a curious look. "It has a letter addressed to you."

"Oh," I said, feeling foolish. Attendants were often used as couriers and messengers, though they could not speak. Nor were they allowed within the Barrows, as their very existence was an affront to our religion. "Thank you."

Neftani nodded. "Blessings of the ancestors upon you, Brother Akhenkatem. And upon your wife."

"Thank you," I said again, and found myself smiling. Not all of the faithful had abandoned Bahlanni.

Though all the unliving servants of Albastine were uniformly masked and anonymous, the Attendant awaiting me downhill from the Barrows was not the one I had encountered the night before. It was shorter and stockier, and its tunic was the patterned white and blue of the Magisterium. That alone was enough to tell me who had sent it.

Its bronze mask smiled cheerily as it extended a hand towards me, the letter clutched between cold gray fingers. *Bellator Gaius Cassius Calvus* was printed on the front in an even, tidy hand.

I tore the envelope open and read the terse message inside with mounting dread.

We found the rest of him.

WHEN I HAD PARTED ways with Lavinia and Drusa, they had been heading to the valley's southern end, attempting to retrace Titian's path during my students' jog last night. Yet according to the address hastily scribbled on the back side of Lavinia's note, his body was in the Pale City's heart.

Specifically, on the Godstreet.

The Old Faith was not the only religion practiced in Albastine, or even the only one practiced by Ayu'li citizens. When the Extorani had been driven from their own homeland, they had brought their gods with them: a pantheon of a dozen chief deities plus hundreds of minor ones, some presiding over concepts as grandiose as time and the ocean, while others governed things as niche as nighttime travelers and childish pranks. Each had particular offerings and ceremonies, as well as the requisite feast days and mystery cults.

Such a vast pantheon would have required temples in the dozens elsewhere, but space in the valley was limited in the extreme. An eminently practical people, the Extorani had long ago found a workable solution in the form of the Godstreet.

A long, narrow stretch of cobblestones, it ran half a mile from the Senate hilltop down to the market district below. Walking up the hill from the valley, one passed all twelve temples to the major Extorani gods on the right, each carved directly into the mountainside. On the left stood the minor gods, each sculpted from the valley's white marble in a pose and style characteristic of their personality and purview. The one at the base of the ridge was Perseverance, staring stern and determined uphill. Next in line was his twin brother, Chance, a crooked grin on his face and a pair of dice resting in his open palm. After the twins stood their elder sister, veiled Misfortune, and so on.

I shivered as I climbed the Godstreet, pushing past the crowd of onlookers that had already formed beyond the magistrates' cordon, craning their necks for a glimpse of the body. Murders were rare in Albastine and inevitably invoked a morbid fascination. Lavinia's people had done the best they could to keep Titian's corpse out of public view, but even as I shoved through the crowd I could tell that was a vain effort. I could already see it.

Pieces of it, anyway.

A magistrate who looked barely older than my Acolytes halted me as I reached the barriers they'd erected. I showed him Lavinia's letter, and he waved me through with a curious glance.

I had expected that Titian's killer would have stashed the body behind one of the statues lining the Godstreet. Some of them were impressively large, considering the narrowness of the street, and a body could have easily been concealed in their lee.

Instead, Titian's body had been put on display.

I approached the statue of Chaos, personified in the Extorani pantheon as a hundred-handed giant. The limitations of stonework meant that this statue had only ten, but each of them held a piece of Titian Candorous.

My stomach churned at the sight of my student's mangled corpse. He'd been dismembered and beheaded, his limbs severed at the knee and elbow joints. Two of Chaos's hands gripped what remained of Titian's torso, the cruel god's posture looking ready to rend it asunder. The head rested in the lowest of the statue's hands, extended towards me in a manner that was almost supplicatory.

Or would have been, were it not for the rigid expression of

shock death had painted upon my student's face, or the line of dark ash smeared across his brow.

"Familiar?" a tight voice asked.

I turned to see Lavinia standing a few feet away, under the shade of a goat-headed statue I didn't recognize. She tapped a finger against her forehead.

Self-consciously I mirrored her, felt the ashmark that was still there.

Lavinia watched me, owlish eyes unblinking. "You ready to go arrest Khefnar, then?"

I tried to answer, only for gorge to rise in my throat. My knees buckled as I doubled over and retched my breakfast onto the cobbled stones of the Godstreet, leaning against one of Chaos's many arms for support.

I'd been a soldier for nearly all of my adult life, commanding legions of Attendants into battle across the Republic's borders. I had watched men die upon my own blade or crashing against the massed spears of my unliving troops. As a Legate I had danced through the charnel fields in a grotesque parody of my ancestral Rites, raising the bodies of those same soldiers to swell the ranks of my own legions. My ears had long since become accustomed to the screams of the dying, my nostrils to the stench of blood. My flesh knew the cut of another's blade, my hands the weight of a dying friend.

Yet any battlefield, however savage, was violence with a purpose. Blood spilled there was shed in defense of one's homeland, or in reprisal against a foe. Amidst the fear and chaos, the clamor and confusion, there was a terrible order to the march of armies, a sick satisfaction in the execution of strategy, even as success was measured by lives taken.

Titian Candorous's death was something else entirely, and infinitely more horrific. He had been butchered, hacked apart. His killing was a senseless waste, the desecration of his body an offense against gods and men alike, and all the more abhorrent for it.

Worse, it had been public. Someone had wanted Titian's body seen, and for anyone who saw him to know exactly who had done it.

I vomited until there was nothing left in my belly, my hands pressed against my knees, shoulders trembling with every heave.

"Here." Lavinia's voice was a fraction less glacial than it had been. She put both hands around my sheathed arm and pulled me to my feet. I tried to shrug her off, but found myself swaying where I stood, so I leaned on her until I could stand under my own power again.

"Thank you," I said, my throat raw.

"Don't mention it." Hand still on my arm, she pulled me away so that we were beneath the goat-headed statue, our backs to Chaos and what remained of Titian. It was a small mercy, but one I found myself glad for. "Definitely your student, then?"

"Yeah," I said, resisting the urge to look back over my shoulder at the grisly sight. "How did...when did you find him here?"

"Maybe an hour ago," she said, glancing up at the sun peering through the clouds. "Acolyte Drusa took me to where she'd run across him last night, near the White Gates. We retraced the path you sent them jogging. There were a lot of footprints—your students', I'm guessing—but she was able to pick Candorous's out from the rest."

I nodded. "Makes sense." Titian was—or had been—the tallest and heaviest of my Acolytes. "Where is she now?"

"Drusa?" Lavinia jerked her head a little ways up the Godstreet, where another group of magistrates had set up a cordon to stop passersby coming down from the hilltop. Drusa sat nearby, perched on a camp chair with a blanket draped around her shoulders. She looked as tired as I felt, with deep bags under her eyes and a haunted cast to her face. Her stare was a thousand miles away.

A pang of sympathy shot through me. Losing a comrade was always hard. I had hoped to spare my Acolytes that pain for a little longer.

I wanted to go over and comfort her, to tell her everything would be all right, no matter how falsely those words might ring. But my duty called me back to the present.

"The White Gates are miles from here," I said, collecting my thoughts. "You tracked his prints all that way?"

"Only back to the city itself." Lavinia's jaw tightened. "It was easy to find him from there."

A sense of deep foreboding settled in my empty stomach. "Why?"

Lavinia looked furtively around, though none of the other magistrates were nearby, and the crowd of curious citizens was still held back by the security cordon.

"More Attendants," she said. "Like last night."

"Sabotaged?" I asked, grimacing at the parallels between the dismembered Attendants and Titian's mangled body. At least the killer was consistent.

Lavinia nodded. "Five of them, spaced almost exactly a mile apart. Each one had had an arm removed."

"Only one?" I frowned. A one-armed Attendant was less useful than an intact one, but there were still tasks it could be set to. It was only a partially successful sabotage.

"Seems whoever's behind this has a sense of humor." Lavinia smiled mirthlessly. "Each Attendant was holding its own hand, pointing it in the direction of the next. The last was pointing up the Godstreet."

Again my stomach threatened to rebel, empty though it

was. "So the same person is responsible for last night and for…this."

"Looks that way," Lavinia agreed. "And what a coincidence that Khefnar and the Sons of Ash returned at the same time."

She pulled the baton from her belt and started down the Godstreet. "You ready to go arrest him?"

I almost said yes. The nausea I'd felt upon first seeing Titian's dismembered corpse was slowly giving way to a deep and abiding rage, one that had been building in the darker regions of my heart since Khefnar had first appeared at the Hour of Refuge to upstage my wife and steal away my people's adoration with false promises. Now someone had added fuel to that growing flame.

They had killed my student. It was no matter that Titian and I had not gotten along. That he had resented me for failing to save his mother, that he had been vocal and abrasive in his disrespect of the heritage I was trying to teach them.

He had been my student. His disrespect was immaterial, as was my dislike. Titian's training was my responsibility, as was his safety. And I had failed him on both counts.

I found myself wishing that I was certain it was Khefnar who had killed Titian, who had mutilated the Attendants as well as having overthrown my wife. How satisfying it would be to place blame for every pain and failing of the last day squarely upon one man's shoulders. How easy.

Too easy, whispered the part of myself not given to flights of rage. It was one thing for the Sons of Ash to speak of secession from Albastine and a return to Ayu, and quite another for them to brutally murder a teenage boy. And though he certainly was no friend to the Republic, Khefnar had spoken nothing of burning it to ashes, as the graffitist had.

Something didn't add up. And I wasn't going to let Lavinia

and her magistrates storm into the Barrows and start a riot until I figured out what that was.

"I don't know," I said to Lavinia's retreating back.

She halted, her cloak fluttering about her. All the frost in her expression returned as she turned around. "Excuse me?"

"*We* don't know," I corrected, stressing the plural. "We don't know that it was Khefnar, Magistrate Caprio. Or any of the Sons."

"We have enough to make an arrest," she said, slapping her baton against her empty palm.

"Respectfully," I said, forcing myself to maintain an even tone, "we don't. All we have is a murder linked to last night's mutilations."

"And Khefnar's reappearance." Lavinia scowled. "I thought you didn't believe in coincidence, Bellator."

"I don't. I think someone might be setting Khefnar up."

Lavinia's scowl deepened. She took a step towards me, baton still in hand. I found myself tensing into a fighting stance, knees bent for quick movement. Ghostfire illuminated the gaps in my leather sleeve. A quick extension of my senses showed me half a dozen Attendants in the immediate vicinity, any of which I could seize control of with a few precise gestures.

Few magistrates, if any, had ever fought a Legate. Our duties confined us to spheres which seldom overlapped, with the Magisterium operating primarily in Albastine itself or other, more urbane parts of the Republic, while Legates commanded armies upon the borders or campaigning into the territory of other nations. And while the nature of the Rites was common knowledge, few citizens knew what each command gesture encapsulated.

Which made Lavinia's response all the more impressive. Her owlish eyes took in the shift in my weight, and she crossed the space between us with an alacrity I could scarcely believe for someone of her stature. In a moment she was within striking range, baton held at an angle used as the opening of several restraining maneuvers.

"You really want to do this in public?" she asked, voice low. Over her shoulder I saw a few of the magistrates maintaining the cordon glance our way before quickly returning their attention to the growing crowd of civilians.

The bruise on my head throbbed viciously. The building rage wanted me to say yes, to strike out at anyone and everyone in reach. To find some channel for my angry grief before it consumed me.

But I would do no one any good brawling with Lavinia. Certainly not poor Titian, now forever beyond my help. Nor his living compatriots, my other students. Nor Bahlanni.

"I don't want to do anything." I forced myself to relax out of my fighting stance, taking in a deep breath. As I exhaled, the ghostfire died away. "I just want to make sure we're examining this from every angle. Including the possibility that maybe there's more than one party at play here."

Lavinia's posture did not change, but she at least lowered the baton to her hip. Dark eyes peered at me with that same unnerving intensity.

"Gracchus warned me this might happen," she said, running a hand through her choppy black hair. "Said you read too deep into things. Told me that after uncovering one conspiracy you'd go bounding off after another, as soon as things got complex."

I bristled. "That last conspiracy turned out to be real."

"I'm aware." She glanced meaningfully at the Senate dome crowning the hill. "To hear Gracchus tell it, you didn't know what to do with yourself once you were out of the legions. Sat at home for months, bored out of your skull. Then one day you find a loose thread in the fabric of our society, and you start to pull on it."

I would hardly have used so blithe a metaphor to describe the assassination of a Senator, nor the bloody chaos that followed.

"By some unhappy miracle it turns out to be exactly the sort of thing the Imperator said your retirement was missing," Lavinia continued. "Purpose. A chance to serve our Republic against her enemies, with the added possibility of dying in the attempt. And here I thought your religion frowned on martyrs."

"Not exactly," I said, not willing to let myself get bogged down in a theological debate—though I did find myself wondering once again how Lavinia, who was plainly of Extorani stock, possessed more than a passing familiarity with the intricacies of the Old Faith. "Let me see if I'm following you here, Magistrate. You think that I'm chasing after shadows in the hope of...what? Being a hero?"

"You tell me," she said, fixing me with that unnerving stare. "How does teaching kids how to keep their Attendants from stabbing themselves compare with leading legions into battle? Or to being lauded as the Republic's savior?"

"Nothing I've ever done has been for glory." Yet even as the words came out I found myself questioning if they were true.

"We all tell ourselves that," Lavinia said. "But we love to hear people cheer our names, all the same."

Her gaze mercifully left mine, tracking instead to the towering figure of Chaos and the bloody pieces of Titian Candorous in its hands. "The simplest answer is usually the correct one. We have reason enough to arrest the Sons of Ash on suspicion—"

An idea leapt from my mouth without consulting my brain. "What if I could give you more?"

Lavinia's gaze jerked sharply back to me. "What?"

"Proof," I said, praying the ancestors would hold my voice steady. "Whether it was really Khefnar and his friends or someone else."

She cocked her head to the side. "Have you been holding something back, Bellator Calvus?"

I shook my head. "Not like you're thinking. But there's a way I can see who killed my Acolyte."

"The gravesight?" Lavinia asked, surprising me again. It must have shown, because one corner of her mouth twitched at my expression. "I take very detailed notes, Bellator."

Of course. That damn tablet and stylus.

"It's not admissible as evidence under Republic law," I said, "but it could show us who killed him."

Lavinia frowned, considering. "I thought you said that the gravesight was unreliable. Didn't it do something ghastly to your wife's apprentice?"

"Hupli was self-trained," I said, glossing over the question. "And the skull in question was long dead. For a killing as recent as this one I should be able to get a clearer impression."

"An impression," Lavinia repeated, manifestly unimpressed. "And how do you expect me to verify that?"

I gave her a thin smile. "You're just going to have to trust me."

She gave me a dubious look.

"Last fall," I said, "before…everything that happened. It was the gravesight that set me on that path in the first place. Pulling those threads, as you put it. If you don't believe me, ask Senator Horatia Aquila. She'll vouch for me."

"Aquila?" Lavinia snorted. "Gods, Calvus. You really aren't working an angle at all, are you?"

I blinked. To the best of my knowledge, Horatia was working actively and tirelessly in the Senate, campaigning to transition Albastine's agricultural practices to be less reliant on

Attendant labor. It had earned her some enemies, but those were a small and vocal minority.

Lavinia must have correctly interpreted my dumbfounded expression, because hers softened to one of droll amusement. "You really don't know?"

I shook my head.

"Horatia Aquila and I were partners for a few years," she said, once again looking past me up the hill. This time, though, her gaze settled on the tall spire of the Magisterium. "Back when we were first starting out. We...didn't get along."

This was news to me. "She never told me."

"Obviously, or you'd never have invoked her name to get me to trust you." Lavinia chewed her lip. "But she was good at her job, I'll admit. Almost as good as me." She considered a moment longer, then jerked her head once in a sharp nod. "Fine. Do your magic dance or whatever it is, Bellator."

I was taken aback by her sudden acquiescence. "You're sure?"

"Yes," she said with an impatient wave of her hand. "Now get on with it before I change my mind."

I turned away and took a deep breath before approaching the towering figure of Chaos and the broken body of my former student.

Titian's face was a rictus of shock, his skin a pale gray against which blue veins stood prominently. His eyes were wide, though filmed over with the glossy haze of death, his mouth slightly open. Gore dangled from the stump where his neck ended, making me perversely glad I had already vomited. The thought of what I was about to attempt was already twisting my insides badly enough without dwelling upon the particulars.

Another steadying breath as I forced myself to stare into

those filmy eyes, then I spoke a word in the tongue of my forefathers.

Titian's eyes were already open, yet something seemed to
flicker in the depths of his blank pupils. Not ghostfire, but
something deeper, stronger, infinitely wilder. I swayed on my
feet as it pulled at me, and suddenly I was falling, falling, down
into the depths of death and memory...

CHAPTER THIRTEEN

I'd used the gravesight only three times previously. The first had been in my late teens, and I had never spoken of that experience to a single soul, save Horatia. The other two had both occurred last fall, during the investigation that preceded the Lightfall Massacre. Each had been as unpredictable as they were harrowing.

When I had peered into Julius Catellus's dead eyes I had witnessed the man's entire life, from his earliest childhood to the very moment of his death. In contrast, using the gravesight on Tycho Terrens had shown me only his final moments before his coconspirator had slit the old man's throat.

But when I had looked into the eyes of my grandfather all those years ago, I had seen myself staring back at me.

Titian's memories took me somewhere else entirely.

THE FIRST SENSATION I became aware of was something soft pressed against me. *A couch*, my waking mind whispered.

Other senses faded in. The lingering aftertaste of wine on

my lips, dry and heady. The scent of incense, pervasive throughout the valley of Albastine. And a voice, pitched so low that it had to be an affectation.

"...and in exchange, we shall endeavor to restore you to your mother's seat."

Sight returned as I swirled the goblet in my hands, eyeing the dark red liquid within.

"Her seat's occupied, though," I said. "By one of those provincial Ayu'li upstarts."

Not I, I reminded myself, *Titian.* It was easy to lose oneself in the depths of another's memories, to forget where the line between the self and the remembered one ended. I had to take care to remember that I was Akhenkatem, Gaius Cassius Calvus, not Titian Candorous.

"It should have gone to me," Titian continued, his words spilling from a mouth that both was and wasn't mine, "inheritance laws be damned. I'm only two years from my majority."

"Laws can be changed," the other voice said from behind me, so low that it was little more than a growl. I wanted to turn my head, to look at the speaker, but of course I could not. "Including those prohibiting Legates from holding office, Acolyte Candorous."

If I'd been in my own body, a shiver might have run down my spine at those words. No one trained in the Rites was permitted to hold elected office. It would be all too easy for an ambitious Legate turned politician to use their command over Attendants to overthrow the Republic by force of arms. For the unseen speaker to even suggest such a thing was tantamount to treason.

Titian sipped his wine. It tasted bitter, though I could not tell whether that was the vintage or some distortion caused by the gravesight. "And all I have to do is cut up a few Attendants?"

I was grateful to be merely an observer in Titian's body,

because if I'd been in control of his faculties I would have dribbled wine all down my front.

"That," the unseen speaker growled, "and one other thing."

"Nothing too illegal, I hope."

"Compared with sabotaging Attendants, it might as well be loitering." A rustle of fabric as the unseen figure stepped forward. They placed a note in my hand—Titian's, I reminded myself again. Both his hand and that of the stranger were several shades paler than my own.

"What's this?" Titian asked with my mouth, setting the goblet down and unfolding the note. As he did I caught a glimpse of the stranger, but only a glimpse—they had retreated back into the corner of the room, their face concealed by deep shadows. A heavy cloak draped about their shoulders obscured their build, so thoroughly that I couldn't even discern their gender.

Then my eyes were torn back to the note in Titian's hand, and I almost forgot about the stranger entirely as we read what was written:

ALBASTINE IN ASHES.

Beneath that, an address, one I dimly recognized as the place where I had first read those ominous words.

"A message," the growler said. "One you'll leave near the Attendants."

Titian held the note up to the lamplight, as if another angle might reveal some secret message. "Who's it for?"

"For the Republic." An edge of dark humor crept into the guttural voice. "A warning of where we are headed if we continue on our present course."

"One would think that a few limbless Attendants would suffice."

"Actions can be misinterpreted," the stranger said, moving into my peripheral vision. The deep hood of their cloak kept their features concealed. "As can words. But when the two are paired together…"

"I take your point," Titian said. "You're certain I won't get into trouble about the Attendants?"

"So long as you're not stupid enough to get caught in the act." The stranger's heavy cloak twitched in what might have been a shrug. "That location is near the Ayu'li district. Their holy day begins at sundown tonight. So long as you do it between then and midnight, the streets should be mostly empty."

Tonight. Titian's death lay mere hours away.

Unknowing, Titian picked up his goblet. "Only mostly?"

"I cannot do everything for you, Candorous." The stranger moved to stand in the doorway leading out of the room, their back to me. "There's another address on the back of the note. Once you're done, go there."

Titian made a noise of assent and flipped the note over. "What happens next?"

"You'll see." I could hear the coldness in the stranger's smile. They made to leave, but halted as Titian called after them.

"What's your interest in this?" he asked. "And don't feed me that line about this secretly being for the good of the Republic. No one *actually* cares about duty that much."

"No?" The stranger's voice softened without losing its gravelly pitch. "Spoken like the truly privileged, Candorous."

I felt Titian's lips curl into a frown. "I won't apologize for who I am."

"Nor should you." A twitch of the hood as the stranger shook their head. "We all have our places in this world. Some are born high, others low. I was the latter, and I scraped and fought for everything I had. Earned my position, my wealth, my power."

"And the ashers took them from you?"

A snort from beneath the hood. "I'd respect them more if they had. No, Candorous. The Ayu'li play at being meek and persecuted. I rather think they enjoy it, in fact. Yet at the same time they complain of their supposed mistreatment, they are constantly asking for more. To be simply given that which I have fought for all my life."

Titian's mouth felt dry. "What's that?"

"Respect." The stranger placed one hand on the door, then paused, heavy cloak swishing against the carpet. "Oh, and one thing more."

I caught the briefest glimpse of a pale face turned in profile, but before its features could register, my eyes were drawn back down to the goblet as Titian retrieved it from the table. I wanted to scream for him to turn his gaze back to the stranger, but I had command of neither my own voice nor the eyes of the body I inhabited.

"What's that?" Titian asked.

"Write it in ash," the stranger growled, and left.

I wanted to turn the memory back for a better look at the half-seen face in the shadows. But as in our waking lives, time in the gravesight marched in one direction only.

Realizing there was nothing of further value to be witnessed here, I withdrew from Titian's memories, though not far enough to pull me from the gravesight. Instead, I watched the intervening hours flicker by in a blur of sped-up motion, taking in a vague impression of their events rather than a detailed recollection. I slowed it only once, when Titian arrived at my class—not because I thought it would help the case, but out of sheer curiosity.

After all, how many of us get the chance to view ourselves through another's eyes?

The man who stood before me—before Titian, that is—did

not cut an imposing figure. I saw myself as Titian did: a dark-skinned man with a shaved head, his build somewhat short but broad-shouldered and muscular. His left arm was noticeably thinner beneath its leather sleeve than the right, which bore its share of scars.

It was a strange sort of vertigo, like looking into two mirrors placed opposite one another and seeing your own reflection repeated infinitely. I had that same sense of being outside myself, an observer in a universe of impossible depth.

"Greetings, Acolytes," I heard myself say, though the voice was oddly different from the one I heard whenever I spoke—higher and less resonant, though still resolutely baritone. "*Enfa tel nakham.*"

"Greetings, Bellator," Titian and his fellows answered in unison. Then, more unsteadily: "*Enfa ro nakhai.*"

Titian's tongue felt heavy and clumsy in his mouth as he formed the Ayu'li words, heat rising in his cheeks as he stumbled through them. I watched through his eyes as he looked down at the Acolyte beside him—Drusa—trying to catch her eye, hoping no doubt to mutter some snide aside I would not hear. A pang shot through me as I wondered whether Drusa's crush on him had been as one-sided as I'd thought.

"Up until now," the Cassius standing before us said, "you have learned the rudiments of the Rites. You have studied the body and its anatomy, have mummified and prepared Attendants for the Rite of Rising, have sutured the bronze masks to the faces of the vessels. You have studied history, learning our Republic's past and values, and the exploits of those soldiers who came before you in her service. Their tactics and stratagems are known to you—at least, I hope so."

A nervous chuckle rippled through the assembled Acolytes, though Titian's face remained a stony mask.

"Acolyte Candorous," the other me said, gaze landing upon

Titian. It felt beyond strange to look into my own eyes. "What was the name of the Legate who commanded the Third Legion in defense of Errant Hill, and against whom?"

I felt Titian's shoulders tense, and he glowered at the call-out. But my mouth spoke with smooth surety: "It was Legate Antonia Hadris. Against a force of Herracian cavalry."

A brief frown crossed my other self's lips, as he no doubt noticed Titian had failed to address him by rank. I remembered deciding to ignore it and press on. "Very good, Acolyte. By what means?"

"Fortification," I said.

"Fortification, *sir*," my double corrected, smiling. "Care to elaborate?"

"Yes," Titian said, and added a grudging, "*sir*. Legate Hadris had her Attendants dig trenches across the hill, from foot to crown. When the Herracian cavalry attempted to engage her forces, they were unable to climb the hill. The Attendants held them at bay while the archers seconded to her legion picked off the Herracians until the survivors routed."

"Very good." The other Cassius nodded. "And can you tell me what led the Herracian general to make such a suicidal attempt?"

Titian shifted his weight uncomfortably. "Sir?"

"It's a stupid general who leads his cavalry against a forti-fied hilltop," my double pointed out. "Legate Hadris's *tactical* plan—fortification—was sound. But why did her Herracian counterpart fall for it?"

I felt Titian's ears burn, as he was unable to supply an answer. Beside him a hand shot up.

"Acolyte Drusa?" my other self said, nodding at her.

"Strategy," was Drusa's immediate answer. "The Herracian army's target was the city of Anquitane, capital of the province of the same name. The terrain surrounding Anquitane is all coastal plain, mostly flat. Errant Hill is the only significant landform for miles. By encamping there, Legate Hadris presented the Herracian general with two options."

"And those were?"

"He could march on Anquitane directly," Drusa continued, "but in doing so would leave his flank exposed to Hadris's legion. Knowing that his forces had the numerical advantage, he chose the other path and attempted to confront her on the field, with predictable results."

"Well said, Acolyte." My double's gaze flickered to Titian. "On the battlefield, you can never make the mistake of assuming your enemy is stupid. Always proceed under the assumption that he is smarter than you, better informed than you, and in command of a larger force. All of these things were true of that Herracian general, yet his men were decimated when he marched them against Errant Hill."

The past Cassius paused, pacing up and down the line of waiting Acolytes. "Legate Hadris's victory came because she was clever, and prepared. But there is one more lesson to draw from her actions at Errant Hill."

Silence. Titian's throat tightened, and I had the impression that he knew the answer but was not willing to say it aloud.

"Sacrifice," my double said after a moment, raising our sheathed hand. "Hadris was outnumbered nearly five to one. If the Herracian cavalry had dismounted and made the charge on foot, they might have been able to climb the hill and swamp her Attendants under their numbers—a rare instance of our foes using our own tactics against us. She and her whole legion could easily have been wiped out that day."

"But they weren't," my mouth protested with Titian's voice.

"No." My other self shook his head. "But Hadris knew that her Herracian counterpart knew they could be. By encamping on Errant Hill, she made herself too tempting a target for him to pass up. Happily for both Hadris and Albastine, the Herracian general took the bait, and Anquitane was spared. But things might have gone very differently for them both that day."

I watched myself square my shoulders, his mouth a grim line. "Someday, Acolytes, you may be called to place yourself in the path of danger in service to a greater cause. If and when that day comes for each of us, let us pray we meet it with the same courage and wisdom as Legate Hadris."

In my peripheral vision I saw several other Acolytes nodding, but Titian merely crossed his arms across his chest. The gravesight did not make me privy to his thoughts, but I knew he must be thinking of his mother. Wondering if she had died with the grace I had spoken of? Or was he thinking that she had been the bait I had used to crush the Republic's enemies, as Hadris had been Anquitane's?

I wished I could have answered those thoughts while there was still time. To tell Titian that his mother's death was a loss and a tragedy, and I would have prevented it if I could. Would have saved her if I could.

But if there is one universal rule of warfare, it is this: you cannot save everyone.

I had failed to save Senator Candorous, just as I had failed to save her son. Yes, Titian had plotted against me; the mutilated Attendants and graffiti of the night before were his doing. But perhaps he would have made different choices had I treated him with more grace.

Either way, it was too late. All I could do was press on and do what I could to spare others his fate.

As I watched myself turn away from my Acolytes, I forced myself to withdraw from the gravesight, the world going gray and muted as my past self began to demonstrate the basic command kata. I watched at a rapid pace as Titian struggled through the movements, culminating in his failure to properly demonstrate The Body Walks for his classmates, and my subsequent chastisement. I fought down the guilt threatening to well up again in my insubstantial form, and slowed my viewing only as he set out along the path to the White Gates, his fellow Acolytes puffing along behind him.

Drusa had been right in saying that Titian was one of the fastest runners in the class. He swiftly outstripped the others, putting his long legs to hard use as the distance between him and his classmates grew. By the time he reached the outskirts of the city proper, none of his compatriots were within view.

Only then did he slow. I watched through his eyes as he scanned the streets, furtively searching for any passersby. The unseen figure had been correct: by this point nearly all the people of the district had departed for the Barrows, leaving the streets empty save for the occasional Attendant. I watched in helpless, horrified fascination as Titian flagged down one of these, then another, and finally a third, commanding each to follow him to the address he'd been provided.

The mist-shrouded courtyard looked no different than it had when I'd first come upon the grisly scene. But of course it didn't—the memory I was seeing now had occurred mere hours before then, perhaps even less.

At Titian's order, the Attendants halted in perfect, obedient unison, statue-still in the mist. Several benches lined the courtyard, and from behind one of these Titian drew the tools of his grim trade: two buckets, each with a brush leaning against it. One was filled with fine gray ash, while the smaller one sat heavy with a sluggish unguent. Between them lay a butcher's cleaver.

For a moment Titian hesitated, as though the sight of the naked blade glittering in the gloom had brought home the reality of the crime he was about to commit. Silently I willed him not to go through with it, to turn around and finish his nighttime jog rather than leap from the cliff upon which he stood. But I was only a witness, and could no more save Titian than I could any of those who now wore the Attendants' masks.

Perhaps Titian too felt uncomfortable with the tasks assigned him, for he undertook the easier one first. He worked slowly, writing out ALBASTINE IN ASHES in unguent across the courtyard wall in long, unsteady strokes. I could feel his hand trembling around the brush, ever so slightly.

A second pass with the ash-coated brush, and the first part was done. Titian stepped back to admire his handiwork. He gazed at the ominous message, then bent to the second and less enviable task of the night.

Don't, I wanted to tell him. But I was a voice without words, an inverse ghost, unable to speak or scream. I could only watch as he bent to pick up the cleaver, feel its weight in hands that were and were not mine.

Titian approached the Attendants, cleaver raised. I wanted to turn away, to close my eyes to what was about to happen. I could do neither, but I could withdraw partially from the gravesight, let this ghastly memory flow past without reliving it in such a visceral manner.

I did not.

This was the moment that led to Titian's end. I had a better idea now of what had led him down this path; having seen myself through his eyes, I knew with greater certainty that I might have kept him from the terrible fate that awaited him. If I had been more patient. If I had provided him a companion in grief, rather than maintaining the careful distance between student and teacher. If I had seen the frightened and lonely boy rather than the façade of a belligerent young man.

Titian was beyond my help now. But I owed it to him to witness the outcome of my failure.

The cleaver rose, fell. Its blade bounced off the Attendant's arm, the leathery mummified flesh stiffer than a living man's. Titian bit back a startled yelp at the impact that ran up his own arm, so jarring that it nearly shocked me from the gravesight.

"Lie down," Titian instructed the Attendant, looking around to see if anyone had noticed. The mists swirled serenely between the buildings, unbroken by human passage.

"All of you," he said, pointing his cleaver at the three Attendants he'd brought into the courtyard, "lie down."

The Attendants complied without hesitation, each stiffly bending until they lay flat against the cobblestones, arms held tight against their sides. I felt a bizarre sort of disappointment that Titian had ordered them vocally rather than using the command gestures. One more way I'd failed him.

Titian knelt over the nearest Attendant and raised the cleaver again. This time his hand did not tremble.

He swung with all his adolescent strength. The cleaver bit into the mummified flesh and through it, sending another shuddering impact up Titian's arm as its point glanced off the cobblestones beneath.

The Attendant did not react to its arm being severed just above the elbow. Nor did any blood flow forth from the stump, only the oozing black liquid that kept the body from rotting.

The cleaver trembled in Titian's hand as the enormity of what he'd just done sunk in. Albastine's society was dependent upon Attendants, almost cripplingly so. To intentionally damage one was an affront to everything the Republic stood for. It was cruel, malicious, wasteful. It served no purpose, other than to harm the society responsible for the creation of the undead servants.

Albastine in ashes, I thought.

Titian drew a ragged breath and raised the cleaver again. Brought it down again.

And again, and again. His hands shook with each blow; by

the time he had finished dismembering the final Attendant he had to grip the cleaver with both hands to keep the blade steady.

Sweat stood out on Titian's brow, prickling and cold in a way the roiling fog was not. He wiped the back of his hand over his forehead, but it was not enough to keep him from shivering.

In utter silence he tossed the cleaver and the brushes into the now-empty buckets, shouldered them both, and took off at a jog across the streets, back towards the high slope where he had left the trail I had set him and his fellow Acolytes to run.

The haze of gravesight made it difficult to tell how much time had elapsed since he had first come to the courtyard, but I did not think it could have been more than an hour. I had not been at the Hour of Rest much longer than that before guilt and panic had forced me to flee into the night, to—

To the strange Attendant.

I would have stopped, had I been in command of the body where my spirit dwelt. But though Titian continued his climb uphill, my thoughts fled back to the courtyard we had just departed.

He had not seen the strange Attendant, nor sent it to seek me out and lure me to the site of his crimes. It had taken me there through the mist and fog, apparently without Titian's knowledge.

It must have been watching, I realized. Observing him unseen from the fog or an alleyway. Hells, it might even have passed within his sight, only for him to dismiss it out of hand— ubiquitous as they were in Albastine, no one ever paid Attendants any mind unless they had something that needed to be done.

The stranger, I realized. My unseen adversary, the one who had set Titian upon this suicidal course. If they were a Legate, as I suspected, it would have been easy enough for them to embody their will into an Attendant, viewing the world from behind its bronze mask and puppeteering it directly. In this way they must have followed their pawn to the courtyard, keeping an eye on his work while simultaneously watching for the approach of interlopers. And once his task was complete, they had sent their marionette to me, to draw me into the trap.

It was the only course that made sense, but I had little time to think on it. Titian had finally reached the mountainside trail he had departed an hour past. Ahead in the distance I could hear the sounds of his fellow Acolytes laughing and ribbing each other as they progressed along their jog, the rhythm of their footfalls suggesting they were taking the course at an easier pace than Titian had.

A bucket in each hand, he set off after them, into the mists.

I watched closely, but the only action of note he took at this point was to venture off the trail at a point where it crossed a gorge. Titian paused for a moment, listening for the approach of his compatriots, but heard nothing. Satisfied, he heaved both buckets and their contents into the gorge. They disappeared into the mists with a clatter, then were gone.

I felt Titian's lips widen into a relieved smile as he ditched the evidence of his crimes.

He resumed his jog, passing his classmates at fairly regular intervals. A few expressed surprise at seeing him this far back, unable to recall when he had lost the considerable lead his long legs had granted at the start of the race. Titian offered them no explanations.

Only once did he acknowledge another Acolyte, not long after he had rounded the White Gates and begun the long race back to the barracks. Drusa came loping along the trail, sweat dripping from her short limbs and broad brow as she ran.

Titian slowed, as did she. They exchanged no words as they

passed one another, but her eyes shone as she regarded him. I wondered if Titian's expression looked at all similar.

They should have had more time, I thought, and was glad Titian's pace picked up once they had passed one another. I had no body of my own, yet the burning in his muscles was an outlet for my anger all the same.

He had only been fourteen. So much life had lain ahead of him, both heartbreak and joy. The mistakes he had made should not have robbed him of that future. Yet someone had taken it from him, all the same.

Titian's jog took him back to the outskirts of the city, to a warehouse on the river's edge. Squatter and broader than Albastine's more typical towers, it stood out from the surrounding buildings like an ugly wart.

The moment of his death was drawing near. I could feel it in the tightening of the gravesight, an indescribable sensation that the world was narrowing down to a single point. Like rushing towards a crescendo or falling towards an inevitable shock.

Inside, the warehouse was dark, the sconces on the walls unlit, and there was no sound save for the settling of timbers. The air stank of dust and grain. And beneath those smells, something acrid. Oil?

"Hello?" Titian called, only for the word to be echoed back at him from the corners of the room.

He took a step further in, glancing over his shoulder at the open door behind. Only mist remained outside, slowly spilling over the threshold.

"I did what you asked," he said to the darkness. "The words and the...and the Attendants."

A rustle of fabric came from somewhere in the shadows, then the guttural voice. "Were you seen?"

"No," Titian said, shoulders tensing. There was no relief in his voice at the discovery that he was not alone in the warehouse. "I mean, I don't think so."

"Followed?" The voice echoed around the warehouse, making its source difficult to determine.

"No," Titian said, turning defensive. "None of the other Acolytes were anywhere near me."

"Good." A pause. "You've done well, Acolyte Candorous."

"Wasn't hard," Titian said, but the bravado in his tone was undercut by the shivers creeping down his spine. "I held up my end of the deal. Still waiting on yours."

"Alas," said the voice, suddenly very close at hand, "you'll be waiting a while yet."

A hand on Titian's shoulder, steely strength beneath its fingers. A hot flash across his neck.

He tried to say something, mouth working soundlessly, but something was wrong. He could not get enough air, and something hot and wet was spilling down his chest, a spreading stain across his tunic.

Titian pressed numb fingers to his throat, just as a bloody bubble burst from his lips. I felt his pain and shock as if they were my own, but I could do nothing for him.

With his last strength he tried to turn around, but the cold fingers on his shoulder stopped him.

"I'm sorry," the adversary's voice growled in his ear. "Truly. But die knowing that your sacrifice will help to save our Republic."

Titian made no reply. Only pitched forward, the floor rushing up to meet him, and behind it an impenetrable darkness roaring up to swallow me whole—

I tore myself screaming from the gravesight, my good hand clutching at my neck. I could still feel blood pouring down my front, still sense the ragged slash across my throat. Yet my clothes were dry, my neck whole and unhurt.

Pain, I thought numbly. *Pain and fear.* The last things Titian Candorous had ever felt, and the slowest to recede from his body. Their indelible impressions crashed against my waking mind like a tide battering a dike, demanding I lower my guard to let them drown me.

But they were only feelings, and could do me harm only if I let them. I summoned my will and pushed them aside.

"Bellator?" an uncertain voice asked.

I opened my eyes. Drusa stood just out of reach in a half-crouch, looking ready to run. I could hardly blame her now that I knew what the gravesight looked like to an observer. After seeing what it had done to Hupli.

The thought of Bahlanni's wayward apprentice made me shiver. My grandfather had told me that the gravesight should always be cut short before the moment of death. That witnessing the great void was not something a man could experience and still retain his sanity. This was the closest I'd yet come, and I had no desire to tread any nearer to that indelible border between this world and the other.

But had anyone warned Hupli of such dangers? By his own admission, he had learned the gravesight through study alone. I had attributed the harrowing experience of his gravesight to a combination of inexperience and an improper vessel—Ostakri had been dead for months, perhaps years, whereas the oldest corpse I had ever attempted to use the gravesight on had died only hours prior.

Had Hupli been able to tear himself away from Ostakri's skull before witnessing his death? And if he had not, what lasting harm might it have done to him?

"Bellator Calvus?" Drusa repeated, drawing my attention back to the present. "Are you...?"

"I'm fine," I said, pulling myself to my feet. I did not remember falling, but there was a bloody scrape down my good arm from where I'd hit the cobblestones.

"You screamed," Drusa said, still looking wary. "Did...did you see?"

"Titian?" I closed my eyes. "Yes."

Drusa's voice was small. "Who did this to him?"

"I don't know," I said. Three words, yet each of them cost me more than I could say. "I...he didn't see them."

"Oh." I felt Drusa's hand on my shoulder and had to fight the urge to flinch away, recalling a different hand on a different shoulder. "It was pointless, then."

"Not completely," I told her, opening my eyes. At least now I knew who had sabotaged the Attendants, as much as the revelation pained me. "Where's Lavinia?"

"Magistrate Caprio?" Drusa's brows rose in surprise. "She left."

"She *what*?" I looked around, expecting to see the diminutive magistrate examining the crime scene or helping her fellows secure the cordon against curious citizens. But she was nowhere to be seen.

"She left," Drusa repeated. "Almost right after you started the...you know, the gravesight. She took three of her magistrates with her. Said they were going—"

"To arrest Khefnar," I finished, my heart sinking. Drusa nodded.

Cursing, I turned and took off at a run down the Godstreet.

"Bellator!" Drusa shouted from behind me. "Where are you going?"

"To the Barrows!" Behind me I heard Drusa give chase, but I hardly noticed as I pushed through the security cordon, eliciting cries of surprised outrage from citizens forced to flatten themselves against the rocks as I came flying down the Godstreet.

My feet pounded down the cobblestones as I ran, silently cursing myself for letting Lavinia play me so easily. She had displayed nothing but hostility towards the Old Faith and its trappings throughout our brief acquaintance. I should have suspected something was up when she'd acquiesced to using the gravesight upon Titian.

"Calvus!" Drusa's voice, surprisingly close behind. "What about me?"

What indeed. She'd shown more courage than I'd expected of her, first in coming to me with news of Titian's disappearance, and now with her evident willingness to help further, even after witnessing the fate that had befallen her fellow student.

All the same, I could not afford to divide my attention between stopping Lavinia from starting a riot at the Barrows and babysitting one of my students. And, as a fresh pang of guilt reminded me, her safety was my primary responsibility. I could not—would not—allow what had happened to Titian to happen to her, or to any of my remaining students.

"Go to the Barracks," I ordered, slowing just enough for her to catch up. "Make sure nobody else has gone missing."

"Is that a concern?" Drusa asked, the fear in her voice plain to hear.

"Could be." Titian's memories showed me that he had acted alone on behalf of my unseen adversary. But that didn't preclude the possibility that they had recruited others to work for them. Nor did I think it coincidence that they had chosen one of my students to aid in their plans. After all, the presence of the strange Attendant indicated a Legate's involvement. And while none of my Acolytes possessed the skills necessary to control an Attendant to such a degree, even their rudimentary grasp of the Rites could be put to sinister use in the right hands.

"Once you're there," I continued, jogging past the many-faced statue of Duplicity, "make sure none of them leave. Bellator's orders. Can you do that?"

"Yes," Drusa said, coming to a stop. She pressed her fist against her chest. "Sir."

We reached the end of the Godstreet and went our separate ways: her to the barracks, me to the Barrows. I did not know how much of a lead Lavinia had on me, but I needed to make every moment count if I was going to catch up in time to prevent bloodshed.

I slowed my pace enough to reach out with my will, summoning Attendants to my side with short, direct gestures. Ghostfire flared along my arms as the Attendants came to me, bronze masks smiling serenely. I did not stop calling them until I had over a dozen silent servitors trailing behind me, their tunics bearing the emblems of city couriers, laborers, and private estates alike. Whatever tasks I had plucked them from, there were greater things at stake.

Yet even as I neared the Barrows I told myself that I could still prevent outright violence. That I had called these Attendants to me sheerly as a deterrent, not to stop Lavinia by force. None of my unliving followers were armed, I reassured myself. No one else needed to die today.

The thought rang hollow. The greatest lies are the ones we tell ourselves.

I MADE IT IN TIME, **but only barely.**

My legs were burning with exertion by the time I crested the final rise on the mountainside trail leading up to the Barrows, my Attendants following behind in eerie silence. Ahead of me the mists cleared, revealing the familiar bronze gates and the stone sphinxes flanking them.

Lavinia and her magistrates were climbing the hill. I was dismayed to see that each of them carried a gladius in addition to the baton already in their hands. Within the valley walls, only magistrates and soldiers were permitted to carry bladed weapons, and even then they had to apply for special permission to do so. Given Lavinia's rigidity, I had no doubt she had filed such an application well before she had left me alone on the Godstreet.

Had she been expecting violence from the start? Or had she convinced herself that the short sword at her side was a preventative measure, a deterrent against true violence, just as I had told myself the Attendants trailing behind me were?

At the top of the slope the Ayu'li guards crossed their bronze-tipped staves, denying entrance to the Barrows.

"Halt!" Neftani's voice rolled downhill through the fog. "Who approaches the temple of the Old Faith of Ayu?"

"Lavinia Caprio," she called back, not slowing her climb.

"Magistrate of Albastine, by the grace of the Republic and appointment of the Senate, come to you with a warrant of arrest for one Khefnar Djaru on suspicion of murder."

"None save the faithful are permitted behind these walls," the other guard said, as though he had not heard Lavinia's accusation. I suspected that the Sons of Ash had forewarned the guards that the magistrates would attempt Khefnar's arrest before the day was out, and not to believe whatever charge was brought against him. For those already inclined towards Khefnar's distrust of the Republic, it would be easy to imagine that the Magisterium would invent a crime to arrest him.

That's the problem with believing in conspiracies, I thought as I jogged up the hill, my Attendants trailing in my wake. *Once you believe that someone is secretly working against you, you start to see them in every shadow.*

I decided not to dwell on what that said about me and my own search to uncover the conspiracy behind Titian's death.

Lavinia strode up to the guards, ready to argue her point. But as they turned their staves towards her, one of the magistrates caught sight of me charging uphill and cried out. "Caprio!"

She whirled, baton raised in a warding stance, her other hand falling towards her gladius. Her face curdled as she caught sight of me.

"Stop!" I shouted, but it came out more of a wheeze. "Everyone, just stop for a minute!"

"Calvus," Lavinia said in a tone of exquisite distaste, at the same moment as Neftani frowned and said, "Akhenkatem?"

"Me," I confirmed, resisting the urge to double over and catch my breath. Instead, I forced myself to straighten, glancing over my shoulder. I had just emerged from the thick bank of fog, behind which the Attendants I'd brought with me remained concealed. I flicked my wrist in a silent command for them to halt, not wanting to escalate the situation unless forced to. The ghostfire running along my sheathed arm died down to a dull glow.

"Bellator Calvus," Lavinia said, in the voice of exaggerated calm I was becoming all too familiar with. "What are you doing here?"

"Stopping you from making a terrible mistake," I said, raising my voice and my eyes to the guards. "Stopping all of us, in fact."

"Brother Akhenkatem." Neftani nodded in greeting, though his staff remained pointed at Lavinia. "This magistrate is attempting to breach the Hours of Remembrance."

"To arrest a known criminal," Lavinia fired back, though her gaze remained locked on mine. "Believe me, Bellator, I have no wish to set foot inside your temple, but the laws of the Republic supersede those of your religion."

"Khefnar didn't murder Titian Candorous."

Identical expressions of surprise plastered the faces of the trio of magistrates Lavinia had brought with her. They looked questioningly at her.

"So," she said tightly, "the gravesight worked."

A sharp hiss of breath from Neftani, but I could no more spare a glance at him than Lavinia could look to her magistrates. There was no one in the world but us, each striving in a contest of wills to sway the other from their chosen course.

"It did," I said, taking a deep breath to tell her all I had seen.

"Let me guess." Lavinia's lips curled into a sardonic frown. "You saw who murdered Titian Candorous, and they weren't Ayu'li at all. Was it a Herracian mercenary left over from Light-fall? Or maybe the same Wodeman who took your arm?"

"How *dare* you." Anger flared to sudden life within me. But Lavinia was not done.

"Don't tell me," she said, raising her baton, "an Attendant

killed your student, and you want me to help you track down the rogue Legate who—"

Rage drove my feet forward without my mind's consent. Lavinia drew her gladius with her free hand. Steel rasped through the fog as her fellow magistrates mirrored her. Behind them, Neftani and the other guard took a step back, staves still raised.

Lavinia's companions spread out, moving warily to flank me, though the narrowness of the mountainside path limited their maneuvers. No matter. There were only four of them.

I raised both hands and let ghostfire rise from my heart to race along my arms, flickering along my fingertips. By some twist of fate, the fog bank behind me dissipated just as I sent the silent command.

One of the magistrates gasped as my ragtag collection of Attendants came marching up the hill towards them, unarmed but grimly uniform in their bronze masks. Even Lavinia turned pale, but as I closed the distance between us, her mouth twitched into that familiar, knowing smirk.

And in that briefest moment, I realized how close I was to making an already dire situation unspeakably worse.

You're playing into her hands again, a distant, calmer part of myself realized. *Just like you did last night, when she tried to bait you. But if you attack her now, you're not the only one who's going to get hurt.*

I forced myself to a halt a few yards downslope of Lavinia, lowering my hands. The ghostfire died down but not away as my Attendants stopped.

"So." Lavinia broke the silence, looking over my shoulder. "I see you came here intending to start a fight."

"To prevent one," I said, then forced myself to focus. "I used the gravesight on Titian. You saw that I did."

"I saw you hold a staring contest with a severed head, and

some spooky lights. Nothing worth waiting around for while the murderer drums up a rebellion behind those gates."

"Khefnar didn't murder Titian," I repeated. "I saw his memories, Magistrate. His killer wasn't Ayu'li. They were Extorani."

"How convenient for you."

"I also saw that Titian was the one who cut up those Attendants."

Real surprise flashed across Lavinia's face, and I pressed on before she could muster a reply. "Someone hired him to do it. The same person who killed him. I didn't see their face, or even whether it was a man or a woman. But they had pale hands, Extorani hands."

Lavinia's face was a portrait of disbelief, but she hadn't interrupted me yet. Nor was I about to give her space to. "This person, this...Adversary told Titian that if he cut up those Attendants they'd see to it that he'd assume his mother's seat in the Senate."

"That seat's occupied." For the first time I heard uncertainty in Lavinia's voice. "And he couldn't hold office if he was going to be a Legate—"

"I know," I said. "They were lying, telling him what he wanted to hear so that he'd do as they said. And once they were done with him they killed him, then set it up to look like it was the work of the same person behind the mutilations."

I looked past her, at where Neftani stood before the Barrows gates. His companion was busy banging his staff against them, summoning more guards. I had perhaps a minute, maybe two, before this entire situation exploded into violence.

"Khefnar is a threat to the Republic," I said, returning my attention to Lavinia. "But he didn't kill Titian. He didn't have any *reason* to. The Sons of Ash are no friends to the Republic, but their goal is to leave Albastine behind, not burn it down.

Someone's setting them up, and they killed my student to do it."

Lavinia was silent for so long that I fancied I could hear running Ayu'li feet echoing down the Barrows tunnels. She nodded, very slowly, and for the briefest moment hope flared in my heart.

"That's a lot of weight to place on your word and a dead boy's memory," Lavinia said, her voice flat. "In my experience, Citizen Calvus, the simplest explanation is usually the correct one. Khefnar and the Sons of Ash sabotaged those Attendants and killed Titian Candorous. Now, if you'll excuse me, I have an arrest to make."

She turned, cloak billowing behind her as she started towards the gates.

"No!" The word tore itself from my lips as I rushed towards her, ghostfire flaring to sudden life again as my Attendants surged forward behind me.

Lavinia whirled, quick as thought, her gladius whirring as it cut through the mist. I stopped short, just beyond the reach of her swing. Lavinia settled into a low crouch, gladius pointed towards me, baton held in a guard position.

"Ma'am—" one of her magistrates began, but she shook her head.

"I've got this," she told them. "You go tell those guards to let you in, unless they want to join their prophet in his next exile. As for you, Bellator Gaius Cassius Calvus, I am hereby placing you under arrest for assaulting a magistrate. Do not resist."

"Lavinia, *think,*" I said, taking a step back even as I commanded two of my Attendants forward, flanking me. "You said you don't believe in coincidence. How come I ended up discovering those Attendants right before you did?"

"I was on patrol," she said, moving towards me, "doing my job. What's your excuse?"

With a flick of my wrist I sent one of my Attendants forward, interposing it between us, arms outstretched towards her. Lavinia easily ducked out of its reach, hooked her baton behind its ankle, and came up in a roll, taking the Attendant's feet out from beneath it.

"There was an Attendant—" I started, but realized it was no good. "You wouldn't believe me anyhow."

"Probably not," Lavinia agreed as I sent a second Attendant towards her, and a third. I was really moving now, ghostfire lighting up the mists as I danced through the kata, controlling the Attendants directly.

Lavinia snarled a curse as my Attendants grabbed her. One's cold fingers wrapped around the wrist holding her gladius, the other's around her offhand shoulder, pinning her baton to her side. She struggled, but could not free herself.

Relief flooded through me as I glanced uphill to see that the bronze gates stood closed and barred, Neftani and the other guard having retreated inside. The three other magistrates were looking warily between me and their leader, who struggled to free herself from my Attendants' restraint.

"Don't come any closer," I told them, even as I performed a complex series of motions. I was rewarded with a yelp of pained frustration from Lavinia as one of the Attendants bent her wrist back, forcing the gladius from her grip. It clattered against the stones below. "I don't want to hurt you or her—"

Lavinia's yelp turned into a snarl that sounded like it came from the throat of a feral wildcat. No longer bothering to fight for control of the hand holding the gladius, she yanked that arm across her body in a slashing motion. The Attendant, fingers still locked in a death grip around her wrist, collided with its compatriot. There was a crunch of breaking bone as the two Attendants slammed against the stony wall of the mountainside, and I felt my control over them waver for a moment.

A moment was all Lavinia needed to worm her way free of their loosened grips, baton still in hand. She dove from between the Attendants, flying at me like a furious black bat as her cloak rippled out behind her.

She hit me in the middle, knocking the wind from my lungs and my feet from beneath me. Rocks bit into the exposed skin of my arms and face as we went tumbling downhill in a confused pile of limbs, struggling blindly against each other.

Another impact knocked the breath from me as we collided with the remaining Attendants I had brought, bowling through several of them before their massed bodies brought us to a stop.

I tried to make a gesture of command, only for pain to erupt across my living arm as Lavinia slammed her baton against my forearm. I gave a wordless cry as she clawed her way on top of me, still gripping her baton. I covered my face with both arms, knowing that one good blow to the head would take the fight right out of me.

There was no pain as her second blow landed, only a dull throbbing through my leather-sheathed arm.

"Getting real tired of that trick," Lavinia said, raising the baton over her head for another blow. I tried to reach for it with my good hand, only for Lavinia to sucker punch me in the jaw. Blood exploded from my lower lip, stars bursting in my vision as my head slammed against the unforgiving stone. All sensation in my left arm abruptly vanished as I lost the concentration animating it, the ghostfire guttering out.

Lavinia brought the baton down again.

An unliving hand wrapped itself around her wrist, halting the baton's descent. Lavinia snarled and turned, raising her other hand to ward off the Attendant's interference.

The Attendant grabbed her other wrist, its hand darting out with a speed and fluidity nearly the equal of a living man's.

Lavinia tried to shake it free, but the fingers around her wrists were corpse-stiff.

"How are you doing this?" she snarled down at me.

I looked down at my left arm, which lay limp and useless beside me, devoid of the flickering ghostfire. "I'm not."

Lavinia's struggles ceased for a minute, her expression twisting into one of utter shock.

"See?" I said, nodding up at the smiling bronze-masked figure standing over us. "I told you there was an Attendant."

CHAPTER FIFTEEN

"I can't believe I'm doing this," Lavinia muttered as we followed the Attendant through Albastine's omnipresent mists.

"Which part?" I asked, pressing two fingers to my split lip. They came away bloody. "Letting an Attendant controlled by an unknown Legate lead you into what's almost certainly a trap? Or working with an Ayu'li?"

Lavinia sniffed. "The first part, obviously."

"Could have fooled me."

The Attendant's head turned as though it were listening to us. I supposed whoever was controlling it was doing precisely that.

It had made no further attempt to communicate after intervening in the fight between Lavinia and me, only beckoned for us to follow it down the hill and back into the mist-shrouded streets of Albastine. Baffled but wary, Lavinia and I had agreed to an uneasy truce, on the condition that her magistrates remained stationed outside the Barrows gates. Seeing as the vast majority of the faithful were already cloistered inside for the Hours of Remembrance, I gave my reluctant consent. I could only hope that within those walls Bahlanni was successfully persuading our people not to follow Khefnar into disaster.

"I know you won't believe this," Lavinia said, "but I truly don't have anything against your people, Calvus."

"No?" I did not slow my strides, forcing her to keep pace. Nor did I bother concealing my anger. "You've assumed the worst of me at every turn. First last night, with the graffiti. You attacked and arrested me without giving me any space to explain. Tried to coerce me into a false confession after. And just now, you accused me of lying about the gravesight to keep you from arresting Khefnar. So tell me, Magistrate, is it all Ayu'li you hate, or just me specifically?"

Lavinia regarded me with that owlish, knowing gaze. "If I hated all Ayu'li, I wouldn't have married one."

I nearly tripped over an uneven stretch of cobblestones. "Married?"

"Don't sound so surprised."

"Given your charming personality, I suppose I shouldn't be. Hells, there must have been dozens of Ayu'li lining up to be your husband—"

"Wife."

This time the hitch in my stride had nothing to do with the stones underfoot. "Oh."

"Oh," Lavinia agreed, a bitter smile stretching over her face. "You begin to see, Bellator Calvus, why I bear so little love for your faith or those who profess it?"

"Your—"

"Wife," she repeated, more emphatically. "Khessia. She is my wife, and she is Ayu'li, but she is not of the Old Faith. Not any longer."

"I'm sorry," I said, and found that I meant it. "She's welcome to return if she ever—"

"Why would she ever want to return to those who cast her out?" Lavinia snarled. "Why go where she's not welcome?"

"All are welcome among the ancestors," I said, though that felt an inadequate defense. "And the Old Faith has done me good. It could do her—"

"Harm," she spat. "That is all your faith has done my Khessia, Gaius Cassius Calvus, Akhentem, or whatever secret name you call yourself."

She turned and strode after the Attendant, which seemed somehow relieved to be moving again.

We pressed on through the mists in silence for a time, until abruptly Lavinia spoke again.

"We grew up together," she said, her voice tightly controlled, "Khessia and I. Our parents were friends. From my earliest memory I loved her. We played games together, went everywhere together, did everything together. Our parents were glad we had such a strong bond. At least at first."

Ahead of us the Attendant had picked up its pace, as though even it wanted to be away from this conversation.

"We grew older," Lavinia continued. "I loved her, the same as I ever had. The kind of love that makes you want to wrap yourself around her like a blanket, to feel your body pressed against hers until there's nothing left between you. You know?"

I nodded, not trusting myself to speak.

"When I was young I thought that was the sort of love all girls share with their best friends," Lavinia continued, her eyes locked on the Attendant's back. Perhaps it was easier for her to talk about these things when she wasn't looking at me. "Only when we stopped being girls and started becoming young women did I realize that my feelings were...different. That what I wanted was more than friendship."

"Did Khessia feel the same way?" I asked softly, wary of frightening her out of this unexpected vulnerability. If I could build some sort of connection with her, could reach her as a person, maybe she might not take such a hard-line approach to the Sons of Ash.

"She did." A genuine smile flashed across Lavinia's face, like a glimpse of sunshine through fog. "All the gods of earth and sky be praised, Khessia loved me the same as I loved her. We still went everywhere together, did everything together, but the games became kissing games. Just silly girls playing at being grown-ups, at first. Until suddenly we were grown up, and no longer playing."

"You're lucky," I said, thinking of kissing games I had played when I was young. I did not regret the choices that had led me to marry Bahlanni, not anymore. But it had not been her I'd played those games with.

"I suppose," Lavinia said as we followed the Attendant into a narrow alleyway. Her hand dropped to her baton, dark eyes scanning the shadows for threats. "Lucky that we found each other. Less so in what came after."

"You married her, though."

"I did." Her smile faded and grew bitter. "With my parents' blessing. But not hers."

"Oh," I said, feeling stupidly inadequate as I said it. Marriage between those of the same gender had been practiced by the Extorani since before the days of their exile, back when they had ruled over an empire of their own. My own people, however, had not always been as accepting of such unions.

"That's the thing about a religion centered around ancestor worship," Lavinia continued as we approached the end of the alleyway. "All that emphasis on bloodline and descent makes it so that your prospective in-laws aren't thrilled about the idea of their daughter marrying another woman."

"That's hard," I said, feeling that another refrain of

sympathy would ring hollow. "No one should have to go through that."

"We did anyway." Lavinia shrugged. "Maybe I'm wrong about you, Calvus. Maybe you're a decent man. But that doesn't change the harm your religion has done to the woman I love."

I had no answer for that. Nor did I need one, for we emerged from the alleyway to behold the second murder scene that morning.

The corpse lay slumped between a pair of pillars separating the alleyway from a small piazza, mouth hanging open, staring up into the fog. Or would have been, had its eye sockets not been empty.

"Gods," Lavinia said, pulling her baton from her belt as she ran towards it. But the body was obviously already as dead as an Attendant.

More so, I corrected, glancing at the Attendant that had led us to the horrific sight. It had retreated a few yards away, observing us with its masked head tilted to one side. Once again unnerved by its eerily human gesture, I had to remind myself that this was merely the influence of whatever unseen Legate was controlling it.

Sensing my attention, the Attendant nodded towards where Lavinia knelt over the corpse, as if to say *get on with it.* Thoroughly spooked, I nonetheless complied.

"How bad is it?" I asked, knowing the answer before she said it.

"Bad." Lavinia pointed to the ring of black bruises around the man's throat. "Strangulation. Messy way to go."

I flinched, recalling a memory that was not my own: Julius Catellus, once a Senator, struggling for his life against the implacable hands of a dead man, the serenely smiling bronze mask the last thing he would ever see. I fought the urge to turn back to the Attendant who had brought us here.

"That's what killed him?" I asked. "Not the...?"

I made a vague motion towards my eyes.

"No." Lavinia shook her head and pointed at the empty sockets. I forced myself to look into those dead black holes of nothingness staring back out at me. "The incisions were too clean. Either the killer drugged him first, or he was already dead when they took the eyes."

"Any idea who he was?" The victim's dark skin was unmistakably Ayu'li, though the lack of ash upon his brow indicated that he was not an adherent of the Old Faith.

"Not yet." Lavinia glanced over her shoulder at the Attendant, still waiting with its arms folded. She rested a hand on her gladius. "But at the moment I'm more concerned with why we were brought here."

"And who sent him." I nodded at the Attendant, then realized what I'd just said. The Attendant was just a tool of whoever was puppeteering it, possessing no will or cognizance of its own.

"Agreed," Lavinia murmured, striding through the mist to where the Attendant stood. I trailed behind, glancing warily around at the fog roiling between the buildings. Surely if the Attendant had brought us here to stage an ambush, we would have been attacked by now.

Unless the ambushers are taking their time getting into position, I thought with an unpleasant shiver.

"You." Lavinia's voice cut through the fog as she strode up to the Attendant, craning her neck to stare into the serene bronze face. "Whoever you are behind that mask, why did you bring us here?"

The Attendant tilted its head, then pointed at the eyeless corpse.

"Right, to show us the body." Lavinia waved her hand

dismissively, as though blinded murder victims were an everyday occurrence in her line of work. In actual fact, most magistrates went their entire careers encountering fewer homicides than she and I had in this single day. "Why, though? Did you kill him?"

The bronze mask glinted as the Attendant shook its head from side to side, the gesture startlingly human. Whoever was controlling it was doing so with greater skill than any Legate I had ever encountered, save for two: my grandfather, Octavio Calvus, and the ancient retiree Tycho Terrens, whose bitterness had consumed him until he'd betrayed the very Republic he had spent his life in service to. But they were both dead.

Both dead, part of me whispered, *and both Attendants. But Grandfather carried secrets with him back from Ayu...*

"Who are you?" I asked, moving to stand beside Lavinia.

The Attendant went very still, and for a moment hope soared in me, desperate and absurd, that it was indeed my grandfather standing before me, impossibly returned from beyond the veil.

Just as swiftly, that hope was dispelled by a ponderous shake of the head behind the bronze mask.

"You can't tell us?" Lavinia asked, brows furrowed together.

A nod, markedly more emphatic.

"I hate guessing games," Lavinia muttered before addressing the Attendant again. "Okay. Whoever you are, you're a Legate. Not Calvus, unless he's much, *much* better than I think he is."

"You just caught me on a bad day," I said, then turned my attention to the Attendant. "But you brought us here. To show us the body?"

An even more empathic nod.

"Why?" Lavinia asked.

It pointed at her, or more specifically, at the silver magistrate's badge clasping her cloak across her shoulders, then at me, to the flickering ghostfire running along my sheathed arm.

"Because of our jobs," I realized. "Magistrate and Legate—I mean, Bellator. You wanted us to be the ones to find the body."

Nod.

"If you didn't kill him," Lavinia interjected, "did you see who did?"

This time the Attendant hesitated before nodding.

"Who?" I blurted.

Lavinia shot me a look of annoyance, silently reminding me that the rules of this bizarre game demanded yes-or-no questions. Yet to our mutual surprise, the Attendant raised an accusing finger and pointed it directly at me.

"Me?" I said stupidly. Lavinia's face turned grim, her hand falling to her gladius.

I was saved by another shake of the Attendant's head, so fervent I half expected the mask to fly from the dead face, despite it being sutured to the skull beneath. Lavinia's hand left her sword.

The Attendant jabbed its finger at me again, so close it nearly poked me in the forehead. Only then did I realize it was pointing not at me, but at the ash smeared across my brow.

"The killer was Ayu'li?" I guessed. "Of the Old Faith?"

A terse nod of confirmation.

Lavinia's eyes narrowed. "Still think Khefnar and his Sons have their hands clean, Bellator?"

"I never thought that," I said. A thought occurred to me. "How long has he been dead?"

"Not sure," Lavinia admitted reluctantly. "Let me check."

She examined the body, testing the stiffness of its joints. Once her back was to me I leaned in and whispered the question that had been burning on my mind since the strange Attendant had reappeared. "Have you been following me?"

The bronze mask tilted towards Lavinia, saw she was preoccupied, then gave the swiftest of nods. My heartbeat stuttered.

"Why?"

Very quickly, the Attendant pointed at my chest, then thumped its fist against its chest, right above its unbeating heart, in the traditional Albastinian salute. It pointed at the ashmark on my brow again, then let its hand fall to its side.

It was as short and unambiguous a message as could be mutely communicated. *You,* it had pointed at me, then saluted. *Serve.* Pointing to the ashes, the symbol of the Old Faith.

You serve the Ayu'li.

"I serve the People," I said, mouth dry. The Attendant shrugged minutely, as though it saw no distinction between the Ayu'li in specific and the people of the Republic as a whole.

Lavinia rose, wiping her hands on her pants as she came over.

"Dead about four hours," she said. "Rigor mortis of the neck and jaw, less so around the limbs. Puts time of death at a little after sunrise, I think."

"Right after the Hour of Refuge," I said, frowning.

"In other words," Lavinia said, giving me a grim little smile, "not long after Khefnar and his friends made their triumphant return."

"Not long at all," I admitted. "Everything was chaos after he came back. Any of the faithful might have snuck out and done this without anyone noticing."

Though the Barrows' entrance was shut and guarded, it was only sealed during the ceremonies for each Hour. In between them, congregants were free to come and go as they wished. Any one of them might have departed after the Hour of Refuge, committed this murder, and then come back in time for the Hour of Rending with no one the wiser.

"For a man who claims to have no love for the Sons of Ash," Lavinia observed, "you're awfully quick to find alternate explanations for the crimes that keep happening around them."

I'd become inured enough to her suspicions that I almost let that one slide. Almost.

"I told you," I said, against my better judgment. "Whoever killed Titian wasn't Ayu'li, they were Extorani. I saw it in the gravesight—"

My breath hitched in my throat. I turned around slowly, drawn to the body lying against the marble pillar. Wide black holes leered at me from the pale face.

"That's why they took his eyes," I breathed, my stomach churning at the revelation. "They knew I'd find him, and they didn't want me to see who they were."

Which meant that the killer was someone I knew.

"Wait a minute." Lavinia frowned. "You said that your wife's apprentice used the gravesight on a skull. Don't tell me it still had eyes."

"It didn't," I said, my voice tight. "And the experience nearly killed him."

"I thought you said that was because the skull had been dead too long."

"That's part of it," I admitted. "But the lack of eyes couldn't have helped."

Lavinia ran a hand through her hair, huffing in annoyance. "So once again, we find ourselves with a murder that conveniently can't be linked to the Sons of Ash. Not unless we're willing to take the word of an unknown Legate—"

"Fine," I snapped. "I'll do it."

That shut Lavinia up. She stared at me, dark eyes wide. "You'll—"

"Use the gravesight," I said, bending over the corpse as ghostfire flared up my left arm. "Just don't run away this time."

Lavinia said something else, whether in protest or acquiescence I could not hear. I was already speaking the Old Ayu'li word of command, already falling down into the black voids where the dead man's eyes should have been. Falling, falling, into...

CHAPTER SIXTEEN

*P*ain.

Pain, roaring through my body like the ocean, drowning out all sensation of sight or sound. Pain like a tightening noose around my throat squeezing the life from my lungs, unknown fingers digging themselves into the soft flesh of my neck until I could feel the bruises blossoming purple. Pain growing like a cancer until it was my world, until I could do nothing but scream in a voice that held no breath—

"Calvus!"

I struggled towards the waking world from beneath the weight of the dead man's strangled final thoughts, their pressure weighing down against me like the tide. I burst free and heaved in a ragged breath as my consciousness returned to my body, collapsing onto the street.

Lavinia caught me, putting her shoulder under mine, bearing me up with surprising strength for someone so slightly built. I leaned against her, all pride and dignity forgotten as my whole body trembled.

"Calvus," Lavinia said, softer than I'd ever heard her speak. "Are you...did you..."

"Still here," I croaked. My throat felt raw. Had I been screaming? "Still think that I'm faking the gravesight?"

"No." Lavinia's voice trembled. "No, I...I believe you. Did you see...?"

"Nothing." The word came out in a ragged whisper. "Nothing but pain."

"Okay," she said, almost gently. "Okay, Calvus. I'm sorry I doubted you. Can you stand?"

I nodded, but as soon as I tried to take my weight on my own two feet my knees buckled. Lavinia eased me into a sitting position against the nearest wall, disquietingly similar to the posture of the eyeless corpse lying mere feet away.

"So," she said after a moment of silence, "this gravesight. It's reliable?"

"Not enough for a court," I admitted. "But enough to follow where it leads."

She made a noise of acknowledgment. "And if we can believe our anonymous friend— oh, gods *damn* it!"

Startled, I followed her gaze to where the Attendant had been standing. It was gone, faded back into the mists like a ghost.

I'm not crazy, I reminded myself. Lavinia had seen it too.

"It'll be back," I said, my voice still ragged. "Whoever's controlling it wanted us to see this. Wanted us to know that it was an Ayu'li who did this."

Privately I wondered whether that person and the Adversary who had killed Titian were one and the same. Both crimes had been performed to paint the Ayu'li as murderers, if the Attendant was to be believed.

"Except he was an Ayu'li, too." Lavinia nodded at the eyeless corpse. "If this is the Sons' work, why would they kill one of their own?"

I wanted to tell her that I didn't know, that this was just further proof that the Sons were being played by the Adversary, just as we were. But as I opened my mouth a darker possibility occurred to me.

"No ashmark on his brow," I pointed out. "He wasn't one of the faithful."

"Making an example of the apostate?" Lavinia guessed.

"Maybe," I admitted reluctantly, looking around at the mist-shrouded buildings. Like most Albastinian architecture, they were stately spires, narrow but tall, climbing into the fog. "But something else is off. The graffiti, the mutilations, Titian. What did they all have in common?"

Lavinia shrugged. "Criminality?"

"They were all public," I said, forcing myself to look once more at the eyeless corpse. "Titian was instructed by this...this Adversary to dismember those Attendants where they would be found. And didn't you say there was a line of carved-up Attendants pointing the way to Titian's body?"

"Pointing with their own severed arms," Lavinia said, lips curling in distaste. "Someone wanted to make a statement."

"Exactly." I nodded down at the corpse. "Look how this body was wedged between the pillars. His killer at least made the attempt to hide him."

Lavinia grimaced. "I don't like the idea of there being *two* killers running around the streets, but you're right. It doesn't line up with the other murder or the mutilations. But there's a thread connecting them."

"The Attendant," I said, recalling how it had first appeared to me outside the Barrows the night before, in what already felt like a memory as remote as any the gravesight had shown me.

"Exactly." Lavinia nodded. "Whoever is controlling it—"

"Magistrate!"

Someone was running down the alleyway towards us, a shadow in the fog. Lavinia raised her baton, while I extended my will in search of any Attendants in the vicinity. I found none.

The shadow resolved itself into a young Extorani man whose tousled brown hair lay plastered against his forehead by mist and sweat. He slowed to a halt, pressing his fist to his heart.

"Magistrate Caprio," he said, breathing heavily. I dimly recognized him as one of the junior magistrates who had accompanied her to the Barrows gates, whom Lavinia had ordered to remain stationed there while she and I followed the Attendant back into the city streets.

"Magistrate Elan." Lavinia nodded, holstering her baton. I relaxed, letting the ghostfire along my bad arm fade to its usual flicker. "I thought I told you to remain outside the Barrows."

"You did, ma'am. Magistrates Abbate and Sala are still there." He glanced to the side and did a double take at the sight of the blinded corpse lying not three feet to his right. Under less macabre circumstances it would have been comical. "Gods! Is that—"

"A dead body," Lavinia said calmly. "You've seen them every day of your life, Elan. This one just isn't walking around, yet. Now, I'm assuming you have good reason for abandoning your post?"

"Yes, ma'am." Elan held out an envelope. "This came for you, not long after you left."

Lavinia took the envelope. It had been sealed in black wax bearing the open eye of the Imperators.

"Abbate and Sala and I drew lots," Elan continued nervously as Lavinia broke the seal and her eyes scanned over the contents. My stomach dropped as her face darkened. "I came up short, so they sent me to find you."

"How did you find us?" I asked as Lavinia stared down at the letter. "We didn't even know where we were going."

"You didn't go far," he replied, glancing up at a gap between the nearest of the towers surrounding us. The steep cliffside leading up to the Barrows was just barely visible through the fog. "And I, ah, heard screaming. Sir."

I winced, recalling how the gravesight had backfired on me.

"Thank you, Elan," Lavinia said, folding up the letter and putting it back into the envelope. "I have a new assignment for you."

His nervous chatter was replaced with a startled "Ma'am?"

"Watch over this body," she said, pointing at the eyeless corpse. "Make sure no one interferes with it. I'll be sending someone from the mortuary to retrieve it for an autopsy shortly."

"Yes, ma'am." Elan saluted, though the green tint to his features suggested he did not relish being left alone with the body.

"Bellator Calvus," Lavinia said, already hurrying down the alleyway, back the way we had come, "if you'll come with me?"

I caught up to her, restraining myself from asking the burning question until I was certain we were out of Magistrate Elan's earshot.

I nodded down at the envelope in her hand. "Gracchus?"

"Who else?"

"What'd he say?"

She thrust the envelope into my hands without breaking stride. I struggled to reopen it and walk at the same time; the dexterity of my dead hand was still not what it had once been. I doubted it would ever be.

Such thoughts of self-pity were driven swiftly away by the words written in tidy black script:

Magistrate Caprio,

Meet me in the central marketplace as soon as you are able. More Attendants have been sabotaged.

—Imperator Antonin Gracchus

I looked at Lavinia, whose sharp-featured face was drawn tight. "Still think there's only one killer out there?"

"If there is, they're covering a lot of ground." We emerged from the alleyway onto a side street devoid of traffic save for a pair of courier Attendants, neither of which were the right build to be our mysterious visitor. "I need to handle this. Can't leave the Inquisitor waiting."

"Good luck," I told her, and was surprised to find I meant it. Despite her other faults, Lavinia had proven willing to change her approach when confronted with new evidence. I doubted she fully believed my assertion that there was a shadowy Adversary manipulating events to cast further suspicion on the Sons of Ash, but she was slowly coming around to the possibility. At the moment, it was the best I could hope for.

"Thanks," she said, turning onto a main street. "And you?"

"Me what?"

"Don't play dumb, Bellator. I don't expect you to sit on your hands while I'm busy inspecting the latest bunch of butchered Attendants."

"You want me to go with you?"

"Waste of time," Lavinia said without rancor. "I think the investigation's better served if we divide and conquer."

"So we're on the same side now?" I asked. "You've been pretty clear that you don't trust me."

"That was one murder and several mutilations ago," Lavinia fired back as we hurried up the main street. She glanced up at the marble towers around us, practically synonymous with Albastine itself. "We *are* on the same side."

Still in the Ayu'li part of town, the street was largely empty, but here and there we passed a citizen on their way to lunch, a meeting, or to work. I found myself peering into their faces, trying to discern if a killer's mind lay behind any of them.

"Consider this an olive branch," Lavinia continued. "We pool our resources, share what we find. Figure this out together."

It was a tempting offer. And more than that, it would get her off my back, at least for a while. With the certainty that she wouldn't go storming the Barrows and incite a riot by arresting Khefnar, I'd have some breathing room to reconnect with Bahlanni and devise our own plan for ousting the Sons of Ash with minimal chaos.

"Okay," I said, slowing to stick out my good hand. "Partners?"

Lavinia laughed, tight and incredulous. "Don't get ahead of yourself."

We clasped arms, her fingers tight around my wrist.

"Talk to your wife," she said. "Find out if there are any Legates other than you currently in the city."

As high priestess of the Old Faith, Bahlanni was one of a handful of officials granted access to the Census, the regularly updated list of all citizens currently residing within Albastine. Given the inherent threat that a rogue Legate could pose to the Republic's social integrity, their residential status took top priority. Whoever was puppeteering our rogue Attendant would have their name on that list.

"Consider it done," I said, but then another, worse thought occurred to me. "Khefnar and his disciples managed to slip into the city undetected. What if whoever's behind the Attendant did the same?"

"Well then," Lavinia said, her grip on my wrist tightening even further, "you'll just have to ask the Sons of Ash how they managed it."

PART FOUR
RECKONING

CHAPTER SEVENTEEN

I returned to the Barrows just past noon and was relieved to see that the fragile truce between the guards and Lavinia's magistrates had not devolved into further violence.

Actually, four of them sat in a loose circle before the bronze gates, taking turns rolling a pair of pewter dice in a cup. A small pile of denarii lay on the ground between them. One of the magistrates cursed as his dice came up snake eyes.

"The ancestors are with me today!" Neftani crowed, hauling the pile of coins towards himself.

"Clearly," I said from behind him.

He started, a few denarii slipping from his fingers as he turned and scrambled to his feet. "Brother Akhenkatem! I hadn't—"

"Expected to see me back? You're not the only one." I glanced down at the dice game. One of the magistrates jerked his hand guiltily back from where he'd been reaching for Neftani's dropped coins. "Busy work standing guard, I see."

"Sorry," Neftani said, his cheeks coloring.

"Don't worry about it." Ancestors knew I'd engaged in many a surreptitious bout of gambling during the long, boring stretches of a campaign abroad. "I have something more important to ask about."

Neftani relaxed. "What?"

"Has anyone entered the Barrows since the Hour of Rending began?"

The Hour of Refuge began at sunup and ended three hours later. After that came the Hour of Rending, during which there was neither sermon nor festivities. Instead, the faithful retreated to their familial shrines, offering prayers of consolation to the ancestors they had lost and reflecting upon the homeland that had been torn from us. No one was permitted entry or exit until the Hour's conclusion, and not even Khefnar's revanchist crusade could breach that solemnity.

"Of course not." Neftani grimaced. "I mean, some left after the Refuge ceremony. Families without shrines, folks with errands to run. Like you. But they all either came back before Rending started or stayed away."

I nodded, trying not to let my frustration show. Whoever had murdered a man and taken his eyes must have been among those who'd left after the Hour of Refuge, if the Attendant could be believed. But in the confusion following Khefnar's reappearance, I doubted Neftani had kept very close track of the comings and goings.

"What about the Sons of Ash?" I asked. "Have any of them left the Barrows?"

"No," the other guard said, also standing. Rithokh, I remembered. "Brother Khefnar and his followers have been within ever since the Hour of Refuge."

"When you let them in," I said, narrowing my eyes.

"On the orders of Brother Hupli," Neftani interjected, even

as his compatriot lifted his chin. "Anyone who pledges to wield the bronze staff is sworn to follow the orders of the priesthood, Akhenkatem. You know that."

He was right, of course. The fault lay with Hupli, not the two guardsmen. Anger built in me as I silently resolved to find out how long he'd been in communication with the Sons of Ash and how much persuading it had taken for him to turn against Bahlanni—if any.

I turned my glance skywards, to the sun shining bright and high above the white valley. "Am I allowed in yet?"

Neftani followed my gaze and nodded. "The Hour of Rending should be ending now. Reckoning is at hand."

As I entered the bronze gates, I could only hope those words were not an omen.

SONG STILL ECHOED through the halls of the Barrows, but there was a marked difference between the gentle, melancholic hymns that characterized the Hours of Rest and Refuge and the driving, altogether more savage rhythms of the Hour of Reckoning. These were not songs of lamentation for a lost home and a sundered past. These were the angered cries of a people wronged, the furious dirges whose pulsing, implacable beat was drawn directly from the drumbeats that had accompanied the Ayu'li of old as they marched into battle.

For our ancestors had not simply rolled over and let invaders oust them from their homeland. So much of our modern identity was tied to our status as exiles that it was easy to forget that we had not always been so. That once we had dwelled in our homeland and raised armies to defend it.

And defend it they had. Clad in bronze armor and wearing

battle masks that would one day be replicated for the Attendant legions, the Ayu'li of centuries past had won many battles against the invaders—but lost the war. Town by town, city by city, our homes were sacked and burned, our territory shrinking like an oasis whose spring had run dry. Until the final battle, the one we called the Reckoning, in which the last vestiges of our soldiery were slain in a desperate final stand, leaving the civilians to flee into the desert, shepherded only by the surviving priests.

All peoples want to believe they are peaceable, that they would never raise a fist in anger, only in defense of their spouses and children, their lands and their neighbors. Yet paradoxically all nations, however much they claim to value life and prosperity, glorify conflict. Those societies who most loudly proclaim the nobility of their causes and the safety of their citizens esteem martial excellence far above all pursuits of invention or artistry.

I was a soldier. It was not and had never been my place to judge the morality of military force or the necessity of its employment. Small and surrounded by our enemies as we were, that was not a luxury that any citizen of Albastine could enjoy.

Yet as I walked the halls my ancestors had shaped, listening to the battle marches that their own forefathers had followed into bloody defeat, I found myself wondering how righteous their defense of their homeland had truly been. The desert people whose descendants proclaimed themselves sultans and caliphs had been invaders, yes. But for years before that they had been Ayu's neighbors, their relations with the children of the river relatively cordial. What had soured those relations, until we were driven out by the sword and cast upon the wandering winds?

For the first time in my life, I wondered whether the oft-repeated claim that the Ayu'li of old were evil necromancers held any truth to it. So much had been lost to the ravages of time, so many holy rituals forgotten. Through the Rite of Awakening, we could temporarily call the souls of our ancestors back from their dwelling places beyond the veil of death. Could the ancients have called back other souls, those with whom they shared neither blood nor love?

Beyond Albastine's borders vile rumors spread about the valley of necromancers, as the barbarians styled us. A particularly infamous one was that we bound the souls of those we killed to the masks of our Attendants, consigning them to the Pale City's eternal service. I had always dismissed such outrageous accusations as superstition, no doubt arising from our battle doctrine of raising the fallen of both sides to serve as new Attendants.

But what if there was more truth to the rumors than I'd dared believe? What if my ancestors really had imprisoned the souls of their enemies—or worse, forced them into service as eternal slaves? Attendants were neither living beings nor dead spirits, merely constructs imbued with a fraction of a Legate's will, without souls or consciousness of their own. But perhaps the ancient Ayu'li had not made such moral distinctions. Perhaps the ancestors of the Ghrabeshi and the Emmaiyad princes had not been the aggressors as we'd been taught.

Perhaps the idea to turn the dead into Attendants had not come from the Extorani, as tradition held, but from the Ayu'li themselves.

I shivered as the marching battle chant rose to a feverish crescendo, my heartbeat pounding in time to the pulsing rhythm. These were questions to which I had no answers.

But Khefnar might.

A VEIL of gauzy red silk had been draped across the entryway to Bahlanni's ancestral shrine in remembrance of the ancestors fallen in battle. I glimpsed my wife's silhouette through it, swaying and stepping in time to her own soft humming. Yet it was not the savage beat of the Reckoning marches that drove her feet and raised her hands. This was slower, gentler, yet prone to sudden lifts leading into equally sudden refrains, each moment building upon those prior to reach a crescendo as unexpected as it was moving.

I had not meant to watch more than a moment, to pause out of respect as Bahlanni rehearsed the steps of the Rite of Awakening. But once I had begun to watch I could not look away. The red silk separating us transformed her into a shadow backlit by candles. She might have been the very ancestors she sang to, dancing her way across the Quiet Fields to these bitter lands, until only a thin veil separated us from one another. My breath caught as she reached for it, fingers twining in the silk as she pulled it aside.

"Akhenkatem?" My name spilled from my wife's mouth in a gasp, her chest rising and falling heavily. All Rites were demanding performances, and none more so than that of Awakening.

"Sorry," I said. "Didn't mean to startle you."

"If you wanted to watch," she said, grinning, "all you had to do was ask."

It was good to see her smile again after our confrontation with Khefnar and his Sons. Hopefully she had regained some inner peace; it seemed that she now felt more in control of the situation with something to channel her energy towards. Or perhaps it was just that it was very, very hard to maintain a bad mood and dance at the same time.

"I didn't want to interrupt," I said, ducking under the veil and into her shrine. A canticle scroll lay unfurled at her ancestors' carven feet. On it lay Old Ayu'li pictograms, interspersed with diagrams showing the very steps she had just danced. Many of our ancient rituals had been lost in the fall of Ayu; those who had fled had wisely committed what Rites they still knew to paper.

I nodded at the scroll. "How's it going?"

"Difficult," Bahlanni admitted, her grin fading. "It's a hard dance to learn. Even harder now, without a teacher…"

She abruptly stopped, glancing at the scroll like a child trying and failing to ignore the broken cookie jar shattered on the floor.

"Wait a minute." I frowned. "Harder? Did you attempt it before?"

"I…" Bahlanni hesitated. "Your grandfather showed me how to do it, once. Back when I first apprenticed under him."

"Did it…" I swallowed, my mouth suddenly dry. This was the first I'd heard of it. "Did it work?"

Bahlanni gave me a look that was equal parts embarrassment, apology, and defiance. "Yes."

The combination of shock and exhaustion made the world swim around me. My grandfather, Octavio Calvus, had been mentor to both me and Bahlanni, first as a Legate of Albastine and then as the high priest of the Old Faith. From him I had learned the value of duty, of honor, of the Republic and its laws. To learn he had violated one of the most fundamental of those laws, even in secret, was akin to discovering he'd had an affair.

"Who?" I shook my head, trying to clear it. "Who did you see? When he…"

"My parents," Bahlanni said, her voice trembling only a little as she looked to the stone faces of her mother and father, standing benevolently near the entryway of their shrine. "It was a year after they'd…"

I squeezed her hand, not wanting her to relive those memories. Bahlanni squeezed back, soft fingers tight around my own.

"His gift to me," she whispered. "A last goodbye."

I could not fault either her or my grandfather for wanting that. Had I not attempted the same with the gravesight after his passing?

But I would not speak of that again, not even to her.

"I've danced it since," Bahlanni continued. "Every year on their passing, in fact, in this very chamber. Not as well as your grandfather did; I could never call them back. But to honor them, so if they hear me on the far side of the veil they will know that they are remembered."

I nodded. It was human nature to cling to rituals great and small in remembrance of our dead, to honor their memories in whatever ways we could.

"I never knew," I said, once more feeling the sting of our separation.

"One thing more for us to discover about one another," Bahlanni said, pressing her lips to my fingers. "The last time I danced it was while you were recovering from your ordeal at Lightfall."

That recently? But of course it had been; her parents had died in early winter.

"That's good," I said, hoping to cover up my surprise. "It means you'll have an edge on Khefnar when the Hour of Revelation comes."

Bahlanni shook her head. "The Rite of Awakening is not a contest. When Khefnar and I dance it, we will dance together. And so will all the people of the Old Faith."

A familiar unease crept into my heart. "In violation of the Republic's laws, and in public."

Bahlanni shrugged. "They cannot arrest all of us. But you did not come back here to see how well I dance, did you?"

"What if I did?" I teased, but then sobered. "Titian's dead."

Bahlanni's face drained of color.

"Oh, my love," she murmured, putting her hands on my shoulders, "I am so sorry."

I leaned my forehead against hers, letting the ashes on our brows mingle. We stood there, swaying slightly to the dance of the candle flames, no sound but one another's breathing.

"Ancestors," Bahlanni murmured, quietly reverent, "guide the spirit of Titian Candorous across the gray unknown. Lead him to peace in the Quiet Fields, or to the halls of whatever gods he worshipped in life. Let him find comfort in his mother's embrace as they dwell together forever in the mansions of rest prepared for them by those who have already braved that last unknown."

Her prayer was well-meant, but it brought me no peace. There could be none for Titian or me while his killer still haunted the Pale City.

"Thank you," I said, and took a deep breath. "But there's more."

I told her about Titian's brutally desecrated body and what his gravesight had revealed to me: he had been the one to mutilate the Attendants I'd discovered last night, and the half-glimpsed Adversary had persuaded him to commit those grisly crimes and then disposed of him in bloody fashion. I told her how Lavinia had nearly breached the Barrows in her attempt to arrest Khefnar, only to be stopped by the intervention of the enigmatic Attendant. The Attendant that had led us both to the eyeless corpse, which it claimed had been the work of one of the Old Faith.

Bahlanni did not interrupt, only listened attentively, squeezing my hands or rubbing my arm. I took comfort in these silent assurances, gentle reminders that she was here with me.

"And now there are more mutilations," I finished. "In the central market, or near to it. Lavinia went to investigate them."

"And you came here," Bahlanni said. "For the Census?"

I had not gotten that far, but my wife was a clever woman.

"That's right," I said. "It's got to be a Legate controlling that Attendant. I'm hoping the Census can tell us who."

"That might be a vain hope," Bahlanni cautioned, even as she turned to the far wall, where a niche for important documents had been wedged in between statues of ancestors. These were common in Old Faith shrines; it was hard to know what ancestor you were worshipping without a comprehensive family tree near at hand.

After a moment's searching, she pulled a thick scroll from the niche and unfurled it, her eyes scanning the neat rows of text. The Census was organized by occupation, beginning with Senators and other elected officials. It did not take Bahlanni long to find the section she was looking for.

"Bad news," she said, handing the scroll to me. Underneath the subheading LEGATES was listed a single name. My own.

"That can't be," I said, staring at the scroll as though I could force it to divulge the unknown Legate's identity through sheer force of will. "*Someone* has to be controlling that Attendant."

"I agree," Bahlanni said. "But whoever they are, their name isn't on the Census."

"So whoever it is, they entered the valley illegally." By law all Legates were required to submit their application to enter Albastine a full month prior to their arrival, allowing time for the Census to be updated to reflect their visit. "Just like someone else we know."

"What if they're the same?" Bahlanni frowned, voicing the very question I'd been thinking. "Khefnar was never trained as a Legate. But if he has learned to dance the Rite of Awakening in Ayu—"

"He might have learned more than that," I finished. I leaned in and pecked Bahlanni on the cheek. "Keep dancing, flesh of my flesh. I'll see you at the Hour of Revelation."

"Where are you going?" she asked as I pulled the veil aside.

I paused. "To find out how Khefnar and his friends snuck into the Pale City."

CHAPTER EIGHTEEN

Like Bahlanni's, Khefnar's ancestral shrine had been divided from the adjoining tunnel by a red veil. Unlike her crimson silk, his was a thick woolen sheet, presumably to keep out the chill of those chambers exposed to the mountain heights.

Also unlike Bahlanni's shrine, Khefnar's was guarded. The two female Sons of Ash stood shoulder to shoulder before the entrance. They carried no weapons that I could see, but their backs stiffened at my approach.

"Sisters," I greeted them in the traditional Ayu'li fashion. "Blessing of the ancestors upon you."

"And on you," Shahkti said after a moment's hesitation. "We did not expect to see you here again."

"I didn't expect to be here," I said. "May I enter?"

"No," the larger of the two women said immediately. "Brother Khefnar is indisposed."

Practicing the Rite of Awakening, no doubt. From within the chamber I could hear baritone voices singing to the same rhythm Bahlanni had danced to.

"What if I said I'd come to set our grievances aside?"

"Then I would ask if you also had a bridge in Zantyum you were looking to sell me," Shahkti snorted. "You and your wife made your positions quite clear, Brother Akhenkatem. If you wish to address Brother Khefnar, approach him after the ancestors have made their will known at Revelation."

Before I could get out a word of argument, the curtain drew aside. Laurent peered out, his bushy white brows lifting as he caught sight of me.

"Cassius!" he said, grinning, then corrected himself. "That is, Brother Akhenkatem. Thought it was your voice I heard out here."

The larger woman frowned. "Brother Imnatt, he is attempting to interrupt Brother Khefnar's—"

"Of course he is, Tyshett," Laurent said, emerging onto our side of the curtain. "After what we've put him and his wife through, can you blame him?"

My shoulders tensed. Was he speaking only of the Hour of Refuge, or had he just let slip that the Sons of Ash *were* connected to the mutilations and murders plaguing the valley?

If so, Laurent gave no sign of it.

"Come, Cassius," he said, shouldering his way past Shahkti and Tyshett into the tunnel. "There's something I've been wanting to show you ever since I laid eyes on you."

He took off up the tunnel, towards the furthest chambers on this high level of the Barrows. I hesitated before following. I'd seen more than one theatrical production where the unsuspecting victim followed their murderer to an isolated location. Even in those poorly written dramas, the killer's pretense was usually not so thin as "I want to show you something."

But it was either that or try to fight my way past Shahkti and Tyshett, just to ask Khefnar a question. Sighing, I followed Laurent up the tunnel, trying to reassure myself that I could overpower the old man if I had to.

"How long have you been a Legate?" Laurent asked as we made our way along the tunnel. The moaning wind echoed off the walls, the scant candles turning the dimly lit passageway eerie.

"I'm retired," I said, flexing the fingers of my bad hand. "A Bellator, now."

Laurent looked at the leather sleeve. "How bad is it?"

"Bad." I was sensitive about my dead arm, unable to avoid feeling like a bug under a glass whenever I caught someone staring at it. Yet somehow Laurent's interest did not bother me, despite his affiliation with Khefnar. Perhaps it was because he had known my grandfather.

"It's useless unless I'm animating it," I said as we climbed. "The nerve endings are almost completely severed. The chirurgeons wanted to amputate, but I..."

"Couldn't go through with it," Laurent guessed. "You cover it well, though. If it weren't for the ghostfire, I'd scarcely be able to tell you were using the Rites to move it."

"It was hard at first," I admitted. "Still doesn't feel natural. But it's close."

"That's good." Laurent grunted as we climbed a short flight of stairs some long-forgotten hand had carved into the rock. "Most Legates never figure out the trick of using the Rites on anything other than an Attendant."

I nearly tripped on the stairs.

"You *can't* use the Rites on things that aren't Attendants," I protested, recovering my balance.

"No?" At the top of the stairs Laurent turned back to look down on me, one bushy white brow raised. "And your arm's an Attendant, then?"

"More or less," I shot back, disliking the turn this conversation had taken. "It was—is—functionally useless. I had it undergo the same alchemical processes that we use to make bodies into Attendants in the Rite of Rising to keep it from atrophying further. It's essentially just a small, arm-shaped Attendant that happens to be permanently attached."

"Good," Laurent said, surprising me. "That'll make this next part easier, then."

Before I could ask what he meant, he turned down the tunnel. I hurried after, just in time to see him duck into one of the adjoining chambers. Uttering a silent prayer to all the ancestors that he wouldn't be waiting inside with a knife, I followed.

The chamber had been divided into two portions by a red woolen sheet identical to the one outside Khefnar's chamber. I glanced at Laurent, who had already seated himself cross-legged on the floor on the nearer side of the curtain.

"It'll make sense in a minute," he said, adjusting into a more comfortable position. "So, Cassius Calvus, grandson of Octavio, you came here to ask a question?"

No point beating about the bush. "How did you slip into the valley undetected?"

I expected him to protest, or deny, or prevaricate.

"That's it?" Laurent chuckled. "That's all you wanted to ask?"

"That," I said, "and which of you is a secret Legate."

His chuckle died away, replaced by a deep frown. "Secret Legate?"

"I figure it's either Khefnar or you," I said. "Both of you spent the longest time in Ayu, other than Nakmond, but the Ghrabeshi sultans would never have permitted one of their own to study the Rites. And if Khefnar learned the Rite of Awakening during his time there, he could have learned how to control Attendants as well—"

"Cassius," Laurent said, his creaky old voice suddenly so

authoritative that I reflexively stopped talking. "*Think.* There are no Attendants in Ayu. The things Khefnar learned there were the ancient Rites: gravesight, Awakening, and so on. Not the watered-down versions you teach your Acolytes."

I hesitated, considering the old man's point. The gestures of command the Legates used to control the Attendants were descended from those more ancient Rites, true, but learning the latter in no way conferred mastery of the former. They were related branches of study, not interchangeable.

"Besides," he continued into my silence, "if Khefnar counted a Legate among his followers, he'd have no need of your assistance."

Assistance for what?

"If he wanted that, maybe he shouldn't have upstaged my wife."

"I agree." Laurent's laugh was bitter. "I tried to counsel him out of that, to approach you both before the Hours began. But he wanted his return to have the greatest possible impact upon the faithful. Maximize the drama of the thing. He's always been something of a showman, I'm afraid."

"So I've noticed," I said, rubbing my scalp. "But what's that got to do with me?"

"I'll tell you," Laurent said after a momentary hesitation. "Just like I'll tell you how to sneak into the valley. But first I need you to indulge me in an experiment."

I frowned. "Is whatever this is what you wanted to show me?"

"It is." He gestured at the woolen sheet. "I want you to tell me whether there's an Attendant behind that curtain or not."

An incredulous laugh slipped from my lips. "Attendants are forbidden in the Barrows."

"Indulge me." I reached for the curtain, but Laurent clicked his tongue. "Not with your hands."

I closed my eyes and extended my will beyond myself like a man reaching blindly in the dark. Almost immediately it found purchase in an Attendant not ten feet from me, on the far side of the curtain.

I turned to Laurent, openmouthed. "How did you manage to smuggle an Attendant into the Barrows?"

The old man's smile glimmered with mischief. "See for yourself."

I made a command gesture, ghostfire dancing along my arms. My will poured into the Attendant on the other side of the veil, turning it into an extension of myself, just as my dead arm was. Another command gesture—*come forward.*

The curtain parted, and the Attendant came.

Except it was not an Attendant—at least, not like any Attendant I had ever commanded before. This was no unliving corpse, mummified and anointed and gilded with a bronze mask. The nearest comparison I could find was a marionette, albeit one slightly larger than a child. It had been carved of wood, its rough limbs cunningly replicating the joints of human anatomy to an impressive degree. It had a head but no face, only a dull block of wood.

It stood, as still and obedient as any Attendant, awaiting further instruction.

"What in the name of all the ancestors?" I breathed.

"Go ahead," Laurent said. "Tell it to do something."

Frowning, I gestured for the marionette to raise its left hand. It did, as smoothly and unhesitatingly as any Attendant I'd ever commanded.

I went through a rapid series of other gestures, testing its limits. The wooden Attendant obeyed adroitly, raising its right hand, then both at once, then standing on one leg. Only this last gave it any trouble; unbalanced, it toppled to the chamber floor.

"It's not perfect," Laurent admitted. "Lighter than a traditional Attendant. Not as sturdy, either. Makes it a touch more difficult for them to stand upright."

"A traditional Attendant," I echoed, swallowing. "This...you made an artificial one?"

"I had it made before we left Ayu," Laurent said. "The craftsmanship is Emmaiyad; they're famous the world over for their marionettes. It wasn't much of a stretch for the carver I commissioned to scale one up to something approaching man-sized."

"How does it...?" I flexed the fingers of my sheathed hand, involuntarily sending a signal to the marionette on the floor. It twitched unnervingly. "It responds just like an Attendant."

"Of course it does." Laurent knelt, gathering the puppet in his arms and setting it carefully upright. "I had it treated with the same alchemical process used in the Rite of Rising."

"That shouldn't be enough for it to respond to the Rites," I said, though even as the words came out I knew I was arguing against the evidence before my eyes. "They let us raise bodies, not...whatever this is."

"That's where you're wrong, young Calvus," Laurent said, tugging at his beard. "The Rites form a sympathetic link between the Legate and the Rite's object. Ordinarily this object is a dead body—it's the right shape, for one. For another, it's spent a lifetime performing most of the actions an Attendant will: standing upright, walking, manipulating objects."

I stared. "You're not saying that they remember?"

"Not in the way you or I do." Laurent shrugged. "But repetition carves its way into the very matter of the body, just as it does the mind. Suffice to say that while bodies are the most suitable vessels for an Attendant, others may be used."

"That still doesn't explain this," I said, gesturing at the marionette. "The alchemical treatment only staves off decay."

"It does more than that." Laurent's smile was self-satisfied.

"It took some experimenting, but I discovered that the treatment could be modified to mimic the blush of life in an object that had never lived. To imbue it with the same recollection of consciousness every human body carries, which the Rite of Rising repurposes into the Attendant's driving force."

He rested a hand on the marionette's shoulder, like a proud father. "For all intents and purposes, this is a small Attendant."

My head spun with the implications of what he was telling me. The ability to craft Attendants by hand would fundamentally alter the shape of Albastinian society. But it was not a question about the future I found myself asking. "Why show me this?"

"For one thing, I figured that if anyone was going to appreciate this thing, you would." His mouth quirked. "For another, I needed to see whether it would actually work."

"You didn't know?"

"Not for certain." He shrugged. "The final step in the Rite of Rising is the investment of a Legate's will into the prepared vessel. In this case, the marionette."

"So you tricked me into making it an Attendant."

"Don't sound so defensive," Laurent admonished. "You just took the biggest step forward in Albastine's history. You and I" —Laurent punctuated his point by tapping the marionette's chest, sending a hollow reverberation through the chamber— "just rendered the Attendants obsolete."

I stared. "You can't be serious."

The Attendants were the cornerstone of Albastinian society, every bit as fundamental to our identity as our democratic ideals. To imagine the Republic without them was to imagine a living body without a skeleton.

"Why not?" Laurent challenged.

"The Attendants are the backbone of the Republic," I

protested. "They work our fields, raise our buildings, carry our messages."

"All of which other nations have managed to do without relying upon the dead," Laurent pointed out.

"Our smallest neighbors boast ten times the population of Albastine and all her provinces," I argued. "Besides, what of the army? The vast majority of our forces are legions of Attendants. Without them there is nothing to defend us against the Wodes, the Herracians—"

"You misunderstand," Laurent said, holding up a hand. "I am not calling for the abolishment of the Attendants. Merely for their replacement."

"With this?" I gestured at the marionette standing at attention. "One puppet isn't going to replace thousands upon thousands of Attendants."

"What about thousands of puppets?"

I stared. Laurent's smile widened.

"They're not as hard to make as you'd think," he said, adjusting the marionette's elbow joint. "I brought the schematic back with me from Ayu. Here."

He produced a thick sheaf of papers from his robe and handed them to me. I opened them to see a series of detailed diagrams illustrating the process of creating the marionette, step by step. Though the captions were in the smoothly flowing script of the Emmaiyad rather than the familiar Extorani alphabet, the illustrations were comprehensible enough.

I looked up to see Laurent gazing at me expectantly. "If you can train Acolytes to prepare a body for the Rite of Rising, you can put them to work mass-producing these. Given a few years, you could replace the Attendants entirely."

"Why, though?" The idea was not without a sort of appeal —the entire catalyst for the Lightfall Massacre had been a dwindling supply of Attendants. Skirmishes on the border and the natural march of time had kept that issue from becoming acute, but months later it was hard not to notice that there were fewer of the unliving servants wandering the streets of Albastine than I remembered from my childhood.

"Because using corpses for vassals is unnecessary," Laurent said with sudden heat, taking the schematics back. "The Attendants were born from bitterest need. In the early days of Albastine's founding, when the Autumn Sickness killed so many people—"

"There were not enough left alive to bury the dead, or to farm the fields." I nodded, impatient. Every child of Albastine was taught the story from their earliest schooling. "So the priests of the Old Faith decided to share their secret rituals. From the Rite of Awakening they formulated the Rite of Rising, raising the bodies of the dead but not their souls. Everyone knows this."

"They do," Laurent agreed. "But what they overlook—what we have *all* overlooked, these last three centuries—is that the ancients only chose to make such automata out of corpses because the dead were the most readily available resource. Had they been blessed with an abundance of iron, perhaps they would instead have turned to building men of metal. Don't you see? The Republic has grown beyond its need for Attendants."

I tried to imagine the future he spoke of, with the silent, bronze-masked corpses replaced by wooden constructs like the one before me. Would they be able to perform the same tasks as the Attendants? Most likely, given that they were of similar shape, if not size.

"You could make them to any specification," I realized aloud. "Larger models for construction. Build them light and fast for couriers."

"Exactly!" Laurent nodded vigorously, his old eyes alight. "The possibilities are infinite. Within a few years this valley could be full of Attendants purpose-built for every task imaginable. You'd hardly miss the old version at all. Hells, maybe the city will finally stop smelling so strongly of incense—"

"What do you mean?" I cut him off.

Laurent coughed. "I mean, it's not a *bad* smell, per se, and when you spend all your time around it you get used to it. But for those of us who've been away it can be mighty pungent—"

I shook my head. "Not that. You said we wouldn't miss the old Attendants. But even if we started making the artificial ones today, they wouldn't fully replace the unliving ones for many years, if ever."

"Well." Laurent smiled apologetically. "That's the thing, young Calvus. I'm not offering these as a gift. I'm proposing a trade."

My stomach lurched. Laurent had said Khefnar wanted my help. Now I knew why.

"You want the Attendants." The words sounded absurd even as I spoke them. "The ones we have now."

"Smart boy," Laurent said. "All of the Attendants currently in service to the Republic, in exchange for the capacity to manufacture an infinite supply in the future. It's more than fair."

I choked out a disbelieving laugh. "You're wasting your time. The Senate would never go through with it."

"Good thing I'm not asking the Senate, then."

It felt as though the floor of the chamber had been pulled from under me, leaving me falling hundreds of feet to the valley below.

Laurent had not brought me this proposal merely because he'd been on good terms with my grandfather, once upon a memory. He had come to me because I was a Legate. If I agreed to his terms I could seize control of every Attendant within the valley, as soon as the deal was struck.

"Earlier," Laurent said, very quietly, "you said you would

not lead the Ayu'li back to their homeland without an army to protect them. But there's one already awaiting you. All you have to do is lead them when the time comes."

I wish I could say that I told him no immediately. That I rejected his proposal out of hand, my heart hardened against such temptation by upwards of a decade of service to my country.

But no beating heart is wholly undivided. How we navigate our conflicting desires and duties defines who we are. I was no exception in that regard, and though I thought I had long since reconciled my dual identities as Ayu'li and Legate, I found myself tempted all the same.

What would it be like to command legions of Attendants in direct defense of my people? To shelter them through a wilderness of hostile nations and perilous terrain, to stand at their head as we reclaimed the lands that had been stolen from us generations prior?

I could see myself clearly in my mind's eye: no longer Gaius Cassius Calvus, dutiful Legate, but Akhenkatem, prophet and savior of the Ayu'li, the warrior-priest who led his people back to their ancient homes. I imagined glories heaped upon me, the praise and adoration of the people whose service I had fully committed myself to, body and soul.

I saw us build a house, Bahlanni and I—not the cold stone estate of my forefathers situated in this misty valley, but a warm little house of yellow brick by the banks of the River Ayu. We could raise children there, in the land that the river god had promised would be ours forever. Worship our forebears as we pleased, without the strictures of an Extorani-dominated government to restrict us. Perform the Rite of Awakening together, recalling those we had lost to the sunlit lands once more, to laugh and dance and cry with each other as we always should have done.

I could see my grandfather again. And my parents. Everyone I had ever lost.

Tears stung my vision, sudden and unexpected as summer rain. I blinked them away, hoping Laurent had not noticed.

"Well?" he asked, the tenderness in his voice dispelling that hope immediately. He stuck out his left hand. "Is it a fair deal?"

To my shame, I reached for his hand. Ghostfire flickered along the sheathed arm.

I froze, feeling as though I'd just awoken from a wine-soaked dream. I had lost that arm in defense of Albastine, fighting to save the Republic from forces threatening to tear it apart from within. What was the point of that sacrifice if I absconded with the Attendants that same Republic relied upon for its defense, leaving it vulnerable to any of a dozen hostile neighbors?

Nor was my arm the only thing I had lost in service to the Republic. The grinning face of Quintus Aquila rose in my memory, handsome, laughing, and forever dead. Horatia's brother, my closest friend, fallen in battle alongside me as we fought to protect our homeland.

For Albastine *was* home. Though my faith might proclaim Ayu as our destined refuge, I had never set foot upon those lands, had never drunk from the waters of that mighty river. My home was the steep valley cliffs, the unending mist, the cool rush of the Providens.

So it was for the rest of my people. Ayu might have been the place from which our forefathers fled, but Albastine was the place they had chosen. Here they had joined with their fellow exiles and made a home unlike any other in the world.

Albastine. The Republic. The Pale City.

My home.

"Sorry," I told Laurent, and meant it. "No deal."

CHAPTER NINETEEN

"You're certain?" Laurent's voice was flinty.

"I am."

"Think carefully, Calvus." He held the schematics over one of the candles lining the room. A thin line of smoke rose from one corner of the paper as its edges blackened and curled. "This is a one-time offer."

"You're bluffing," I said. "Burn that and you have nothing to bargain with."

"Smart boy." A smile tugged at the corner of Laurent's mouth, bitter and rueful. But he did not lift the schematics from the candle. "Are you willing to risk Albastine's future on it?"

"I'd be risking her future if I agreed," I said, keeping my eyes fixed on him and not the curling edge of the papers. "If I absconded with the city's Attendants today the entire valley would be engulfed in chaos by morning."

"In which case the Magisterium would no doubt step in to impose order," Laurent said, turning over the schematic so that the candle's flame licked at another side of it. "Besides, some instability might be exactly what your precious Republic needs to discover how badly it needs to wean itself off the Attendants' labor."

"People could die."

Flames glimmered in Laurent's eyes. "People *will* die on the march to Ayu, Cassius Calvus, unless you are willing to take your rightful place as a servant of the Faith and safeguard their passage."

By this point the corner of the schematics was really starting to catch fire. I forced myself to keep my eyes on Laurent as I clasped my hands behind my back, hoping he could not see the ghostfire flaring up my arms.

"Why now?" I asked. "If these constructed Attendants are Albastine's future, why not wait until the Republic has an ample enough supply of them? What is happening in Ayu that Khefnar is so focused on bringing our people there now?"

"Politics," Laurent sneered. "The Ghrabeshi sultans have always been fractious, but in recent months they've been practically at war. Nakmond's father, Nizar an-Swerati, believes that—"

What Nizar an-Swerati believed I never discovered, for at that moment I flung both arms forward in a command gesture.

The wooden Attendant hurled itself at Laurent. Small as the construct was, I had half expected it to merely bounce off the old man, but it had been carved of dark ironwood, dense and heavy. Instead, it knocked him to the ground, the smoldering bundle of schematics flying from his hand.

"Damn you!" Laurent spat, clawing for the fallen papers. I reached them first, beating the singed sheets against my chest to smother the flames.

"Sorry," I told him, taking a step back. I halfway meant it. Opposed though we were in the power struggle for the hearts of the faithful, Laurent had been friends with my grandfather and had seemed to genuinely like me.

Besides, ordering an Attendant to attack an elderly man hadn't exactly felt heroic.

"Coward," Laurent snarled, disentangling himself from the wooden Attendant's limbs. "Thief."

"I'm not stealing these," I said, tucking the sheaf of papers into my robe. "I'll make sure the Senate compensates—"

I did not so much hear the blow coming as I sensed a change in the air. Instinct honed by years of training sent me sprawling to the floor as a bronze-tipped staff thrummed through the space where my head had been not a heartbeat earlier.

I turned my duck into a spin, knees bent, coming up behind my assailant—Tyshett, snarling and already throwing a backswing.

I should have expected the Sons of Ash wouldn't trust me alone with one of their own.

"Get him!" Laurent yelled, pulling himself to his feet. "He has the schematics!"

Tyshett lashed out again, but the close confines of the chamber caused her staff's bronze tip to bounce off one of the statues lining the walls, cracking it. She barked out a curse and drew back for another strike.

I grabbed the red woolen curtain hanging from the ceiling, pulling it in front of me just as the blow fell. The staff bounced off the taut fabric. A dull *thwump* echoed through the chamber as it rebounded against Tyshett's skull.

I yanked at the curtain as she cursed. The fabric tore, a sizable portion coming away in my hands. Balling it in my fists, I turned and fled from the chamber, the shouts of the Sons of Ash following me down the tunnel.

My heartbeat was a rush of blood in my ears as I ran, not daring to look back. Had this been some commedia performed in the market square, Tyshett smacking herself in the face with her own staff would have taken her out of commission. But the rules of combat are not the same in real life as they are on stage, and Tyshett's echoing footfalls told me that the big woman had recovered enough to give chase. With her longer legs, she would likely close the distance between us in a matter of seconds.

I put my head down and put on speed, skidding around a turn and vaulting down one of the flights of stairs Laurent and I had climbed mere minutes prior. Out of the corner of my eye I glimpsed Tyshett charging after me, a huge angry shadow chasing me like every monster in every nightmare I'd ever dreamed.

Another flight of stairs, shorter this time. I jumped them, letting out a sharp grunt as pain tore into my knees at the landing.

The chanting of low voices echoed off the walls: Khefnar and Nakmond. Ahead of me the tunnel was a straight stretch, terminating in the long flight of stairs that would take me back down to the main level of the Barrows.

Except that my way was barred.

Shahkti and Hupli stood in the tunnel outside the entrance to Khefnar's family shrine, apparently deep in conversation until they had turned to look at me. Surprise flickered over Shahkti's face, followed swiftly by grim understanding. Like Tyshett, she held a bronze-tipped staff in her hands.

Hupli followed her gaze. His eyes landed on me, but showed neither surprise nor recognition, nor any emotion at all.

The sound of a woman-shaped avalanche crashing down the stairs behind me propelled me to further motion. I tore down the tunnel, unbunching the rolled-up curtain still clenched in my fist. I gripped its corners with both hands and raised it over my head, letting it trail out behind me like a cape as I ran. Ahead of me, Shahkti gripped her staff, settling into a wide stance. Perhaps deciding that discretion was the better part of valor, Hupli retreated into the chamber.

Time slowed.

Blood singing in my ears, I ground my heels against the stone floor. My feet skidded along the tunnel as I slowed, still hurtling towards Shahkti. The bronze cap of her staff grew to the size of a mountain as she began to swing.

I hurled the red curtain forward, exactly as I had once seen a bullfighter do in the sandy arenas of Zantyum. It flew from my hands, unfurling like a flag caught by a sudden breeze.

Straight for Shahkti.

She flinched, trying to adjust her swing at the last moment to bat the sheet away from her. Red fabric wrapped around her staff, her chest, her face. At the same moment, my heels went out from under me, but fate or the ancestors or sheer blind luck were still smiling on me, for my momentum carried me forward, and I slid along the tunnel's smooth stone floor. Shahkti's wool-wrapped staff passed harmlessly above my head, her muffled cries of dismay following me down the tunnel as I regained my feet.

"After him!" Tyshett bellowed.

Nothing's ever easy, I thought, and kept running.

I SHIED AWAY from the more heavily trafficked tunnels and thoroughfares of the Barrows, avoiding the stretches where gathered families of the faithful were even now paying their respects to the ancestors lost in the Reckoning. I fled down narrow access corridors and half-deserted tunnels, and our echoing footfalls drowned out the distant rhythms of worship songs.

Had it been anyone else pursuing me, I might have tried to

lose the Sons of Ash in the maze of twisting turns and dead ends that made up these more obscure regions of the Barrows. It would have been easy to slip into some shadowed alcove and wait for them to pass me by, then double back and sneak away unnoticed.

But Hupli's voice echoed down the corridors after me, shouting directions to Tyshett and Shahkti whenever a corner or sudden turning took me out of their sight. As junior priest, he knew the Barrows with an intimacy even I could not hope to rival.

Speed, not cunning, would decide this race.

My lungs and legs were both burning by the time I reached the broad, straight stretch of tunnel leading to the gates. My every muscle ached for rest, however brief, but I forced myself to keep moving, each step bringing me nearer to the bronze gates and the sweet release of freedom.

And what then? The decision to steal the schematics from Laurent had been the choice of a moment. I was not certain how much faith to put into his assertion that the creation of artificial Attendants would obviate the need for the traditional versions, but it would serve no one to have those schematics destroyed. Better to deliver them into safer hands until a decision could be made regarding what to do with them.

I wished I knew exactly whose hands those were.

My feet pounded over the stone floor, the half-muffled shouts and cries of the pursuing Sons of Ash not far behind. The bronze gates loomed ahead of me, the candlelight making the glyphs inscribed into them dance and glimmer. My stomach dropped as I saw a heavy timber beam laying across them, barring them shut.

I slowed to a stumbling jog, the cries of my pursuers echoing after me. I reached the gates and tried to lift the wooden beam. It barely budged.

"There he is!" Tyshett's bulky form loomed against the candlelight at the far end of the tunnel, Shahkti and Hupli close on her heels.

I cursed and squatted, putting my back and shoulders against the bottom of the beam, pushing with all my might. My legs ached from the chase, but with a creaking groan the beam slowly began to lift.

Candlelight sent shadows dancing up the wall alongside my pursuers, like demons that had joined in the chase. Sweat beaded on my forehead as I strained, lifting the wooden beam from the sconces that held the great bronze doors closed. The Sons of Ash were drawing nearer, and in Hupli's hand I caught the gleam of metal.

A knife? But weapons were forbidden in the Barrows...

The beam came free of the sconces with a final complaint. I let it fall, already pushing the great bronze gates forward with every bit of strength I had. The Sons of Ash were so close that I imagined I could feel their collective breath against my neck, hot and hungry.

The gates opened with a terrible grinding, letting in fine wisps of mist. I stumbled into the cool air of freedom, heart still stinging, legs still aching.

"What in all the ancestors—" Neftani shouted, hauling himself to his feet above the dice game. His fellow gamblers did likewise, reaching for their own weapons.

"Stop them!" I yelled, not stopping in my headlong flight downhill. My voice came out in a ragged wheeze. "They're trying to—"

"Guards!" Hupli's voice was so high as to be a screech, more emotional than I'd ever heard him. "Stop that man, by order of the priesthood!"

Neftani and Rithokh looked at each other, then at the pair of magistrates, then at me. On the faces of all four men conflicting loyalties warred.

This was the start of it, I realized. Until now the struggle between Khefnar and Bahlanni, between the Magisterium and the Sons of Ash, had been relatively bloodless—save for the murders and mutilations, which I remained unconvinced were Khefnar's doing. If things devolved into violence now, with the guards obeying Hupli's orders and the magistrates following mine, things would spiral out of control until there was no hope of a peaceful resolution.

Incongruously, I recalled Titian's final lesson: Legate Hadris and her willingness to sacrifice herself on the altar of the Republic.

I had done as she had done, time and time again. I thought I had paid my dues, that my obligations of service had ended when I had lost the use of my arm, or when I had nearly died stopping the Lightfall coup.

But duty, I'd discovered, did not end with the completion of a task or the retirement of a title. It was an ever-hungry thing, always demanding more, so long as there was anything left of me to give.

One day, I knew, I would run out of self to give. I could only hope it was not today.

The Sons of Ash were closing in behind me, weapons in hand. To my left rose the steep slope of the mountainside, while to my right it fell away, to the winding switchback trails leading down from the Barrows. Ahead of me, guards and magistrates alike tensed, uncertain in their allegiances now that the moment of conflict could no longer be forestalled.

Unless I took that choice from their hands.

Steeling myself as best I could, I took a deep breath and threw myself down the mountainside.

CHAPTER TWENTY

The drop from the path leading up to the Barrows was not a sheer one, though the incline was steep enough that the trail was broken into a series of long, narrow switchbacks steadily climbing the mountainside. My feet hit the slope with a painful jolt, then I was half sliding, half falling down the rocky slope. Dirt and stone and plant matter scraped and tore at me as I slid, sending up a miniature landslide as I plowed a furrow down the slope. I gritted my teeth against the pain and closed my eyes, fearful that some upflung pebble might strike me blind.

From overhead came dismayed shouts, though the roar of earth around me prevented me from discerning whose voices they were. Not that it mattered. I had more pressing concerns.

I was picking up speed, my stumbling slide down the slope rapidly nearing a true fall rather than a semi-controlled descent. I thrust my left hand out behind me, my gloved fingers clawing against the cliffside for any sort of purchase. Scree and stone slipped through them, tore at them. Had I tried this with my other hand it would have been flayed raw.

It worked. The cold grip of my bad arm arrested my

momentum enough that when I hit the first of the switchback trails I did not smash into it like a bird against a window. Instead, my whole world exploded into bright starbursts of pain as I hit the trail and kept going, rolling side over side towards its far edge. I lashed out blindly with both hands, clawing for whatever purchase I could.

I found it in the upthrust root of a half-dead tree overhanging the trail, clinging stubbornly to the cliffside despite the inhospitable terrain. I clung to that root with similar tenacity, coming to a rolling stop with my head hanging halfway over the side of the trail.

I opened my eyes and immediately wished I hadn't. The second switchback was much, *much* farther below me than the first had been, no more than a pale line snaking its way along the mountainside. It was not a fall I could have survived.

I scrambled away from the edge, not stopping until my back was pressed against the cliff wall. Adrenaline still had my heartbeat racing frantically, but it was no longer enough to dull the dozens of bruises flowering all over my body. I tried for a deep breath, felt instead a sharp stitch in my side.

"Gods," I hissed, feeling for the injured spot. I found it, sending another lance of pain through my sides. A broken rib, or at the very least cracked.

I closed my eyes, breathing in through my nose. I wanted nothing more than to lie there and drift off to sleep, letting time and oblivion heal the injuries I was rapidly accumulating. But I heard shouts falling from above, muffled by the mists.

The Sons of Ash were still after me, though none of them had been stupid enough to risk replicating my extremely rapid —and extremely foolish—descent. Instead, the mountainside echoed with the clatter of stones as they raced along the trail, closing what little lead I'd gained on them.

I felt gingerly inside my robe, careful not to aggravate my

injured rib. My questing fingers found the schematics, miraculously still there even after the long fall.

Biting my lip to keep myself from screaming as another stab of pain jolted through my side, I pushed myself to my feet and hurried down the trail, my mind swimming with pain and shock that I had survived the fall.

The city, I told myself as I made my way downhill in a stumbling jog, going as fast as I dared without worsening the pain in my side. *All I have to do is make it to the city.*

Save for the years I had spent abroad in the legions, I had lived in Albastine all my life. Once I was within those misty streets it would be trivial to lose myself in the maze of winding alleys and thoroughfares, to disappear into the throngs of citizens who did not hold to the Old Faith. My pursuers possessed no such intimacy—Shahkti and Tyshett had both been abroad for years. As for Hupli, I could count on one hand the number of times I had seen him outside the gates of the Barrows.

Like when he let the Sons of Ash through those same gates. A queasy feeling settled in my stomach as I remembered that I had failed to accomplish what I had gone to the Barrows to discover. The Census had no record of any other Legate entering the valley lately, which meant that whoever was controlling the enigmatic Attendant had come here under the same clandestine auspices as the Sons.

The price of that knowledge had been too high. I wondered why Laurent had ever expected that I might abandon the Republic I had served faithfully all my adult life—and found myself disquieted by the possibility that perhaps he had expected there to be more of my grandfather in me than there was.

Octavio Calvus, my grandfather, had been priest of the Old Faith from the time I was very young until his passing in my early adulthood. Yet before that, he had served as a Legate, defending his country against our barbarian neighbors for nearly thirty years. Not for the first time, I wondered how he had reconciled the apparent conflict between his patriotism and his faith, between the society he had devoted his life to and the religion it oppressed.

Had he felt that oppression more bitterly in his later years, when the laws of the Republic he had fought and bled for kept him from performing his priestly duties? How badly had it galled him that he could not perform the Rite of Awakening, could not commune with his ancestors for guidance and succor?

Not only the ancestors. My grandmother, my mother and father—all had preceded him to the Quiet Fields and whatever lay beyond. Only I had been left to him, and though he had raised me with all the care and wisdom he had, I wondered whether he had not felt more than a twinge of bitterness at the separation between us and those who were gone.

A bitterness Laurent had been willing and ready to exploit, had it manifested as deeply in me as he thought it had in my grandfather. But the old man had been mistaken. My loyalties were not divided enough to make me abandon my principles.

At least now I had a fuller grasp of Khefnar's plan. He had not intended to lead the Ayu'li out of Albastine unattended—quite literally. Instead, he had meant for me to be the general at the head of an Attendant army, safeguarding the passage of the faithful on their long pilgrimage home to Ayu.

And despite my moment of temptation, it was a patently absurd idea. I would no sooner abandon Albastine than cut off my remaining arm.

Mist kissed my face as I descended lower into the valley, rounding one of the switchbacks. Through the fog, Albastine's white spires loomed like silent sentinels.

No, I thought. It would take a far greater offer than mere power to turn me against my city.

THE HURRIED FOOTFALLS and muffled cries of the Sons of Ash, still uncomfortably close at hand, faded into the mist behind me as I reached the bottom of the trail. Despite the throbbing pain in my side, I put on a final burst of speed, the pounding of the cobblestones against my feet a welcome relief.

Once again I felt at my side, checking that the schematics for the artificial Attendants were still secure. They were. I doubted Laurent had been wholly honest in his assertion that they could replace the true Attendants entirely. For one thing, producing the constructs en masse would require a great deal of timber, which the valley did not have. For another, the poor balance and relative delicacy of the marionette Laurent had shown me did not suggest they would make passable soldiers.

Yet their usefulness could not be overstated. Even mummified and treated with alchemical solutions to ward off the ravages of decay, the Attendants were still corpses. The Rite of Rising slowed their decomposition but did not halt it entirely, necessitating the omnipresent incense that kept the entire city from smelling like a summertime charnel house. On average, each Attendant lasted ten or twelve years before it was too rotted to be of service to the Republic.

But artificial Attendants could be built from more durable materials. Wood, yes, but what of ceramics, or metal? I thought of Laurent's suggestion that the first Albastinians might have built their Attendants from iron if the valley had been readily supplied with ore rather than corpses. An iron man would be almost too heavy to move, but one built of sturdy timber and merely armored with iron plates...

"He's right," I said aloud, drawing a curious glance from a pair of women hurrying by, sculptors' tools lining their belts.

The introduction of man-made Attendants would be a turning point for the Republic. No longer would we be wholly reliant upon the dead to farm our fields, raise our buildings, and wage our wars. Instead, those duties could be turned over to a newly created class of automata, sturdier than their unliving predecessors, purpose-built for whatever role was required of them. Admittedly, they would sacrifice much of the current Attendants' versatility in exchange for more specialized functions; the class of construct built for war would necessitate a vastly different shape than its agricultural counterpart. But when a single farming construct could do the work of a dozen Attendants...

I pressed my hand against my side, wincing as it brushed my probably broken rib. The sheaf of schematics remained there, nestled safely against my heart. The thick stack of papers seemed oddly heavy, as though the weight of their importance was a physical thing.

I was struck by the sudden, absolute certainty that comes only in the rarest moments of clarity. These papers were the most important documents in Albastine's history. Greater than our founding charter, greater than any bill signed into law. Greater even than the canticles in which my people's sad and noble history were written.

Those were all things of Albastine's past. The schematics were her future. A future free of Attendants as we knew them now. A future wherein there would be no need to outlaw the Rite of Awakening, allowing the Ayu'li to practice the Old Faith in full. At last, we would be able to dance the steps long denied us, to rejoice in communion and fellowship with the souls of our departed.

Khefnar had come to the Barrows bearing prophecies of our

glorious return to Ayu. Of recapturing the stolen homeland he and his alone had set foot upon in living memory.

He claimed to be the harbinger of our salvation. He was right. He just didn't know that he had already brought it with him.

I laughed at the irony, though quietly enough not to draw stares this time. If the Sons of Ash had only stopped to think their actions through, they would have realized that the key to solving the Ayu'li's problems was with them all the while.

Except it was not love of their people that drove them. Everything they had done was born as much from resentment of Albastine as it was from love for Ayu. Khefnar and his acolytes could no more separate the former from the latter than they could remain in the valley. They did not seek peaceful cohabitation with the Extorani in the nation we had built, but departure from it.

Perhaps Laurent had meant to turn over the schematics to Albastine, but I could not see Khefnar allowing such a trade to take place. Even if I had agreed to his terms and donated the designs to the Senate, he would have orchestrated events so that they would mysteriously vanish, or tragically catch fire, or meet any of a dozen other unfortunate fates. His bitterness ran too deep.

And that was the problem, I reflected as my feet led me to the rushing flow of the River Providens. Not with Khefnar alone, but with the Sons of Ash and their entire crusade to return the Ayu'li to Ayu. No future built upon a foundation of bitterness could last. At best it would crumble and collapse, unable to sustain itself without a foe to direct its energies against, turning instead upon its own people and devouring them like an ouroboros. Or worse, it would seek new enemies to devise grievances against, conquering and consuming in the name of righteousness and empire.

My robe kept out the chill of the ever-present fog, but I found myself shivering nonetheless. Khefnar spoke much of his ambition to return our people to our homeland, but he had never claimed that those ambitions stopped at Ayu. That he had allied himself with Nakmond an-Swerati—coupled with the latter's conversion to the Old Faith—meant that his intent was not to wholly uproot the Ghrabeshi and Emmaiyad peoples who had settled there in the intervening centuries. Did he seek to enforce some sort of cohabitation between those peoples and our own, whether as uneasy neighbors or as conquering overlords?

Unless Nakmond's conversion is genuine rather than political, I thought, *and he would willingly stand by as his people were put to the torch.* I did not know enough of the man to judge which was the case.

But if Khefnar really did intend to drive out the people who had been living in our ancestral lands for better than three hundred years, how was he any different than their own ancestors? How were any of us, if we followed him into holy war?

The sins of the father, I thought as I strode alongside the river. Ahead the lights of the central marketplace had been kindled against the fog, warm and inviting. Perhaps the wrongs done to our ancestors could never be redressed, and we would never resettle in Ayu. But I thought it no terrible thing to break the cycle of violence and dispossession that had begun all those centuries ago. To look at last towards a brighter future instead of a grim and blood-soaked past.

Yet even as I thought it, I knew that past could not be escaped any more than the bloody present. Before I could hand the schematics to the artificial Attendants over to those who would know what to do with them, I had to deal with the murders and mutilations plaguing my city.

The latest of which was quite literally staring me in the face.

CHAPTER TWENTY-ONE

Deeply absorbed in my thoughts as I was, I had not immediately noticed the mutilated Attendant standing in the middle of the street, just before the open gates leading into the central marketplace. Yet it was not wholly my distraction that kept me from realizing that the figure standing before me was not alive.

This Attendant wore no mask.

That jarring realization sent a creeping revulsion crawling across my skin. To see an Attendant unmasked was more than distasteful; it was a violation of the Republic's very principles, as repulsive as the mutilations and murders I had come here to investigate.

For the smiling bronze masks were not merely decorative. They kept the Attendants anonymous, dampening any curiosity over exactly whose corpse it was that swept your halls or delivered your letters. More than that, the masks obscured the grim reality of the Attendants' nature—inured to the dead though we Albastinians were, the sight of rotting flesh was no more palatable to us than to any other people.

So integral were the masks to the Attendants' existence

that steps were taken to ensure they could not be unmasked; each was carefully sutured to the skin beneath. Jagged tears at the edges of this Attendant's mummified face indicated that this had once been the case, before someone had torn the mask free from the putrefied flesh. No blood seeped from the wounds, for the Attendant's heart had long since ceased beating.

My feet felt unsteady beneath me. Like the limbless Attendants and the pieces of poor Titian, this was an affront to everything I believed in, and just as intentional a violation.

And like those crimes, this one was also a statement, for the tears where the mask had been ripped away were not the only bloodless wounds it bore. Someone had carved long, jagged cuts across its face, stretching from each temple to the opposite jaw in a crude X, exposing the stringy white muscle beneath.

Only then did I see the face beneath the vicious wounds. The Attendant had been someone I knew.

The eyes of Venaria Hestis, once Triarch of Albastine, stared at me. In life those eyes had been gray, and in death they remained so, but now they were the foggy, glaucous eyes of a corpse.

"Grisly, isn't it?"

Ghostfire raced up my arms as I instinctively reached for an Attendant to defend myself. The corpse that had been Venaria turned as I did to regard the shadow approaching us from the fog.

That shadow resolved into the diminutive figure of Lavinia Caprio, striding from the marketplace into the circle of light cast by the lantern hanging from the archway above us.

"Easy," she said, glancing from me to the Attendant. "I see you've found our perpetrator's latest message."

"Not as clear as their first," I said, thinking back to the graffiti that had been the start of all this. *Albastine in Ashes.*

"No?" Lavinia frowned, looking critically at what had once been Venaria. "How do you figure?"

"You remember what she did," I said, quiet amidst the fog. "At Lightfall."

"I do." Lavinia's frown deepened. "Tried to get herself appointed tyrant by the Senate. Then started the whole bloody coup when that didn't pan out."

"That's not all of it," I said, then hesitated. The full details of the Lightfall Massacre were known only to a few—myself included, since I had been the one to inadvertently uncover the entire conspiracy. Yet I did not know how far beyond the halls of power such sensitive information went.

"You mean her reasons for doing so," Lavinia said, guessing at the reason for my recalcitrance. "Venaria's wanting to start a war so that Albastine would have a fresh influx of new Attendants?"

"How did you know?"

"Gracchus briefed me on it when I took this assignment."

Interesting. I had never met a man less willing to share information than the dour Imperator. Had he been less mistrustful of me while I investigated the murder of Julius Catellus, the Lightfall Massacre might have been prevented entirely. If he had told Lavinia the truth behind Venaria's betrayal of the Republic she had been elected to lead—a betrayal born from her own twisted sense of duty—then he must have thought it relevant to the current investigation.

"I get it," she said, interrupting that line of thought with a nod at Venaria's corpse. "If it was just her, it would seem like the mutilator was making a statement about her betrayal."

"But she isn't the only Attendant they did this to?"

"Of course not." Lavinia's mouth twisted into a grim smile. "There are three more, one at each entrance to the marketplace. And just like our dearly departed Triarch here, all three of them held public office before they died. Two Senators and a provincial governor."

"All with wounds like these?" I asked, gesturing to the gashes crisscrossing Venaria's face.

She nodded. "Exactly. Like I said, not a lot of ambiguity to carving an X across the faces of politicians, living or dead. Though I suppose we've all been tempted to do the same, at one point or another."

Caught off guard, I barked out a laugh. "Gods, Magistrate Caprio. Who knew you had a sense of humor?"

She shrugged. "You see some pretty awful things in this line of work, Bellator. You either learn to laugh in the face of it, or you let it eat at you."

"It's the same in the legions," I said. If there was one thing every soldier I'd ever known shared, it was gallows humor.

I looked around and saw that we remained alone in the mists. "How come it's just you out here? You had a cordon set up around Titian's body."

"It's not just her." Gracchus's voice, oily smooth as ever, glided to us out of the mists. The man himself followed, stopping just outside the circle of lanternlight. He nodded at me. "Bellator."

"Imperator."

"The other two gates have a cordon set up," he continued, gesturing behind him. "But by now word has reached the wider city of the other mutilations, and of poor Titian's murder. The Magisterium is stretched thin trying to maintain a visible presence."

"All patrols have been doubled," Lavinia added. "But that leaves us with only a handful available to help with the case directly. Since the north gate is the least heavily trafficked of the four..."

She shrugged, a gesture which somehow conveyed the futility of trying to maintain order in a city gripped by fear.

"So it's just bad luck that I wandered into the one entrance you left unguarded?" I asked. "And that it happened to be the only one where the Attendant is someone I have a history with?"

"Is that so surprising?" Gracchus asked, his voice dry. "You have already demonstrated an unenviable capacity for bad luck, Calvus. But come. Now that you're here, we might as well continue this discussion out of the elements."

He turned and strode back into the marketplace, not waiting for Lavinia and me to follow.

Albastine's central marketplace lay very near the heart of the city, and of the valley itself. Situated at a bend in the Providens, it was bordered on its western side by the river, which slowed there enough for a series of docks to be constructed, allowing for downriver travel. The other three sides lay in a sort of bowl formed by the surrounding hills, which had been further enclosed by the construction of a tall stone wall, with arched gateways to north and south. Westward, a bridge stretched across the Providens upriver of the docks, though it too was gated.

Ordinarily the market would be a medley of sounds and smells from Albastine and beyond: foreign traders hawking their wares, exotic spices scenting the air, the faint musk of livestock driven into the city from the outlying farmlands. Yet now the afternoon was strangely quiet, the stalls and tents erected across the marketplace unnervingly empty.

"You closed off the entire market?" I asked as we walked between vacated shopfronts. Most were separated by piles of lumber: kindling for the communal hearths dotting the market-place. Even in early spring the chill of winter still lingered in Albastine's alpine climate.

"Of course we did," Lavinia said. "It's a crime scene."

"For how long?" Bahlanni and Khefnar's showdown at the Hour of Revelation had been meant to occur in the amphithe-ater at the marketplace's heart. I was still uncomfortable with the idea of my wife performing the forbidden Rite of Awakening there, but before Khefnar's arrival had thrown everything into chaos it had been her intent to use the public venue as a way to promote the practices of the Old Faith to the city, showing that we were neither as insular nor as hidebound as those outside the faithful believed us to be.

Bahlanni would be crushed, but maybe it was better this way. If she still intended to perform the Rite of Awakening, better it be done in the privacy of the Barrows, where the Magisterium could not immediately arrest her and Khefnar for violating one of the Republic's most foundational laws.

"Only a few hours," Gracchus said, shattering my brief hopes. We passed by a stall laden with dozens of ceramic urns, the acrid scent of oil emanating from them. "Rest assured, your people will still be permitted to hold their religious services here at sundown."

He gave me a significant look as he said it, and I wondered whether he knew exactly what Bahlanni and Khefnar were planning to do this evening.

"Why so brief?" I asked, hoping to divert the conversation to safer grounds. "I mean, if the Attendants were dismembered here—"

"They were not," Gracchus said. "The mutilations were performed elsewhere, then the Attendants sent here. They caused a good deal of commotion when they came walking unmasked from the mists."

I shivered, recalling my own unease at the sight of Venaria's mummified and disfigured features. It was a minor miracle that four such Attendants converging on the marketplace at once hadn't caused a riot.

We emerged from the maze of merchants' stalls into the empty amphitheater, its tiered seats descending to the open space at its foot, a stage at its center. Behind it the hills rose in a sheer cliff, backing up to the city's towers. I swallowed the sudden fear that came rising up my throat at the reminder that my people's fate would be decided in this very place, a scant few hours from now.

"Any idea where they came from?" I asked.

"No." Lavinia shook her head. "But our suspect pool is growing narrower."

"How so?"

"Because of who these Attendants were in life," Gracchus answered, gazing pensively down the rows of seats. "Politicians."

I caught on. "Whoever mutilated them knew where to find their bodies."

"And given the importance of Attendant anonymity," Lavinia said, "the list of people who could identify and locate a particular person's Attendant is vanishingly small." She counted them off on her fingers. "Morticians, priests—"

Gracchus gave me another significant look.

"—and imperators," Lavinia finished, glancing at her superior. Gracchus's lip twitched, but he did not smile.

I looked at Gracchus. "Something you want to confess?"

"Not to you." He adjusted his cloak. "I hear that your wife's apprentice has publicly declared his support for the Sons of Ash, however."

Reflexively, I opened my mouth to protest, but could think of no rejoinder. Hupli had made his allegiance known—and hadn't I seen a knife in his hand as he chased me through the Barrows? Had that same knife carved the mask from Venaria's dead face?

And there was the matter of the mysterious Attendant, who had silently claimed that the eyeless corpse it had led us to had been murdered by an Ayu'li of the Old Faith...

I glanced past Gracchus to Lavinia, standing behind him. Understanding shone in her dark eyes; she was thinking of the circumstances under which we had last parted. Neither of us had mentioned that particular crime in Gracchus's presence.

Holding my gaze, she gave the slightest shake of her head.

So that omission had been intentional. If Gracchus was playing his hand close to the chest, so would we.

"I saw Hupli not long ago," I told Gracchus, deciding to leave out the precise details. "The timing would have been questionable."

Gracchus shrugged. "That does not preclude the crime being committed beforehand and the Attendants ordered to come here after."

"Maybe not," I admitted, then remembered something else. Like many memories, it was prompted by scent—namely the acrid smell of oil from the stall full of urns we had passed. I had smelled that same scent not long ago, though not in my own memories. "But I have an idea of where it might have been done."

Gracchus's dark brows lifted. "By all means, share your theory."

"I used the gravesight on Titian Candorous." Gracchus showed no reaction to that; Lavinia must have told him as much already. "He was murdered in a warehouse. Not far from here, I think. It was by the river..."

I gave as detailed a description as I could, which Gracchus

absorbed without comment. I had long suspected the man had an eidetic memory.

"I believe I know the place," he said once I had finished, turning to Lavinia. "Magistrate?"

"I'll head there now," she said, but hesitated. "Bellator Calvus. Was there anything else you've discovered since we last parted ways?"

It was a clumsy attempt at obfuscation, but she could not ask me outright if I had managed to discover whoever was behind the mysterious Attendant. Not with Gracchus staring hawklike at us.

Yet the identity of the Legate behind that Attendant was a deeper mystery, as was their agenda. Clearly they were working at cross purposes to Khefnar and his Sons of Ash; elsewise they would not have revealed the eyeless victim to me, nor claimed that it had been the work of an Ayu'li. Besides, if they *had* been working with the Sons of Ash, Laurent would have had no need to approach me about Khefnar's plan to abscond with the Attendants.

Don't tell them about that, I thought, avoiding Gracchus's and Lavinia's expectant gazes. If word of that scheme got out, it would only heighten the tensions between the Old Faith and the rest of Albastine—and might lead Lavinia to make another attempt at storming the Barrows to arrest Khefnar, which would inevitably result in the riot I was working so hard to avoid.

The weight of the schematics lay heavy against my chest. For a moment I was tempted to reveal those documents to Lavinia and Gracchus, to share the good news of the bright future they portended. To let someone else take the burden of their stewardship from me. Wasn't I under enough pressure as it was?

But the foundation of what little trust Lavinia and I had

built was still shaky. And while Gracchus was as committed to the Republic as I was, in his peculiar fashion, he was no visionary—I could not trust that he would not see the creation of artificial Attendants as a threat instead of the opportunity it was.

For the time being, the secret of the schematics and the invention they contained was still mine to safeguard.

"No," I said, the lie leaving a bitter taste on my tongue. "I haven't found anything important."

CHAPTER TWENTY-TWO

I followed Gracchus and Lavinia to the marketplace's southern gate. Beyond the archway a harassed-looking group of magistrates struggled to hold back a crowd of merchants, many of whom were laden with what wares they had been able to grab before those same magistrates had escorted them from the market. No doubt they had already disposed of the three Attendants that had been mutilated in the same fashion as Venaria.

"Coming, Calvus?" Gracchus asked, halting beneath the gated archway. Lavinia drew to a stop beside him. The lantern directly overhead cast both their faces in shadow.

I hesitated, surprised to find myself torn. I wanted very badly to go with them to the place where Titian's life had met its abrupt and untidy end. To find who had killed him, and why.

To avenge him, if I could. Or at the very least to keep the rest of my students from suffering as he had.

My other students. I had not heard from them since sending Drusa back to the Barracks. I could only hope that was a sign that the Adversary's interest in the Acolytes had been limited to Titian, finding him a convenient lackey for their goals.

I took a deep breath before answering Gracchus, wincing at the pain that lanced through my side. Encountering the Attendant that had once been Venaria had been such a shock that I'd practically forgotten about my injured rib.

Reflexively I pressed my hand to my side, felt the sheaf of papers nestled there. Remembered everything they portended.

Duty was not a monolithic thing. My obligation to Titian was important, but so was my duty to my people and their future.

"No, Imperator." I shook my head. "I have...other leads to follow."

"Oh?" Gracchus cocked his head. Shadowed as his face was, I could not see his eyes. "What, precisely?"

"The Sons of Ash." They were the first thing to come to mind. "They're in the city right now. Or at least, some of them are."

"I thought they'd cloistered themselves away," Lavinia said, frowning. "Hiding in the Barrows, with those big metal gates and a few thousand Ayu'li between them and us."

"They had," I admitted. "But a few of them chased me out after I...confronted them. Things got violent."

"I thought that was what you were trying to prevent Magistrate Caprio from doing," Gracchus observed, glancing down at Lavinia.

"I'm *trying* to prevent a riot," I countered, grinding my teeth. "Me getting into an altercation with the Sons is a fair sight different than the magistrates storming our temple during our holy day to arrest a self-proclaimed prophet."

"He's right," Lavinia said, to my surprise. She turned to Gracchus, squaring her shoulders. "Our duty is to uphold order in the city, Imperator. The Barrows is as much a part of Albastine as this marketplace."

Surprise gave way to relief. I could have hugged her, had circumstances been less tense.

Gracchus, however, felt no such solidarity. "I thought you of all people would welcome a chance to confront these Ayu'li extremists, Magistrate."

"I do," she assured him. "But under the right circumstances."

He stared at her for a long moment, then at me. "You've devised a plan, I take it?"

"*We* have," I said, putting the slightest emphasis on the pronoun. I waved over my shoulder, where the amphitheater lay somewhere in the mists. "Bahlanni still plans to lead the Hour of Revelation here, in the marketplace. Khefnar will challenge her for leadership of the Old Faith."

I hesitated, waiting for them to ask precisely how such a challenge would be conducted. If either guessed that the most forbidden Rites lay at the heart of my plan, this would be the moment to voice their suspicions.

To my surprise, neither did. Gracchus and Lavinia merely stared, expectant.

"Bahlanni will win," I continued, hoping I sounded more confident in my wife's success than I felt. "Once she does, the Old Faith is hers again. Khefnar will be discredited, and you can arrest him without provoking a riot."

"It's the perfect place for it," Lavinia said, cutting off whatever Gracchus's response might have been. She gestured at the gate above us. "Three entrances, easily sealed off. No way in or out."

"And no chance of their escape," Gracchus said, rubbing his chin. "You said several of the Sons are at large in the city now?"

"Two," I said, thinking of Tyshett and Shahkti chasing after me. Hupli had followed them out of the Barrows, but had he pursued further? I had not seen and could not recall. "Possibly three."

Gracchus was silent for a moment, apparently deep in contemplation.

Lavinia glanced at me, silently asking if I'd been able to find the mystery Legate. I shook my head as slowly as I could, not wanting the Imperator to catch on to our wordless conversation.

"Very well," he said at last. "Our efforts will be better served if we divide and conquer. Magistrate, with me. There's a warehouse in need of our attention."

Lavinia saluted, fist to her chest. Gracchus turned to me with a curt nod—the most respect he'd ever shown me. "Good hunting, Bellator."

With a whirl of dark robes, he turned and strode into the foggy afternoon, Lavinia hurrying after him. As he reached the magistrates' cordon, he gestured for them to allow the merchants back into the marketplace. The beleaguered magistrates stood aside, and with a chorus of relieved shouting the merchants began streaming through the gates. But many of them remained lingering outside, hoping for a glance at the Attendant standing in the midst of the magistrates, its mutilated face hastily covered by a cloak.

I turned and hastened back through the marketplace, knowing it was only a matter of time before the place filled up with vendors hawking their wares and citizens looking to buy. The Attendants sent by the Adversary as a message would not dampen the spirit of trade; if anything, morbid fascination would draw more people to the marketplace than would otherwise be there. Coupled with the rare public performance of an Ayu'li religious ceremony, I had little doubt that the amphitheater would be completely full by the Hour of Revelation.

Bahlanni, I thought as I hurried through the rows of empty carts and stalls, *you wanted the citizenry to see the Old Faith at work among them. Looks like you'll get your wish. I only hope—*

A movement in the fog was all the warning I received before something hard slammed into my gut. The air fled my lungs and I doubled over, wheezing. Somehow they'd missed my injured ribs, but a second blow caught me between the shoulder blades, knocking me to the ground. Pain shot up my side at the impact.

Letting out a wheezing moan, I rolled aside to avoid the next hit. Something dully metallic slammed into the dirt where my head had been.

I kept rolling until I felt myself bump up against the legs of a vendor's stall. I pulled myself to my feet as Tyshett's hulking form came running at me out of the mists, bronze-tipped staff clenched in both hands like a bat.

I turned, barely managing to duck a swing from Shahkti, who'd crept up on me almost soundlessly. Her own staff slammed against one of the support beams of the vendor's stall with a splintering crack.

I threw myself at Shahkti, ghostfire flaring along my dead arm. Her swing had overbalanced her, and there was nothing to block my fist from colliding with her nose. Another crack split the fog, this one sickeningly wet.

Shahkti cried out in pain, clutching her nose. Blood streamed from between her fingers as I shoved past her, back into the maze of the marketplace. If I could slip into the crowd of returning merchants, I could lose Tyshett and Shahkti—

Another figure stepped from between the market stalls, taller than Shahkti, thinner than Tyshett. A knife glimmered in his hand.

"Akhenkatem," Hupli said, stepping into my path. "I advise you stop—"

I turned, darting between the nearest pair of stalls. Hupli

gave a startled shout and headed after me, but I was already zigzagging through the narrow alleys formed by the close-packed rows of booths. Labored breathing nearby told me that my other pursuers were also closing in.

As I ran, I pulled crates and urns and any other vessel I could lay hands on from the stalls I passed, leaving a cacophony of shattering ceramics and splintering wood in my wake. I was rewarded by muffled grunts and stifled curses from my pursuers.

Judging from the low volume of their voices, they were trying to keep from calling the attention of the merchants filtering back into the marketplace. They had taken a great risk in following me here at all; within the Barrows they were protected, but beyond its confines they could be apprehended and arrested by Lavinia and her magistrates.

They'd come in through the north gate, the sole unguarded entrance, and followed me through the marketplace at a safe distance while I talked with Lavinia and Gracchus, shrouded from view by the mists and ample hiding places.

"Akhenkatem!" Tyshett called, daring to break the silence. She sounded startlingly near at hand. "Don't make us hurt you! All we want is—"

"The schematics," I growled, feeling that the sheaf of papers was still nestled against my heart, impossibly heavy for something so small.

I took a sharp turn, darting between a pair of stalls. One of them sold fresh vegetables, the other little votive statuettes of the Extorani pantheon—miniature replicas of those stone figures lining the Godstreet. I reached out to knock them from their table, but stopped when I found that my hand had settled on Vigilance, her sword and lantern upthrust against the foggy gloom.

I knew whom to entrust the schematics with.

Shouts came from either end of the aisle of stalls as Hupli ran towards me from one side, Tyshett from the other. I leapt over the booth, ignoring the protests of my wounded side. Plaster gods scattered and shattered against the ground, but I was already running. Not north, the way I'd entered the marketplace, but west.

Ahead of me the bridge loomed in the fog, a long stone arch rising over the broad sweep of the unseen river below. Every pounding step and ragged breath brought me closer. As Hupli's and Tyshett's shouts grew fainter, a surge of triumph coursed through me, lending me speed. I was going to beat them to the bridge. I was going to make it—

A lone shadow detached itself from one of the merchant stalls flanking the bridge. Shahkti, her mouth and chest caked with blood, staff gripped tight.

I tried to slow, but I was too close, my momentum carrying me forward even as I dug my heels into the dirt.

Shahkti sneered, teeth startlingly white against blackish blood, and swung the staff.

I raised my left hand. Even its deadened senses were not enough to dull the pain that shot up my arm as the bronze tip connected with my wrist, a dull thwack reverberating in the fog as metal met leather.

The force of it sent me sprawling, feet flying out from under me. For a half second I hung suspended in the air, before a shriek of pain tore from my lips as I hit the dirt. I tried to draw breath, but all I inhaled was pain.

Shahkti loomed over me, her beautiful, bloodied face set in a snarl. Behind us the pounding feet of Hupli and Tyshett drew nearer.

"You should have taken Khefnar's offer," Shahkti said, her voice thick with blood. She raised the staff above her head. I tried to shield my face, but the pain was too great for my injured arm to respond to my commands, its ghostfire extin-guished. All I could do was close my eyes and turn away from the impending blow.

It never came.

Instead, there was the sound of something hard hitting flesh and the crunch of breaking bone. Shahkti let out a cry of pain, and the staff clattered to the dirt beside me.

I opened my eyes in time to see a tall woman with red hair swing a magistrate's baton at Shahkti. Not once but three times, the blows rapid and precise as she struck Shahkti in the arm, the side, the head.

The female Son of Ash swayed on her feet and tried to throw a counterpunch. Her attacker sidestepped it easily, hooked the baton around the back of Shahkti's knee, and twisted. There was a small explosion of dust as Shahkti joined me in the dirt, gasping for air.

"Come on, Cassius." The redheaded woman stood over me, reaching with her free hand. I forced down the pain, channeled my will into my arm, and gripped her living hand with my dead one.

As she pulled me to my feet, the running footsteps abruptly halted. I turned to see Tyshett and Hupli slowing at the sight of their fallen comrade, and us standing over her.

"Come on," my rescuer said, stepping back into a fighting crouch and brandishing the baton. "See if you fare any better."

Tyshett started forward, but Hupli seized her by the wrist. She whirled on him, eyes flashing, but he shook his head.

Voices filtered through the fog—the chatter and clamor of the merchants returning to the marketplace, filing through the maze of stalls to their own booths. Already I could hear shouts of dismay from those whose stands I had wrecked in my attempt to slow my pursuers.

Tyshett turned back to us, Shahkti lying bleeding and

groaning at our feet. The big Ayu'li woman gnashed her teeth, but Hupli's hand remained tight on her wrist. She looked down at him, then back at Shahkti one last time before the two turned and disappeared into the mists.

I waited until I was certain they were gone before turning to my rescuer.

"Cassius," Horatia Aquila said, smiling at me, "let's get you cleaned up."

CHAPTER TWENTY-THREE

"Ow!"

"Stop being such a baby, Calvus," Horatia chided, examining my injured side. "I'd think you were used to the pain by now."

"Evidently not," I hissed as she pressed a finger against my rib, sending a fresh wave of agony blossoming across my side. "Gods!"

We sat in her office, a high-ceilinged room off the Senate rotunda. It was easily three times the size of Lavinia's cramped little office across the street in the Magisterium, though in contrast to many of her Senatorial colleagues, Horatia's taste in interior décor was distinctly spartan. The stool I perched on was the only thing approaching a visitor's chair I could see, implying that Horatia wanted her guests to cycle through with as much alacrity as possible.

"Definitely broken," she noted, withdrawing her hand.

"I could have told you that." I winced. "Are you done playing chirurgeon?"

"That depends."

"On what?"

Horatia pursed her lips. "Whether you're done playing magistrate."

"Look who's talking," I said. "Coming out of the dark swinging that baton like she'd never turned in her badge."

And thank the gods she had. I still wasn't sure if the Sons meant to kill me, but Hupli's choice of weaponry had indicated they weren't opposed to the idea. Thanks to Horatia's timely rescue, he and Tyshett had fled into the night, while Shahkti was cooling her heels in one of the Magisterium's few prison cells.

"What were you doing patrolling the streets with your baton, anyway?" I asked, glancing over at where that weapon hung on a hook beside the door. "Getting nostalgic for the old days?"

"Hardly," Horatia said. "I heard about your Acolyte. The late Senator Candorous's son."

"Oh." My throat constricted.

"Sorry for your loss," she said.

"Thanks." I considered telling her the true circumstances of Titian's death and my complicated feelings regarding the matter.

"I figured you'd be investigating," she continued, saving me from explaining myself. "So I did a little digging. Found out about the sabotaged Attendants last night. When I heard there were more I decided to come see for myself."

"Lucky for me that you did," I said.

"Yes," she agreed, smiling slightly, "lucky you."

I could think of nothing else to say, and we lapsed into an uncomfortable silence.

Growing up, Horatia and I had been as close as brother and sister, and we'd retained that friendship into adulthood. During the period where Bahlanni and I had separated, it had grown into something more, though neither of us had possessed the courage to act upon it. And now that I had returned to my marriage, it was too late to do so.

We had decided to become friends instead, Horatia and I. But the last few months had left us with little time to foster that friendship. As one of the new Senators following the Lightfall Massacre, Horatia had had her hands full keeping the Republic from fraying apart at the seams. Meanwhile I had been preoccupied with recovering from my injuries, and later with growing into my new role as Bellator. We had seen each other only occasionally in the intervening months, and the ground we trod was still uncertain.

A knock at the door, its rhythm dully mechanical, saved us from further awkwardness. Horatia jumped up and hurried over to open it.

An Attendant stood there, bronze mask smiling cheerily. I stared hard at it, trying to discern whether it was the Legate-controlled Attendant that had led me to two separate crime scenes.

There was an easier way to tell, of course. I reached out with my will, just as the Attendant reached its own hands towards Horatia, holding a cloth-wrapped bundle towards her. Something wet and red dripped from it and fell splashing to the tiled floor.

Blood.

I thrust my hand forward, ignoring the bite of pain in my side. Ghostfire flared along my arms, arresting the Attendant's motion as my will pushed into it, meeting no resistance. The bloody bundle stopped an inch from Horatia's hand.

"Cassius?" She glanced over her shoulder, eyebrows raised. "What are you doing?"

This Attendant was under no one's control but my own. I exhaled through my nose, releasing my control as I did so. "Nothing."

Frowning, Horatia plucked the proffered bundle, then turned back to me, dismissing the Attendant with a wave of her hand. It retreated, closing the door behind it.

"You thought it was another message," she said, looking down at the bloodstained cloth. "Like those other Attendants, or your poor apprentice."

I smiled weakly. "Can you blame me?"

"I suppose not. Here."

The bundle was wet but surprisingly firm. I unwrapped it to see that it was no dismembered Acolyte or Attendant, but a half-frozen steak. "I'm not hungry."

"Good," she said, smacking me lightly upside the head. "My office doesn't have a kitchen. It's for your side, dummy."

I pressed the cold slab of meat against my injured rib, the initial discomfort swiftly replaced by a spreading numbness. "I was joking."

"Uh-huh." Horatia leaned against her desk, arms folded across her chest. "And with that Attendant just now?"

I opened my mouth to answer, but was cut off by a sudden hammering at Horatia's door.

"Aquila!" a muffled baritone shouted. "I know you're in there!"

Ghostfire lit the room as I reached out my will, searching for the Attendant that had delivered the steak. It could not have gone far...

"Stop being dramatic," Horatia hissed, putting a hand on my sheathed arm. "There's no danger here. Just politics, which is worse."

I flushed and released my will, the ghostfire dying down to its usual low flicker. Horatia smoothed down the front of her robe and returned to the door, which the knocker seemed to think he could batter down with his fist.

"Senator Aquila!" he shouted. "We need to discuss the—"

She threw open the door. "Logistics of repurposing Attendant soldiers from the Herracian border to civil service. I know, Senator Mithran."

Senator Mithran was revealed to be a short, red-faced Extorani in late middle age, one fist still raised to pound at the door. Caught off guard, he peered past Horatia, brow furrowing at the sight of me. "Then what are you—"

"Doing in conference with Albastine's resident Bellator?" Horatia asked archly. "Addressing the issue, obviously. Who better to help coordinate the transfer of Attendants from front-line service to civic works than a former Legate?"

"I..." Mithran's mouth worked soundlessly as he searched for a diplomatic way to course correct. "I see. Yes. Glad that you're keeping abreast of things."

Horatia gave him the most forced smile I'd ever seen. "That's the job, Senator. We can discuss it more over dinner tonight."

"Yes." Mithran nodded, visibly relieved to be back on solid ground. "Sunset at the Oyster Lodge?"

"Absolutely," Horatia said, her smile growing a touch less forced. "I'll see you then, Julius. Give your husband my love."

She shut the door without waiting for his response and leaned against it, eyes closed.

"Enjoying the new job?" I grinned.

"Not the verb I would use," she said, opening her eyes and strolling over to her desk. "Endless fancy dinners and inane small talk, all while trying to push your projects forward by making deals and compromises you hope won't hamstring your overall agenda further down the line."

"Poor you," I said. "Too many oyster dinners over a bottle of Zantyan red. Eating out every night on the taxpayer's dime—"

Horatia balled up a paper from her desk and threw it at me.

"I can see the headlines now," I said, raising my hands in

mock surrender. "'Senator Assaults Veteran with Projectile—' *Ow!*"

This last as she tossed a stylus at me. It bounced harmlessly off my shoulder to the floor.

"For the record," she said, coming over to retrieve it, "I pay my own way. And so do the rest of the Senators, now. Pushing through a new anti-graft law was one of the first pieces of legislation we voted on after..."

She trailed off, expression growing somber.

"Lightfall," I finished. Horatia nodded.

"I still think about it," she said, her voice carefully level. "The blood and the killing. And I wonder if there was any other way. If we had been faster, or..."

I leaned forward and squeezed her hand, careful to do so with my living one. After a moment she squeezed back.

"Me too," I said quietly. "But we can't, you know? Can't change things."

"I know that." Horatia swallowed. "It's just...by the time I convinced Gracchus of what was happening, you were locked away in Venaria's basement. And even then, when he proposed I take Quintus's place in the Senate, I dragged my feet. Didn't want the responsibility." She gestured around at her office. Minimal as its comforts were, they were still considerably more lavish than what she'd been used to as a magistrate. "You can see how that worked out."

"Horatia," I said, "you took an oath. So did I."

She gave me a humorless smile. "All Serve the People. I know."

"And this is how we serve." I gestured with my dead hand at the office around us. "Neither of us chose the roles we play now, not really. But that doesn't really matter, does it?"

"No." She shook her head and wiped at her eyes with the

back of her hand, though I had seen no tears. "What matters is that we serve as best we can."

"Right," I agreed, reaching into my robes and pulling out the sheaf of papers. "Which brings me to this."

She took them gingerly and opened to the first page. Frowned. "Puppets?"

I shook my head. "More than that."

Horatia paged rapidly through the schematics, eyes widening as she realized their true importance. "These are... gods, Cassius, where did you get this?"

I glanced out the window, gauging the time by the position of the sun. An hour or two past noon, which meant that the next of the Hours of Remembrance was not far off. "How much time do you have?"

"Plenty." Horatia smiled thinly. "I won't lose any sleep over postponing dinner with Julius Mithran."

I barked out a laugh and began.

One thing I had always admired about Horatia was her capacity to absorb information without the need to interject her own thoughts. She listened as I filled her in on everything that had transpired over the last day or so, starting from my last lesson with Titian Candorous. I told her about fleeing the Hour of Rest, the strange Attendant that had led me to the site of the graffiti and mutilations, and my subsequent arrest. Only then did she interrupt.

"Magistrate Caprio?" she asked with narrowed eyes, unable to restrain herself. "Lavinia?"

"A former partner of yours, I hear." Then, because it had been nagging at me: "Can I ask what happened between you two?"

Horatia ran a hand through her auburn curls. "I'd rather not rehash ancient history, Cassius."

"Believe me," I said, thinking of Khefnar's crusade to return the Ayu'li to Ayu, of the solemn commemorations of the Hours of Remembrance, "I empathize."

Sighing, Horatia sat on her desk, looking out the window at the misty city below.

"We were both young," she said. "Deputy magistrates paired together on a beat. Walking the city, writing citations for littering or petty vandalism. That sort of thing."

"And she wanted more?" I guessed.

"We both did." Horatia smiled wryly. "That was the heart of the problem, I think. We were too much alike. Both young and ambitious, without any family ties to the Magisterium to put us ahead." She hesitated. "Or so I thought."

"Ah." No need for her to fill in the details—Horatia was an Aquila, one of the noble families that could trace their lineage all the way back to the ousted ruling class of the Extorani's ruined empire.

In contrast, Caprio was a surname derived from the nomadic goatherds who had lived in the mountains surrounding the Albastine Valley, gradually mingling with and eventually becoming part of the Republic alongside their Extorani cousins. And now that I thought about it, I realized that Lavinia spoke with a carefully neutral accent, the sort cultivated by those attempting to suppress a more rural native speech.

"In hindsight, I probably *did* have it easier than she did," Horatia continued. "But you know what it's like being twenty. The whole world's already out to get you, to prove that you're no good, that you're going to fail at whatever dream you're chasing."

"So when she inevitably accused you of nepotism you got defensive."

"Exactly." Horatia's smile was bitter. "At first it stayed mostly under the surface—sniping at one another, little intimations here and there, that kind of thing. She never said as much, but I knew she thought I'd bought my way into the Magisterium." She plucked at an imaginary speck of dust on her robes. "I was...unkind to her, in my retaliations. Classist, though I didn't realize it at the time."

Between her clash with Horatia and the way her wife had been spurned by her fundamentalist parents, I was beginning to understand Lavinia's combative attitude. "Did things ever come to a head?"

"Naturally," Horatia snorted. "We were tracking a smuggling ring bringing goods in and out of the city. We'd gotten ahold of one of their suppliers, squeezed until he told us their route and schedule. I wanted to plan an ambush, but Lavinia insisted on arresting the supplier then and there. She thought we could nab him and the smugglers at once if we moved fast enough."

"But you didn't."

"No." Horatia drummed her fingers against the desk. "The smugglers smelled that something was off and scattered to the winds. Best we could do was retroactively pronounce them exiled. But that was like closing the door of a burning house behind you."

"So what happened with you and Lavinia?"

Horatia barked a short, humorless laugh. "Things got ugly. Physical. Afterwards we were both placed on administrative leave for a week."

"I'm guessing you weren't partnered together after that."

Horatia shook her head, auburn curls bouncing. "Assigned different beats as soon as our leave was up. Better for both of us, really."

"I don't doubt it," I said. "Do you think we can trust her?"

"You're asking this about a woman who's struck both of us," Horatia said, but her frown was one of consideration.

"She's headstrong and ambitious and more than a little reckless."

"You forgot overconfident."

"That too." Horatia's gaze traveled to the window, to the white spires rising from the fog, the afternoon sun painting the whole valley gold. "But she's got integrity. Believes in the law enough not to break it, even when it'd be to her advantage to do so. Honorable, in her own way."

"That'll have to be enough," I said, and proceeded to tell her the rest of the story. Of Gracchus's intervention and "request" that I assist Lavinia with her investigation into the Sons of Ash. Of my initial refusal and the subsequent appearance of Khefnar and his disciples at the Hour of Refuge. Of Hupli's betrayal and the gravesight he should never have attempted.

"You don't think he's the one behind that Attendant?"

I shook my head. "Different disciplines. Just because he learned one ancient secret doesn't mean he could control an Attendant with that level of precision. I mean, it practically moved like it was alive."

"But there is someone out there," she pressed. "Someone controlling this Attendant. Why?"

"I don't know," I admitted, frustration creeping into my voice. "Whoever it is, they're not working with the Sons. They wouldn't lead me to the sabotaged Attendants. And Lavinia and I both encountered that Attendant later on, and it led us to another body. An Ayu'li, but not one of the faithful. The Attendant told us that that murder had been done by one of the ashmarked."

Horatia's eyes widened. "It spoke?"

"Of course not. We played charades with whoever was behind it."

Horatia laughed another mirthless laugh. "So, both times you've seen this Attendant it's been pointing to the Sons of Ash as the culprits. And so far I haven't heard any compelling reason to think otherwise."

"You're about to." I told her about Titian's murder, what I had seen in his gravesight, and the Adversary.

"And you don't have any idea who it could be?"

"Someone influential." I shrugged. "They promised Titian that they could restore his mother's senatorial seat to him, even if it required the laws prohibiting Legates from taking office to be rewritten."

Horatia snorted. "That kind of resolution would never make it to the Senate floor."

"I know that." But I had been thinking hard on that very issue. "But maybe Titian didn't."

"Meaning?"

"Meaning that it didn't really matter whether or not they could get that legislation passed," I said, "only that Titian believed they could."

"Right." Horatia chewed her lip. "What's the point to all this, though? If the Adversary is so opposed to these Sons of Ash, why not just wait for the Magisterium to forcibly eject them from Albastine? Why go to the trouble of perpetrating all these crimes in their name?"

"Because it's not just about the Sons of Ash," I said, reaching up my living hand to brush the ash painted across my brow. "It's about the Ayu'li."

Horatia caught on quick. "There are more of you in the Senate now than at any other point in history."

"And more of those are adherents of the Old Faith than before, too." I stood, careful to keep the thawing steak pressed against my side, and moved to the window, looking out at the city spread out below. "We're in the middle of a cultural resurgence, Horatia. One Bahlanni's striving to take full advantage of, by sharing our religion with the rest of Albastine instead of keeping it locked behind bronze gates. One the Adversary feels threatened by."

"So our Adversary is Khefnar's opposite number," Horatia concluded. "An Extorani who resents the changing status quo."

"Entrenched powers always have the most to fear from upheaval," I agreed. "Which brings us to those schematics."

The schematics Horatia still held in her hands, as though afraid they'd go up in smoke as soon as she let go of them. I swiftly filled her in on how I had acquired them from Laurent and my subsequent flight from the Barrows, followed by my time in the marketplace.

"...and then you showed up and chased them off," I finished, turning back from the window to face her.

Whatever I'd been about to say next died on my lips. Horatia's already fair complexion had turned pale beneath her freckles.

"What is it?" I asked.

She looked down at the schematics. "You said his name was Laurent? Laurent Ignatus?"

The sun through the windows had warmed my back, but not enough to stop a chill from creeping down my spine. I hadn't told her Laurent's surname.

"That's right," I said, mouth dry. "How did you know?"

Horatia looked at the papers, then back at me. "He's one of the smugglers Lavinia and I apprehended, all those years ago."

"That's why he was away from Albastine," I said, feeling foolish for not realizing it previously. "He was exiled."

Another, more disturbing thought. "How was it that these smugglers were bringing goods into the city?"

Horatia joined me at the window, looking out at the white-capped mountain peaks on the far side of the valley. "They were using an old goat trail. Narrow little path winding through the mountains. Very dangerous, but smugglers aren't exactly risk-averse by nature. We collapsed the trail after they fled, but…"

"Any smuggler worth their salt has more than one route," I finished, following the train of thought where it led. "That's how the Sons of Ash snuck into the valley undetected. Laurent brought them in through one of his old routes, one you hadn't found."

"Which means our mystery Legate could have done the same," Horatia said. "Unless…"

She looked at me, and I saw we had come to the same realization at the same time.

"Unless Laurent *is* our mystery Legate," I said, the pieces of the puzzle falling into place. Laurent had been close to my grandfather. He had no doubt seen him perform the Rites many times, and while I doubted Grandfather had ever formally trained his old friend, Laurent might have picked up enough rudiments of the Art to approximate it. And if he had spent years in Ayu learning more esoteric Rites, was it such a leap that he had learned to fully embody his will into an Attendant?

"But if that's the case…" Horatia began.

I completed the thought. "Then Laurent's a double agent."

PART FIVE
RUIN

CHAPTER TWENTY-FOUR

"Say Laurent *is* working for the Adversary," Horatia said. "He would have given them advance notice of Khefnar's return to Albastine. That explains both the timing of the dismembered Attendants and the one that led you to them."

"Further evidence that this was always a setup," I said, leaving the window to pace Horatia's office. I'd always thought better while in motion. "Hell, the Adversary might have *lured* the Sons of Ash here."

Horatia frowned. "Why?"

"Instigation." I ran my hand along her desk. "Say you come from an old Extorani family whose proud history dates back to before the Republic, with all the wealth and influence that entails. You've never had to question your station in life, because you've always been on top."

"I'll try to imagine," Horatia said drily.

"Then at Lightfall," I continued, "all of that's upended when two-thirds of the Senate is killed, alongside all three Triarchs. Only the Old Faith Ayu'li's intervention saved the day. Now they've risen to new prominence in the Republic, with their leaders pushing for greater recognition of their religious rituals."

"The same rituals whose performance conflicts with one of the most basic tenets of our society," Horatia said. "If you're the Adversary, the only way to reverse their progress is to villainize them."

"By bringing in an extremist faction," I said, pacing the perimeter of her office. "You reach out to your man on the inside—Laurent—and tell him to bring Khefnar and his disciples back to the city. Probably you tempt Laurent with a pardon, the same way you promised Titian his mother's seat."

"Laurent and the Sons of Ash return to Albastine," Horatia said, picking up where I'd left off. "Khefnar's already got his own man on the inside in the form of Hupli, who he must have reached out to in secret before their return."

"Right. They come back at the Hours of Remembrance, and Khefnar whips the Old Faith into a frenzy with his proposed crusade back to Ayu. Just as the Adversary was hoping he would. Meanwhile, Attendants are being dismembered all over the city, with evidence pointing towards the Sons of Ash. So once the Old Faith emerge from the Barrows to perform the Hour of Revelation in public…"

"They're not a respected minority sharing their culture," Horatia said. "They're a cult full of zealots. Or at least that's how the Adversary's hoping they'll be seen."

"Exactly." I nodded. "The Adversary's already laid the kindling for the city to burst into fear. All they need to do now is light it."

"There's one thing I don't understand," Horatia said. "Say we're right, and this Adversary is some reactionary fighting to return the Republic to its old status quo. Why send Laurent with the schematics to make an artificial Attendant?"

That *was* a significant wrench in the theory. Laurent had

claimed he needed a Legate's investiture of will to complete the creation of his artificial Attendant. But if he *was* a Legate –in ability if not in title—then he would have already done so, and my participation was unnecessary.

Which meant that he had *wanted* me to see the artificial Attendant.

"What was he smuggling?" I asked. "Back when you and Lavinia tried to apprehend him."

Horatia twirled a ringlet around her finger, thinking. "Fresh fruit," she said after a moment.

"Not exactly contraband," I said, a smile tugging at the corner of my mouth.

"Spoken like someone who hasn't had to worry about how high import duties are," Horatia said, sounding for the moment very like the senator she was. "Laurent and his gang specialized in evading exactly those taxes."

"What kind of fruit?"

"All kinds." She thought another moment. "But they had a special fondness for persimmons, I recall."

I laughed. Albastine's high, cold climate was less than ideal for cultivating most fruits, making them a coveted delicacy. But persimmons had grown abundantly in Ayu and were found in many a traditional dish among the Old Faith.

"What's so funny?" Horatia asked.

"He's devout," I said. "Laurent's adherence to the Old Faith is real."

She scratched the back of her head. "Why go along with the Adversary's plan, then?"

"Because Laurent has his own agenda." I pointed at the sheaf of papers in Horatia's hands. "The Adversary doesn't know about those or the marionette back in the Barrows. Laurent *meant* for me to get ahold of the schematics, but he had to do it in a way that wouldn't arouse suspicion from the other

Sons or alert the Adversary to what he was doing. He pulled it off, and now here we are: in possession of a set of designs that will free Albastine from its reliance on the Attendants forever."

"He outplayed the Adversary at their own game." Horatia's tone was one of grudging respect. She looked down at the papers, leafing through them again as if to reassure herself that they were real. "But that only solves our future problems. Khefnar's still set on leading the Old Faith out of Albastine."

"Which will only happen if he and Bahlanni successfully perform the Rite of Awakening."

"And if the spirits of your ancestors align themselves with him over your wife." She chewed her lip, hesitating. "Who do you think they'll choose?"

"I wish I knew," I said, pinching the bridge of my nose. "Honestly. Bahlanni's a good leader. She's served our people with wisdom and grace for years. But Khefnar promises a return to Ayu, and that's..."

I shook my head, struggling for some apt comparison. The Extorani grieved little for their deposed empire or their lost homeland.

"Holy," Horatia said softly.

I nodded. "I suppose it doesn't matter. I've gotten Gracchus and Lavinia to agree to hold off on apprehending Khefnar until after the ceremony, but once the magistrates realize that it's the Rite of Awakening, they'll both be arrested. The only question is whether the ancestors will have taken a side before that happens. If it's Bahlanni, the faithful will stand down when she tells them to. But if the spirits choose Khefnar, and he orders them to resist..."

"It'll be a bloodbath," Horatia said.

"Unless..." I paused in my pacing as an idea took shape. "Who's commandant of the Magisterium now?"

"Severna Raffine," Horatia answered immediately.

"What's she like?"

"Very grounded. Apolitical."

"How much sway do you have with her?"

Horatia's eyes narrowed. "What are you asking, Cassius?"

"Nothing too drastic," I lied. "Gracchus and Lavinia have already promised to delay sending their magistrates into the marketplace to arrest Khefnar until after the Hour of Revelation concludes. I just want you to talk to Raffine and make sure she holds to that."

"That's no small ask."

"But an important one," I countered. "Can you do it?"

Horatia's eyes roved about her office, settling on the one personal effect that graced its otherwise austere confines: a marble bust beside the door, carved in the likeness of her late brother and my best friend, Quintus. This had been his office, once. Before he had died in my arms on a distant battlefield, fighting to defend the Republic.

"I'll have to call in a few favors," Horatia said, "but I can make sure that Raffine holds the magistrates back regardless of what Gracchus and Lavinia might say."

I let out a breath I hadn't realized I'd been holding. "Thank you."

"Of course. Now..." Horatia crossed to the far corner of the room, to a heavy ironwood chest with dark metal clasps. She drew a key from her robe, unlocked it, and placed the schematics inside.

"They'll be safe in there?" I asked.

"Safer than anywhere else in the Republic," she said, closing the lid with a heavy *thunk*. "It's fireproof and damn near unbreakable. You could swing an axe at this thing and it'd bounce off."

"Anyone else have a copy of that key?" I asked as she turned it in the lock.

"Only me," Horatia said, returning it to her pocket. She glanced out the window. While we'd talked the day had drawn on to late afternoon. "The Hour of Revelation is at sunset, right?"

"Correct," I said, following her gaze. We were closing in on the Hour of Ruin, the time of fasting and symbolic destruction meant to evoke the Ayu'li's losses in the wake of Reckoning.

"That doesn't leave a lot of time." She frowned. "If I'm going to grease the palms I need to in order to get Raffine to cooperate, I should get started yesterday."

"Of course," I said, feeling a well of guilt rising inside me. Horatia's duties as Senator were multitude, and I had just taken up hours of her day. "I should leave you to it."

"Where are you going?" she said as we both moved to the door. "You need rest, Cassius. Especially with that rib."

"That Hour's already passed," I said, shaking my head. "I need to confront Laurent."

She glanced down at me, brows raised. "After he and his friends chased you from the Barrows, pushed you down a mountain, and then tried to murder you in the marketplace?"

"No one pushed me," I protested. "I jumped."

"Not helping your case," she said, hand on the doorknob.

"Listen," I said, putting my hand over hers. My deadened hand so that I could not feel the warmth of her fingers beneath mine. Horatia flinched but did not pull away. "Whatever the Adversary's planning for the Hour of Revelation, I doubt it's as simple as pointing the magistrates at the Ayu'li and hoping a riot breaks out. If the dismemberments and murders are any indicator, they'll want to help things along."

Horatia pursed her lips and gave a grudging nod for me to continue.

"Laurent knows who the Adversary is," I continued. "Or at least has been in contact with them, somehow. If nothing else, he can point me in the right direction. *Especially* if he's actually working against them."

"And that's the easiest way to discover the Adversary's identity?" Horatia's eyebrows were threatening to disappear into her hairline.

"Can you think of a better one?"

"Yes, actually." She turned the doorknob. I didn't stop her. "You're a Legate, Calvus. Every Attendant in the city is yours to command, if you focus hard enough."

It took me a moment to realize what she was implying. When I did, it hit me like a fallen statue.

"You think there'll be more mutilations."

Horatia nodded approvingly. "And if you pour your will into enough Attendants quickly enough, you might catch them in the act."

"I..." What she was suggesting was possible, but only barely. There were thousands of Attendants within the city at any given time, spread over an area of miles. I had never extended my reach so far, or into so many Attendants at once.

"You can do it, Cassius," Horatia said, squeezing my shoulder, careful to touch the one that wasn't bound in leather. "Think of it as gravesight in reverse."

That forced an uneasy laugh from me. "How do you figure?"

"You're looking out from the eyes of the dead to see the present." She glanced over her shoulder at the window. "I really do have to go."

"Of course." I removed my hand from hers and stepped out of the way so that she could leave.

Horatia sidled past me, looked over her shoulder. "Stay safe, Cassius."

"You too."

She gave me a last smile I couldn't quite read, then closed the door. I waited until I heard her footsteps retreating down the hall before I moved to the window, looking down at my city.

A year ago I would have said that what Horatia was suggesting was beyond the capabilities of any Legate, but that was before I had met Tycho Terrens.

Terrens had been close to a hundred, blind and infirm, dwelling in isolation within the dusty depths of his familial estate. Or so I had thought upon first meeting. In reality he had honed the Rites all throughout his retirement, refining his control over his household Attendants until he could pour his will into all of them simultaneously, a single mind with many bodies.

This ability had not been limited by distance or to those specific Attendants. Terrens had seized control of another Attendant shortly after my first encounter with him, and he'd used it to murder Commandant Nestoris, Horatia's former superior. That killing had occurred in the Magisterium, halfway down the valley from the Terrens estate.

Terrens had been killed in turn by his coconspirators not long after, but his very mode of existence had forced me to reexamine the limits of what the Legate's Art could accomplish. Over the last six months I had steadily worked at pushing my own capabilities, extending my will over progressively greater distances—first simply to see how far out I could sense the presence of Attendants, then, as I grew more comfortable exploring those limitations, to control them.

That had been practice. This was the real thing—the chance to discover where the limits of my powers truly lay. But the attempt would not be without risk; Tycho Terrens had been quietly mad by the time I'd met him.

I closed my eyes and felt the warmth of the sun on my face, magnified by the glass. A wave of fatigue washed over me, as if momentum alone had been carrying me forward ever since I'd fled the Hour of Rest.

My stomach growled, and I wondered when I had last eaten. Not since my predawn breakfast before the Hour of Refuge, when everything had gone so wrong.

A meal followed by a long nap were the only things I wanted at that moment, but they were as far beyond my reach as the sun peering through the window. Soon it would set, and the Hour of Revelation would come. When it had passed, the fate of my people would be decided.

I opened my eyes and turned from the window, heading for the door. My aches and bruises protested every step, but I fought down the pain and held the thawing bundle of steak close to my side.

Rest could wait.

CHAPTER TWENTY-FIVE

The slender architecture of Albastine's mist-shrouded spires was regarded the world over with as much admiration and envy as our Attendants were with fear and mistrust. Even before settling in the valley, the Extorani at the height of their empire had been master stonemasons, and they'd long since devised an alchemical process to help strengthen stone that would otherwise make for poor building materials. As the Albastine Valley was rich in limestone but little else, it swiftly became the trademark building material of the burgeoning Republic, giving us our most famous sobriquet: the Pale City.

Or, I reflected as I made my way between white buildings shrouded in gray mist, *maybe that's just because of the fog.*

Due to the spatial limitations of living in a narrow mountain valley, our forefathers had built upwards instead of out, giving Albastine's architecture its characteristic spires. A popular misconception bandied about in other nations was that ours was the only city taller than it was long. Ludicrous, of course, but the considerable height and narrow breadth of the many towers certainly gave that impression.

I was making my way towards one of the most famous of those, an edifice dating back to the second century of our settlement, popularly known as the Mushroom due to its domed cap. It had other, less flattering names, of course.

It was not the tallest of the Pale City's spires. Rather, its significance lay in its location: as close as possible to the valley's geographic center, with the view from its bulbous dome commanding most of the city, making it an ideal place for what I was about to attempt.

There were more people treading the cobblestone streets than there had been earlier in the day, but few of them walked alone. Instead, they hurried about in pairs or small groups, huddled together against the fog. Here and there I caught someone looking sidelong at me, their gaze invariably drawn to the ghostfire flames shining through the cracks in my leather sleeve. Or—more distressing—to the ash smeared across my brow. Evidently, despite the Magisterium's best efforts, word had spread through the city about the mutilations and the apparent connection between those crimes and the more extreme members of the Old Faith.

We're the same, I wanted to tell them. *Ayu'li or Extorani, it makes no difference. Before anything else, we are citizens of the Republic.*

Yet how could I protest that when the Attendants we relied upon were being dismembered? When their fellow citizens were being murdered and dire warnings splashed across the walls of their city?

Guilt settled uneasily in my gut. If I was to restore these people's faith in their Ayu'li brethren, I would have to do it tonight.

Like most of Albastine's towers, the Mushroom was primarily a residential structure, each floor belonging to a particular family. Typically the topmost floors were reserved as a common space for the residents, but due to its centrality and impressive view, the Mushroom's domed upper level was open to the public. From there I could find a quiet spot to perform the Rite of Communion, pouring my will into as many Attendants as possible, as rapidly as I could.

There was only one problem.

"Godsdamned stairs," I muttered as I struggled up the narrow, winding spiral staircase at the tower's heart. Ordinarily I could have climbed to the top and broken only a mild sweat, but that would have been on a day I didn't suffer from a broken rib, painfully little sleep, and an empty belly to boot. Instead, I clung tightly to the railing, halfway pulling myself up each step. By the time I reached the topmost floor I was drenched in my own sweat, my legs aching. The raw steak I still held against my side had thawed completely, leaving a trail of blood spattered across the staircase.

They'll get an Attendant to clean that up, I thought as I surmounted the final step at last, onto the tower's uppermost floor.

A ray of sunlight stabbed at my eyes. I raised both hands to shield them, blinking sunspots from my vision. By the time I did, a merciful cloud had hidden the sun from view, and I found myself looking out upon a vista so spectacular that for a moment all the pains of my body and heart were forgotten.

Beyond the tall windows stretching from the floor to the dome, the Pale City lay spread out beneath me. The valley mists were a golden cloud below, roiling and spreading gently as the currents of air shifted and churned. The white marble towers that rose from the mist were painted fiery reds and oranges by the lowering sun, making them look less like skeletal digits and more like frozen flames.

"Albastine in ashes," I murmured, imagining real flames licking the sides of those stately spires, the fog below turned to smoke. A vision inconceivable in its horror, yet all too plausible, as events appeared set to spiral out of control.

Unless I stopped them.

I turned so that the sun was no longer directly in my eyes, stepping gingerly across the open floor to another window. To my immense relief, the Mushroom's top floor was wholly unoccupied. No one there to witness me in my exhaustion as I leaned against the window frame, staring down at the mist-shrouded city.

I stood there, swaying, as I focused on my breathing. Deep breaths, in and out. Just as I'd instructed Titian, in the last lesson he had failed to learn. Fresh guilt stabbed through me, though perhaps it was merely the stitch in my side or the trouble of breathing with a broken rib.

"No time for that now," I told myself, and was relieved that I could say the words without wheezing.

Dwelling on the past would do no one any good, Titian least of all. Yet I found myself thinking back on that final lesson all the same.

Inhale strength, I had said. *Exhale power.*

I closed my eyes, feeling the sun against my face, and breathed in deep, imagining that the air itself was strength gathering in my lungs.

The Body Walks, I thought, and breathed out power as I moved into the opening steps of the kata.

The command gestures, kata, and Rites passed down from Legate to Acolyte comprised a highly structured, regimented system. Each motion had a specific purpose, either as a physical shorthand to issue simple commands to an Attendant, or as an exercise of deeper control, allowing us to impose our wills on those Attendants directly. As our military doctrine was wholly reliant upon Attendant infantry, Legates past had designed these systems to be rigid and inflexible, permitting no variation from the learned maneuvers.

But before there had been Legates, there had been priests. And before there had been Rites or gestures of command, there had been funerary dances.

So I danced.

I began with The Body Walks, the steps of the kata comfortably familiar, as natural to me as walking. Once I reached its end I flowed smoothly into the next kata in the sequence, The Oxen Labors.

There were thirty kata in the Acolytes' curriculum. I moved through them all, sometimes with eyes open, sometimes closed. My side still ached, but I felt the pain only distantly, focusing instead upon my movements as they flowed from kata into dance. I deviated from the rigid structures of the Rites, incorporating more baroque motions from the celebrations of the Hours, adding in hand movements and steps from the funeral dirges we had carried from Old Ayu.

Each step became an expression of myself: Ayu'li and Legate, citizen of the Republic and adherent of the Old Faith. There was no contradiction in my identity, for none of my facets could amount to my whole being. They were the roots from which the tree of my life sprang, grounding me in the overlapping virtues they exalted: duty and honor, loyalty and sacrifice.

Ghostfire flared along my arms, but as I danced it spread over my body: down my legs, across my chest, and up my neck, crowning me with a wreath of spectral flames. If anyone had been there to see me I would have looked like a fiery phantasm dancing in the empty tower. But I was alone, with my fears, my doubts, my regrets. I banished them all, one by one, building up my power and will with every breath.

I took a step, raised both hands in a posture of supplication, and extended my will.

There was a rushing sensation—not falling, but rising, as though I were being lifted from the earth by a cord. Though my body remained where it was in the dome atop the Mushroom, my will soared through the city. I sensed the Attendants in their thousands, their alchemically treated bodies shining in my mind's eye like beacons in the night.

Previously, the maximum distance I could extend my will in search of Attendants to control was half a mile, but over the past six months I had steadily tested the limit of my powers, pushing myself until I could reach considerably further, though it was a strain to do so. Located at the approximate geographic heart of Albastine, the Mushroom provided me the greatest reach to extend my will in search of any Attendants currently being sabotaged by our Adversary.

I dove into the nearest of the Attendants with a sensation of vertigo followed by a gentle halt, as though I had fallen backwards and landed upon a pliant mattress. My will was fully embodied within the Attendant, which was busily engaged in washing one of the windows several floors below me. I moved its hands as though they were my own, watched from behind its mask as it froze mid-scrub, suds dripping down the glass.

I wanted to laugh, and perhaps I did. My will was disconnected from my body, my consciousness resting within the empty vessel of the Attendant. I untethered myself from it, seeking out another. This one was also in the Mushroom, in one of the residences. I pushed my will into it, found myself mechanically mopping the floor of a cramped kitchen. Sound filtered through the Attendant's dead ears, vague and distorted —though not enough to disguise the moans and sighs emanating from the next room.

I exited that Attendant posthaste.

As swift as thought I became an untethered will once more,

floating over Albastine. Attendants dotted the valley below like stars, each one a light crying for my attention.

Obviously neither of those first two was being assaulted by the Adversary. But ancestors willing, I would find the ones which were.

My consciousness dove into another Attendant, this one shoveling nightsoil into a cart. I was instantly struck by overwhelming nausea, making me thankful not to be in my own body. I fled that Attendant nearly as swiftly as I had the previous one, wondering what the point was of restoring the Attendants' sense of smell to their bodies alongside sight and hearing.

And another, and another, and another. Couriers, cleaners, builders, servants. Working the city's elegant spires or trudging her narrow alleyways, threading through the throngs of merchants and shoppers in the marketplace or laboring in the fields at the valley's southern end.

At first I tried to take note of where each Attendant was, what they were doing. But I swiftly realized that doing so was a waste of time; there was no way I could check them all for signs of the Adversary's presence at this rate. Instead, I sped through them, my consciousness flitting from body to body, inhabiting each just long enough to verify that they weren't what I sought. The result was a dizzying kaleidoscope of sensations, images and sounds and scenes flickering past at a rate too fast to comprehend.

If I'd had time for introspection, I might have worried what effect this detachment of mind from body was having on me, or what leaping from one vessel to the next was doing to my sense of self. But I had neither the time nor the energy to focus on such doubts.

I could not say how long I spent in that strange limbo space jumping from one Attendant to the next, nor whether my battered body continued to dance as my mind wandered. It might have been minutes or hours; it felt like an eternity.

Until, without warning or preamble, I found what I was looking for.

I was staring down at my hand. Except that it was not my hand, but the gray hand of an Attendant. I tried to lift it, but succeeded only in raising my forearm. The hand, severed just below the wrist, lay flat and lifeless upon a wooden table.

"What in the hells?" a familiar voice breathed.

I turned—or rather, the Attendant whose body I had commandeered turned. Through its lifeless eyes I gazed out from behind the bronze mask, into a face I knew well. A face over which an expression of horror and realization had begun to dawn.

"Oh, gods," Drusa swore. "Bellator Calvus?"

CHAPTER TWENTY-SIX

"Drusa?" I tried to say, but no sound came from the Attendant's mummified vocal cords.

"Shit." Drusa backed away, knife in hand. "Shit, shit, *shit.*"

I reached for her with the Attendant's remaining hand. She slashed wildly, missing by several inches. I urged the Attendant forward, raising the stump of its other hand to ward off her backswing. This time her knife carved a gash down the Attendant's forearm, but the wound drew neither blood nor pain.

Drusa's eyes were wide and wild with fear as she thrust the blade at me. I caught it between the Attendant's fingers, wrenched it from her grasp. She stumbled away as I sent the Attendant towards her.

We were in a warehouse, thick with the same acrid smell of oil as the one Lavinia and Gracchus had gone to investigate. But it could not be the same one, for one wall lay open to the river-front, letting in fog from the Providens. Several small boats used for carrying goods up and down the river lay moored inside, empty of cargo.

Drusa was backing towards those boats, pulling down

stacks of pallets after her to slow my Attendant's pursuit, just as I had done to hinder Hupli and Tyshett not long ago. Despite her evident betrayal, I had to admire my onetime Acolyte's resourcefulness. The Attendant I'd embodied moved slowly and could not swim. If Drusa unmoored a boat she would easily escape.

I withdrew my will fractionally, just enough that my senses were no longer fully intertwined with the Attendant's. Immediately the warehouse lit up with the presence of nearly a dozen other Attendants, each a beacon to my untethered mind.

For a moment I hesitated, daunted by the thought of what I was about to attempt. But the stakes were too high for such doubts. I banished them and poured my will into every Attendant in the warehouse.

My senses fractured as I took in the scene from a dozen pairs of eyes, heard Drusa's panting breaths and the lapping of water against wood through a dozen pairs of ears. The dizzying flood of sensation was not wholly unfamiliar. I had first experienced it when diving into Tycho Terrens's memories to view the world as he did: a blind man using his Attendants as his eyes. And again at Lightfall, when I had poured my will into my small army of Attendants, defending the Senate with dozens of bodies when my own would not suffice.

It took me only a moment to reorient, but that was long enough for Drusa to reach the nearest of the boats moored to the warehouse. Her trembling fingers fumbled at the ropes tying the craft to the wooden pylons.

I sent the Attendants after her. All of them.

Wooden floorboards creaked as unliving bodies surged towards her from every corner of the building. Drusa's gasp echoed through the warehouse, the moorings slipping from her fingers as looming shadows stumbled towards her from the gloom. Her hand fell to her side as they bore down on her, each closing in from a different angle. Dismay flickered over Drusa's face as she remembered that I had deprived her of her only weapon.

Even then, she did not surrender without a fight. A strange admixture of annoyance and grudging pride coursed through me as she closed her eyes, centering herself. She took in a deep breath of the misty air, just as I had taught her, and made a gesture of command to the nearest of my Attendants.

To my surprise I felt it: a sensation like a sharp tug, insistent and unignorable. But my will was stronger than hers. I shrugged her off with little effort, and my Attendants' forward march continued unabated.

Drusa's eyes opened wide, her face going pale as she saw that her last attempt had failed. She turned away from the Attendants' reaching hands, poised to throw herself into the boat.

I would not permit her to escape so easily.

The first and nearest of my Attendants seized her wrist with its single hand. She struggled, trying to wrench free, but her adolescent strength was no match for the iron vice of the dead man's hand.

The other Attendants closed in, turning Drusa's struggles more frantic, more violent. She clawed at the one holding her with her free hand, her raking nails scoring bloodless gouges down its arms, across its neck. Impervious to pain, my dead grip did not loosen.

More unliving hands groped for her, finding purchase in her robes, stiff fingers clawing hooks into her garments. Drusa shrieked and struggled, but the sheer weight of the bodies pressing in on her bore her down, pinning her to the floor of the warehouse.

Controlling so many Attendants at once was taxing, but I had no time to worry about what strain such extended effort might be taking on my own body. I forced myself to think of each Attendant as one of my fingers, each separate but working in concert towards a single end.

Namely, restraining my traitorous pupil.

Several minutes and a considerable amount of effort later, Drusa sat on a wooden cable drum in the center of the warehouse, her arms bound securely to her sides at the elbows and wrists with some spare mooring rope I had found coiled in a corner. Her legs were similarly bound.

I felt a touch of perverse pride as I surveyed my handiwork through a dozen viewpoints. Attendants were not as dexterous as the living; the alchemical treatments that fortified their dead flesh against the ravages of necrosis also stiffened their joints. Tying Drusa up had required fully half the Attendants I was possessing to hold her down while the remainder fumbled with the ropes. The resulting knotwork would have made any professional boatman hang his head in shame, but the fact that I had been able to successfully bind her at all was a testament to both my growing finesse and my wearied patience.

"If you're going to kill me," Drusa panted, thrusting her chin at the nearest Attendant, "just do it."

I'd left her ungagged; this close to the marketplace, crying out for help would only lead the citizenry of Albastine to investigate, rather than the Adversary she was working for.

Besides. I needed her to be able to speak.

"What are you waiting for?" she demanded, looking around at the Attendants crowding around her. I was reasonably certain that the knots I'd tied were sufficient to hold her for now, but if she managed to loosen them I'd need all hands to restrain her again. "You found me. I'm the one who's been cutting up the Attendants. That's what you want, right? A confession?"

I focused in on the Attendant standing directly before her,

the same one she'd been in the process of dismembering. I made it shake its head, slowly and deliberately.

"You don't want a confession?" Drusa looked skeptical.

Another shake of my Attendant's head. Drusa's nostrils flared in frustration as she tried to puzzle out whether that meant no, I didn't want a confession, or the opposite.

Fortunately, I had learned from the frustrating game of charades with Laurent's Attendant.

Another Attendant approached and held up a slate in front of its chest. The one-handed one took a piece of chalk from a third Attendant, and at my command, it slowly scratched a single word onto the slate.

WHY?

Comprehension dawned. "Why'd I do it?"

My Attendant nodded.

"Because you're a good teacher."

That caught me off guard. My Attendant cocked its head to the side, expectant—a reflexive motion, not one I had consciously meant for it to perform. Silently I chastised myself for allowing my own actions to seep into the Attendant's. No good could come from blurring the lines between my body and theirs.

"Because I believe you when you talk about our duty to the Republic," Drusa continued, licking her lips. "About how everything we do should be to uphold its traditions, its democratic systems. Its laws."

I waved the Attendant's stump at her.

"Heh." Drusa laughed wanly. "Right. You remember one of the first things you ever taught us about tactics? That sometimes it's necessary to sacrifice a squadron to save a platoon? Same thing. To save the Republic I had to break some of its laws."

I wiped the slate clean with an Attendant's sleeve and scratched out a new question.

FROM WHAT?

"From you." Drusa's eyes narrowed. "From your wife, specifically. And the Sons of Ash and their sympathizers, and everyone else who follows the Old Faith."

I'd never heard her spit out words with such venom before. My knee-jerk reaction was to protest, to counter that we Ayu'li and our religion had been as responsible for the Republic's foundation as the Extorani and their ordered society, that we could not be separated from one another. But I could not speak, and those thoughts were too complex to articulate through a chalkboard.

And Drusa was not done.

"I told you when I snuck into the Hour of Refuge that I don't follow the Old Faith," she reminded me. Now that I had gotten her talking she seemed unwilling to stop. "None of my family have since my great-grandmother. They worship the Extorani pantheon on my dad's side. Gods that don't tie you forever to a past you can't escape from. A past that's constantly threatening to drag you and everything you care about down with it."

I chalked a new question. HOW?

"Look around, Bellator." She nodded at the Attendants surrounding her. "Albastine *needs* the Attendants. They're the core of who we are. Not gods, not ancestors, not even democracy. When people think of the Republic, they think of Attendants. Of the one nation in the world too frugal to waste their dead. But your religion will not stop until you've put them all back into the Barrows, more useless than the ones I've cut up."

There was a confessional tone beneath her anger. I wondered how long Drusa had held these feelings. When had the Adversary first learned she'd harbored such resentments, as Titian had?

They had both been my students, and both the Adversary's pawns. I had failed them spectacularly, but there was no time to dwell on that now. Guilt would uncover none of the answers I sought.

I scribbled a name on the slate. Drusa's bravado crumbled, and she cast her eyes downward.

"Titian," she murmured. "I...Bellator, I...I didn't know. Didn't know that he was going to do...that..."

At my behest the Attendant made a cutting motion across its throat. Drusa nodded, tears shaking free from her eyes.

"He said that Titian had been too obvious. That the magistrates were onto him, and that if they discovered what he'd done—what we'd planned—they'd torture him until they had their answers. That his death was—"

Her shoulders shook, though no more tears fell. She sucked in a ragged breath, though when she spoke again her voice still trembled.

"That it was necessary. For the plan to succeed. To keep us safe."

He said. So the Adversary was male.

I was perversely glad not to be in my own body as I chalked the next words. Attendants' hands were not prone to shaking.

WHO SAID?

Drusa bit her lip, her eyes wide and shining. "I can't tell you."

I moved in, my dozen bodies crowding in around her, eyes staring at her from behind the smiling bronze masks. Drusa flinched away, but I had surrounded her. Even if she'd been unbound, she had nowhere to flee to.

"I can't!" she protested, voice cracking. "I can't tell you, Bellator! He said if I did he'd kill me—"

LIKE TITIAN?

Drusa closed her eyes, too overcome by grief and guilt to answer.

So she did not see the next words I painstakingly scratched out, the longest thought I'd articulated yet using the Attendant's clumsy hand, until I placed that same hand on her shoulder.

Drusa started at the cold touch. Her eyes flew open, scanned across the slate.

LIED TO T. ALWAYS MEANT TO KILL HIM. LYING TO YOU TOO.

She read it again, then looked up at my Attendant looming over her. It drew its hand across its throat once more, and this time I did not need to write out the message for her to understand.

"Oh, gods." Sweat beaded her brow. "He's going to kill me too."

I put the Attendant's hand on her shoulder again. She looked up into the bronze mask as I shook its head from side to side, carefully deliberate.

"You still think you can stop him." Drusa choked out a disbelieving laugh. "He's been steps ahead of you this whole time, Bellator, playing you just like he played the Sons of Ash. That's his *job*."

I knew then—had perhaps known ever since she'd confirmed the Adversary's gender. But I had been so busy trying to keep the situation from spiraling out of control that I'd been unwilling to confront the possibility that I was being moved around a chessboard like everyone else.

"Gracchus," Drusa said, her voice shaking. "Imperator Gracchus. He came to me and Titian. He knew we were your students, knew we were both from families who weren't happy with how you were putting pieces of the Old Faith into our training. Told us about your wife and that her goal was to legalize the Rite of Awakening. To get rid of the Attendants, ultimately. Gracchus said that if we were real patriots—if we really wanted to serve the Republic—we could help him stop her. Stop you."

No wonder Gracchus had agreed to my request to keep the magistrates from entering the marketplace to arrest Khefnar during Revelation. It was a lie.

It had all been a lie.

Gracchus had practically said as much to my face. That his job was to protect the Republic, to uphold order within its bounds. At the time I had thought that meant upholding its laws, but I realized that he would break those laws without hesitation if it meant securing his idea of order. We had been allies of convenience at Lightfall, aligned against a common threat to the Republic.

But with that threat removed, he had turned his sights inward, seeking new ones, and settled on the Old Faith. I recalled the words he had spoken to Titian, the disdain in which he had held our demands for equal respect. Of course he had seen our newfound cultural and political power as the first steps down a long road that would end in the dissolution of the entire Attendant system.

And so Gracchus had set his plan into motion. His desperate mission to restore the status quo that had been irrevocably shattered when Venaria Hestis had ordered the mass murder of the Senate in her bid to become tyrant.

Yet even Venaria had been motivated by a twisted sense of duty. Her entire plot had been concocted because of the steadily declining numbers of Attendants in the Republic's service, as our economy and our military would both eventually founder without enough corpses to power them. So she had hatched a plot to start a needless, interminable war, securing enough fresh bodies for generations to come.

That was the commonality between the two. Gracchus and Venaria both sought to preserve the Republic as they had known it—more than that, in the image they had made it. They were both Extorani, making it all too easy for them to disregard the way the Republic as it stood had disenfranchised those who practiced the Old Faith. It was an arrangement that was perfectly acceptable to them, for it would never harm them as it did me and mine.

Another commonality: they were both willing to kill in order to uphold that status quo.

I felt a sudden stab of fear at the thought of Lavinia alone with Gracchus in the warehouse where he'd murdered Titian. Wondered if she would meet the same fate—one more casualty in the Imperator's mad quest to keep the Republic stagnant.

I wiped the slate clean and scribbled frantically with dead hands, discarding punctuation and grammar completely in my haste.

HIS PLAN

"I..." Drusa stared into the eyeholes of the Attendant's mask, trying to see me behind it. "He didn't tell me. Not everything, I mean."

Impatient, I tapped a dead finger against the slate. HIS PLAN.

"It's something to do with tonight," she said, panic creeping into her voice, "with the Hour of Revelation. I don't...I don't know exactly what. But he said something about Khefnar getting the martyrdom he's been chasing—"

The world swam around me. Assassination. That was Gracchus's masterstroke. Gather the Old Faith into the marketplace, alongside a sizeable number of curious onlookers, let Bahlanni and Khefnar conduct the Rite of Awakening—word of that must have reached him by now—and then arrange for Khefnar to be murdered at the climax, sparking as bloody a riot as the streets of Albastine had ever witnessed.

I looked down at Drusa, at her shoulders trembling as she fought back the sobs threatening to course through her thin frame. I wondered how readily she had turned against me, at how easily she had fallen into Gracchus's schemes. Whether she had tried to back out or had been coerced into going along with it.

Drusa had betrayed me. Framed my people for crimes against the Republic and helped conceal the murder of her fellow student. Yet somehow I could muster no anger for her, only a strained pity. She was not the first susceptible young person to be recruited into an extremist's cause, too inexperienced in the world to understand the extent of the harm she was doing. Especially when she'd been swayed by someone as domineering and deceitful as Gracchus.

Instinctively I put a hand on her shoulder. Drusa flinched away, and I remembered belatedly that an Attendant's cold touch was no comfort.

Again I chastised myself for blurring the lines between this body and my own. The longer I spent in that state, the more my sanity would fray at the edges.

Fortunately, I needed stay that way only a little longer. All I had to do was find out how Gracchus planned to carry out Khefnar's assassination. A knife in the crowd? An archer on the rooftops? Or something more insidious?

I ran a sleeve across the slate, clearing it for what I hoped would be the final question. Gripped the chalk between cold fingers, scratched out the beginning of the question—

Pain hit me like a sledgehammer between the ribs.

The dozen bodies I occupied doubled over as one, clutching at their middles as agony rolled over me in waves. Before I could react, another invisible blow came down on my shoulders, sending all the Attendants I controlled sprawling to the floor, like puppets with their strings abruptly cut.

The world swam, the already bleary sight and hearing of the Attendants becoming a muddled haze. My grip on them loosened, my will slipping from two or three of their bodies as I found myself unable to maintain the connection.

"Bellator?" Drusa's voice, high and frightened. "Calvus, what's happening? What did—did he find you?"

Her words cut through the fog. Someone had attacked me, back in my own inert body at the top of the Mushroom, while my untethered mind was far away.

Fear wrapped itself around me like a shroud. What would happen if I died like this, my spirit still uncoupled from its mortal shell? Would I find myself sped away to whatever existence awaited us on the far side of death? Or could the soul persist after the death of the body: a ghostly presence roaming the streets of Albastine, unseen and unheard? And if it did, could I still possess the body of an Attendant, or would that ability be lost alongside my own body? Would I even want to cling to such a crude facsimile of life?

Questions better left unanswered, for there were more pressing ones at hand. What was the method by which Gracchus intended to assassinate? Perhaps with more time I might have been able to glean some hint of the truth from Drusa, but that avenue was closed to me, as I was forcibly reminded by another wave of pain tearing through my scattered bodies.

I released my grip upon the Attendants. The warehouse dimmed, then dissolved like a desert mirage as my soul fled through the city, racing like an invisible comet across the sky.

CHAPTER TWENTY-SEVEN

Falling, falling, a dizzying drop from unimagined heights back into myself.

I choked down a ragged gasp, my limbs jerking like those of a resuscitated drowning victim as life flooded them. My eyes flew open, vision swimming back into focus as I fought to concentrate on the two faces standing over me.

"He's back." Hupli's voice, strangely shrill. Was he angry?

"Not for long," Tyshett's voice answered, and something huge and dark devoured my sight. Pain followed in the dizzying starburst of knuckles slamming into my temples, in the sickening crack of my skull rocking back against the stone floor. It was echoed by a high-pitched ringing in my ear.

"Don't!" Hupli shouted, the shrill note climbing into a shriek. "Don't, you'll *kill* him—"

"I have to!" Tyshett snarled, rounding on him. "Shahkti's been arrested! The magistrates are probably on their way to the Barrows as we speak!"

Hupli's counterargument was drowned out by the pain pressing down on me like a physical weight, the persistent ringing in my ears its musical accompaniment. It would have been so easy to lie there and suffocate beneath it.

But pain and I were old friends of long acquaintance. And in one respect, my body was no different from those of the Attendants I commanded: it was an instrument of my will.

My world whittled down to nothing more than my arms as I forced myself up on my elbows. Ignoring the screaming protests of my battered side and shoulders, I half crawled, half kicked myself away from the two Sons of Ash, the stone floor cold against my forearms.

"Not like this!" Hupli was arguing, gesticulating with a wildness thoroughly at odds with his ordinarily stoic demeanor. "I was promised that I could do with him as I pleased!"

Tyshett spat. "The time to persuade Akhenkatem and his wife has passed, Brother Hupli. They are merely obstacles in our path now. And if you cannot remove them, I will."

My vision had finally begun to clear, just in time to see the big Ayu'li woman turn away from Hupli and lumber towards me, flexing the fingers of her huge hands.

The thought of those fingers digging into my throat sent me scrambling even faster, only to bump up against something hard and unyielding. One of the stone pillars lining the domed room, the windows to either side looking down upon the city laid out below. No escape on either hand, save for a long drop and a short stop.

Groaning, I braced myself against the pillar and pushed myself to my feet, just as Tyshett reached me, one fist already flying towards me in a right hook. Ghostfire flared along my sheathed hand as I caught the blow, though the force of it nearly knocked me to the floor again.

Tyshett's other fist collided with my liver, doubling me over as I heaved a thin line of bile onto her feet. Tyshett made a disgusted sound and swung again, a wild uppercut I managed to slip out of pure luck.

The world tilted crazily beneath me as I tried to dart away. I managed only one lurching step. Tyshett seized my shoulders with both hands, slamming me against the marble pillar.

"How'd...find me?" I managed to choke out, staring up into her dark eyes. Every moment spent talking was another moment I could use to find a way out of this mess.

"After you refused our offer to lead our people home, we figured you might decide to take control of the Attendants and set them against us." Her gaze darted past me, to the misty city laid out below us. "Hupli thought this would be the best place to do it."

Inwardly I cursed myself for abandoning the security of Horatia's office. The Sons of Ash were wrong in their assumption that I'd come here to create my own Attendant army, yet they'd successfully deduced that the Mushroom's centrality would lead me here. I silently thanked the ancestors that I'd at least had enough of a head start to discover the truth behind the mutilations.

"Listen," I said, desperate to keep Tyshett distracted as Hupli paced agitatedly behind her, "we're being played, both of us. There's still time to—"

Burly hands wrapping about my throat cut off what I'd been about to say next.

"Enough," she growled. "We gave you a chance to choose your people over this farce of a Republic. To save us from our oppressors and lead us back to the homeland we've dreamed of since we were children!"

She was shouting, her spittle flecking my face. I tried to answer, but her fingers tightening around my windpipe indicated she wasn't interested in making this a conversation. Hupli drew up behind her, peering at me with an odd, almost dazed expression.

"Instead, you threw it back in our faces!" Tyshett shouted, lifting me bodily from the floor. My legs spasmed and kicked as I clawed at her hands, but her grip was as tight as any Attendant's. "Ran back to your masters and begged them to stop us. As if anything could keep us from our prophesied destiny—"

There might have been more, but all I heard was a tearing sound, followed by a shocked, croaking gasp. Tyshett's grip around my neck slackened, and I pried her fingers free.

A jolt of pain shot up my legs as I landed on the stone floor, stumbling away from the two Sons of Ash, struggling to make sense of the scene before me.

Tyshett was turning around, her motions oddly sluggish. Blood trickled freely from a pair of jagged tears in her robe, coating the knife in Hupli's hand. Tyshett looked down at it, then back up to him, confusion written all over her face.

Hupli stabbed her again. Another wet tearing echoed through the chamber as flesh parted beneath the knife.

"Bastard!" Tyshett roared like a wounded bull, shoving him away. The blow knocked Hupli from his feet, sending him sprawling against the floor.

Do something, I told myself as Tyshett charged her downed comrade, unarmed save for her massive swinging fists. But the pain had caught up with me, and all I could do was lean against the stone pillar, desperately trying to breathe.

Tyshett reached Hupli just as he was pulling himself to his feet, and she swung at him with a wide left hook that would have sent him to the floor again, had it connected. Instead, he stayed crouched, rolling under her hook and coming up behind her with a speed and grace I would never have expected of the gangly priest.

Tyshett spun to face him, but too slow. Hupli's knife flashed again. Arterial blood sprayed from her neck, painting the lower half of Hupli's face red.

Tyshett pressed one hand against the spurting wound, blood pouring between her fingers. With her other hand she reached for Hupli. I could not tell whether the gesture was one of supplication or a final desperate attempt to avenge herself.

I would never know. He stepped out of her reach, the movement somehow contemptuous. Tyshett tried to step forward, then collapsed like a felled tree. I could have sworn that the stone floor beneath me shook with the force of the impact, though that may have been my own unsteady feet.

Tyshett rolled over, clutching desperately at her bleeding throat with both hands, a pool of red steadily growing beneath her. Her mouth opened and closed with a mechanical rhythm, like a fish out of water. Hupli stood over her, staring down impassively, heedless of the blood smeared across his face.

My enemy though she was, I could not help feeling a pang of stricken grief coursing through me as Tyshett lay dying upon the floor. Her goals and mine may have been incompatible, but they both stemmed from the same source: a love of our people, a cherished reverence for our faith.

I wanted to go to her, to provide some comfort in her final moments. To say some words to ease her passing, and though I was no priest, to grant her last rites. But my legs were made of cement, too heavy to take even a step from the pillar I leaned against.

Hupli was a priest, yet he stood over her without speaking, staring down with predatory patience as Tyshett slowly died. Watching in helpless, horrified fascination, I saw the moment it happened: the last jerk of her limbs before they stilled, the final wheezing exhalation from her torn throat. The light fading from her eyes, last of all.

Only then did Hupli crouch over her, but he gave her no last rites, no requiem to speed her spirit along its journey to her ancestors. Instead, he cupped her face in both his hands, leaning down so that they were scarce inches apart, the dead woman and the living man. For a single sickening second, I thought he was going to kiss her.

What he did was worse.

Light returned to Tyshett's eyes, but it was not the light of consciousness. Instead, two swirling vortexes of ghostfire appeared, growing larger with each passing moment. Hupli's eyes reflected their light as he leaned in, his forehead resting against Tyshett's. Tendrils of ghostfire leaped from her eyes to spear his. Hupli let out a low, shuddering moan.

Gravesight. The thought came sluggishly through the haze of pain, but it was enough to send a chill down my spine. Just as he had done at the Hour of Refuge, Hupli was drinking in Tyshett's memories, absorbing everything that had made her who she was.

And still I could not force myself to move.

I do not know how long that scene lasted: Hupli hungrily devouring the dead woman's life as I leaned helplessly against a marble pillar, unable to flee or tear my gaze away from the grisly sight. Time seemed to stretch and distend, the horror of the moment disrupting the ordinary march of seconds and minutes.

For it was a horror. Not the death itself, though that had been messy and painful enough to haunt my dreams, should I live long enough to have any. It was Hupli's misuse of the gravesight that set my empty stomach to roiling. It was a ritual meant to ease the loss of the departed's loved ones or to glean wisdom from the remnants of a life well-lived. What Hupli was doing was an act not of reverence but of desecration.

The bridge of light connecting their eyes faded, then went

dark. Hupli let out a shuddering breath, still crouching vulture-like above her body.

"You killed her," I heard myself say.

Hupli turned his head to me, lazy and languid. The ghostfire had gone out of his eyes, leaving them so hugely dilated that I could see no hint of iris ringing his pupils. He licked his lips.

"Yes," he said, a strange inflection to his voice. "We killed her. And in killing her, we saved her."

He had dropped his knife shortly after using it to end Tyshett's life. Now he retrieved it, both the blade and his hands coated in her blood. Straightening, Hupli turned away from his victim and walked towards me, his steps slow and measured.

Cold shock hit me as I realized what had changed about his behavior. Early in my career I had traveled to the city of Zantyum, crossroads of the world, where anything could be bought or sold for the right price. There I had witnessed dens of iniquity thick with the smoke of poppies and hashish. The dreamlike expression plastered across Hupli's face matched those of the addicts I had seen there exactly.

"Hupli," I said, backing away as he advanced on me, knife held loosely in one hand. "Hupli, how many times have you used the gravesight?"

"Four." I had never seen Hupli smile before. But he did now, a wide and almost innocent expression of wonder. "No, five. Twice to prepare for Khefnar's return, on bodies in the mortuary before they put the masks on them. Once you saw, at the Hour of Refuge. After that..."

A full-body shudder wracked his thin frame. I thought wildly of charging him in that moment, while his guard was down, but when I tried to take a step the ground swayed beneath me.

I did not fall, though. I took that to be a good sign.

"I found a corpse in an alleyway," I said, seizing hold of a sudden intuition. "One without eyes. That was you, wasn't it?"

Hupli licked his lips and nodded. "We couldn't stop, after Refuge. Not with Ostakri joined to us. He is...louder than the others. What he showed us...we wanted more."

"We," I repeated, staring into the dark void of his eyes. "How many of you are in there?"

Hupli's laugh echoed weirdly off the domed ceiling. "First Hupli, all alone. Then joined by Caius and Panaea and Ostakri. Then Iktan in the alleyway, and now Tyshett makes six."

My head swam. The few times I had used the gravesight it had been difficult to differentiate my own sense of self from those of the person whose memories I'd relived. But I had been trained to do so, whereas Hupli had been self-taught. He had not maintained such barriers, and their memories had bled over into his own.

Six personalities and six lifetimes, all vying and contending with one another in his head. No wonder he had taken to referring to himself in the plural. I was no longer speaking with Hupli, my wife's ambitious young apprentice, nor even with the zealous priest who had aligned himself with the Sons of Ash and their doomed crusade. I was dealing with a mad chimera.

"Why kill her?" I asked, nodding down at Tyshett's corpse. The longer I could keep him talking, the better prepared I would be when he decided to use the knife.

Hupli stared at Tyshett's body as though he had only just noticed it. Then he turned back to me, frowning, as though it were a simpleton's question. "She was going to kill you. I...we could not have that. Not yet."

Cold sweat beaded on my brow. "What do you mean, not yet?"

"Not until we've taken them from you." A grin like a sawblade spread across Hupli's face. "The others. How many are in you, Akhenkatem? How many souls dwell behind your eyes?"

"Only my own," I said, heat rising unbidden in my voice. "Hupli, listen to me. You're sick. The gravesight's not to be used like this—"

"Sick?" Hupli barked, his tone eerily reminiscent of Tyshett's. "No, Akhenkatem, we are not sick any longer. Hupli was...incomplete. A part of him was always missing. He did not laugh, or cry, or rage. Even when his parents died he felt nothing, though he honored their spirits and performed the funerary rituals as was expected."

Hupli's icy demeanor had always unsettled me, but I had never suspected it ran so deep. "Why become a priest, then?"

"Because he saw a need," Hupli answered, looking down at the knife in his hand. "A station he could perform, a role he might fill. Just because he did not feel as others do did not mean Hupli was immune to seeking satisfaction or the need to belong. But when he first braved the gravesight..."

He licked his lips, a mad gleam in his black eyes. "Imagine a blind man suddenly seeing the world in all its vibrant color. A deaf man hearing a symphony for the first time, or a cripple rising to dance the Rites. An entire world of sensation denied him, suddenly revealed as he lived the life that had belonged to Caius Antonitian. He...I wept, Akhenkatem. For the first time in my life, as the feelings of another spread through me."

He stared down at the knife, suddenly pensive. "But it was not enough. You have performed the gravesight. You know that the memories do not fade with time, yet a man cannot live in memory alone. So I...he...Hupli sought it out a second time. Another body not yet reduced to an Attendant, its memories still fresh. Panaea, her name was. And for a time that satisfied. Until Khefnar and his Sons of Ash came to me seeking entrance to the Hours of Refuge, just as we had planned"—he licked his lips—"bearing the skull of one who had seen things beyond my imagining."

"Is that why you sided with Khefnar against Bahlanni?" My gaze darted to Tyshett's body, still lying in a pool of her own blood. "Because they promised you Ostakri's skull?"

"We allied ourselves with the Sons of Ash because Brother Khefnar is *right*." His voice had shifted again, its speech taking on a slight accent. Ostakri, I presumed, wresting control of Hupli's body from the cocktail of personalities dwelling within. "He is chosen by the ancestors of Ayu, Akhenkatem. Our prophet and our savior. You were wrong to oppose him, and now you must pay the price."

He advanced, knife held in both hands. I sucked in a shallow breath, sending a stitch lancing through my side, letting ghost-fire gather along my outstretched arms. Behind Hupli, Tyshett's body twitched.

"Blasphemer," Hupli said, his stride unbroken. "To use the holy rituals of our faith for such mundane ends. Do you really think such sacrilege will save you now?"

I did not answer, pouring all my concentration into raising Tyshett's body. I made a gesture of command, but pain flared to life in my side where she'd pummeled my liver, forcing me to double over and dry heave. The ghostfire guttered out, leaving my bad arm hanging dead and useless at my side.

Tyshett's corpse stilled.

"You see?" Hupli's crazed grin widened. "The ancestors do not favor you, Akhenkatem, prodigal son that you are. Whereas I am their chosen vessel."

He raised both hands. Ghostfire flamed along them, glimmering off the bloody knife. "And I have learned more than one secret from them."

Sheathed in its leather sleeve, my left arm jerked and spasmed, fingers clenching and unclenching without my consent. I tried to focus through the haze of pain, but to my horror I found my will running up against the wall of Hupli's own.

Hupli let out a high-pitched cackle, utterly crazed. "Time to sow what you reap, Legate Calvus."

The fingers of his free hand curled into claws. He made a swiping motion, and suddenly my own fingers were at my throat, squeezing.

I tried to gather my will again, but the black spots bursting in my vision made that impossible. Desperate, I clawed at my dead hand with my living one, but I had no strength left.

Dead fingers tightened on my throat as Hupli reached me, both hands clenched into fists. I tried to flee, only for the room to sway around me as my knees buckled. Another dull throb of pain as I hit the floor, my head inches from Hupli's feet. Through my blackening sight I glimpsed movement behind him and wondered fleetingly if he had succeeded in raising Tyshett's body where I had failed.

"Do not fight it, Akhenkatem," Hupli said from high above me. He crouched over me, just as he had crouched over Tyshett in her dying moments. The knife glinted in his hand. "It will not hurt for much longer. Soon you will join us. You, and all the lives residing within you, until we are many souls in one vessel. All your fears and doubts will be washed away in the glory of our union."

Cold steel kissed my cheek as he ran the blade slowly down my face, resting the point against the place where jaw met throat. "You'll see soon enough."

My vision had narrowed to a tunnel. I closed my eyes, not wanting Hupli's crazed face to be the last thing I saw, and awaited the bite of steel.

Instead, there was a rush of air, a startled cry. The sound of a body hitting stone.

The knife stopped pressing against my jaw, the grip on my throat slackening. I clawed at the dead hand with my living one, tore it free as I dragged down huge gasping breaths. I half crawled, half rolled away from Hupli as grunts and groans and sharp gasps of breath echoed from above me.

My sight returned, revealing Hupli slashing at a small, dark-haired figure with his knife. She raised her baton against the blow, its length flat against her forearm, and the blade bit into wood rather than flesh.

"Lavinia?" I croaked.

She grunted an affirmative as Hupli drew back the knife and stabbed at her. Fast as thought, Lavinia sidestepped his thrust and performed a complicated maneuver with the baton. Hupli let out a strangled cry as the knife spun out of his grip.

Unarmed, he threw a punch, but whatever skill in boxing he had gleaned from Tyshett's memories did not translate to his thinner frame. Lavinia ducked the blow and came up with a sweep of her baton. A sharp *snap* echoed through the chamber as she brought it down on his wrist.

Hupli howled, backing away. But there was nowhere to run. Lavinia stood between him and the spiral staircase, and the room had no other exit.

"Citizen Hupli Kiaton," she said, panting only slightly, "you are hereby under arrest for murder, attempted murder, and desecration of a corpse. Get on your knees and place your hands behind your head."

Hupli's eyes were wide enough that I could see the whites at the edges of his hugely dilated pupils. His gaze darted from Lavinia to me, from me to Tyshett's body.

"No," he croaked hoarsely, sounding more like himself. "No, I didn't—"

"Save it." Lavinia brandished the baton. Hupli took a step back, only to bump up against the glass of the floor-to-ceiling window. The lowering sun outlined his silhouette in a fiery halo. "I heard everything, Citizen Kiaton. Your illegal use of the gravesight ritual and the murders of Citizen Iktan Thalonitus and the exile Tyshett. It made for a pretty complete confession. Wouldn't you agree, Bellator Calvus?"

"I would," I managed to wheeze as I struggled to my feet. The world spun as I joined Lavinia where she stood between Hupli and the spiral staircase, blocking off his avenue of escape in case he tried to make a run for it.

"Akhenkatem," Hupli said, looking over Lavinia's head at me. Despite the pleading note in his voice, he sounded more like himself than ever. "Akhenkatem, think. If word of this gets out, all Albastine will turn against the Ayu'li. The Old Faith will be condemned, our people ostracized and outcast."

"Your people didn't do this," Lavinia said, speaking as much to me as to Hupli. "The punishment for your crimes falls on you alone, Hupli Kiaton. Now, on your knees."

His gaze remained fixed on mine, and I was shocked to see tears gather at the corners of his eyes. "Akhenkatem, *please*. Don't let her tear down all we've built."

"No." My mouth was desert dry as I shook my head, condemning him. "You did that yourself, Hupli."

He swallowed, nodded slowly. "You're right. I was only trying to help. Will you tell Bahlanni that when you see her? That I was only trying to lead our people home."

Something in his tone sent a sick sense of dread crawling through me. I stepped forward, reaching for him. "Hupli—"

Lavinia glanced back at me, putting out a hand to keep me from coming any closer.

It was all the distraction Hupli needed.

He cupped his fist in his hand and drove his elbow back against the window, putting all the force in his thin frame behind it. A spiderweb crack ran up the glass, but it held.

"NO!" Lavinia darted forward, free hand reaching towards Hupli. He drove his elbow into the glass again, this time turning his hips and shoulder into the motion.

The window shattered.

A gust of cool air blew in, blowing Lavinia's short hair back from her face as she reached for him. Hupli did not take the proffered hand. Instead, he leaned back, heels hanging over the ledge of the broken window. His eyes met mine for a final time.

"Tell her," he said, and fell.

PART SIX
REVELATION

CHAPTER TWENTY-EIGHT

Lavinia dove for Hupli, but he was already falling from the tower, the wind tearing at his robes as he plummeted like a stone towards the city below. She halted on the edge, arms windmilling wildly as she struggled not to lose her balance and topple after him.

Adrenaline drove away the pain as I surged forward, wrapping both arms around her middle and hauling her bodily away from the ledge. We landed in a sprawling heap, both breathing heavily as we stared up at the domed ceiling above us.

"He jumped," Lavinia said wonderingly. "Why did he jump, Calvus?"

I pushed myself up onto my elbows, wincing. "Cassius."

She looked up at me, uncomprehending. "What?"

"Cassius," I repeated. "Anyone who saves my life gets to call me by my given name."

She choked out a ragged laugh. "Call me Lavinia, then. But—"

"He thought it was the only way," I said, staring out through the broken glass at the sun lowering towards the western mountains. "If he's dead, he can't confess. The only proof that the gravesight had anything to do with his murders is what he said to us."

"Meaning what's in my report," she said. "And in your witness statement."

I said nothing.

"Calvus," Lavinia said, then corrected herself. "Cassius. You know I have to report this."

"Do you?" The words slipped out before I could stop them. "Even knowing what it means for my people, for your wife if this gets out?"

Lavinia made a frustrated sound in her throat. "I have a duty to uphold the law, Cassius. I can't break that, for you or anyone."

"But you could bend it."

She did not answer. Instead, she clambered to her feet, dusting off the bits of broken glass that had clung to her robes, then turned to me and offered her hand. I did not take it.

"Bellator," she urged, reverting back to stiff formality, "the Sons of Ash are still out there, and the Hour of Revelation is nearly here. We've got maybe an hour until sundown, if that."

The evening sky silhouetting her gave proof to her words. But I did not take her hand.

"Cassius," she said, almost gently, "we can address Hupli's crimes later. Right now there's still the Adversary to deal with."

The Adversary. Drusa's betrayal. Titian's murder. Tyshett's attack and Hupli's madness had driven those concerns from my mind, but now they came flooding back—and with them, the chill fear of facing the enemy who'd been a step ahead this entire time.

"Gracchus," I said, seizing her wrist and staring up at her. "Gracchus is the Adversary, Lavinia."

Her hand tightened on my wrist, but her face betrayed no surprise. "I know."

My brows shot up. "How?"

"He tried to kill me," she said, and though her tone was even I could sense the suppressed rage beneath. Lavinia Caprio was not the sort of woman to take betrayal lightly.

"When?" I asked, letting her pull me to my feet.

"While we were investigating that warehouse. He slipped up, said something that made me realize he'd already been there, and recently. Tried to backtrack and caught himself in his own lie." Her expression grew sour. "Not before he tried convincing me to throw in with him, though."

Asking why she hadn't would have been an ungrateful repayment for saving my life. Instead, I forced a smile. "What'd he offer you?"

"Tried to appeal to my sense of duty, first." Lavinia smiled too, though hers looked even more brittle than mine felt. "Or my resentment, depending which way you cut it. Told me the Old Faith was tilting rapidly towards the radical stance the Sons of Ash represented. All but said that if I didn't help him stop your people that they'd...*cleanse* Albastine of people like me before going back to Ayu."

"We'd never—" I protested, then shook my head. "You didn't believe him."

"No." Lavinia's bitter smile faded to something sadder. "I told you before, Cal—Cassius. I grew up with Khessia and her family. That's long enough to see the good in people as well as the bad."

"I'm not sure I follow."

"I mean," Lavinia said, "that the Extorani have married men to men and women to women for the entire time we've lived in this valley, and none of the Ayu'li ever attempted mass violence against us before. That's not your way. No matter what Gracchus said."

I nodded, not trusting myself to say the right thing. "I take it he didn't handle your rejection well."

"Hardly." Lavinia ran her hand through her hair. "Once he realized that tack wasn't working he shifted to bribery. Went on about how the Senate's been dismantling the estates of the wealthy who died heirless at Lightfall and portioning them out to the citizenry, about how that's disrupted the balance of power."

"He gave Titian a similar speech," I recalled.

"I'm sure he did," Lavinia said. "But I'm not an entitled teenager. And our favorite Imperator was the client of one of those fallen Senators. When they divided up her estate, his lodging got lost in the shuffle. You can imagine what going from a life of wealth and comfort to having nothing does to a man like that."

"No wonder he's holding a grudge," I said. "He told you that?"

"Said that if we put things to rights, he could ensure that I'd be just as well off. So long as I helped him put the Ayu'li in their place." Lavinia's expression turned sour. "But he overstepped himself, there. Forgot who I was married to."

"How'd you get away?"

"Lots of places to hide in a warehouse. Turned it into a real cat-and-mouse game." Lavinia pulled her baton from its holster and spun it around her wrist. "Managed to trip him up and slow him down long enough to slip out of there. After that..."

"You came looking for me?" I gave her a tired smile. "I'm touched."

Lavinia snorted. "Don't be. He's put out an arrest warrant on both of us, framing us for Titian's murder. It's what I'd have done in his place."

"Me too," I admitted. I looked down at the spiral staircase. "How'd you know where to find me?"

"I got desperate enough to swallow my pride," she said, looking out the window. Not at the sun, but at the shining dome of the Senate across the valley. "I know you and Horatia Aquila are...close. I figured if there was anyone in the valley who could get word to you it would be her."

"She told you what I was planning to do?"

"That you were trying to see out of as many Attendants as you could. Sounded crazy, but then, this is you we're talking about."

I smiled thinly. "And you guessed where I was going to do it."

Lavinia shrugged. "Didn't take a genius. If I wanted to reach as much of Albastine at once as I could, this would be the place to do it from. Figured the same principle applied to your Rites."

"Good thinking," I said. "Otherwise Hupli..."

I closed my eyes, not wanting to contemplate what he'd been planning to do to me. As far as I knew, the memories contained within the gravesight were just that: memories, lingering afterimages of the sensations the dead had experienced in life. Hupli's belief that they were the real, conscious souls of the departed dwelling in his mind was a product of his madness, his lack of preparation to use the ancient ritual resulting in his being unable to delineate where his self ended and the others' began.

Or so I hoped. The alternative was too terrible to contemplate.

"Hey," Lavinia said, gentler than I had ever heard her. "Cassius. Worry about that later, alright? We have a job to do."

She was right.

"The Hour of Revelation," I said, moving for the spiral staircase. "Gracchus is planning to assassinate Khefnar there and spark a riot."

I was going to say more, but we had to move around the

pool of blood surrounding Tyshett's body. In death she looked strangely small, somehow deflated.

One more lost soul to lay at my door, I thought. Tyshett's actions had been driven by Khefnar's extremism, but even that had sprung from the same love of her people and faith that now guided my own steps. Fleetingly I wondered how such similar values could have led us to such very different actions.

I stood over her, closed her eyes, and murmured a quick final rite. Despite her aversion to the Old Faith, Lavinia stood by respectfully until I had finished.

"We'll send a magistrate to tend to the body," Lavinia said once I was done. "Assuming they don't arrest us first, anyway."

I nodded and followed her down the spiral staircase. My bruises ached with every step, but I didn't think any new bones had been broken by Tyshett's fists. Small mercies.

"How did you know?" Lavinia asked, huffing a little as we hurried down the stairs.

"Know what?"

"About Gracchus." She glanced up at me over her shoulder. "He didn't try to kill you too?"

I shook my head. "Not yet. But he wasn't working alone. Drusa was helping him."

"Your Acolyte?" I could hear the frown in Lavinia's voice. "I thought she was Ayu'li, like you."

"She is," I said, not bothering to clarify that Drusa's heritage was mixed. "We're not a monolith. Some of us adhere to the Old Faith, some don't. Some are even opposed."

"I know." Lavinia's answer was short, and for a few moments we traversed the stairs in silence.

"I'm sorry," she said suddenly, slowing only a little.

"For?"

Lavinia glanced over her shoulder, biting her lip. "For letting my feelings cloud my judgment."

She turned away and continued down the stairs, apparently considering the matter settled. But I wasn't about to let her get away so easily.

"What feelings?" I called down after her.

Lavinia halted on one of the landings that lined the staircase at intervals, leaning against the railing with her arms crossed. I joined her, only too glad of the excuse to catch my breath.

"I think," she said slowly, "that we were both played from the start. Me as well as you."

"How do you figure?"

"I was put on this investigation for a reason." Lavinia ran a hand through her inky hair. "Triarch Ferra appointed me to head the case into the Sons of Ash, but clearly Gracchus already knew they were on their way to Albastine. No doubt he pulled some strings to make sure I was the one Ferra chose for the case."

"It would explain how he showed up so fast after you arrested me," I said, rubbing at the spot on my head where she had hit me. Hard to believe that had only happened last night. "And why he was playing good magistrate to your bad magistrate. Trying to work us up against one another from the start."

"We barely needed the help," Lavinia said drily. "I...haven't been fair to you, Cassius. I knew who you were, what you'd done at Lightfall. Was one of those who couldn't help noticing how much your actions had benefitted the Ayu'li in general, and your religion in particular."

"You're saying Gracchus could have recruited you outright?" I said, not bothering to dance about it.

To her credit, Lavinia did not shy away from the accusation. "Maybe he could have if I was ten years younger. Like your Acolytes. But I've been a magistrate for years. I thought I could separate my prejudices from my profession."

She thrust a hand towards me. "I was wrong."

I looked down at Lavinia's hand, then back at her. For a moment her mask slipped, and behind her owlish gaze I saw real apprehension.

I took her hand in both of mine—not the comradely soldier's grip she had clearly been expecting, judging by the consternation and confusion that flickered across her face, but gently, as though her hand were a small bird that might fly away at any moment.

"I'm sorry too," I said.

Lavinia blinked. "For what?"

"For the harm my faith has done you and your wife." I shook my head, cutting off whatever protest she was about to voice. "Religion should be a source of meaning. Of community. Joy. Not something that drives people away and condemns them. No one should have to suffer what you suffered, and I'm sorry for that."

"Bellator," Lavinia said, then corrected herself. "Cassius. You didn't—"

"Doesn't matter," I said, squeezing her hand as much as I dared to. "It's my religion, Lavinia. My community, and my faith. I'm a member of that body, as much as I am a citizen of the Republic. I own a part of every action that they do, for good or bad." I released her hand and stepped away, giving her space. "And for whatever harm the Old Faith has done you, I apologize. If there's anything I can do—"

For half a heartbeat I thought she was about to hit me, just like she had at our first meeting. I flinched away from the blow that never came, instead finding her arms wrapped tight around my middle. Pain flared through my side, but I ignored it as long as I could, putting my arms awkwardly about her shoulders.

"Watch the rib," I said, when I could bear the hug no longer.

Lavinia separated from me instantly, a sheepish flush climbing her neck. "Sorry. I forgot."

"It's alright," I said, resisting the urge to press my hand against my protesting side. "I'm just fragile."

"Poor thing," Lavinia said, grinning widely. "You want to take a nap here, let me sort out Khefnar and his bunch?"

"Not on your life," I said, moving past her to the stairs. "Race you to the bottom."

"Just don't cry when I beat you," she said, and we took off.

IT WASN'T A RACE, not really—we were both too cognizant of the weight of our mission to risk breaking our necks falling down the narrow steps. But we hurried down them with as much speed as my injuries allowed, Lavinia having the good grace to slow enough for me to keep up.

We emerged from the Mushroom into the cool chill of early evening. The sun hovered just above the western mountains, and though I knew that the Hour of Revelation would not properly begin until it had fully set beyond the distant horizon, the thought nevertheless lent speed to my steps.

"Come on," Lavinia said, tugging at my sleeve as she hurried up the street. The urgency of the hour was weighing upon her as well.

I raced after her, each step sending a thrum of dull pain through me. I fought it down and pressed onwards as we threaded our way through the maze of streets back towards the central marketplace.

We weren't the only ones. Several streets away I could hear the commotion of marching feet and raised voices, and here and there snatches of song: the faithful making their way from the Barrows to the marketplace, alive with the excitement of the culmination of the Hours. Even from here I could smell the incense and spices, the herbs and sweet fruits that grandparents and cousins had cooked up to serve their relations during the final Hour.

Where Rest was the time of quiet reflection and Reckoning that of righteous wrath, Revelation was the Hour of promise. A time to look forward with hope towards the future proclaimed by the canticles: a return to Ayu, and restoration of all that we had lost.

My body was battered and bruised, my mind and heart still reeling from the far darker revelations I had uncovered in rapid succession: Titian's murder, Drusa's betrayal, Khefnar's schemes, Hupli's crimes. I felt like a climber who thinks he has summited a mountain, only to realize upon reaching the heights that the true peak is still far, far above him.

But strangely, the thought of all I had yet to face no longer daunted me. Perhaps it was the rich scent of holiday foods in my nose, or the familiar refrains of hymns sung by the children of Ayu. Perhaps it was even the nearness of the ancestors, who were said to dwell nearer to the border between the living world and the Quiet Fields upon this night than any other.

"Come on," I said, seizing Lavinia by the wrist and pulling her towards the sounds of merriment.

"What?" she protested, half jogging along as I raced through the streets towards the swelling music. "Cassius, what are you—"

"We're joining the procession!" I shouted over my shoulder, but we were getting so close to the chanting, dancing march of worshippers that I wasn't sure if she heard me.

We raced down an alleyway and emerged onto one of the main streets leading to the marketplace. And there they were.

My people. The sons and daughters of Ayu, each with ashes smeared across their brow, their arms and wrists adorned with bangles and jewelry that had been passed down through the generations: cherished heirlooms, some with histories older than Albastine itself.

They danced together, sometimes in the holy ritual steps, sometimes simply swaying however the music moved them. White teeth shone in dark faces bright with laughter, hands clapping to the rhythm of the song moving through them.

I was smiling too, my heart lifting as I moved towards the parade of faithful dancing their way through the streets of my city. They were more than those who shared my faith, more than my fellow citizens. They were my family.

"Come on," I said again, pulling at Lavinia as my heart pounded in time to the music. But she stayed resolutely where she was, unmoving.

"Cassius," she said, shaking her head, "I can't."

"I'm not asking you to join in the worship," I said, though it took a conscious effort to resist swaying in time to the song. "This is our best chance to get into the marketplace undetected, if Gracchus has put out a warrant for us like you said."

Lavinia looked over my shoulder at the crowd streaming past. Dozens of Ayu'li, all wearing robes not too dissimilar from mine or Lavinia's. So long as we avoided calling attention to ourselves, we stood a good chance of slipping into the marketplace with the rest of them.

Still Lavinia hesitated. "It's not my faith, Cassius."

"But it's mine," I said, turning to face her. I waved my sheathed hand at the crowd marching behind us. "What it should be, Lavinia. Not the reason your wife's parents refused to accept you, but what it is at its heart. Family. Community. A place to belong."

I held out my hand. "You're going to save these people. *We're* going to save them. Together."

Lavinia still hesitated, but the faintest trace of a smile

tugged at the corner of her mouth. "Can you imagine the look on my in-laws' faces when they find out I helped save their congregation from an assassination?"

"I won't have to," I said, grinning. "I intend to be there when you tell them."

Laughing, Lavinia took my hand, and we dove into the press of worshippers marching up the streets. The crowd absorbed us instantly, the eyes of those closest lighting with pleasure at the unexpected addition of their high priestess's husband to their ranks.

"Akhenkatem!" shouted a pair of grinning, wrinkled older women I recognized as two of Bahlanni's aunts once removed. A gaggle of younger relatives and their even younger children trailed in their wake as the crowd parted before them.

"Auntie Nyberu," I greeted them, bowing my head. "Auntie Khatori. Blessings of the ancestors on you both."

"And on you!" returned Nyberu, stick-frail and stooped but still grinning widely. "We had thought you would already be within the marketplace with our niece."

"We were delayed," I said, glancing at Lavinia.

"But who is your friend?" demanded Khatori, a head shorter and twice as big around as her sister. She beamed broadly at Lavinia with undisguised curiosity. "A convert?"

Lavinia reddened, though whether from indignation or embarrassment, I couldn't say. I stepped in before the well-meaning aunties could make things worse.

"No," I said hastily, putting a hand on Lavinia's shoulder. "This is my friend, Lavinia Caprio. Magistrate of Albastine."

"Blessings of the ancestors upon you, Magistrate!" Khatori practically squealed, seizing a bemused Lavinia's hands in hers and kissing them on the knuckles.

"And on you as well?" she replied, her sidelong glance at me turning it into a question.

I nodded my approval. "Honored aunts, we were hoping we might arrive at the marketplace unannounced...?"

As soon as the aunts had turned their attentions to Lavinia I had begun wracking my mind for plausible reasons for us to want to infiltrate the marketplace unremarked. I needn't have bothered. The aunties exchanged a knowing look, then turned to us with identical grins.

"Can't blame you," Nyberu chirped, her smile revealing missing teeth. "If more folks recognize you, they'll all want to thank you for what you did last autumn. Everyone wants to say hello to the Hero of Lightfall."

Now it was my turn to flush, despite the chill of the evening. Lavinia glanced at me, mouthing the words "Hero of Lightfall?"

"All to say," Auntie Khatori chimed in, sparing me further embarrassment, "by the time they'd be done with you, the Hour of Revelation would be long over. And we can't miss watching our niece show that renegade Khefnar who really leads the Old Faith, can we?"

"Exactly," I said, seizing on that last part. "Thank you for understanding, aunties."

"Don't you worry," Nyberu said with a sly wink. "We'll get you there in record time."

With that she turned and hollered to several of her younger relatives, who formed a sort of impromptu honor guard around us as we rejoined the flow of the parade. As they crowded us from prying eyes, Khatori procured a set of hooded robes from her son-in-law and draped them over Lavinia and me, obscuring our faces from anyone not looking too closely at us.

As we marched and danced towards the marketplace, the constant song was intermingled with the aunties' incessant pleasant chatter, switching apparently at whim between Old Ayu'li and the common speech of Albastine. I answered their questions as best I could—little nothings about my and

Bahlanni's married life, when we might be having children, and all the other intrusive questions older relatives long to discover the answers to.

"And you?" Khatori asked, turning to Lavinia, who tensed subtly. "Are you married?"

Lavinia nodded curtly. "I am."

"Children?" Nyberu asked, pausing in the middle of haggling with a passing kebab vendor.

"We're thinking about it," Lavinia admitted, then took a deep breath. "My wife is more in favor than me, though."

Even as we swayed in time with the crowd, Lavinia's posture was that of a woman bracing against a storm.

"Oh, children are a delight!" Nyberu crowed, turning from the vendor to press kebabs into our hands. "Eat up, dears, you're both too thin."

That was truer in Lavinia's case than mine, but I had barely thanked Nyberu before my hunger overrode politeness and I began digging into the richly spiced skewer of meat.

"Thank you," Lavinia said, staring at the aunties even as she accepted the kebab. "You don't—"

"Nyberu!" Khatori nudged her sister. "The poor dears haven't brought any heirlooms with them to the Hours."

"So they haven't," Nyberu agreed, frowning. "That won't do. Here."

She pulled a pewter chain from around her neck and placed it over my head, careful not to disturb the hood concealing my features. Beside her, Khatori was pulling rings from her thick fingers and slipping them onto Lavinia's much daintier ones.

Before we could get so much as a word in edgewise, they'd laden us down with small items of jewelry.

"What was all that?" Lavinia asked as the aunties were momentarily pulled away by a crying grandson. She looked down at her hands, now adorned with topaz bracelets and copper rings.

"A gift," I said, adjusting one of the pewter chains they'd draped around my neck. "They saw you—well, that *we* didn't have any heirlooms, so they gave us some of theirs."

"Generous," Lavinia said, looking dubiously at the topaz bracelet. "Why, though? They can see I'm not Ayu'li."

"You're married to one, though."

She looked at me, then back at where the aunties were keeping pace towards the back of our little knot of extended family members. Then looked down at the rings that had joined the one she already wore. "I said I had a wife. They didn't... They heard me, didn't they?"

"Not all the faithful believe as your wife's parents do," I said, offering her a kebab. "The Old Faith's emphasis on the ancestors has less to do with bloodline and more to do with the family itself. In Ayu, men married other men nearly as often as they did women, and vice versa."

Lavinia took the kebab. "But that would mean the end of the ancestral line. Wouldn't it?"

"Adoption," I said. "Family is family, by blood or choice. It says that somewhere in the canticles, though it's a lot prettier in Ayu'li."

Lavinia absorbed this in silence as we marched up the street, drawing nearer to the lights of the marketplace and the Hour of Revelation. The sun was just beginning to crest the western mountains.

"So my wife's parents are just assholes, then," she said at last.

"They are," I said, eliciting a terse laugh. "After we were driven from Ayu, we were a nomadic people, few in number. Many of the Ayu'li became fixated on trying to repopulate, but this was hampered by the fact that we could never settle in one place very long before being driven out by our new neighbors. So when we finally reached Albastine and put down roots…"

"They thought that couples of the same gender weren't pulling their weight by popping out lots of Ayu'li babies?"

"It's always been a minority opinion," I said, waving around at the crowd buoying us along. "We're not in any danger of dying out, as you can see. But as is often the case, the loudest voices in the room are usually the ones whom the fewest agree with."

"True," Lavinia said. She took a bite of the kebab and munched noisily. Her brows shot up, her expression of surprise swiftly giving way to one of pleasure.

"And your aunts," she said through a mouthful of kebab. "They didn't care that I'm not Ayu'li?"

"Bahlanni's aunts," I corrected. "And as far as they're concerned, being married to one counts."

Lavinia shook her head. "You know I'm not going to convert, right?"

"Not trying to." I shook my head. "Just showing you that there's a place for you and your wife here if you ever decide you want it."

"I…" She frowned, but it was a thoughtful one. "I'll think about it. Really."

"Good." I looked ahead at the gates leading to the market-place. "We're nearly there."

An early fog had settled on the streets, but that did not deter the gathered throngs of faithful Ayu'li. Lanterns flickered amongst the crowd like stars, adding to the festive atmosphere.

We let the procession carry us along, keeping to the center of the crowd lest any stray magistrates catch us at its edges. Over the noise of their excited chatter, I could hear the distant reverberations of the first hymns from the amphitheater.

The walls of the marketplace kept out the worst of the

evening chill, though mists rising from the dockside meant that even within those walls Albastine's pervasive fog remained. As we approached the gates I saw a handful of Attendants waiting on either side, having been dismissed from the marketplace proper in deference to Ayu'li custom. As subtly as I could, I reached out with my will, feeling to see if any of them were under Laurent's control.

"Cassius!" Lavinia hissed, tugging at my arm, where the ghostfire had begun to glow bright enough to rival the lanterns around us. "I thought the whole point of joining this parade was to be sneaky?"

I nodded and withdrew my will, the Attendants by the gates going slack once more as the ghostfire on my arm faded to its usual dull glow. None of the bronze masks housed another's mind.

We passed beneath the gates unmolested, following the stream of citizens as they made their way between merchant stands, skirting the communal firepits already lit to keep out the chill. The press of bodies was so thick that I found myself scraping against the splintery logs of piled kindling that interspersed the booths.

"So what's the plan?" Lavinia muttered as we took a shortcut between a bookseller and an oil merchant. "Do you have any idea when Gracchus is going to try and assassinate Khefnar?"

"At the climax of the ceremony," I said, emerging from our shortcut into another stream of citizens. Not only Ayu'li worshippers, but nearly as many Extorani, come at Bahlanni's invitation to view the performance of our holy rituals. *A display of good faith from the Old Faith,* I thought, and wondered bitterly how wrong things were going to go tonight.

"Dramatic," Lavinia said. "But why wait? I mean, if he's

trying to spark a riot, wouldn't it be better just to kill him as soon as the opportunity presents itself?"

I shook my head and dove into the crowd, forcing Lavinia to keep up. I had not revealed that Khefnar and Bahlanni planned to settle the question of high priesthood by means of the Rite of Awakening to anyone save Horatia, and for good reason. Lavinia might have come to tolerate me as an unlikely ally and perhaps even to reconsider her stance against the Old Faith and its adherents, but such magnanimity would not extend to publicly violating one of the Republic's most foundational laws.

"Cassius!" Again she caught me by the arm, halting me as the faithful and the curious flowed past. "Talk to me."

"Come on." I tried to pull away, but Lavinia's grip was surprisingly strong.

"Cassius," she repeated, forcing me to turn and meet her gaze. Her owlish eyes were flinty. "Tell me what you're hiding."

I shook my head, about to conjure up some denial, but she forestalled it with a raised hand. "If we go into this keeping secrets from one another, things *will* go wrong. Badly wrong. And all these people are at risk." Her hand tightened on my wrist. "Tell me what you know."

She was right. Gracchus certainly already knew about the Rite of Awakening. I could only hope that Lavinia would forgo arresting Bahlanni and Khefnar in favor of stopping the assassination.

"It's the Rite of Awakening," I forced myself to say. Lavinia's brows rose, but she waited for me to continue. "They're going to summon the spirits of the ancestors. Of the other high priests, specifically. Let them decide who deserves to inherit their mantle."

I expected shock, outrage, or disgust, but to my surprise Lavinia's only reaction was to lower her hand from my wrist to my hand.

"Your grandfather was high priest," she said softly.

"How'd you know?"

"I did my research on you," she said with a tight smile. "He also raised you, from what I understand. No wonder you didn't tell me."

That wasn't it at all—or at least, I hadn't been willing to admit that the chance to see Grandfather again had factored into my decision to keep the Rite secret.

"What are you going to do?" I asked.

Lavinia squeezed my hand. "Stop the assassination, of course. Now come on."

Relief washed over me, as cool as the evening mist against my forehead. Before I could utter so much as a word of gratitude, Lavinia was pulling me along, towards the amphitheater at the market's heart.

By THE TIME we reached the amphitheater most of the seats were already filled—or would have been, had anyone been sitting. Instead, the Ayu'li danced in place, swaying and singing to the rhythm of the age-old hymn echoing across the valley. Hands clapped and feet stomped as we made our way through them. A strange pang shot through me as we passed an Extorani family, both parents and children doing their best to mimic the motions of their Ayu'li neighbors.

Nor were they the only Extorani infected by the jubilant atmosphere. Even those who did not sway in time to the music were on their feet, though this might have been so they could see over the heads of those standing in front of them.

Lavinia and I made our way down the long aisle of narrow stairs to the pit: the open space between the front row of seats and the stage itself. This too was crowded, though almost entirely with the devoted faithful, dancing with such fervor that the ground practically trembled beneath them.

And there, upon the stage, was Bahlanni.

My wife stood with arms thrust to her sides, head thrown back and eyes closed, her mouth wide as she sang the high, ululating notes of the welcoming hymn. Gold bangles dangled from her wrists, while intricate spiraling patterns of dye snaked up her bare arms and down her legs. A golden amulet that her most ancient predecessors had carried from Ayu itself was clasped about her neck, with a bright topaz shining at its center.

"She looks like a goddess," I whispered, and only Lavinia's murmured agreement made me realize I had said it aloud.

Khefnar stood opposite her, his posture a mirror of hers. Unlike Bahlanni, he was naked above the waist, revealing a broad chest thick with muscle. Save for the pair of enameled bronze bracers he had borne from Ayu, he wore no jewelry. While the lantern light glittering off Bahlanni's adornments turned her into a bright and shining star, the gathering fog clung to Khefnar, making him a brooding shadow.

They stood before the crowd, two visions of the Ayu'li people. One dark and wrathful, eager to redress the wrongs dealt us that we carried with us each and every day. The other bright with the warmth of community, her face shining with the light of the promised better future.

Revelation, I thought, *the shape of things to come.*

And now, on the stage before us, that shape would be revealed.

"Come on," I said, pulling Lavinia close to me as we shoved our way through those dancing in the pit. Bahlanni and Khefnar were not alone upon the stage; hooded guards stood behind them, bronze staves reflected in the lantern light. I caught a glimpse of Neftani's face beneath one shadowed cowl, and beneath another's—

My breath caught as my eyes widened in recognition. She could not be here. She was securely bound, locked away—

Her eyes widened as she caught me looking, dismay chasing recognition across her beautiful face. I pressed towards the stage only a few yards away, knowing that if I could reach her in time I could save not only Khefnar, but every soul around me.

A hand caught my shoulder, heavier than Lavinia's. At the same moment, something sharp pressed itself against my back, hard enough to draw blood.

"Easy, son," Laurent whispered in my ear. "Let's wait and see how things play out."

I looked to Lavinia, only to see her in similar straits. Nakmond an-Swerati stood with his knife pressed against her middle, low enough that the dancers around us could not see it —just as Laurent held his own blade to me.

I turned back to the stage, making eye contact with the woman who should not have been there. In front of her, Bahlanni and Khefnar held the final, piercing note of the welcoming hymn, their arms outstretched in greeting to the faithful.

But Shahkti had eyes only for me.

CHAPTER TWENTY-NINE

"Brothers and sisters," Bahlanni began, greeting the crowd with a wide smile, "welcome to the Hour of Revelation, the penultimate and most sacred of our Hours of Remembrance. Tonight I invite you all, not only those who follow the ways of the Old Faith, but our fellow citizens of this Republic, to join us in celebration..."

Her voice was clear and resonant, augmented by the amphitheater's natural acoustics. But the rush of my own blood through my ears drowned her out as Shahkti's presence loosened a cascade of revelations.

When last I had seen her, Shahkti had been locked up in one of the Magisterium's cells by Horatia. Khefnar had no influence over the magistrates that could compel them to release her.

But as an Imperator, Gracchus did.

I'd miscalculated. Laurent had not been Gracchus's mole within the Sons of Ash. It had been Shahkti—had to have been, or she would still be under lock and key, not standing onstage awaiting her master's signal to assassinate Khefnar.

But that makes no sense, I thought, combing my memory for what I knew of Shahkti. She had joined Khefnar upon his pilgrimage to Ayu after her intended husband turned down their arranged marriage. Why would she agree to murder the man who had taken her away from that shame, had shown her the place from which our people had come all those years ago?

The answer was cold water down my spine.

My only proof that Gracchus intended to murder Khefnar tonight was Drusa's word. And just as he had lied to Titian, knowing that my proximity to the Acolyte would lead me to glean information from him, so too had he lied to Drusa.

"She's going to kill Bahlanni," I said aloud.

"No one's killing anyone," Laurent growled in my ear, digging the knife in just a little deeper. "We're going to watch this play out, and the ancestors will make their will known. And that, my boy, will settle this once and for all."

"You don't understand," I said, straining against his hold as much as I dared. "Laurent, we're being set up. All of us. The Imperator—"

"Can't stop the Rite," Laurent cut me off. "Look around you, Cassius. All these people came to join us in the Hour of Revelation. There aren't enough magistrates in the city to stop them. Watch."

He prodded me with the knife, forcing my gaze back to the stage, where Bahlanni and Khefnar had begun to dance the Rite of Awakening. Their voices rose and mingled together, Khefnar's low and rolling like thunder, Bahlanni's high and sweet, ethereal as the roiling mists. A stab of unexpected jealousy pierced me as I watched my wife and her rival upon the stage, their differences set aside in this moment of worship.

The eyes of everyone were upon them, even those who were dancing the Rite in imitation. Fleetingly, I wondered whether their participation would aid the ritual's completion or hinder it. My only small solace was that thus far, no magistrates had appeared to arrest anyone. Horatia had come through.

Onstage Shahkti tensed, her hands ducking into the voluminous sleeves of her robes, where her own knife was no doubt hidden. But she made no move towards Bahlanni or Khefnar, for I had been right in one assumption only: Gracchus intended the assassination to occur at the most dramatic moment possible.

He was here too, somewhere. Gracchus's pride was too great to allow him to let his machinations succeed from afar. He would want to witness the fruits of his labor firsthand and to intervene personally if things went astray.

Lavinia and I needed to find him. But we could not do that with knives pressed against our backs.

The crowd swayed around me, the rhythm of the Rite slow at first, but building in tempo with each verse of Old Ayu'li as Bahlanni and Khefnar's song echoed the cries of our ancestors: cries for succor and respite, the cry of every child longing for its parents to come and sweep aside the world's hurts, to wrap them in their arms and whisper everything would be all right. I found myself blinking back sudden tears at the remembrance of my own parents, now little more than faded memories themselves, and of my grandparents, their own deaths each a blow to my young heart.

Someone sniffled behind me. A few feet to my right I saw a young Extorani man with tears shining bright across his cheeks and knew that the truth of the song had found its way home in a way mere words could not.

Laurent made a strained noise in his throat, loud in my ear. The knife against my back did not waver, but his hand trembled on my shoulder. If he would only give me an opening…

"The schematics are safe," I said, hoping it would distract him.

"Good," Laurent grunted. "Would have been a waste of everyone's time if they were lost."

Out of the corner of my eye I saw Lavinia watching us warily, having guessed my intentions. When the time came to act, we would make our move together. Even if it ended with both of us bleeding on the amphitheater floor.

"So you were bluffing with the candle, then," I said to Laurent.

"Had to," he said, lowering his voice so Nakmond could not hear. "Only way to get the schematics to someone who could actually use them."

"Why?" I asked, my eyes fixed on the stage. Still dancing, Bahlanni and Khefnar circled one another in a way that made them look more like gladiatorial champions than priests offering devotions to their ancestors. "What was the point if you're still on Khefnar's side?"

"Because I agree with him that the Ayu'li should return home," Laurent muttered in my ear. "And that we'll need an army of Attendants to get there. What I don't agree with is the idea of leaving whoever stays behind high and dry. The Republic has its faults, but its people don't deserve to suffer."

"So you made sure we'd have the means to replace the Attendants you're going to steal," I said, licking my lips. "Kind of you. I take it you'll be Khefnar's Legate general?"

"What are you talking about?" Laurent asked, his voice full of sincere bewilderment. "I'm no more a Legate than your magistrate friend."

Then who was behind the strange Attendant? I wanted to ask, but before I could, a miracle occurred.

Onstage, Khefnar and Bahlanni drew together. They reached out their hands, and to the gasping wonder of the crowd, ghostfire sparked in the space between them.

No, I realized through my shock, not ghostfire, but the magic of the holy ritual in its purest form. The ethereal ball of light glowing and growing like a teal sun between them was to my pale ghostfire as the holy dance was to the brutal simplicity of my command gestures. This was the real thing, the truth, against which all the Legate's arts and techniques were mere shadowy imitations.

Bahlanni's voice trembled, her eyes widening at the display of ancient magic before her. Across the circle Khefnar continued unwaveringly, his eyes locking on hers. He gave her the slightest nod, and for the briefest moment something like kindness lightened his features. Bahlanni resumed the song, her voice ringing out stronger and clearer than ever.

The spectral orb grew steadily larger, spreading out so that it engulfed first Bahlanni and Khefnar, then all those standing upon the stage. Before I could react, it had reached us and passed us, though I felt nothing but the rush of a damp breeze against my cheek as it radiated outwards, filling the amphitheater and the marketplace beyond.

Just as swiftly it dissipated, leaving behind traces of pale, glimmering light in the air around us. It took me a moment to realize what I was looking at.

"The fog," Lavinia said, her voice heavy with awe. "As I live and breathe, it's lit up the fog."

So it had. Each droplet of mist shone with light, turning each speck of fog into a tiny, glimmering star.

And they were moving.

Onstage where the orb had first appeared, the shining fog roiled and swayed, amalgamating itself into a recognizable shape. As I watched, the shining light materialized into a body —not a solid form, but illuminated in countless pinpricks of light. It became a tall, elegant figure, with a face I knew as well as my own.

"Khaimesu?" Bahlanni whispered, and though I was too far away to hear her, I could see her mouth shape my grandfather's name.

She reached for him, fingers trembling, but her hand came away empty and damp. A sad smile graced my grandfather's misty features as he shook his head.

"You cannot touch me," he said in a voice made of whispers and fog. Despite the softness of his tone, my grandfather's voice carried throughout the amphitheater. *"But I am here, Bahlanni, my apprentice, dear as daughter. Come back from beyond the Quiet Fields."*

Nor was he the only spirit materializing from the mists. Others were forming onstage beside him, the mists swirling and shifting into the shapes of people. The first of these was a rotund, grandmotherly woman I vaguely recalled from my early youth as Syoris, Grandfather's predecessor, while beside her a younger man took shape, the dewy mists sparkling in his beard.

Our people had always been strongly tied to the river that was our namesake. And though the Rite of Awakening was little understood in these latter days, it placed primacy upon recalling the soul back to its body, for that was what it had been most strongly tied to in life.

But our bodies are not the only places where our souls dwell. We leave little pieces of ourselves behind in every place that we love, from the warm spot in our bed where our spouse sleeps to our favorite chair beside the hearth, to the mountaintop where we once sat and watched the sunrise. Like footprints, traces of ourselves linger, imprinting themselves upon the stones of our homes, the bricks of our churches, the very air we kiss with every breath.

And no substance holds memory better than water.

This, then, was the secret Khefnar had carried with him back from Ayu. I could have laughed, were it not for the knife against my back.

Bahlanni's eyes remained wide as she looked upon the faces of those who had borne the mantle of the Old Faith's high priesthood before her. Judging from the surprise and awe upon her face, even she could hardly believe the Rite of Awakening had worked.

But, I supposed, that was the difference between expectation and faith. One draws upon past experience to intuit the shape of the future; the other draws upon hope to do the same.

Spirits continued to manifest from the mists, a crowd of sparkling phantasms forming between Bahlanni and Khefnar. The leader of the Sons of Ash showed none of Bahlanni's surprise, only smug satisfaction. He must have done this before—summoned ancestral spirits from the waters of Ayu, older by far than the shades of these priests.

"Honored ancestors," he said, his booming voice echoing through the amphitheater, "we have come here tonight to beg your judgment in a matter concerning your progeny. Not only those you see gathered here before you, but their children yet unborn, and their children's children, from now until the end of days. For the question we bring before you concerns the future of every child of Ayu: who is to lead us, and to what end?"

He turned, facing away from the spirits and to the assembled crowd filling the amphitheater. "Are we to linger forever in this narrow valley, subject to the wills of those with whom we share neither blood nor faith? Or shall we return proudly to the lands our ancestors were driven from with fire and sword, long lost but unforgotten?"

Shouts from the crowd—some in favor of the former, but many more yelling for the latter. I saw the parents of the Extorani family nearby shift uneasily, looking about at their Ayu'li neighbors with fear in their eyes.

That fear sparked a deep rage in me, twin to that I had first felt at Khefnar's overthrow of Bahlanni's place before her congregation. The Republic was not two peoples, but one, blended together. The Ayu'li could no more separate themselves from it than we could divorce ourselves from our heritage. For what was a culture, if not heritage in the present tense?

The spirits onstage—fully a dozen of them—murmured in ghostly whispers too soft for living ears to catch. The world stilled as every soul in the marketplace leaned forward, holding their collective breath as they awaited the pronouncement of the dead.

Every soul save one.

Shahkti stepped forward from among the other guards onstage, their eyes too fixated on the returned spirits among them to notice the knife slipping free of her sleeve. Bahlanni's back was to her.

"Hey, Nakmond," I called over to the Ghrabeshi prince, breaking the silence. He turned to me, surprise written across his bearded face.

I gestured to the spirits gathered on the stage. "Think Tyshett will join them?"

Surprise was replaced by shock, then rage as he realized what I was implying. His knife jerked towards me, blade flashing.

It was all the opening Lavinia required.

She jammed her elbow into Nakmond's ribs, startling a breath from him. Before he could use the knife, she rocked her head back, her skull colliding with his nose with a wet snapping sound.

Laurent let out an inarticulate cry of distress, his grip on my shoulder loosening slightly. It would have to be enough.

I tore free of the old man's grip and surged forward, fighting my way through the press of bodies between me and the stage. I was rewarded with a bright streak of fiery pain across my side —not a stab between my ribs, but a long cut across my hip. It hurt like hell, but not enough to kill me nor slow me down.

Onstage, Shahkti was moving towards Bahlanni and Khef-nar. A frightened shriek split the night as someone finally noticed the glimmer of steel in her hand.

I shoved my way through the crowd, heedless of their shouted protests, fighting desperately to make my way to the stage. Shahkti broke into a full sprint, charging at Bahlanni.

Time seemed to slow as I caught my wife's eye. Recognition dawned there, followed by confusion, consternation, and at last, understanding. Bahlanni turned about, moving as though she were underwater, as Shahkti rushed her with the knife.

Reading the alarm on Bahlanni's face, Khefnar turned, his big fist already swinging even before his eyes saw Shahkti. Quick as a snake, she ducked under the blow, leaving nothing but the insubstantial spirits between her and Bahlanni.

Yet Khefnar's swung fist had given a slight figure in a dark robe enough time to clamber onto the stage, just ahead of me. A glance over her shoulder revealed another face I recognized.

"Drusa," I breathed, but by the time I reached the stage lip she was already in motion.

Bahlanni flinched away as Shahkti thrust the knife at her heart, a million spectral points of light reflected off its blade.

Drusa threw herself between Bahlanni and the killing blow. For a moment she hung suspended in the air, illuminated from all sides by the ghostly lights of the resurrected ancestors.

Then Shahkti's dagger pierced her heart, and she dropped to the stage like a stone.

A wordless scream tore from my lips as I pushed myself onto the stage, clambering on all fours towards Bahlanni as Shahkti drew the bloodstained blade from Drusa's body.

Ghostfire flared along my bad arm as I swung it towards Shahkti, her blade bouncing harmlessly off my leather sleeve. I kicked at her leg and she went down hard, her lower back slamming into the lip of the stage. I saw panic written on her face as she slipped from it headfirst, then disappeared from view.

Shahkti screamed once, short but loud. Then there was a sickening snapping sound, and her cry died as she did.

"NO!" Khefnar roared, leaping to the edge of the stage. I peered over it and saw what he did: Shahkti lying upon the pit with limbs outspread, her neck twisted at a stomach-churning angle.

I turned back to Drusa, who lay on the stage with her hands pressed against her middle. The light was growing all around us now, making it almost too bright to see. Dimly I registered more shapes appearing in the fog—not only the ancestral spirits of the high priests and priestesses, but others too, called back to the world of the living by the Rite of Awakening.

But I had eyes only for Drusa and the blood pooling beneath her.

I dropped to my knees, taking my former Acolyte in my arms. She weighed surprisingly little.

"Bellator?" she whispered, eyes finding mine. Her face had gone pale, both hands pressed against her middle, red and sticky.

"Shh," I said, shifting her to a more comfortable position. "Shh, let me see."

She moved her hands, only for more blood to come gushing forth. And beneath it, something white that made my stomach churn.

"It hurts," Drusa said, trembling in my arms like a frightened bird. "Oh gods, Calvus, it *hurts...*"

"I know," I murmured, tucking a loose strand of hair out of her eye. "I know. Just lie still, okay? We'll get help—"

Drusa gave a violent shake of her head and drew in a rasping breath. "I'm sorry. For...for Titian, and for...for—"

"Don't worry about that now," I said, pulling her closer. "You did the right thing, okay? You saved Bahlanni's life."

Blood trickled from the corner of Drusa's smile. "Do I…get… candied date?"

"Yeah," I said, blinking the tears from my own smile. "Yeah, I think you've earned it."

"Good." Drusa breathed, resting her head in the crook of her arm. The light of the spirits that had gone before shone like stars in her eyes.

Then her own light went out, and she was gone.

CHAPTER THIRTY

Grief pressed its suffocating weight upon my shoulders. But I was given no time to mourn.

"Shahkti," Khefnar murmured, staring disbelievingly at her broken body lying before the stage. "Shahkti, first of my disciples, why?"

But she did not answer, could not answer.

Khefnar threw back his head and howled, a wordless cry of grief and rage that echoed through the amphitheater.

"Her death is your doing, Khefnar, son of Feri and Yadennu."

My grandfather's shade still spoke softly, but its watery voice whispered directly into the ears of all present, drowning out Khefnar's basso roar.

"Shahkti followed you," another of the spirits said, this one a grizzled old battle-axe who looked more like a soldier than a priestess. *"She drank in your words of retribution and reconquest by the sword, until the sword was the only tool she knew. Yet vengeance is a blade with two edges."*

"I..." Khefnar faltered, and for the first time I saw doubt cross his scarred features, swiftly replaced by indignant outrage. "I did not cross a thousand leagues of peril to spill

Ayu'li blood! I do not know what drove Shahkti to attack Sister Bahlanni, but rest assured, honored ancestors, that it was not in accordance with my will."

"That remains to be seen," my grandfather's spirit said, and for the briefest moment his misty eyes rested on me. *"But as for you, Brother Khefnar, speak the reason you called us forth."*

"Yes." Khefnar nodded, moving so that he and Bahlanni stood on opposite sides of the circle of departed priests. "We have danced the Rite of Awakening together, Sister Bahlanni and I. The first to do so in generations."

"We have called you forth," Bahlanni said, her eyes fixed on the spirits before her, "to settle the question of your successor. And of the future of our people."

She paused, but my grandfather's shade gestured for her to continue with an impatient wave of the hand that pierced my heart with its familiarity.

"In life I was your apprentice." Bahlanni sank to her knees and raised her hands to the ancestors in a posture of supplication. Khefnar remained standing. "I have tried to honor your teachings. To serve as a shepherd for the faithful, to provide them with what wisdom and guidance I can. I have done my best to honor the memories of those who came before us, while seeing to the needs of those still with us."

Her eyes flickered to Khefnar, her mouth and shoulders tightening. "If I have done wrong in this, if I have neglected the future in favor of past and present, I ask your forgiveness and for you to select a worthier leader for the children of Ayu."

She bent so that her palms and forehead were pressed against the stage floor: the bow of deepest respect employed only in the presence of the most revered ancestors.

"And you, Brother Khefnar?" My grandfather's glittering shade turned to the towering Son of Ash. *"What claim do you*

make to the high priesthood of the Old Faith? You were no apprentice of mine, nor of any of those assembled here."

"No," Khefnar admitted, raising his head proudly. "I am appointed prophet and savior by those who were dead centuries before the eldest among you drew her first breath. In the waters of Ayu itself, which few have seen since the Reckoning, I was baptized and anointed by the spirits of our ancient prophets, our forgotten monarchs. They do not wish for our people to be sundered any longer from the land of their birth. They commanded me to lead us home, to reclaim Ayu from those who stole it from us." He glanced at Bahlanni, still bowed. "Not to beg for table scraps from a people who condemn our holiest acts even as they steal and corrupt those parts of our religion they find useful."

Silence reigned over the amphitheater, save for the susurrating murmurs of the shades conferring amongst themselves. At last they turned back, a dozen insubstantial forms facing the assembled crowd.

"Brother Khefnar." They spoke in unison with a single voice, soft yet irresistible. *"Your faith is not of the religion we brought with us out of Ayu."*

Khefnar's jaw worked soundlessly, but before he could voice any protest, the ancestors continued.

"Yours is the faith of those who lived before our ancestors were driven out. The faith that viewed the children of Ayu as ascendant above all, the chosen people of the river who had conquered death. In their mastery over it they made it their plaything, subjecting those peoples who were their neighbors to the tyranny of deathless sorcerer-kings. These are the forgotten monarchs who have declared you their champion: bloodstained conquerors, hungry to recreate their unnatural empire."

"I..." Khefnar shook his head, his expression troubled. "They said nothing of such sins. Nor is anything written of it in the canticles."

"Nor would it be," the shades said in their one voice. *"All people are swift to forget their own sins, even as they treasure their grudges against those who have wronged them in turn. Yet we who dwell upon the far side of the Quiet Fields have spoken with the shades of those who name you their champion. Those who in life called themselves not Ayu'li, Ayu's children, but the Ayu'ra, Ayu's masters."*

My grandfather's shade came forward, the others falling silent as he spoke. *"Look out upon the faces of those gathered here today, Brother Khefnar. Are they the faces of conquerors and slavers?"*

Khefnar turned slowly, as though dragged towards the assembled crowd by a will other than his own. His eyes roved the amphitheater. I looked and saw as he did.

Not warriors or crusaders, but simply people. They stood alone or in little knots of family groups, with their partners or with their friends. Old and young, they watched the events unfolding onstage with hope and wonder, fear and disbelief. The soft glow of the spirits' light washed their faces in pale aquamarine, and the only way to tell Ayu'li from Extorani was to see who had dark smudges of ash across their brows.

Not two peoples, I thought, *but one.*

"But..." Khefnar faltered, staring at the crowd as though seeing them for the first time. "The Hour of Revelation foretells that Ayu is destined to be returned to us. That it is our home." A muscle worked in his jaw. "All I ever wanted was to lead us home."

"Khefnar," my grandfather said in a gentle tone I knew achingly well, *"that is what Ayu means, in the old tongue. Home. Our ancestors lost theirs, but their descendants formed a new one. Ayu is not a distant river, but here, in this valley. In the faces*

standing before you. You have sown strife and discord amongst them, but it is not too late to make amends."

"Amends," Khefnar repeated. Something of the old fire burned in his eyes as he raised his head. "Yes. There will be amends. Amends from the Extorani who drove us to such extremes. Who turned us against one another, when they were our enemies and our oppressors all along. But for them, Shahkti might still be alive."

"Shahkti betrayed you, Khefnar."

The familiar voice was startlingly close at hand. Another shade was materializing from the mists, her visage identical to the cold figure in my arms.

"She served the same master I did," Drusa's shade said, her whispery voice echoing through the amphitheater. *"The master who lured you here, using her voice to tell you that it was time to claim leadership of the faithful for yourself. The one who is everything you fear and hate about Albastine, in the form of one man."*

She pointed a finger made of light and fog into the crowd. I followed it and saw his pale face as she spoke his name. *"Imperator Antonin Gracchus."*

There was a commotion from the audience as Gracchus turned to flee, followed by shouts and the louder scuffle of blows being exchanged. The civilians around him cleared a space, and within a few moments he was being hauled onstage by the combined efforts of Lavinia, Laurent, and Nakmond.

A kick from the Ghrabeshi prince sent Gracchus sprawling at Khefnar's feet. He tried to rise, but the warning smack of Lavinia's baton against her palm kept him down.

"The enemy reveals himself," Khefnar growled. He bent so that his face was inches from Gracchus's. "Is what the shade says true, Extorani?"

"That your disciple betrayed you?" Gracchus spat. The Imperator was paler and more haggard than I had ever seen him, yet his voice carried through the amphitheater. "No. Shahkti was my creature from the outset."

Khefnar flinched. "You're lying."

"Am I?" Gracchus turned his gaze to Lavinia, who held her baton warily towards him as he rose, holding his palms out. "Her husband-to-be broke off their engagement, which your people thought so deeply shameful that she could not appear in public among you. Small wonder that she approached me when she heard you planned to venture to Ayu. How else do you think I was so well-informed of your arrival here?"

"And the mutilated Attendants?" Lavinia asked. "They were never the Sons' work, were they?"

"*They were mine.*" A murmured gasp spread through the crowd at Drusa's words. "*You recruited me into your scheme, as well as Titian Candorous. Told us the Ayu'li meant to abolish the Attendant system, and it was our patriotic duty to stop them. Had us carve up those Attendants and make it look like the Sons of Ash were responsible.*"

Shocked murmurs rippled through the audience, but Drusa was far from finished.

"*And when you saw that a few limbless Attendants wouldn't be enough, you murdered Titian and tried to make it look like Khefnar had done it.*" A strained smile graced her insubstantial lips. "*You would have murdered me too, if you'd had enough time.*"

Gracchus drew in a deep, shuddering breath and turned to Bahlanni. "Priestess. You have conjured these ghosts through illegal magics, forbidden under the laws of our Republic. In its name, I place you—"

The crowd let out a low, threatening rumble, a chorus of booing voices as those nearest the stage surged forward, making their displeasure known. Amongst them I heard scattered shouts of "Liar!" and "Murderer!"

Gracchus raised his hands, still looking to Bahlanni. "Am I permitted to defend myself against these insinuations?"

She glanced at me, then back to Gracchus. *Don't,* I wanted to say, but could not voice it.

"Speak," my wife said, "if you think it will absolve you of your crimes. The Republic deserves to know what you have done and why."

Gracchus turned back towards the assembled crowd. Albastinian faces stared back at him, Ayu'li and Extorani alike, flat and stony.

"I have served the Republic for three decades," he said, his voice shaking with barely suppressed emotion. "I have fought threats from the shadows most of you have never dreamed. I have foiled the schemes of Zantyum assassins and Herracian spies. Sabotaged alliances between our bitterest foes. Halted Venaria Hestis's plot to crown herself tyrant."

Restless murmurs spread through the crowd. No few of those assembled had lost family at Lightfall.

"Yet of all these threats," Gracchus continued, "none so endangers our society as what you see upon the stage before you. Ayu'li necromancy, its practice forbidden centuries ago by our forefathers and theirs so that it would not undo everything they—and we—have worked to build in this valley.

"The Republic was founded upon the backs of its dead. Of those whose bodies were reclaimed as Attendants, to till our fields and raise our towers. They are our servants and our soldiers, as integral to our way of life as breath is to a body. Our strength. Without them, Albastine will wither and die."

He turned to Khefnar, both men regarding each other like wary predators. "You have heard it from the Ayu'li's own mouths. Their faith is incompatible with the Republic's very foundation. These Sons of Ash seek to lead their brethren across the trackless wastes, taking our Attendants with them, leaving

Albastine defenseless." Gracchus's voice rose to a high and reedy shout. "Citizens of the Republic, will you permit this? Will you join me in upholding the order of our society?"

My breath caught in my throat. Here at last was the dreaded moment I had been striving all day to prevent—a riot against the Old Faith, the Pale City's streets flowing red as the Ayu'li defended themselves against a populace stirred to fear and frenzy by Gracchus's mutilations and murders.

And there was nothing I could do to stop it.

A murmur swept through the crowd as they looked uneasily at one another. Once again I was struck by how the pale light of the spirits bathed each face in soothing tones, muting the difference between Ayu'li and Extorani.

"No," someone called.

Just that single word, without any heat or vehemence behind it. The simplest of refutations, yet it seemed to break the spell that Gracchus's words had cast over those assembled in the amphitheater. Other voices joined it.

"My husband is Ayu'li!"

"So are my neighbors!"

"Who cares whether they worship the gods or their ancestors? We're all citizens! All serve the People!"

That last cry was taken up, echoed in chorus. My lips curled into a smile as the crowd began to chant the Republic's ancient motto in a single voice.

"All serve the People! All serve the People! *All serve the People!*"

Onstage, others joined in. Lavinia was the first to take up the cry, but after a moment's hesitation Neftani and the other guards added their voices to the chorus. But the death knell to Gracchus's ambitions came when Bahlanni took up the chant in her high, clear voice, and the remainder of the Old Faith followed. Only Khefnar, Nakmond, and Laurent abstained.

Gracchus's face turned the color of curdled milk. He lowered his hands in disgust, shaking his head.

"Fine," he said, softly enough that only those of us onstage could hear him. "We'll do this the other way."

Something in his tone sent fear pulsing through my veins, but before I could rise to my feet Gracchus had thrown his head back and howled in a high, manic voice:

"BURN!"

His shriek echoed through the fog, cutting off the crowd's unifying chant. For fully ten seconds there was silence in the amphitheater.

Then the marketplace burst into flames.

CHAPTER THIRTY-ONE

Flickering yellow and orange flames clashed against the softer glow of the illuminated mists. Smoke rose over the amphitheater's natural bowl, mingling with the fog.

"What have you *done*?" Bahlanni gasped, turning to Gracchus.

I didn't wait for his answer. The pieces of his final gambit had been laid out before me all along, like pieces upon a chessboard. I had just been too focused on the next move to keep up with Gracchus, who had plotted each step well in advance.

Smoke stung my nose, and with it the acrid scent of oil. Oil I had smelled in the warehouse where Titian was murdered, and through the nose of an Attendant as I interrogated Drusa in a second warehouse. Even in the marketplace I had passed an unusual number of merchant stalls selling oil in amphoras or big ceramic drums, yet had taken no real notice of them at the time.

From somewhere on the highest level of the amphitheater nearest to the flames, someone screamed.

"Get everyone out!" Lavinia yelled, breaking the shock that

held us spellbound. Yet even as she issued the command, a great groaning of metal on metal echoed across the amphitheater as unliving hands pushed the marketplace gates shut. I recalled the Attendants waiting outside the market walls, and I knew who had ordered them there.

"People of Albastine!" Gracchus shouted over the crackling flames, spittle flying from his lips. "By siding with these dissenters and secessionists you have declared your true allegiance and forfeited your citizenship! There is no place for them in our Republic, nor for those who symp—"

His next words were knocked clean from his mouth, along with three of his teeth, by Khefnar's right cross. Gracchus dropped like the proverbial sack of bricks to the stage floor.

Beyond the stage the crowd was surging up the amphitheater steps, towards the flames lighting the marketplace above. Yet even if they could make their way through the fire, they would have to contend with the gates, shut and no doubt barred. Perhaps some few might make it to the Providens, but if the warehouse Drusa had been in was any indicator, the waterfront would be ablaze like the rest of the marketplace.

Lit by flames, the crowded amphitheater had become a chaotic frenzy. Citizens clawed and struggled to be the first up the steps, fighting and trampling one another in their desperate rush to reach the gates before the fires cooked us alive. Screams of fear gave way to those of rage as the people cast aside their newfound unity in favor of desperate self-preservation.

"Albastine in Ashes," I murmured, looking up at the dancing flames reaching into the sky.

"*Bellator.*"

Mist brushed my cheek as the shade touched me with an insubstantial hand.

"*Calvus,*" Drusa's spirit said, then corrected herself.

"Akhenkatem. You can save these people. All of them. But first you have to let me go."

I looked up and saw her face, made of tears and starlight, smiling sadly down at me.

"How?" I asked, voice hoarse.

Drusa leaned down, her insubstantial lips leaving a constellation of dewdrops on my forehead.

"Breathe," she whispered in my ear, and then was gone, back into the fog.

Closing my eyes, I did as she suggested, long and slow. In the time it took me to exhale, I knew what I had to do.

"I'm sorry," I told Drusa one last time, and laid her body gently on the stage.

I inhaled as much as I could without breathing in smoke, then reached out with my will. Instantly three groups of a dozen Attendants each shone in my mind's eye: one for each of the marketplace's three gates. I sent my consciousness into the bodies of the nearest of these, those by the southern gate.

There was only a slight sense of disorientation as I adjusted to my new surroundings, seeing through the dozen Attendants' eyes at once. The sturdy cedar gates of the marketplace opened outwards, but at Gracchus's instruction the Attendants had barred it with several long metal poles jammed across its frame.

I moved forward with my dozen bodies and wrenched these poles free, not bothering to avoid damaging the gate as I did so. Cedar splintered and cracked, but within a few minutes the gates lay unobstructed. I seized them with twenty-four hands and pulled them open, revealing the inferno beyond.

Relinquishing my control, my mind fled back into my own body, leaving me just enough time to wonder at how easily I'd gotten the gates open. Evidently Gracchus had planned on my death well before reaching this stage of his plot.

As I came back to myself, my ears filled with the panicked

babble of the crowd, underscored by the crackling of flames. Nearer at hand, Lavinia, Khefnar, and Bahlanni were in the middle of an argument that was growing quite literally heated. I rose and went to them, my own plan already taking shape.

"We have to bring them back into the amphitheater!" Lavinia was yelling. "Commandant Raffine and the other magistrates will be working to open the gates once they see the fires, but it'll take time! The people's best chance is to shelter here—"

"Not with the way those flames are spreading!" Khefnar snarled, waving at the top row of the amphitheater, where the wooden benches were already beginning to catch fire. "By the time your magistrates come to the rescue we'll all be dead! We need to find a way through to the gates, or we burn alive in this oven."

"Call them back, then!" Lavinia said, looking out at the teeming masses fighting their way towards their doom. But Khefnar only shook his head.

"They've become a mob," he said, disgust mingling with despair in his voice. "Past all reason—"

"So we find a way to reach them!" Bahlanni shouted, glancing over her shoulder at the growing flames. Nearly the entire marketplace was ablaze. "Anyone who tries to get through is going to collapse from the smoke—"

I stepped towards them through the haze of spirits, whose insubstantial forms parted before me and reformed behind, baptizing me in their light. My grandfather's face smiled at me in the fog.

"We can save them," I said, my voice cutting through their argument as all three turned to look at me. Out of the corner of my eye I saw Neftani and two other guards hauling a dazed Gracchus to his feet. "But we have to work together."

"What do you suggest?" Khefnar asked, looking at me with an odd expression. Respect?

In answer I spread my arms and began to sing.

The words were Old Ayu'li, yet they were familiar—had in fact resounded through this marketplace only minutes before, when the miracle had first occurred. And though I had only watched the steps being performed, my limbs moved through them as though I had been born dancing the Rite of Awakening.

The faces of Bahlanni, Khefnar, and Lavinia all turned to me. I did not break the rhythm of either song or dance, but my eyes found my wife's, imploring her to understand what I was doing. She did. Her feet moved to the rhythm of my own, her clear high voice joining with mine as we sang the song that had seen our people through famine and exile.

All around us the light began to grow as more spirits materialized from the mists.

Lavinia's eyes flashed with comprehension. "Join them," she said, nudging Khefnar in the ribs.

He stared down at her, brow furrowed. "What?"

"Dance!" she said, motioning to Bahlanni and me as we moved through the Rite of Awakening. "The more of you there are..."

Khefnar got it. Without further hesitation he joined us as we swayed and stomped across the stage, two dancers becoming three.

Albastine's constant fogs roiled and churned like a boiling cauldron all across the marketplace. The people who had fled towards the fire found themselves suddenly confronted by shining figures of mist and light, their spectral forms warding the living away from the hungry flames even as their own insubstantial bodies were boiled away. Singly or in groups, the shades of citizens long-departed appeared amongst the fog and fire, herding their living descendants back to the amphitheater.

I had followed Drusa's advice, concentrating on my breathing with every movement of my limbs. Yet each inhalation stung a bit more, the fog mingling with the smoke into a foul soup. I did not know how much longer I could maintain the dance.

I looked up to see the misty forms of the dead shielding the living from the worst of the blaze. I watched a smiling shade dissipate into steam as it threw itself between a pair of children and a leaping tongue of flame, and I knew I would dance until my lungs or my feet gave out—whichever failed me first.

"Everyone!" Lavinia's voice carried across the amphitheater, heavy with the authority of her station. Every head turned towards the diminutive magistrate standing on the stage. Two misty shades stood on either side of her, their features indistinct.

"Everyone!" she repeated, glancing at the spirits flanking her. "They're made of water!"

A rippling murmur from the crowd. In the mingled light of flame and mist I saw a few of them understand.

"Dance!" Lavinia shouted, raising both hands. "All of you, join the dance!"

And, in a miracle greater than any resurrection of the dead, they did.

Lavinia was the first of the Extorani to join, her motions awkward and unsteady. She kept glancing over to Bahlanni, Khefnar, and me, doing her best to mimic our steps.

"*Here,*" one of the spirits beside her said, and though his features had been blurred by the smoke mingling with the fog, I recognized my grandfather's voice. "*With me, daughter of Ayu.*"

His spectral form wrapped around her, the thousand points of shining mist illuminating her limbs as he guided her through the Rite. Lavinia's dark eyes were bright with wonder and dew.

All through the amphitheater more people were joining in,

taking their cue from those of us onstage. Those who bore ash smudged across their brows were the first, for the steps of the Rite of Awakening were not so dissimilar from the ritual dances they had grown up participating in. Their Extorani neighbors soon joined in, making up for their lack of familiarity with an awkward enthusiasm that would have set me to grinning if my whole focus hadn't been entirely upon my own steps.

The amphitheater had become a dome, the air above a mass of teeming gray as smoke and fog mingled together into a noxious fume, lit from below by the hellish firelight and the rival glow of the ancestral spirits. That choking cloud had not yet sunk upon us, but when it did it would kill us as surely as the flames would.

Above the horizon beyond the fire, on the furthest side of the marketplace, another light grew.

At first it was no more than a shift in the color of the smoke, a lighter gray against the near-black of the roiling cloud. Yet as it grew in strength it brightened until it was a wash of cool blue flickering across the smoky sky like the light of an underwater sun.

And awash in that glow, the dead came for us.

Not Attendants, but the spirits of our ancestors—mine and Bahlanni's, Lavinia's and Khefnar's, even Gracchus's. The shades of what must have been every soul to die within the valley's walls, returned from the Quiet Fields to save their progeny from joining them prematurely.

They flowed through the marketplace in a literal wave, for while the shades of the high priests had manifested themselves in the mists, these spirits had taken their forms from the Providens. Each was a rippling, shifting statue of water held together by the will of the returned soul animating it.

They charged forward, their watery voices crying out the names of their kin as they threw themselves unafraid against the flames engulfing the marketplace. The air filled with steam as fire and water met, yet the spirits flooded through the market undaunted, laughing in burbling voices their defiance of a second death.

"Cassius."

I turned mid-step to see my grandfather dancing along with me, the motions of his sparkling limbs mirroring mine exactly. Behind him, Lavinia continued to dance, guided now by Drusa's shade.

"Grandfather," I said, my throat itching from the smoke. Only a concerted effort kept me from stumbling. "I…"

"I know, my boy." His smile was a night sky bursting with stars. *"I know. But this isn't the time. Look."*

Still dancing, I followed his ethereal gaze upwards, to the top of the amphitheater. The watery spirits had carved a path through the towering flames, a narrow aisle between broken market stalls and doused piles of kindling. The fire still raged at either hand.

"They need to go through now," my grandfather's spirit continued. *"We can hold back the worst of the flames, but the smoke will choke anyone who remains here any longer. You understand?"*

"Yes," I managed. "But—"

"Later," he said again, still smiling. *"After we've saved you."*

And with that he disappeared into the fog, along with every other spirit remaining on the stage. I imagined them racing through the mists, diving into the Providens and emerging once more as beings made of water and light.

I turned to tell the others the plan, only to find Lavinia close enough to have overheard everything that Grandfather had said to me.

"Keep dancing," she said even as she stopped, racing over to the others onstage to tell them the plan. Within a minute, we were ready.

"Everyone!" Lavinia shouted, cupping her hands to her mouth again. "We're going to make a break for the gates! But we're going to do so in an orderly fashion!"

She gestured to Neftani and the other guards standing behind her, who'd stopped dancing. "Each of these men and women will move through the crowd. If they touch you on the shoulder, follow them out of here! Until and unless they do, keep dancing! Is that understood?"

"Yes!" someone called.

"Good!" Lavinia hopped down from the stage, the dancers around her parting like the sea. "Now follow me!"

My limbs ached, my every breath thickened by smoke and the sharp pain of my broken rib. Yet even so I forced myself to watch Lavinia moving through the crowd, pausing occasionally to tap a dancer on the shoulder. Whenever she did they would peel away, following her as she climbed the steps of the amphitheater, a trail of people behind her. Something stirred in my heart as I saw that she had made no distinction between Extorani and Ayu'li amongst those she led, and fully two-thirds of those following her were elderly or children.

Lavinia reached the top of the amphitheater steps, standing between the columns of fire before the path the spirits had carved. She looked back over her shoulder, and though she was no more than a silhouette against the flames, I sensed her eyes on mine.

I nodded to her, my throat too raw to speak. *Go.*

She turned and dove into the marketplace and out of sight, her followers hurrying after. I sent a silent prayer to the ancestors who even now moved among us, begging them to keep her safe at the final hurdle.

Beside me, Laurent leapt from the stage, his old eyes burning bright as he moved through the crowd, selecting those who would follow him to safety. Like Lavinia, he made no distinction based on race.

Nakmond followed, and the dozen others upon the stage. With each passage the amphitheater emptied of souls, until only a scant handful remained.

But the danger had not passed. For each dancer that fled, fewer and fewer spirits were able to hold off the flames. What had been a stalemate between the watery shades and the consuming fires was rapidly turning in favor of the blaze, and even from the heart of the amphitheater I could feel the heat beginning to sear my skin.

Thank all the ancestors that Lavinia took the old and the young first, I thought.

I was distracted by a scuffling sound from behind me, echoed swiftly by the sound of bodies striking the stage. I paused mid-dance and turned to see a kneeling Neftani clutching his wrist, now bent at a sickening angle. The other two guards lay beside him, both wheezing and bruised.

Gracchus stumbled away from them, having won free of his captors. He glanced up, his eyes meeting mine, their black depths filled wholly by the reflection of the flames he'd stoked.

Then he was gone, leaping from the stage and pushing his way through the crowd. Neftani half-rose to follow him, only to sink back to his knees, face pale.

"Don't," I said, pausing the dance to help him and his fellow guards to their feet. "It's time to go."

Neftani wheezed. "But Gracchus—"

"With any luck he won't make it to the gates," I said, helping him down from the stage. I found it doubtful that the spirits would shield Gracchus from the flames. "Take the last group of civilians and go."

Looking up at me from the pit, Neftani pressed his fist to his heart. "Blessings of the ancestors upon you, Akhenkatem."

Then he turned, gathering the penultimate group of survivors to himself as they made their way up the amphitheater steps.

Now only a handful of us remained: those fit enough to have endured dancing the Rite of Awakening for this long despite the smoke pressing down upon us, thick enough now to taint every breath. On the stage, only Khefnar, Bahlanni, and I remained.

"One of us has to lead the rest out," I said, my voice little more than a wheeze. "The others need to—"

I doubled over, bent by a wheezing cough as I inhaled a lungful of smoke. Bahlanni broke from the dance to help me, but I waved her off.

"No time," I managed to choke out. "I'll keep...keep dancing. Got to keep the path open—"

"No," Khefnar growled.

Bahlanni and I turned to look at him. The flames danced in his eyes, turning his scarred visage into something almost demonic. But he continued dancing with unflagging endurance, and there was something almost gentle in his hardened features I had never seen before.

"I should—" Bahlanni began.

"The spirits spoke." Khefnar cut her off, but there was no bitterness in his voice. "They showed me I was wrong, Sister. That you nurtured our people while I stoked their anger. Healed their hurts while I fed them bitterness."

He twirled in time with the dance, his braids spinning against the smoke.

"I will never lead them home. Never bring them to the waters of Ayu." Khefnar raised his hands skywards in supplication. "But I can save them. I can save *you*. If you'll let me."

Bahlanni looked stricken. "I—"

"Come on," I said, pulling at her sleeve. Talking was growing more difficult. "Let him...martyr..."

Khefnar looked at me, a knowing smile on his face. "I suppose you're right. I wanted something like this, deep down. Now *go,* and may the ancestors guide your steps."

Wasting no further time, Bahlanni hopped down from the stage, then helped me clamber after her. She put her arm under my shoulder and nodded at Khefnar, who still danced. "May they guide yours as well, Brother Khefnar."

"They already do," he said, smiling as bright points of light glowed in the mist around him, half-seen shades dancing alongside him. They illuminated the stage, empty now save for Khefnar dancing and Drusa's body lying still behind him.

"Come on," Bahlanni said, her voice coming out in a strained grunt as she staggered towards the amphitheater stairs, doing her best to support both my weight and hers.

By the time we reached the stairs the pain in my side had grown into a knife thrust between my ribs. I ignored it as best I could, focusing on the simple repetition of lifting each foot and placing it on the stair ahead of me. Each step set my legs on fire, but I forced myself to keep moving. To focus not on the pain assaulting me from all sides, but on Bahlanni's breath in my ear, the warmth of her body against mine as she hauled us both up the amphitheater steps.

"Bahlanni," I rasped as we reached the top of the amphitheater. "I..."

"Shh, blood of my blood." Her voice was soft comfort in my ear. "Save your strength. We've done well, but we have a ways to go, yet."

I looked up and saw that it was true. The path between the fiery remnants of the market stalls remained open, though only barely. A line of watery shades stood sentinel at either hand, keeping the flames at bay even as the heat sizzled their forms into steam.

"Here." Bahlanni tore two strips of cloth from her robes and approached the nearest of the shades—Syoris, the last high priestess before her.

"Apologies, honored ancestor," Bahlanni said, and plunged both cloths into the shade's watery body. With them thoroughly soaked, she wrapped one cloth around her mouth and nose, the other around mine. I inhaled a ragged breath, but tasted no smoke.

"Smart," I rasped.

She smiled slightly. "Now let's go."

She started down the path cleared by the shades, keeping low to avoid the smoke. I followed after, bent almost double as the flames closed in at either side, steam and smoke turning the world into a gray haze.

I was caught in every hell I had ever lived through. It was like being back in the Silva Incognita, where the fog had hung too thick for our scouts to detect the approach of the Wodemen's army until it was too late. And like my hurtling blind flight through the catacombs beneath the Senate in pursuit of the traitor Venaria, guided by intuition and feel instead of sight.

My heartbeat raced in my chest, the familiar strangling hand of panic threatening to rise up and throttle me. My breath hitched as I recalled the panic that had pressed against me from all sides at the Hour of Rest. The walls were closing in on me again, but here they were made of fire.

"Akhenkatem," Bahlanni shouted over the crackling flames, her hand tight in mine. "Stay with me."

I clung to her hand with all the strength in me, with the terror of a drowning man slipping under the waves. But I would not drown. Bahlanni would not let me.

We fled hand in hand through the narrowing corridor of clean air between the fire and smoke, my wife and I. Her presence was as solid and real as the shades steaming into nothingness beside us were insubstantial, her heartbeat racing as mine did. We moved in hobbling sync, supporting each other as we ran through this inferno. Together.

The marketplace wall rose before us, its gate a looming gap in its stone face. It hung open to the night beyond, foggy but mercifully clear of fire and smoke.

"Come on!" Bahlanni shouted through the cloth over her face. "We're nearly there!"

Hope surged in my heart, lending my feet a final burst of speed from some deep-buried reservoir of strength I hadn't known I possessed. We were going to make it. We were—

My attention was caught by a shadow against the smoke. Gracchus, clambering across the burning wreckage towards the gate. Unguarded by the shades, he must have gotten turned around in the smoke and confusion, but now he was running as fast as he could towards the empty night ahead.

If he escaped, how long before he attempted something like this again?

"Bahlanni," I wheezed through the cloth over my mouth. "Bahlanni, I have to..."

"Come on!" she yelled, still supporting me. "We're nearly there. Just a little—"

"Bahlanni," I tried again, my eyes fixed on the fleeing shape of Gracchus, "live well."

Then I was off, flying on a path to intercept the fleeing Gracchus. Bahlanni shouted something from behind me, but my whole world had winnowed down to my quarry as he ran for the gate.

Hearing my pounding footsteps, Gracchus turned, eyes widening. He slowed, trying to correct course, but not fast enough.

I collided with the Imperator in a flying tackle, knocking him off his feet. Tongues of flame licked at me as we crashed into the burning ruin of a merchant's stand.

Gracchus writhed eel-like from my grasp, his spindly fingers wrapping about a burning plank of timber.

Sputtering and coughing, I tried to pull myself to my feet, only for Gracchus's improvised club to come hurtling at my head. I turned, and the blow glanced across my shoulders instead, forcing a grunt of pain from me.

"Ayu'li filth!" Gracchus screamed, hefting the timber for another blow. There was no trace of his former silky tones, only a shrieking madness as he swung at me. I ducked and rolled away blindly, further into the burning wreckage.

Gracchus came at me again, the burning plank of wood still tight in his hands. The fire had transfigured the Imperator into something better suited to our infernal surroundings. Half his scalp had been burned away, the bitter tang of burnt hair joining the disgusting mélange of smells assaulting my nose. The flesh beneath was pink and glistening, warped and twisted by the heat. Those parts of his face that were not burned were covered by a thin layer of ash.

"Gracchus," I said, my voice coming out hoarse. "You went *into* the fire?"

His face twisted into a horrifying grimace, a nightmarish parody of a smile. "Couldn't finish you with everyone on your side. Had to get you alone."

He swung the burning timber again. I raised my arms over my head, and by some stroke of fortune it bounced off my leather sleeve.

"Never enough for you, was it?" he snarled as I backed away, looking for a way out and seeing nothing but fire. "You and all Ayu'li. Couldn't be satisfied with what you had. Always pushing for more."

"Not more," I rasped, settling into a fighter's crouch, ready to dodge his next swing. "Just what everyone else has. And you know what?"

No longer caring about the smoke, I lowered the cloth so that he could see my smile.

"We won. Everyone who survived tonight made it out because of the ancestors. Because of the Rite of Awakening. You really think the Senate is going to vote against it now?"

Gracchus's only answer was an insensate howl as he swung the burning timber at me. I tried to dodge, too slow. It hit me like a falling mountain.

The next thing I knew I was lying on my back, choking in breaths that tasted of soot and smoke. The world above me was black and orange, broken only by the shadow looming over me. Gracchus swooped down on me like a carrion bird.

"Without Attendants," he hissed, fingers that had burned and twisted like candlewax clawing at my throat, "the Republic we knew is dead. Let's die with it, Legate."

His hands squeezed, cutting off my air. I could not even summon the strength to try and pry them free. Black spots played in my vision as I wondered which would kill me first: Gracchus or the flames.

Not like this, I prayed. *Dear ancestors, not like this.*

But it was not the ancestors who answered.

Not at first, anyway.

"Hands off him!" called the sweetest voice I had ever heard.

The flames closest to us were extinguished as no fewer than four shades threw their river-formed bodies against them. And through the gap they formed my wife came dancing, every inch of her covered in shining droplets of mist.

Bahlanni, high priestess of the Ayu'li Old Faith, parted the flames before her as she danced, her body surrounded and suffused with the spirits of what seemed like every ancestor ever to dwell in the Albastine Valley. They formed an honor guard around her, keeping the flames at bay as she moved towards us, swaying and stomping in time to the rhythm of the Rite of Awakening.

"Release him," she commanded Gracchus, her voice cutting through the roar and crackle of the blaze. "I will not ask a second time."

"Come to die with your husband?" Gracchus sneered. "Romantic, Priestess. If only—"

Bahlanni wasted no further time on him.

A flick of her wrist sent the nearest of the shades billowing towards Gracchus in a steaming cloud. Where they touched him his skin reddened and bubbled as they pressed their boiling bodies against his.

Screaming, Gracchus loosed his hold on me, clawing at the spirits assaulting him. But all he succeeded in doing was burning the last of the flesh from his fingers.

I sucked in a greedy breath and rolled over, turning my back upon Imperator Gracchus as the Ayu'li spirits boiled him alive. I crawled on my elbows and knees through ash and ruin, my vision tunneling until all I could see was Bahlanni standing in an island of calm amongst the inferno.

I reached for her with trembling fingers. Hers wrapped around me tightly, and as my vision swam I saw bright pinpricks of light slide down her wrist and onto mine.

"Akhenkatem," she said, her voice sounding very small and far away. "Cassius. Blood of my blood, hang on. Hang..."

The last thing I saw before the darkness took me was her face, shining like a star descended to earth.

CHAPTER THIRTY-TWO

In the end, Albastine was not reduced to ashes that night.

At least, not the entire city. The marketplace burned for two full days, so hot that the unmortared stones of its walls were fused together by the time it subsided. The valiant efforts of a brave crew of firefighters and their Attendants managed to keep the blaze from spreading beyond those walls, though the nearest neighborhoods had to be evacuated due to the constant danger of smoke.

Even their all-hours bucket brigade failed to do more than contain the fire, which ultimately defeated itself. Having devoured everything within the marketplace that could possibly burn, the fire ran short of fuel and ultimately succumbed to the damp air of the valley's constant fog. Even then, it was weeks before the marketplace was deemed safe to enter, and only then by crews of Attendant laborers working all hours to clear the debris.

Miraculously, all of those Lavinia and the others had led from the marketplace survived the ordeal. The cleanup revealed only four bodies among the wreckage, reduced by the fire to little more than charred bones: Shahkti, Drusa, Khefnar, and Gracchus.

A smoky haze hung over the valley for nearly a month afterwards, necessitating a general mandate for the citizenry to remain indoors whenever possible. Those displaced by the fire were offered refuge in the Barrows, where Bahlanni and volunteers of the Old Faith converted unused chambers and smaller family shrines into temporary abodes. I was certain this must have ruffled some feathers amongst the more conservative members of the faithful, but they could hardly gainsay their high priestess after she'd personally called their ancestors back to the land of the living.

All of this I found out later, though, as I spent most of that first week unconscious.

I HAD BEEN LUCKY, allowing for a charitable interpretation of the word. I had keeled over due to a combination of lack of air and sheer exhaustion, rather than inhaling a fatal amount of smoke. For several days every breath was an exercise in pain, but the chirurgeons assured me that my lungs had suffered no permanent damage.

Those first few days were little more than a haze of disjointed impressions of faces and voices and hands: chirurgeons tending to me, visitors checking in on me. Bahlanni's smile, Horatia's red curls, Lavinia's dark eyes.

When I slept, they were replaced by others: Drusa and Titian, Khefnar and Hupli, alternatively chastising me for failing to save them or begging my forgiveness for their failings. I could not tell which of these visitations were their departed souls come to haunt me and which were products of my fevered subconscious. Nor did I want to know.

The first day I felt remotely human, I awoke to one of the last faces I'd expected to see.

"Not dead yet, eh?" Laurent asked, his grandfatherly face wrinkling in a grin.

I tried to say something, but all that came out was an ugly, hacking cough.

"Here," the eldest surviving Son of Ash said, handing me a wineskin. I took it and drank greedily, soothingly cool water rushing down my throat.

"Not so fast, now," Laurent advised, taking it from my protesting fingers.

I wet my lips. "Why...you?"

"Why am I here, you mean?" Laurent raised an eyebrow. I nodded. "To thank you."

"For?"

"For giving Khefnar the end he wanted." Laurent's tone sobered. "Always knew he was going to make a martyr of himself, all the way back to when I first met him."

"In Ayu?" I managed to rasp.

"That's right," he said. "A young man full of anger and zeal, determined to die for a cause. I thought I could...I don't know. Temper him, maybe? But I think Khefnar had more of an effect on me than the reverse."

"Not..." I coughed, but forced the words out anyway. "Not your fault."

"I know." Laurent smiled sadly. "Like I said, this was the end he wanted. At least this way he didn't take our people with him."

"At least," I agreed. "What..."

My throat wouldn't cooperate enough to form more complex thoughts, but a burst of will that sent ghostfire running down my left arm got the point across.

"The artificial Attendants?" Laurent asked. I nodded, and

his smile grew a shade less sad. "Well. It's been a bit lost in the wake of the fire, but the Senate voted to begin production of a prototype batch of them this week. They're going to test how well they perform, compare them against the standard version. It'll take a while, but in time they might overtake the dead as Albastine's workforce. You can thank your Senator friend for that, by the way."

"I will." I waved feebly at him. "You?"

Laurent shrugged. "There was some debate as to whether or not Nakmond and I should be punished for crimes against the state, but ultimately any sentencing was waived in consideration of our actions at the Hour of Revelation. Hell, they even revoked my exile from my smuggling days, if you can believe it."

"Anyone know..." I sent another pulse of ghostfire down my arm. "Fakes?"

"That I was the one who gave you the schematics?" Laurent shook his head. "They wouldn't have believed me anyway. Believed you, maybe, but you were busy napping."

"Sorry."

"Don't be." He gave a dismissive wave. "Way I hear it, Senate's considering lifting the prohibition against the Rite of Awakening entirely, after what happened in the marketplace. If the artificial Attendants work as well as I hope they do, there'll be no reason to use bodies at all. That's thanks enough for my part."

"What...do?"

"Seeing as I'm no longer an exile," he said, rubbing at his beard, "I considered staying for a while. But I think I've still got at least one journey left to make."

"Where?"

His gaze traveled to the window. "Back to Ayu. Nakmond is returning home. Wants to bury Tyshett beside the river, I expect."

Ordinarily all bodies that died within the Valley were summarily made into Attendants, but in all the chaos of the preceding days I was sure Nakmond would succeed at sneaking his lover's body past the mountains. Especially with an old smuggler's assistance.

"Anyway." Laurent stood, his mood evidently soured by talk of his dead friend. "Wanted to thank you. For giving Khefnar what he wanted. And the Attendant thing."

He turned away, putting his hand on the doorknob.

"Laurent?" I called after him, fighting the urge to cough. "You were never controlling the Attendant, were you?"

He turned, his face a mask of puzzlement. "What Attendant?"

Then he was gone, leaving me with one last unsolved mystery.

"You look terrible," Lavinia told me a few days later.

"Thanks," I said, folding my hands over my stomach. My throat was still painfully raw, but it no longer hurt just to breathe. Sitting up in bed helped.

Lavinia might have said more, but she was interrupted by a loud snore. Both our heads turned towards Horatia, who lay sleeping in one of the chairs at my bedside.

"Surprised that you two can stand to be in the same room with one another again."

"We decided to put our differences aside to visit a friend in need." Lavinia shrugged. "Besides, she's better company this way."

Horatia snored again. I fought back a laugh, knowing it would feel like sandpaper against my throat.

"So we're friends now?" I asked instead.

"I think we are," Lavinia said, leaning against the windowsill. Beyond it, Albastine lay spread out below us, white spires shining in the light of a rare fogless day. "Can I ask a question?"

"Sure."

"How did you know it was going to work?" Her gaze tracked to the place where the marketplace had been: a ruined splotch of dark gray soot amongst the alabaster towers. "The Rite, I mean. Getting everyone to dance it. I mean, hell. Half of us weren't Ayu'li."

"I didn't." I reached over to my bedside and took a sip from the cup waiting there. "But when I saw that Bahlanni and Khefnar alone were able to summon the old priests and priestesses from the fog, I figured the rest of the ancestors could materialize from the river. Couldn't think of a better way to keep the fire at bay."

"So you took it on faith," Lavinia said, glancing at me.

I only smiled.

"That's another thing I don't understand," she said, turning back to the window. Her eyes followed the winding course of the Providens. "The whole reason the Rite of Awakening is outlawed is because it's calling the spirits back into their bodies, which we need to use as Attendants. But that wasn't the case that night."

"No," I agreed. "Any other night of the year, I don't think we could have done what we did. But the Hours are held when they are for a reason."

"Six months past Lightfall." Lavinia frowned. "The spring equinox?"

I nodded. "Right on the money. At times of transition, the border between the living world and what comes after is...thinner. More permeable. And water retains memory better than any other substance, save the mind itself."

"Speaking of," Lavinia said, "I didn't mention Hupli's gravesight in my report."

I straightened up as much as my reclining posture allowed. "You didn't?"

"No reason to." She shrugged. "I never *saw* him doing it. And he had already aligned himself with the Sons of Ash. As far as I —and the Magisterium—are concerned, he murdered Tyshett after arguing how to deal with you."

Which was true, broadly speaking. "And his other victim?" I asked. "The eyeless one?

"Citizen Iktan Thalonitus," Lavinia said. "Death attributed to Hupli Kiaton, motive unknown."

"I..." I hesitated, not knowing what to say. "Isn't that breaking the law? Leaving out the gravesight?"

"Bending it, as I recall." Lavinia smiled thinly. "It won't do anyone any good including it in my report. The people we rescued from the marketplace are overwhelmingly well-disposed towards the Old Faith, but reactions in the wider Republic are...mixed. Not everyone loves the idea of a bunch of ghosts parading through the streets."

She ran a hand through her hair, a gesture I somehow found endearing now. "I thought it prudent not to give them any more reason to distrust your religion. Not unless we want more people to think like Gracchus did."

"No," I agreed. "Thank you."

"Don't mention it," Lavinia said seriously. But a smile tugged at the corner of her lip. "Unless you want me to lose my job."

"Perish the thought."

"Good." Lavinia left the window and retrieved her belongings from the chair beside the sleeping Horatia. "Speaking of, I need to head out. Stay well, Cassius."

"You too," I said as she put her hand on the door. "Lavinia?"

"Yeah?"

"Just so you know," I said, my throat gone dry and scratchy, "if you and your wife ever...ever wanted to come to the Barrows. To worship, or just find a quiet moment. You'd be welcome. If you want."

Lavinia's shoulders tensed, and for a moment I worried that I'd overstepped my bounds. But when she looked back at me her dark eyes were gentle, almost shy.

"I'll think about it," she promised. "Really."

"WHERE ARE WE GOING?" I asked a week later as my wife led me by the hand through the lower valley.

Spring had finally come to Albastine. Though mornings and evenings were still chill with fog, the daytime hours were warm enough to wear tunics, leaving us free to stroll through the valley with the sun warming our bare arms.

"To show you the future," Bahlanni said, ducking under a low-hanging branch. Though most of the lower valley was farmland, the slopes leading up to the mountainsides remained relatively untouched forest.

"So you really are a prophet now?" I teased.

Bahlanni turned to grin at me, walking backwards. "What else do you call a miracle worker?"

"In my case," I said, grinning back, "wife."

Her laugh echoed across the valley. I caught up to her, threw an arm about her shoulders, and pulled her close as we walked beneath the dappled light filtering through the trees. "And how are our people, o prophet?"

"Growing," she said. "You'll see some new faces by the time you're well enough to attend services again."

"Converts?"

Bahlanni nodded. "Turns out a lot of people are more willing to entertain the idea of religion when they participate in one of its miracles. And since the Old Faith doesn't directly contradict the worship of the Extorani pantheon, we've got a growing population who adhere to both faiths."

I frowned. "But the Extorani don't revere their ancestors like we do."

Bahlanni smiled. "Well, turns out that seeing them come back from the dead to rescue your children changes some people's views on the matter."

"Turns out," I agreed. "I...do you think we'll ever be able to do it again? The Rite, I mean."

"Very probably, once the artificial Attendants are numerous enough." We rounded a bend in the trail, and broad acres of farmland spread across the valleys below came into sight. Bahlanni lifted her hand and pointed at the nearest of these. "Look."

I followed her finger and saw.

The fields closest to us were not being tended by Attendants —or at least, not by the repurposed bodies I'd been surrounded by my entire life.

Instead, these were constructs, similar to the marionette Laurent had smuggled into the valley. Built of metal and wood, they were taller and spindlier than that prototype, the tools required for the task of tilling the fields already built into their limbs. I watched in breathless fascination as one larger than a horse made its slow, lumbering way across the fields, scoring deep furrows in the soil with the plow-like limbs trailing behind it. Smaller, many-legged ones followed after, their strange undulating gaits sowing seeds into the freshly dug plots.

"They work," I whispered. Bahlanni nodded.

"Exceedingly well, from what I hear. It'll take time before

they can replace the old version completely, but..." She turned to me, smiling. "There's already talk of repealing the prohibition on the Rite of Awakening. We'll be able to use the Rite on the bodies of our deceased, just like we were always meant to."

I looked out at the new breed of Attendants laboring, taking in their strange inhuman forms.

"The deceased who still have bodies, anyway," I said. A lump was rising in my throat.

Bahlanni reached out and took my hand, her thumb stroking my knuckles.

"I miss him too," she said, speaking of my grandfather. "It was...good to see him again."

"It was," I agreed. "I just wish..."

"That we had more time," Bahlanni said softly. I nodded, not trusting myself to speak.

"We all wish that, my love," she said, squeezing my hand. "More time with the ones we care for. Before they're gone, and after."

"He said he'd see me again," I whispered. "That we would have time to talk. Later. I...I wanted to believe him."

Silence for a moment.

"Akhenkatem," Bahlanni said. "Love of my life, flesh of my flesh. You are immeasurably stupid."

I stared at her. "What?"

She tucked her hand under my chin. "Did your grandfather ever lie to you while he was alive?"

"Of course not."

"Then why would he after death?" she snorted. "It's most of a year until the next Hours of Remembrance, but of what concern is time to those who dwell beyond the Quiet Fields?"

Bahlanni took both my hands in hers. "Next year we will perform the Rite of Awakening once more, by the waters of the Providens itself. Everyone who wishes to will be able to meet with their departed loved ones once more. And Khaimesu will surely be there to greet us."

Smiling, my wife put my hands on her belly. It was warm, and smooth, and just slightly rounder than when last we'd touched one another.

"All three of us," Bahlanni said, and kissed me.

PART SEVEN
RETURN

EPILOGUE

Somewhere in Albastine, an Attendant stood before a mirror.

Sutures littered the floor around its feet, brass staples broader and brighter than the dull bronze of its mask. The Attendant had removed these one by one, prying them free as carefully as the rigid joints of its withered fingers would permit. Now only one remained.

The final suture was located at the crown of the Attendant's skull, right where the hairline would have been, had the Attendant still been possessed of hair. Slowly, it worked the staple free, taking care to damage the skin beneath as little as possible. Not out of vanity—the Attendant was a years-dead corpse, and nothing could be done to improve upon its appearance.

No, the reason for the slow care and precision with which it pried free the suture was the dead flesh tearing beneath. Toughened and leathery though it was compared to that which it had worn as a living being, the Attendant's skin was no longer capable of growth or self-repair. Any damage it incurred would last for as long as it did. That was a lesson the Attendant had learned already.

For unlike the other resurrected bodies that roamed the streets of the Pale City, this Attendant was capable of thought and memory. It remembered having a name once, back before it had awoken from a pleasant dream of quiet fields and found itself in a body that could not breathe.

A tearing sensation told the Attendant it was moving too fast, that it had torn the skin of its forehead in its rush to remove the final suture. Not pain, just a dull sensation of separation. One more scar, forever unrepaired.

The Attendant would have grimaced if it could, but its facial muscles were as rigid as the bones beneath them. And even if they had not been, the Attendant had a strange intuition that the expression would have been wrong, somehow. Like wearing a glove that was too small for its fingers.

That was how it felt, to be a body whose heart did not beat. Or perhaps it was this body in particular, ill-fitting to the mind now dwelling within. Unfamiliar. Alien.

The Attendant had assumed at first that this was simply a result of whatever curious circumstance had called it back to the streets it had once walked, or of the alchemical process that had transformed the corpse into an Attendant in the first place. But even as it had grown slowly more adept at walking and running—even at fighting—in this dead body, the dysphoric feeling did not fade. If anything it had steadily intensified, like an itch that could not be scratched.

So now the Attendant did what it must. What it knew it should have done at the first, when it had awoken from death into this crude unlife. Fear could hold it back no longer, for whatever the terrible truth was, the need to know it had eclipsed fear long ago.

The final suture fell to the floor, clattering against the marble.

Perversely thankful that its nerveless fingers could no

longer shake, the Attendant raised its hands to either side of the bronze mask that clung to its face. Through the two eyeholes it could see that mask reflected in the mirror, the serene smile on the blank features antithetical to the Attendant's own feelings.

The mask made a moist tearing sound as the Attendant lowered it from its face, again feeling the dull sensation of leathery skin tearing free—little strips of its face coming off with the mask after years spent adhered to the cold metal.

The Attendant did not notice, nor would have cared if it had. It lowered the mask and stared into what the mirror revealed.

Its features were sunken and hollow, the shape of the skull clearly visible beneath skin that had faded until it was very nearly white. Thin stitching through its lips tied its mouth firmly shut, and its ears were little more than shriveled pits in the sides of its head. A thick band of scarring encircled its hairless scalp like a crown, showing where the skull had been cut away by diligent chirurgeons to operate on the brain beneath.

None of that was what made the Attendant stumble back from the mirror, fear racing through its body in place of blood. Had its lips not been sewn together and its vocal cords removed, it might have screamed.

It had expected to see a corpse staring back in place of the reflection it had known in life. Had prepared itself as best it could to look at its own features transfigured by death, its skin stretched tight across the face that had been its own. But that was not what the Attendant saw.

The face in the mirror was not its own. It was someone else entirely, someone who had borne a long scar down one cheek, whose features were heavier and rounder than those the Attendant had had in life. It was a stranger's face.

It knew, then, beyond doubt or fear, the terrible truth that had dogged it each day in this strange limbo as a thinking mind trapped within a dead body.

A body that was not its own.

The Attendant turned away from the mirror, buried its face in its cold hands, and wished with all its unbeating heart that it could still scream.

THE END
The Ashen City
Rites of Resurrection Book 2

THE ADVENTURE CONTINUES...

... in *The Awoken City (Rites of Resurrection Book 3)*.

BOOKS AND REVIEWS

If you loved *The Pale City* and would like to stay in the loop about the latest book releases, deals, and giveaways, be sure to subscribe to the Shadow Alley Press Mailing List.

www.ShadowAlleyPress.com

Sign up now and get a free copy of our bestselling anthology, Viridian Gate Online: Side Quests! Your email address will never be shared and you can unsubscribe at any time.

Word-of-mouth and book reviews are beyond helpful for the success of any writer, so please consider leaving a rating or a short, honest review on Amazon—just a couple of lines about your overall reading experience. Thank you in advance!

You can also connect with us on our Facebook Page where we do even more giveaways: facebook.com/shadowalleypress

BOOKS BY SHADOW ALLEY PRESS

ENTER THE SHADOW ALLEY LIBRARY to take a peek at all of our amazing Gamelit, Fantasy, and Science Fiction books! Viridian Gate Online, Rogue Dungeon, Snake's Life, Dungeon Heart, Path of the Thunderbird, School of Swords and Serpents, the FiveFold Universe, and so many more... Your next favorite book is waiting for you inside!

ABOUT THE AUTHOR

Marshall J. Moore is a writer, filmmaker, and martial artist who was born and raised on Kwajalein, a tiny Pacific island. He has trained a professional mercenary in unarmed combat, sold a thousand dollars' worth of teapots to Jackie Chan, and was once tracked down by a bounty hunter for owing $300 in overdue fees to the Los Angeles Public Library. He lives in Atlanta, Georgia, with his wife Megan and their two cats.

An active member of the SFWA, his short stories have appeared in collections from Flame Tree Publishing, Mysterion, Air and Nothingness Press, and many other publishers.

Find him online at:
linktr.ee/marshalljmoore

facebook.com/kwajmarshall

twitter.com/Kwaj14
instagram.com/marshalljmooreauthor
tiktok.com/@marshalljmooreauthor